Running From Love

(Formerly titled Running Out Of Fear)

Sandy Loyd

Published by Sandy Loyd
Copyright © 2013 Sandy Loyd
Cover by Kelli Ann Morgan at Inspiration Creative Services
Edited by Pam Berehulke at Bulletproof Editing
ISBN: 978-1-941267-01-1

For more information on the author and her works, please see www.SandyLoyd.com

This book is also available in print from some online retailers:

Other books by Sandy Loyd

Contemporary Romances
The California Series
Winter Interlude – Book One
Promises, Promises – Book Two
James – Book Three
Dancing with an Angel – Book Four

Second Chances Series
Tropical Spice – Book One

Romantic Suspense
D.C. Bad Boys Series
The Sin Factor – Book One
Raising The Stakes – Book Two New Release

Running Series
Running Out Of Fear – Book One

Deadly Series
Deadly Misconceptions – Book One

A Matter of Trust – New Release

Kicker's Legacy – New Release

Prologue

With the eyes of a circling hawk, he noticed her the moment she stepped off the Greyhound and took a furtive glance around. Though she looked older than his usual prey, her assets—a firm butt sheathed in skintight jeans and a perfect bare waist showcased with a skimpy top that did nothing to hide full breasts—convinced him to hang around the Nashville depot. She stopped at the glass enclosure and spent a long moment engrossed in what she read.

Yep. He'd bet any amount of money she was looking for a job. Most likely had visions of becoming a star, joining the throngs of women with lofty dreams, hoping to break through the competition. That worked for him. Those dreams provided a steady stream of fresh talent. He was always on the lookout, as fresh talent kept them in business.

He started toward her. "Hi. I notice you're looking at the want ads. You need a job?"

She eyed him warily. "I might."

Definitely not naïve, just as he'd thought. But that was okay. He knew his way around caution, using charm with the skill of Michelangelo crafting a marble statue. Charm went a long way in dispelling caution, especially with women. He offered a smile, one that displayed his dimples. One that women found fascinating because his smile reminded them of a lost little boy. Or so he'd been told. Yet, he was far from lost. He knew exactly where he was going and exactly how to get there with women like her in tow.

Soon! Soon, he'd have her within his grasp. After a month of the hell he'd put her through, she'd forget all about caution and her dreams would no longer matter. His would. So what if she endured a few nightmares in the process? He never concerned himself with trivialities. Not when fulfilling his dreams was what mattered most. It was all part of the game.

"You a singer?"

Her gaze narrowed, her expression closing tighter as she slung her guitar further behind her shoulder. Even better. He enjoyed a fighter…anticipated the challenge…of first luring her and then breaking her. An interesting challenge honed his skills. He loved the thrill of the chase and when the chase was thrilling, he loved winning even more.

"I'm only asking because my sister hires talent for a nightclub about an hour up the interstate. She's always searching for new voices." He shook his head, sighing. "The ones she breaks in tend to move on to greener pastures within a matter of months. Pay's decent. It's a good starting place if you're interested." He whipped out a card. "Her name's Ivy. Tell her Jerry sent you."

"Thanks." She nodded and took the card. "I'll think about it."

He tipped his cowboy hat and flashed his dimples one more time. "Don't think too long, darlin'. I've given her card to three others so far today and she can only hire one this week."

Whistling as he went, he strutted off, but not before catching her reconsidering glance telling him she'd make the call. Once she got an idea of the area's rents. They all underestimated the cost of living. Just because Nashville was considered a Southern city, didn't mean it was a cheap place to live. Quite the opposite, and jobs, even menial ones, were hard to come by.

Yep. Nashville was the land where dreams came true. At least his, anyway.

Chapter 1

Forgiveness isn't meant for the forgiven. It soothes the forgiver's soul and channels negative energy to positive. As Shelly Matthews paced, her mother's words echoed in her mind.

The glaring summer sun beat against the pavement. Though in the shade, heat from the blacktop seeped into her sandals, the soles growing hotter with every step.

Shelly glanced at her wrist, then wiped at the sweat trickling on her brow.

Damn. Where was Kiera? She'd orchestrated this meeting, so why was she late?

She took another look around. Birds chirped and cicadas buzzed, but no other sound marred the quiet in the high school parking lot, deserted this time of year.

"Remember why you're here," she muttered, and resumed pacing. "To hear Kiera out, so you can move on and embrace your future."

According to her mom, Shelly couldn't do that until she resolved her past, and forgiveness was the first step. Since time had a way of dulling anger and hurt, forgiving Kiera had seemed so easy…in theory. Unfortunately, implementation was much harder than just driving back to the one-light town she'd sworn never to set foot in again. All around her were reminders that dredged up bleak days she'd spent too long forgetting.

Funny, even the faint smell of lavender from the butterfly garden she'd helped plant as a high school junior drew unwanted memories…memories of lonely weekends spent planting and weeding and nurturing flowers that nobody cared about but her and a few other outcasts.

She glanced at the well-tended garden at the end of the school's main building, then smiled. Besides the purple lavender, she could see that red and yellow lantana, pink verbena, and even pinker foxglove were in full bloom. Mrs. Hendricks, the sponsor, must still be around. The woman was a saint, in her opinion. Her friendship had been something to treasure and definitely worth remembering. Yet, having a teacher as her sole friend—once Kiera had left for college—stained those memories with loneliness. It certainly hadn't helped her fit in. Neither had Shelly's love of gardening. Both had only set her more apart from her peers back then.

She expelled the dismal thoughts in a deep exhale. How had Kiera ever talked her into returning to this rinky-dink town? Wasn't Kiera the guilty party needing forgiveness? Shelly should have insisted, at the very least, that her ex-best friend make the drive to Atlanta for this meeting after her out-of-the-blue call. Kiera had seemed to be worried about something, so Shelly had caved, as if that summer hadn't happened. Here she was, halfway to a heat stroke. Waiting.

She looked at her watch again, then resumed counting off her eighteen steps in each direction. More memories flooded back, of other times she'd waited for Kiera to follow through on something she'd promised. Was this one of those times?

"Kiera, stop." The shout broke into the humid air. The bird and insect chirps halted.

Shelly stiffened, recognizing a voice she never expected to hear again. Then Kiera appeared around the high school gymnasium's corner and stumbled toward her at a fast clip.

"Shelly, I'm too late." Her voice was barely audible. She was crying and shivering uncontrollably, almost twitching.

"Kiera, what's wrong?" When Kiera almost plowed into her, Shelly reached out to steady her. She held on when a still shaking Kiera collapsed in her arms, then managed to get both of them into a sitting position on the curb.

"I screwed up. I can't finish what I started. He's trying to kill me. May have succeeded."

"What are you talking about?" When she didn't answer, Shelly said a little louder, "Kiera?"

"Can you ever forgive me?" She spoke so softly, Shelly barely made out the words.

The same voice that had intruded earlier rang out in another

4

shout. "Kiera? Where the hell are you?" Jacob Collier then darted out from behind the brick building and charged in their direction. "I only want to help."

Shelly's heart raced. Blood pounded in her head like Indian war drums, their tempo increasing with his every step until he stopped and knelt a foot in front of her.

"Kiera?" He ignored Shelly, who couldn't stop gawking, too stunned to do anything else.

With a concerned expression, he leaned closer. "We need to get you to the emergency room."

"Jake?" Kiera opened her eyes when he tried to lift her from Shelly's arms. "No, wait. I need to tell her." Her resistance roused Shelly from her dazed stupor enough to tighten her grip.

"You're in no condition to—"

"No!" Kiera cut him off and begged into Shelly's ear, "Remember the money tree. Please…" She drifted into unconsciousness, her breathing rapid and shallow.

"Kiera?" She shook her. More shivering was her only response. "Kiera, talk to me." After another moment of silence, Shelly pierced Jake with an accusing glare. "What happened?"

"I think she's OD'd. I have to get her to the emergency room."

His meaning sank in. Shelly released her hold so Jake could heft Kiera into his arms, as their earlier phone conversation replayed. Kiera had begged for this meeting, claiming the last part of her treatment was to atone for her sins, face those she'd hurt, and rectify mistakes if she could.

Was this how she atoned? By overdosing and passing out in her arms? She'd claimed to be clean. Said she had been for years. After what Shelly had just witnessed, huge doubts filled her. Kiera had always had a knack for twisting the truth to get what she wanted. Had she lied?

And what about Jake? Shelly rubbed her temples. Why oh why had she returned? Was she a masochist or what? She should have known Kiera hadn't changed, and the probability of running into him had been greater than great. Geez! He and Kiera were married.

Shelly stood frozen with indecision and debated her options, as he lumbered across the parking lot in the direction of a navy

SANDY LOYD

SUV she hadn't noticed earlier, Kiera a dead weight in his arms.
The impulse to run, to retrace her three-hundred-mile drive, was
a strong one. The idea of actually conversing with him paralyzed
her. She shouldn't go anywhere near the man. Especially after
what she'd discovered the instant she'd heard his voice again. Six
years wasn't nearly enough time to get over Jacob Collier.

She squeezed her eyes shut tightly. Don't be such a coward.
You need to see this through. Kiera said someone was trying to
kill her. Could it be Jake?

She snorted. Like that would ever happen. No. Jake had
always loved Kiera. He damn sure would never harm her. Yett
she'd been afraid of something or someone.

Remember the money tree. What did that mean? Why
mention a bush they'd planted together as kids nearly two
decades ago?

"Wait," she yelled, shoving her jealous thoughts aside and
running after him. Kiera had taken the first step, so she couldn't
back down now. Not when she'd driven so far to give
forgiveness a try. After all, she needed to forgive and move on
with her life, because if anyone's soul needed soothing, it was
her own.

Whether Kiera deserved it or not, Shelly couldn't leave
without at least making sure she was okay. "I'm coming with
you. Shouldn't we call an ambulance?"

~

"No time." An ambulance would take too much time. Time his
ex-wife didn't have, Jake decided. Not if she'd OD'd. Rural and
sprawling Campton, Kentucky, was a tiny dot on the map
compared to Bowling Green, a bigger circle and the closest city,
twenty-five miles south.

"Call 911 to alert Campton Medical Center that we're
coming," he shouted over his shoulder, blindsided with the
shock of seeing Michelle Matthews with Kiera. The entire time
he'd charged in the direction of his car, images of bygone days
flashed in his mind, one right after another.

"Focus on Kiera, not on the past," he whispered, then swore
under his breath and tried to increase his stride, but Kiera's dead
weight staggered him. Next thing he knew, Michelle was behind

6

him, still talking into her cell phone, and he had no more time to ponder her return.

She cut the connection and tucked her phone into her pocket. "They'll be waiting for us."

Now near his Durango, he threw Michelle the keys. "It's frickin' hot. Open the doors."

He did a quick check of Kiera's arms while she ran around to yank doors open to release the heat, before reaching in to stick the key into the ignition and turn it over. The one needle mark confirmed his worst suspicions. He searched her pockets and pulled out a bag of white powder and her cell phone. Hastily, he shoved both into his own pocket without being obvious. Why would she be carrying anything, let alone so much of what looked to be methamphetamine, when she'd been so focused on helping him?

"Is she still breathing?" Michelle cranked up the air conditioner.

Jake nodded. "Just barely." What had gone wrong? He'd kept her involvement secret. Had someone discovered her attempts to ferret out information? Or had she succumbed to temptation?

Jake placed Kiera on the backseat and murmured, swallowing his guilt, "Hang on, Ker."

Michelle climbed in beside her, yanked on Kiera's seat belt and clipped it shut, then fastened her own. She checked for a pulse. "It's rapid and faint, but there's definitely a heartbeat."

"Thank God." He closed both passenger doors, then ran around, slamming the third before sliding inside. Regret over involving her to begin with chewed at his gut.

"Jake?" Michelle's soft tone yanked his attention to the rearview mirror.

They eyed each other for a long second. When he remained silent, she offered a sad smile, the sweetness of it adding to the sincerity in her startling blue gaze.

"Not the best of circumstances for a reunion, is it?"

Remembering their last encounter, he smiled ruefully as he put the car in reverse. "Would you even be in this car right now, if Kiera hadn't collapsed in your arms?" he asked, surprising himself with the question that just popped out, highlighting the obvious. There was a reason they avoided each other.

"Probably not." She blinked back tears, the glaze of them emphasizing her best feature as they continued their stare off in the mirror while he backed out of the space.

Michelle had always had the bluest eyes, making him think a person could get lost in their ocean-like depths. A sliver of attraction sneaked into his mind. He squelched it hard, shifted into drive after braking, unwilling to think of what might have been, if…

"So, what happened?" Her voice cut into the awkward silence and her question registered as he weaved the car through the parking lot toward the high school exit.

"I don't know. I got her call. She wanted me to meet her at Mueller's Cave." Their teen hangout wasn't far from here. "I parked and went to look for her and saw her running. I tried to stop her and…" He broke off. "Well, you were there for the rest."

All he had now were *if only's*. If only he hadn't involved Kiera in the first place. If only two other women hadn't died in the past three months of overdoses. If only he hadn't been desperate to find answers as to how and why. Especially when neither victim had a history of drug abuse and suddenly became users overnight, according to relatives who knew them.

Jake and his partner were investigating the few leads they had. So far, it was as if the two had disappeared into never-never land until their bodies were recovered in Kentucky's backwoods, miles apart, but close enough to consider a connection. Autopsies determined drug overdose as cause of death for both women. Tox screens confirmed lethal levels of an identical designer drug, another connection. Its makeup had amphetamine or meth-like properties, but was considered neither. More like a variant of Ecstasy, but again, not an exact match. And now this.

"Do you think she'll make it?"

Michelle's question intruded on his thoughts once again and he sighed.

"I hope so." Now was not the time to dissect regrets, past or present. He had to keep his focus. Just concentrate on getting Kiera to the hospital. He stomped on the accelerator, racing toward the main highway as fast as he dared go on the narrow lane. Thankfully, there was no traffic. Four or five cars on the road at once in Campton denoted rush hour, and at midday, it was all but deserted.

"She told me she was clean. Was she?"

"Yeah." He nodded. "She has been for years." He'd made sure of it before he'd let her have contact with their five-year-old daughter. He adjusted the mirror, noting Kiera's still form and overall appearance. Other than her pasty white sheen, she looked healthy, nothing like the woman he'd divorced four years earlier, the one who'd chosen drugs over a child and a shot at a happy life with a husband. Her face was plump and round, not gaunt with weight loss.

Kiera had changed. She had been making the right choices. After overcoming all odds, Kiera had wanted to be a mother to Emily, who needed a mother. Though there'd been no chance for a reconciliation between him and his ex—some personal rips just couldn't be repaired with an "I'm sorry"—they'd worked out their differences enough to enjoy a decent relationship.

No way this was an ordinary OD. There had to be a connection to his investigation.

"She wasn't using. I'd stake my life on it." Relying on instinct, Jake had taken a huge risk in trusting Kiera. Revenge and redemption were strong motivators, she'd explained. Helping to close the meth trade in this part of the county so no one else had to endure her pain was something she'd needed to do. Kind of a payback for all the harm she'd caused, as she'd put it.

"Please, Lord. Let her live," he whispered as he braked for a turn.

Once again he'd failed her when he should have been looking out for her. He should have expected the unexpected and kept things from escalating.

Now on the highway's straightaway, he gunned the motor and tore off like an Indy 500 driver. The speedometer touched eighty. He slowed only for curves and when he had to make the turn for the emergency room entrance. The second the car screeched to a stop, he shot out with the speed of an expended bullet with Michelle right behind him.

He nodded to an emergency room technician who came running toward them. "She's in the backseat. Overdose. Meth is my guess."

He needed no other words to act. In minutes, Kiera was strapped onto a gurney as other ER staff joined in the rush to save her life.

"Wait over there," Nurse Ratched at the desk ordered in a terse voice, pointing a bony hand.

Michelle sat while Jake paced and practically wore a rut into the waiting room's bright orange and lime green linoleum floor. The walls were a faded, sickly yellow that reminded him of some of the dirty diapers he'd changed back when Emily was a baby. Who chose the hideous colors? Did those responsible believe the captive visitors wouldn't notice? Hell, that's all he could notice when he wouldn't allow himself to think of anything else.

"I'll be right back."

Michelle's words startled Jake out of his thoughts. He nodded and risked a glance at her as she slipped past him to step into the ladies' room. He studied the door as his mind raced.

What had she been doing at the high school anyway? It had to be something Kiera had planned on her quest for redemption. He'd have to ask her.

Movement out of the corner of his eye drew his attention. His gaze narrowed on a doctor walking down the hall with an intent expression. Was the man searching for him with news? When he stopped near the chair Michelle had vacated, eying the ER without even glancing at this side of the room, Jake relaxed his shoulders and pivoted. His focus returned to the ugly floors.

"Mr. Collier?"

"Yes?" Jake spun around.

The ER doctor who'd taken over from the EMT stood in front of him.

"Ms. Delaney has stabilized, but she's not out of danger yet. It's still too early to tell."

"Thank you." Jake retrieved his cell phone as the doctor retreated. He'd procrastinated long enough in calling Kiera's mother. He punched in Elaine Delaney's number. While the phone rang, he mentally searched for the right words.

"Elaine, it's Jake," he said once she answered. With no way

to keep from smashing her well-ordered life with his news, he just blurted out, "Kiera's OD'd. She's in the emergency room. Campton Medical Center."

He raked fingers through his hair and rested his hand on the back of his neck, rubbing away his discomfort as she asked and he answered the basic questions. "Yeah, I'll wait until you get here. Also, Michelle Matthews is back in town. Looks like Kiera planned some kind of reunion. She's waiting with me." After saying good-byes, he closed the phone, spared a quick glance at the ladies' room door, and renewed his pacing. With his every step, the bag of drugs and Kiera's cell phone weighed heavily in his pocket.

~

"Doctor, how much longer do you think it'll be? My son's been in there for hours."

It took him a split second to realize her words were directed at him. "Shit," he murmured, stiffening as his heartbeat soared and his gaze flew from the ER door he'd been eyeing to his questioner. Then he smiled, satisfied his disguise was still intact.

No one gave him a second thought, including the woman. Too many on the ER staff put in a day a week, traveling from Louisville or Bowling Green, so there were always new faces around. Only minutes ago, he'd slipped out of the locker room wearing scrubs and a doctor's ID with the picture turned to the inside. The urge to stall, because he needed more time, warred with his desire to avoid unwarranted attention. Remembering a name on the roster he'd checked earlier, he said, "I'm Dr. Thomas. I just came on duty. Let me check for you, Mrs.…?"

The one word hung in the air.

She offered a wan smile. "Gardiner. Thank you. My son's name is Wayne Gardiner. He was injured in a construction accident."

Nodding, he refocused on the ER doors. Gardiner. He'd have to remember the name. When the attendant at the desk suddenly left her spot, which was his cue, he said, "I'll be right back."

He nonchalantly walked across the room, glad that the rural medical center was understaffed due to the economy and cutbacks. Since no one now guarded the entrance to the area only patients and hospital personnel were allowed, he stepped behind the desk, pretended to scrutinize paperwork, and listened through the two-inch crack between the ER's double doors.

"She's stabilized for the time being," a man's voice said.

"Good thing, 'cause we just got hammered with casualties," came another. "Pileup on I-65, three incoming. Ambulance just pulled in. Another's right behind."

Ah, right on schedule! He smiled at his well-timed and expected diversion. Planning was everything in his business. His partners had been busy. He pushed through the doors and as he'd hoped, no one noticed him or his interest in the patient in the corner bed. The nurses scurried around like rats in a maze, pulling vials, gauze, and other medical supplies out of drawers and cabinets, adding them to the carts they maneuvered.

He closed the curtain. The space smelled of antiseptic. Soon it would smell like death.

After extracting a full syringe from his pocket, he walked to the bed, injected the contents into her IV, then darted into the men's room just in time. An alarm sounded, indicating her heart had stopped. He waited, eyeing the chaos. At the right moment, he boldly advanced out the ER entrance and sidestepped two parked ambulances left open in the pandemonium. Too preoccupied with saving lives, no one gave him a second glance.

Minutes later, seated in his car, he flipped open his cell phone and punched a preset button.

"She's dead."

"Good. But we may have another problem."

~

Thank God she's stabilized, Shelly thought, staring out of the wall-to-wall windows trying to make sense of everything. How sad to have forgotten what good friends they were at one time. With Kiera now clinging to life, more than a decade of memories consumed her.

"Michelle? Are you okay?"

She jumped when Jake's question registered.

"Yes." She pivoted and met his serious gaze. She wished he'd aged or gone bald or something…anything to take away from his attractiveness. In six years, he hadn't changed a bit, except he'd grown devastatingly more handsome with the sharper edges of maturity etched into his features. He'd always been a heartthrob, in her opinion. But now? He was McDreamy and McSteamy rolled into one, and she'd had a hard time keeping her eyes off his face, off the well-defined muscles of his six-foot physique. If the man modeled for Calvin Klein in *GQ*, she had no doubt sales would triple, and it wouldn't be men doing the buying.

"Don't worry, Michelle. She'll be okay."

Smiling, she took a steadying breath and fought to ignore the tiny burst of pleasure over hearing him speak her given name aloud. Jake was the only person besides her mother who didn't use her nickname. At age thirteen when she'd instructed everyone to call her Shelly, he'd resisted, saying Michelle reminded him of the Beatles' song he liked, one that his mother had always played when he was a kid. Shelly had bought the CD and had immediately fallen in love with the song. To this day it was still a favorite, and back then, she'd prayed to be Jake's Michelle, ma belle. Geez, she'd been filled with silly dreams of him as her Prince Charming at one time. The only problem with such dreams was how easily they turned into nightmares.

Jacob Collier was and always would be Kiera's. How stupid to have forgotten even for a split second. Then remembering their situation, she sobered and shoved all jealous thoughts aside. Jealousy wouldn't aid in her pursuit of forgiving, forgetting, and moving on. If only she could forget Jake, she'd be there already. "Did you get through to Elaine?"

"Yeah."

"How is she?"

Jake shrugged. "As good as can be expected, considering. She's on her way now."

Shelly nodded.

"Where are you staying while you're in town?"

She hadn't expected the question and had to think about how to reply. "Actually, I wasn't planning on staying." She offered a short explanation about Kiera's need to atone, and why she'd come in the first place. Her intentions included driving back to Georgia the moment Kiera finished saying her piece.

Unless forgiveness somehow persuaded her to stay. She'd even packed an overnight bag, just in case. Since that didn't seem likely due to circumstances, it was time to make an exit. "In fact, now that Kiera's stabilized, I should head back to Atlanta." Maybe she'd made a mistake by coming in the first place. "I'll return when things have settled."

"Elaine will need an extra friend. You *are* going to stay long enough to say hi, aren't you?"

"Damn," Shelly muttered under her breath. Indecision swamped her. She hadn't even considered Elaine's reaction. Kiera's overdose would hit her hard. Hadn't she already lost her husband a few years ago from a car accident? If nothing else, Shelly owed her support. The Matthews family owed Elaine much more for employing Shelly's mother, and eventually Shelly and her sister, back when jobs were scarce and money even scarcer.

She nodded, her conscience triumphing over cowardice. "I'll stick around." Heck, the worst had happened. She'd already faced Jake and survived. A few more hours wouldn't hurt.

~

Waiting sucked, Jake thought, returning to the chair he'd vacated earlier. The entire time he sat, his mind waged a bitter battle. His gaze sought out Michelle, whose focus was glued to the windows. He should forget the past and talk to her, find out what she knew, if anything.

Hell, he should be thinking like a DEA agent right now, not a guilt-ridden idiot. He should turn over the substance to Sheriff Baker. Once that thought was out, he discarded it. The damage was done. No one had to know Kiera had it on her. Why make matters worse for himself or those close to Kiera? Including Baker. Didn't matter that he was rationalizing bad judgment and serious repercussions could ensue. He wasn't about to cause his daughter or Elaine more pain and embarrassment.

He'd give it to his partner. Rich had friends who owed him favors. Maybe the chemical makeup of the powder would tell them something. Anything. Maybe Kiera was—

A flurry of activity drew him out of his thoughts as more hospital personnel rushed through the double doors leading into the ER. After eyeing the spot for what seemed like hours, Jake leaned back in the chair and wiped his face in frustration.

"I can't imagine what's taking him so long," said the woman who'd spoken to the doctor earlier and now sat two chairs away from him. She concentrated on the ER doors. "He said he'd be right back and that was almost twenty minutes ago."

"Something must have happened." Jake's gaze followed hers. "There was a lot of hubbub all of a sudden." He stood with the intention of questioning Michelle, when the same doctor who'd given him such an optimistic update burst through the doors, his expression grim.

"I'm sorry." The doctor halted a few feet away. "We did all we could, but Ms. Delaney's heart stopped. We weren't able to resuscitate. Are you her next of kin?"

The unexpected news sliced through Jake's equilibrium. Its finality hit him with the force of a bulldozer plowing through any promise of tomorrow for Kiera.

Jake forced out a strangled, "No." He hadn't been next of kin since their divorce, but he still felt responsible for her. He cleared his throat until the lump of regret lodged in his soul receded enough to speak. "Her mother should be here any minute."

The doctor nodded. "The authorities have been notified per hospital policy on an OD."

Right then, Michelle came up, her expression questioning. When Jake shook his head, she grabbed his arm, a look of horror crossing her face. Her fingers dug into his flesh as the doctor added, "Sheriff's a little busy with an accident on the interstate, but he wants to speak with you. Asked if you could wait."

Of course Baker wanted to see him. "Sure," he murmured.

Remorse over keeping Kiera's participation a secret—against his better judgment—assaulted Jake's senses. He had no excuse, except her determination to remain anonymous. Since she and Baker were dating, she'd been more than adamant about not wanting to worry the sheriff over her involvement.

"I'll wait." He led Michelle to a chair, then sank down next to her. In hindsight, he should have known better than to keep secrets from Baker. They were working together on this case and were already at odds over how to handle it. He damn sure wasn't about to reveal his stupidity this late in the game and create more hostility. Not when he might be reprimanded, taken off the case, or even worse—lose his job. Nothing would stop him from finding out the truth now.

When the doctor turned to go, the woman sitting two seats away asked, "Doctor, did you happen to see Dr. Thomas?"

"I'm sorry. He left for the day…hours ago."

"But he was just here and promised to check on my son, Wayne Gardiner." She nodded toward the ER doors. "Wayne's been in there for over three hours."

The doctor shrugged. "I haven't seen him since early this morning when his night shift ended, but I'd be happy to check on your son."

Michelle let go of Jake's arm as the doctor hurried off. Neither spoke during the strained silence left behind. She was obviously caught up in her own thoughts regarding Kiera's bewildering demise. Thankfully, the doctor reappeared and Jake had something besides death to focus on.

"It won't be much longer," he said. "They're x-raying him now. The ER got deluged with an influx of trauma cases from a pileup on I-65."

He walked away. Seconds later, the double glass doors leading to the street opened. When Elaine stepped into view, Jake stood, mentally preparing the words that would destroy her world, his questions for Michelle all but forgotten, along with the lady and her injured son.

"Have you heard any more news?" Her face twisted in pain as she rushed up to him.

He shook his head. "I'm sorry, Elaine." Facing loved ones of those who'd died so senselessly was shitty. Adding to her torment with his next words only made the task shittier.

"The doctors did everything they could, but her heart stopped and they couldn't revive her." He swallowed hard and added softly, "She died a few minutes ago."

"No!" Tears trailed the sides of her grief-stricken face.

"I don't know what happened." His blink did nothing to wash the blur from his eyes. He wiped at the moisture with his sleeve, using the excuse to break eye contact. "I'm so sorry."

"Dear God, no! Why? When everything was going so well?"

Jake pulled her into his arms. Her gut-wrenching sobs tore into his conscience. What could he say? Not the usual bullshit. He finally understood something about those left behind. If he'd known about the guilt, the denial, the horrible pain of accepting such a horrendous ending, he'd have worked on refining his approach. Yet facing Elaine was easy compared to what was to come when he'd have to inform his daughter. Oh God, how was he going to tell Emily?

Michelle slipped out of her chair and took a tentative step in their direction. "I'm so sorry, Elaine."

"Shelly?" Elaine turned, wiped back tears, and worked at offering a smile. "Kiera mentioned something about seeing you again, and Jake said you were here."

"I just wish I'd come years ago." Tears filled Michelle's eyes. "I'm so sorry I didn't."

"Hush, child. You're here now. That's all that matters."

As the two women comforted each other, an impotent rage filled Jake. The same rage had spurred him into his current line of work after seeing too many of his childhood friends, his ex included, addicted to shit and their lives changed forever.

Something had gone wrong. Kiera wasn't supposed to die. Not from a drug overdose. Not when she'd been clean for years and had too much reason to stay that way.

"I swear, Elaine, if it takes me the rest of my life, I'll find out what happened." He'd damn sure find out who was responsible and nail the bastard. Hard. So other victims wouldn't be drawn in and lose their souls.

Illegal drug trade was a never-ending fact of life, but nonetheless his resolve strengthened. If eradicated, the world would be a better place and the kids who got involved with drugs might be spared misery, as would their loved ones. At the very least, they'd have a brighter future than lying dead on a gurney in the ER or on a slab in the morgue.

~

"I can't believe she didn't make it."

Jake's desolate voice drew Shelly's attention. Though in total shock herself, she wasn't immune to the raw pain echoed in his statement or the heartache his eyes revealed. "It *is* hard to understand." She touched his arm in an attempt to ease his grief.

"I…um…I…" He faltered a moment before clearing his throat. "Such a waste." His gaze returned to the window and he focused on a distant point.

"I thought she had her life on track," Shelly was finally able to get out. Kiera had had it all. Why would she throw it away? Shelly squeezed her eyes shut tight. Damn, she shouldn't be jealous, not of a dead woman. Not anymore. Yet second place still hurt! Even after all these years. To this day, she still believed Kiera had never deserved Jake or his love. But neither had she deserved such a horrible death. No one did. Tears for her friend that Shelly never thought she'd shed blurred her eyes. She blinked them back.

"I'm so sorry, Jake," she said with total honesty. "I know what she meant to you."

"Yeah. It's a goddamn tragedy." His voice cracked. "Now I have to tell Emily her mother died. How do you tell a kid something like that?" He hesitated, then cleared his throat once more before sighing heavily. "Thank you, Michelle, for being here. I really appreciate your help with Elaine. I'm sure this must be hard for you."

Jake's sincerity shot straight to her heart and made her feel like Cruella De Vil for her jealous thoughts. He had no clue how she really felt or that facing him again was much more difficult than even he could imagine. And he never would. Her gaze sought out the distraught woman sitting alone in a chair. "Has anyone arrived to take her home?"

"Yeah." His nod indicated the windows. "Two state troopers just got here. One will follow in her car and the other will drive her home, as well as drop you off at the high school." As he spoke, the double glass doors opened and two burly troopers went up to Elaine, who stood at their approach. "Emily's with a neighbor. We decided it would be better to explain about Kiera's death together." Jake's shoulders slumped. "I'll finish with Sheriff Baker and break away as soon as I can. Then I'd like to talk with you. I have a couple of questions you might be able to clear up. I really appreciate this. I'm forever in your debt."

"Sure, Jake." She smiled wistfully at the thought of being in his debt. She'd much prefer a place in his heart, like Kiera had, but she was done with wishful thinking. "I'm ready to go anytime."

~

Fifteen minutes later, the state police car stopped next to Shelly's parked gray Altima. Shelly hugged Elaine and slid across the leather backseat to open the door.

"You'll at least spend the night before you return to Atlanta?"

Shelly turned around and swallowed her refusal. Elaine's expression was so hopeful, she couldn't outright say no. Not yet, anyway. She sighed. "I'm not sure." She exited, then leaned inside. "I need to call home to tell them what's happened. I'll be there shortly and we can discuss tonight."

Shading her eyes to block out the harsh sunlight, she remained rooted to the spot and watched the brake lights flash brighter before the trooper turned left and finally disappeared.

The oppressive heat added to her sense of doom, as did the weight of indecision settling on her shoulders. She hit the keyless entry and slowly climbed inside. Leaving the door open, she jacked up the air conditioner and lowered all four windows. She reached for her phone, punched in her home number, and resisted another strong impulse to just drive until she ran out of road.

"Mom?"

"Hey, sweetie." Shelly smiled, not expecting her son to answer. "I miss you," she said, in an attempt to focus on Mikey, rather than on what had happened to Kiera or on seeing Jake again.

"I miss you too. When're ya comin' home?"

"I've only been gone since this morning. Still, it's nice to be missed." Her smile stretched in pleasure, and then she sobered. "My trip might be delayed." The horrible death of an ex-friend wasn't something he needed to know. She didn't give explanations, other than, "I'm enjoying my hometown visit. Would you mind if I spent a little more time here?" Just in case she found the courage to stick around.

"Joey's birthday slumber party is in a few days. I need a present."

"Oh, I get it," she teased, striving for levity. "The only reason you want me home is to buy birthday presents."

"Well…" He drew the word out, letting her know that she'd pretty much guessed his motives.

She laughed. Leave it to Mikey to cheer her up under such sad circumstances. Her son never ceased being the silver lining in her cloudy life.

"If I'm not home in time, tell Grandma to pick out a present with blue wrapping." She had a couple of pinks in the pile…for girls. The majority of pre-bought, pre-wrapped gifts she'd picked up at bargain prices were for the six boys in Mikey's class with birthdays coming up in the next two months. Being a single mom required thriftiness and organization, if nothing else.

"I need to speak to Grandma, but before I do, tell me about your day."

They chatted, or rather Mikey did, doing most of the talking. Even if she hadn't wanted his cheerful diversion, Shelly always reached for extra patience when he chose to speak. Since these moments came more infrequently the older he grew, she waited until he finished before she said, "Now can you put Grandma on the phone?"

"Sure. Bye, Mom. I love you."

"I love you too, sweetie."

Maggie Matthews came on the line and Shelly updated her on Kiera's death.

"You say you've seen Jake Collier?" Maggie asked after a brief silence.

"Yes. I saw him." Shelly's back straightened as her grip on the phone tightened. "What has that got to do with anything?"

"You should tell him. Especially now that Kiera is dead. You have no reason not to."

"Please, Mom." Shelly closed her eyes and inhaled slowly. "I can't," she said on the exhale.

"You're making a grave mistake, Michelle. He has the right to know."

"Maybe, but it's my mistake to make." Damn, now she was sniping at her mother. She forced herself to take another deep breath, then smiled into the phone. "I'm sorry. That didn't come out right. I understand you only have my best interest at heart, but you know I have my reasons. Nothing's changed in six years and I won't risk hurting Mikey. Not now. Not ever." Mikey would never experience her pain of not fitting in in this small-minded town, full of judgmental, God-fearing citizens who loved to point out sinners. What better proof of her past sins than an innocent child to remind everyone of her stupidity? As archaic as it sounded, her son would be labeled a bastard. She'd never allow anyone to ridicule Mikey because of his situation. "I'll call later after I talk to Elaine and let you know my plans."

"Well, you know best." Maggie's sigh shot straight to her conscience, something that also hadn't changed in all these years. Her mom had never approved of Shelly's decision to keep Mikey to herself. But Maggie also didn't know the whole story.

Now that Kiera was dead, only Jake and Shelly knew the whole truth of what happened that summer. And only she'd heard Kiera's words. Words filled with hate, but also too much truth. *Who do you think he'd choose between a pregnant you or a pregnant me? You've always been second place behind me and if you don't have that abortion, the whole town will know it every time they see your bastard. You'll be more than pathetic and so will your child.*

"Don't worry about things here," her mother said, diverting Shelly's focus to the present. "Your sister and I can handle the store. Tell Elaine she's in my prayers. It's so sad I've never kept in touch."

They said their good-byes and Shelly cut the connection with the flick of her wrist.

In slow motion, she grabbed her seat belt and snapped it into place, in no hurry to face the next few hours. Today, just as six years ago, the same sense of dread over her decision tore her in two. She'd never intended to see Mikey's father again. Jake had no idea his son existed and she planned to keep it that way, despite her mother's scolding.

They'd all made hard choices. She'd opted against abortion, which meant Mikey belonged to her. Right? Yes, that had to be right. Jake had no claim on her son. Yet, guilt niggled at her peace of mind along with her mother's admonishment.

Shelly pursed her lips and shifted into reverse, refusing to dwell any longer over her decision. Protecting her son was her most important role, and she'd keep her secret with the ferocity of a mother bear defending her cub. She backed out of the parking space and drove past the Jefferson Memorial High School sign. The lettering was faded and one O missing—busted out—most likely from a rock a graduating senior or an incoming freshman pitched on a dare.

Apparently not much had changed in juvenile thrills, she thought, only too glad to have someone else's misdeeds to center on rather than her own.

At Oak and Main, Shelly braked. One way led into downtown Campton, the other to I-65 and home. Her grip tightened on the wheel and she subdued a sudden urge to escape, to turn left and to speed toward the interstate. Had she always been such a coward? Not yielding to temptation, she turned right instead, heading through the center of town.

As she drove, her assessing gaze landed on Campton's only department store, a loose description. Describing Delaney's as a Macy's or Saks Fifth Avenue was like calling a sinkhole the Grand Canyon. Still, Elaine Delaney, the owner, kept up with current fashions. Or she used to. Thoughts of the store and Elaine circled around to the reason she turtled along Main in the first place—Kiera Delaney and forgiveness—or rather Kiera's unsettling phone call.

Why had she called when nothing had really changed? Even worse, why had Shelly jumped like a trained dog at the summons? She'd been surprised to hear from her. The two hadn't spoken since… Shelly closed her eyes, remembering that long ago moment Kiera had unleashed her venom with the speed and accuracy of a poisonous snake, calling Shelly white trash reaching for the moon and accusing her of trying to steal what didn't belong to her.

The words had stung. So much so that Shelly had never forgotten them.

Words were irrevocable. No one could take them back. Not ever. Now, with Kiera's death, she'd probably never get the chance to forgive and to move past them.

Leave the memories in the past, along with your childhood, she chided mentally.

"You're no longer the poor kid living in a trailer. You've moved beyond," she murmured. Or had she? A yellow traffic light yanked Shelly back to the task of driving. She slowed to a stop.

Strung across Main, the traffic signal was the only one in a twenty-mile radius. Yet unlike the light, which changed from green to yellow and then red in a matter of seconds, nothing else had changed in her mind's eye.

Except perception.

Funny, how a nineteen-year-old's viewpoint distorted reality. Tended to make things look larger than life. Campton was definitely smaller, less intimidating, certainly less remarkable than what she'd remembered.

Of course, living in Atlanta could skew any small-town girl's perception, but Campton's crumbling brick, peeling and rotten wood, and empty storefronts invited an obvious conclusion. The decay around her had taken longer than six years to manifest—something a teenager wouldn't notice, especially when ignorant of what treasures lay only hours off the interstate. When your family didn't own a car, five miles in either direction of I-65 might as well be the moon she'd been accused of reaching for.

The light blinked green and she gently pressed the accelerator. An out-of-state license plate was an easy target, and Main Street had always been the speed trap of choice for local law enforcement. Since Kiera hadn't voiced her vicious sentiments to just Shelly back then, Shelly's to-do list didn't include announcing her return via a speeding ticket. She'd hoped to slip into town, take care of business, and then slip out. Unnoticed.

At another crossroad, this one leading out of town on a back road, she turned right and then had to veer into the oncoming lane to avoid hitting an unmarked utility truck blocking the road.

"Jerk," she muttered, steering back to the right after passing at a safe distance. She increased her speed. Her focus moved to the radio. She turned the dial, searching for a decent station.

Seconds later, she glanced in the rearview mirror. The same utility truck was now accelerating, coming up fast. When he got too close, she did what she always did for tailgaters. Eased off the gas pedal. Her next step would have been to tap the brake, but he darted into the left lane to pass on a blind curve without decreasing his speed.

The scene then played out in fast-forward when he steered back over and cut her off just as something burst through the windshield.

An explosion of pain ripped through her shoulder as a loud thump sounded next to her.

"You stupid asshole!" Shelly yelled, braking at the same time to slow her speed around the curve. The car swerved. Instinctively, she turned the wheel, but it was too much, too fast. The late model Nissan Altima plowed through a spot where the guardrail suddenly ended. She veered out of control over an embankment. The car flew a few feet into the air before hitting the ground and cutting through bushes. A ditch finally stopped her momentum.

The airbag exploded and punched her in the face. For long seconds, she only saw stars.

Pinned into place, she was too dazed to move for quite a while. Finally, she gained her wits, unfastened her seat belt, and inched her way out of the vehicle, thankful for the safety devices that let her walk away with only a few bruises.

"Perfect! Just perfect!" Shelly circled her wrecked car. "What else can happen to make this day an utter bust?" Her gaze traveled to the gaping, jagged six-inch hole in the windshield. Upon closer inspection, she saw what had crashed through. A sledgehammer was wedged into the seat inches from where she'd sat.

She stared in stunned amazement as realization set in, then glanced at her fingers massaging the painful lump at the top of her right arm. A nasty bruise had formed that had nothing to do with the collision. Cold terror ran through her veins chilling her insides, despite the heat of the sun beating against her shoulder blades.

Not only had an absolute asshole's reckless actions mangled her car, he hadn't secured his tools. And worse? She'd almost died and he couldn't even be bothered to stop and help.

With trembling fingers, she reached for her cell, about to call 911, then stopped and looked at the wrecked car. She wiped away tears of frustration. At this point, she was an emotional mess and couldn't face a bunch of small-town cops who lived to spread any new gossip.

If she made the call, her intention to slip in and out of town without notice would be history. Heck, her crash would be all over town in less than an hour, providing excitement while halting the tedium of rural living for another day. She'd take pictures with her cell phone and file a police report later, if one was needed. With no way of identifying the unmarked truck or the jerk who'd caused her accident, she'd let insurance deal with the problem.

That left only one person she knew to call. Thankfully, he'd given her his cell number. She ignored the burst of relief at having rationalized the need and brought up the last programmed entry. She steadied the cell phone against her ear when she realized her hands still shook.

"Michelle?"

"Jake? Thank heavens you answered." More tears filled her eyes. She blinked, smiling through the blurry haze.

"What's wrong?" At the worry in his voice, years of hurt evaporated in a nanosecond.

He did care for her. He always had, she suddenly remembered. But only as a friend, and at this moment, considering the emotional toll of the last few hours, Shelly truly needed a friend.

"I didn't know who else to call." Jake would know what to do. She wiped away tears and fought to hold them back, but it seemed the deluge wouldn't stop. "I crashed my car on the way to Elaine's." She spent a moment explaining the accident.

"Shit, are you okay? Do you need an ambulance?"

"I'm fine." Shelly rubbed the knot on her shoulder. "Outside of a few bruises, that is."

"Are you sure? Maybe I should send an EMT to be on the safe side."

"No. I'd rather you not." Local EMTs were just as bad as cops when it came to gossip. "I was able to walk away. I just need a friend."

"Hang on, Michelle. I'll be there as soon as I can break away."

She hung up with the full understanding of why she'd fallen

in love with him in the first place…why she'd never forgotten him. He was the ultimate hero. No man in six years had compared to the idea of him in her mind.

Her shoulders slumped as she hiked up the hill toward the road. She should have stayed in Atlanta. Forgiveness hadn't eased her soul. It only made her heart ache more.

Chapter 2

Jake cut the connection to the cell phone and glanced up.

The sheriff was heading his way, clearly ready to resume where he'd left off. Tom Baker's red cheeks and glaring eyes said it all. Instead of showing what Jake guessed to be grief, the guy hid behind a mask of anger. Blistering anger. He was spitting nails after learning about Kiera's death, even madder to discover how she died.

Okay, so her death affected Baker, and Jake bore some responsibility. That didn't mean he'd let the asshole railroad him. He'd endured over thirty minutes of grilling about the last few hours, starting from the moment he'd found Kiera and had brought her into the ER. Breaking away in order to think was Jake's biggest wish. Unfortunately, the sheriff's intent expression said otherwise. Jake wiped his face in resignation and braced for more questions.

"What're you leaving out? What else did you see or hear in the waiting room?"

"I don't follow?" Jake let the question form in his impatient glare in hopes that Tom would cease with his inquisition. Despite a shitload of capital *T* trouble if ever caught withholding evidence, he wasn't about to offer anything until he fully understood what went down today.

"I just finished with Mrs. Gardiner." Tom's steady gaze bored into his. "Would you like a detailed hypothesis?"

Jake silently eyed him. Why the concern about the lady who sat next to Michelle?

Without breaking eye contact, Tom went on. "Kiera's death is related to the other overdoses. I can feel it." He paused. "This is my town, Collier, and we had an understanding. You play by my rules. I don't need outsiders coming in and taking over."

Jake bit back a retort, stifling the urge to roll his eyes. They might be working together, but the Drug Enforcement Agency was in charge. Small-town sheriffs tended to hold on to their authority with a firm grip and Tom was no different. In fact, the force of their past differences might easily tighten his grip. Jake wouldn't be surprised if he still carried the chip of rivalry on his shoulder. After all, as a high school sophomore, Jake had taken Tom's senior spot as first string wide receiver—stolen was how Tom had viewed it—and Tom had never hidden his interest in Kiera.

"I'm DEA, not an outsider. My main intent is to solve these crimes." The DEA had stepped in to probe rumors of meth trafficking in neighboring counties. Jake had a personal connection to the area and could work with Baker without raising suspicion. His partner had gone in undercover. "You know damn well I don't need your permission to investigate if this is connected. I have a personal stake and nothing you say will stop me." Tom may have been dating Kiera, but Jake had married and divorced her. Despite their rocky marriage, the mother of his child was now dead of an overdose after trying to help him. That made it really personal.

"More reason to let my office handle investigating Kiera's death. This ain't the big city. You federal boys just don't understand rural America," the sheriff said with conviction, as if Jake had been born and raised in Nashville and knew nothing of rural life.

Jake knew plenty. He'd called Campton home for twenty-five of his twenty-nine years. Life, mere miles outside of Nashville where he now lived, was every bit as rural as southern Kentucky.

He flashed a sardonic grin. "And that's why two women—no, make that three—have died of overdoses in the last few months and the DEA was called in? Because you're handling it?"

That was a low blow to hurl at a grieving man, Jake thought, as Baker's lips tightened into a firm line and another angry flush colored his cheeks. But damn it all, the guy deserved the hit.

"No one should've died. Least of all Kiera." Tom's focus went back to his notebook.

"I know." Jake sighed, unable to ignore his despondent

tone. But more than a twinge of guilt nestled in his gut as his instinct kicked in. It never lied. He agreed with Tom's assessment about connections. His mind spun, searching for some link other than dying from an OD.

There had to be something, but right now too many pieces of the puzzle were still missing to figure out what. Jake's thoughts shifted to Tom's sudden turn in his line of questioning. What did this Mrs. Gardiner have to do with anything? He remembered she'd spoken to a doctor right before all hell broke loose in the ER. The timing intrigued him and he had his own questions. Too much didn't add up. Still, he wasn't about to voice his suspicions. Tom would just dismiss them, if only to prove a point.

"Look, I'm sorry." Jake wiped his face. "I spoke out of line. I know this must be tough. Kiera mentioned you two were talking of marriage."

"Yeah, we were." Baker shook his dark head in defeat. His tall, lanky form seemed to diminish as his slumped shoulders instantly added twenty years to his age. "I thought I had a handle on the local meth problem. And now this. I've shut down so many goddamned labs I've lost count, but rest assured." He pounded his pen on the notebook with enough force to poke a hole through the paper. "I won't stop till they're all closed in my county. I *will* find out why Kiera died." Tom met his glance. Jake spied a hint of pain in his pale eyes as the sheriff said, "I don't believe for a second she OD'd accidentally."

Jake rolled the last statement around in his brain, feeling guiltier by the minute. Tom had been closer to Kiera than he had these past six months. If he leaned in that direction, it added credibility to Jake's same conclusion.

"I don't think so either. She wasn't using again. We both know she had too much reason not to." He drew a hand through his hair, rested it on the back of his neck, and rubbed.

He'd fully grasped the magnitude of anyone's daily struggle with addiction. As with any former addict, the risk of relapse was almost a foregone conclusion. Years earlier, Kiera had faltered with a few half-hearted attempts, but when her father died, something snapped into place for Kiera, as if she'd finally grown up. Overnight. After fighting her way to sobriety and staying there, she would have had to have taken a complete one-eighty. In twenty-four hours.

"Emily's been staying weekends with Elaine, part of supervised visitations with her mother for the past year. Kiera wanted joint custody. We were meeting later today to work out the specifics. That just doesn't fit the profile of someone needing a fix."

Nor could he discount the fact that she'd been clean for well over two years with ongoing random drug tests before he'd even allow the visitations, and he'd never let his guard down. He'd known what signs to look for. There were none. He hadn't noticed any other drug paraphernalia on her, nor had he seen her car after spotting her near the high school gym.

She'd come from the direction of Mueller's Cave, the same place Kiera, Michelle, and he had hung out a lot as kids. Jake made a mental note to check it out later. "I wish I'd gotten to the high school earlier. Maybe I could've stopped it."

"Stopped what?" Tom's eyes narrowed and he kept his attention glued to his face.

"I don't know," Jake said honestly, as another question hit him. Michelle was here at Kiera's urging. Would his ex have tossed away the opportunity to square the past with an old friend for a fix? Four years ago, he might have bought it. But now? No way. "I have no idea what went down, but I damn well won't rest until I find out."

"You and me both." Tom's gaze never wavered. "We're working this case together. I don't expect you to go off half-cocked. You got that?" When Jake didn't respond, he added, "I don't need the cavalry riding in, destroying years of hard work, because you're on a vendetta."

Jake snorted. The Tom Baker he remembered had resurfaced. Though Kiera had found him appealing enough to entertain thoughts of marriage, Jake never had much use for him. "I'm DEA, not the cavalry, and I'm not on a vendetta. Not in the way you mean."

Tom Baker's impressive record earned him a far-reaching reputation, and some DEA agents in his division put him on a pedestal. Jake didn't. The past got in the way. He recognized his hidden methods. The sheriff most likely cheated, just as he had in high school, using his strong-arm tactics with more flexibility than a Fed could get away with. County residents would look the other way and vote him back into office because, questionable or not, his methods worked.

Jake shrugged. Wasn't he just as wrong in keeping Kiera's involvement secret and in holding back evidence? After all, they were fighting a never-ending war. Maybe those voters weren't so far off when kids' lives were at stake.

Now with Kiera's demise, he could almost understand their thinking. At least he and Baker held the same goals, and drug use in the county had decreased dramatically among teens.

"Like I said. This *is* personal. For my daughter. I wouldn't be much of a father if I didn't do everything in my power to find out why her mother died." Jake met Tom's unfaltering gaze, let the truth of who was in charge shine in his. "Are we on the same page? Or do I need to go above your head?"

"No need," Tom blew out on a resigned sigh after weighing his response. "Since we're in this together, answer my earlier question." When Jake raised an eyebrow, he said, "What did you see in the waiting room?"

"Nothing."

Tom grunted. "Yeah, right."

Now he was even more intrigued. "I was a little sidetracked. Had an ex-wife dying of an overdose on my mind while I was trying to console her mother, so I wasn't as observant as I should've been." He was also dealing with the shock of Michelle's return, but he hadn't been too overcome not to notice the doctor who'd spoken with Mrs. Gardiner, or the other doctor's comment about the guy supposedly being off duty. Was there a connection?

Jake offered a semblance of a smile. "Why the interest in this woman talking to some doctor? You think he had something to do with Kiera's OD?"

"Just touching all the bases. I'm a thorough man." Tom finished writing in his notebook, then closed and stuck it in his pocket, along with his pen. He glanced up. A hint of anguish flashed in his eyes. "Kiera's body will be transferred to the morgue for an autopsy. I'll wait for the ME's findings." His gaze narrowed, and Jake could see the pain turn to speculation. "Try to remember we're a team. Keep me in the loop and I'll do the same. Are we clear?"

"As glass." Jake nodded. "I take it we're done here?"

"For the time being. If I have any more questions, I've got your cell number."

Jake walked away, swallowing his annoyance and focusing on solving the mystery.

He had a job to do. No good would come from rehashing old rivalries in the hospital waiting room. As he stepped out of the automatic doors on his way to the parking lot, a thought formed. The same one he'd had when he found out about this assignment. How could he work with the guy when he'd never liked him?

Then his brain shifted to Michelle and her accident.

On the way to his car, he called Campton's best and only mechanic. George Dalton also had a body shop on the side. Most who owned businesses in rural areas like Campton were jacks of different trades within the same field to earn a decent living, marginal as it was compared to Nashville. No one got rich, but then one didn't need much with the adjusted costs of living in the middle of nowhere.

"I'm on a call right now, but I can be there within the hour," George said.

"Great." After giving him the specifics, Jake said good-bye, cut the connection, and hit the Durango's keyless entry.

In moments, he sped along the main road leading from town to Elaine's house a few miles out. Jake rounded the bend Michelle had described and tapped the brake. Seconds later he saw her sitting on the guardrail, looking like a vision—the same blonde angel she'd always been—to him, anyway.

Slowing, he guided the car to the side of the road. Michelle Matthews had been as big a part of his formative years as Kiera Delaney had been. She was the antithesis of his ex, a calm and stable beam of light, where Kiera was like a star burning out of control. Growing up, the two friends had been an inseparable study in contrasts, one a willowy blonde with long, almost gawky arms and legs, versus the other who'd developed much too early with full awareness of her dark beauty and sensuality. After exiting, he slammed the car door and turned in her direction.

Michelle stood at his approach. Damn, she'd matured into a beautiful woman. After filling out in all the right places, gawky was no longer an apt description. Though willowy still fit. Grace and dignity personified, he thought, as she seemed to float toward him exuding that serene wholesomeness he'd always attributed to her.

"Thanks for coming." She halted a foot in front of him, stuck both hands in her pockets, and rocked back and forth.

Instantly, the years fell away. He was swept back to that last summer as memories surfaced—memories that were better off left buried—because Kiera still seemed to stand between them. And her death had somehow created a wall neither could scale, least of all him.

Jake cleared his throat and nodded toward the embankment. "Let's go survey the damage."

They stepped around the guardrail.

"I called a tow truck. You remember George Dalton? He had another call to make," he said after an awkward moment. "Should be by soon enough. He can handle things and call us if he has questions. No sense waiting in this heat."

Both remained silent as they trudged side by side down the hill.

A few sounds filtered through the late afternoon air. Trees blew in the breeze, their leaves rustling. Birds chirped, bees buzzed, and cicadas sang, adding to the summer day's ambience. Yet, the atmosphere crackled with more than sounds and heat. Something akin to energy. Invisible sparks of awareness danced in the space around them.

Jesus, he'd barely had time to assimilate Kiera's death, so why did his thoughts keep wandering to Michelle? He didn't want to think of her. He just wanted to forget. Everything. Kiera's horrible death, the heartache of telling his daughter, the chore of dealing with Elaine. He had no time to dwell on his past mistakes. Thankfully, her wreck came into view. He hiked around the tree to reach the front of the car from the other direction.

Suddenly, Jake froze. All thoughts fled as he sucked in a deep breath and eyed the windshield.

He stepped closer for a better view.

"Shit." He blew out the word on an extreme exhale. "You could've been killed."

"I came this close." Flashing a tremulous smile, she held up a hand with thumb and forefinger an inch apart. "My guardian angel must've been looking out for me."

Like a blast of clean spring air after a drizzly, sodden winter, her smile warmed him. Hell, he felt as if the sun had come out of hiding, throwing light and heat over his dark and cold world. He fought to ignore the stirrings. Michelle Matthews was all that was good in the world and he'd never been worthy of such goodness, not with his past sins weighing on his soul.

He sighed in resignation. The feelings of unworthiness were nothing new, nor were they likely to disappear because he was no more worthy today than he'd been six years ago.

"Looks pretty totaled. You should file a report with the sheriff as soon as possible."

Michelle tossed back a handful of hair that had fallen in front of her face. The color, now a darker shade of blonde, appeared like spun gold in the sun and suited her, he thought as she hefted her oversized purse over her shoulder. "I was hoping to avoid the hassle right now. I have no proof. I didn't even get a license number."

"You should still report it."

"I will. Just not now."

"Maybe Baker has an idea as to who owns the truck." He bent to pick up an overnight bag, then offered a hand to help her up the hill.

"I doubt it." She shrugged and grabbed his fingers. "I'll file a report, but it can wait a bit. I'd rather not make a big deal about the accident, if you don't mind. It'll just raise a lot of talk I can't handle right now. I took pictures with my cell and left a message with my agent. When I talk to him, I'll see about getting a rental."

They headed in the direction of his Durango. When he realized he still held her hand, he dropped it as if it had burned him. Smooth move, idiot. Damn, he was more nervous than a kid on his first date and they were simply walking to his car. Get a grip, Collier.

"So, Tom Baker is sheriff now?"

"Yep, pretty amazing, huh?" The topic seemed as good as any, given the atmosphere suddenly turned more strained. "Old man Wellburn retired a few years after you left. Tom happened to be in the right place at the right time." He opened the door and waited until she climbed inside before slamming it and making his way to the other side.

Once belted in, he turned the key and gunned the motor, thankful for the diversion of driving to keep his mind off the woman who sat too close.

~

As Jake expertly guided the SUV onto the main road, the enclosed space seemed to shrink.

Shelly focused on her hands, willing her unease away, then stole a glimpse at his face. She noticed a determined slant to his jaw while he drove. The image of her son flashed. She'd seen Mikey wear the same expression too many times not to recognize the resemblance.

"Do you mind if we take a side trip?" His voice broke into her thoughts.

Shaking her head, she plastered a smile on her face and risked eye contact. "No."

"Good. Something about this scenario doesn't make sense and I want to check out the area where I first spotted Kiera before too much time passes."

Looking him in the eye had been the wrong thing to do. She refocused on her fingernails and murmured, "Sure."

As much as she'd mentally prepared for this, nothing had prepared her for the tremor of longing she'd experienced while watching him exit his car. And after holding his hand? She closed her eyes, sucked in soothing air, and remembered the jolt from touching him. All she could do at the time was walk and pretend the earth hadn't moved.

No! Her fingers curled into a fist. The past would not repeat itself. She'd grown up in six years and nothing of that gawky, naïve kid remained. If that were true, then why did her idiocy from that last summer still bother her?

Sighing, Shelly leaned her head against the rest and focused on the greens and grays whizzing by outside the window. Kiera had died. Tragically. Her heart should be full of compassion, not envy. She must possess a cruel streak, because her compassion wouldn't budge around her recollections and forgiveness suddenly became an impossibility.

A moment later, Jake slowed and pulled to a stop in the wide space alongside the road, less than a block from the school.

She recognized the spot. "You said she told you to meet her at Mueller's Cave?"

"Yeah. And she came running from there, heading for the school." He shut off the ignition and pointed in the direction of the cave. Their cave, about a half mile in from the road. "A few years ago a kid was hurt. Jenkins lives in Florida now and he had the entrance blocked for liability."

Shelly nodded, fully understanding the owner's reasoning in this age of litigation-crazy people. It was sad that no other kids could utilize the caves like they'd done for years. The three of them had spent many hot summer days in the cool underground cavern.

He unlatched his door and climbed out.

She did the same, joining him at the front bumper of the SUV. "What are we looking for?" She pivoted, taking in the familiar terrain, as other unwanted flashbacks surfaced.

"Kiera's car. It has to be nearby. She had to have come from somewhere."

Shelly trailed behind Jake, suppressing more memories. Nothing good would come of wishing that things had turned out differently.

At the mouth of the cave, he stopped. "Maybe we should fan out. I'll head that way toward the high school and then circle back."

Eager to put distance between them, she started off in the opposite direction.

Being around him again in their old stomping grounds was so much harder than she'd ever imagined. Even worse, Jake had mentioned something about staying at Elaine's with Emily, so the next few hours wouldn't get any easier. Without a car, her options were limited as to where she'd spend the night. Not after Elaine had begged this afternoon. Heck, she'd offered her home too many times in her yearly Christmas cards that Shelly couldn't expect a ride to a motel without a fight. No, she was stuck. In hell.

"He's not attractive." She repeated the mantra a few times. Lord only knew she'd never wanted to find him attractive. Not when his heart had always belonged to Kiera.

She'd thought that whatever had attracted her in the past would have diminished by now. Yet time and distance had somehow only suppressed the effects. One car ride and the attraction she'd always felt sprouted forth faster than bamboo grows in the wild.

"How can I be so shallow?" she muttered, rounding the bend. Kiera lay dead, never to see her child or husband again and all Shelly could focus on was how attractive she still found Jake. Yep! That was pretty damn shallow.

As she thrashed through the brush, pushing sticky branches and other vegetation out of the way, the thought of calling home to inform her mom of her accident entered her consciousness.

Without slowing, she pulled her cell phone out and opened it, closing it seconds later because the signal wasn't strong enough. She'd call later. She shoved the phone into her pocket, inhaled, and fought to keep the memories of that last weekend from overwhelming her. She'd been a naïve kid, thinking one night of pure bliss could wipe out years of Jake's single-minded devotion. She'd certainly learned a valuable lesson about men and sex. And drinking one too many beers. Yet, alcohol-induced or not, that night had been the best of her life. One she'd never forgotten. Nor had she forgotten the preceding weeks when she'd had Jake's full attention because he and Kiera had broken up.

Just then she spied bright color ahead. The red object hidden in the brush had to be Kiera's car.

"Jake," she yelled. "I think I found it."

Chapter 3

Michelle's shout interrupted Jake's thoughts.

"I'm right behind you." He glanced at a tree and slowly pivoted, taking mental inventory of his surroundings before heading in the direction of her voice.

Something about the terrain bothered him, but he wasn't quite sure what.

In seconds, he saw her and noticed what drew her shout in the first place.

Why would Kiera's red Camry be so far from the road? Then he noted the dirt ruts, obviously created with tire treads from car traffic. He reached for his cell phone and unobtrusively snapped several pictures while pretending to check for service, without alerting Michelle to his concerns.

Once he cleared the brush away from the car, his gaze hit upon a white pipe sticking out of the ground some fifty feet away. How odd. He walked around the vehicle, clicking off the cell's camera.

After taking a tissue out of his pocket, Jake tried the doors. Locked. He peered inside through the windows. Nothing looked out of place.

"This is definitely her car." Why was it out here? He snapped various pictures of the car's interior to study later. Something was going on in these woods. Whether or not that something had anything to do with Kiera's overdose or the other women's overdoses remained a mystery. Now, more than ever, intuition told him a connection existed. He just had to find it.

"You don't have a key?"

"No," he said. When her gaze turned questioning and she seemed to require some sort of explanation, he added, "We'd grown apart in the last few years and weren't close."

"I see."

She nodded, but more confusion slid over her features. She definitely didn't see. Of course Michelle wouldn't. Not after what he'd told her during their last conversation. She obviously hadn't heard of their divorce. Too late, he'd grasped his huge mistake in trusting his ex. Kiera, a master manipulator, had known exactly how to use his guilt and love against him in order to achieve her own selfish goals.

Yet, she *had* changed since her father's death, so maybe purposefully keeping his distance had been another huge mistake, he realized, as his gaze returned to the bit of white he'd noted moments ago.

Just what he needed. More guilt. More feelings of inadequacy. More reason to believe he'd somehow let his daughter down by not doing all he could to protect Emily's mother.

"Kiera and I haven't…" He broke off with his explanation as the hairs on the back of his neck stood on end.

"What's wrong?" Michelle stiffened, clearly sensing his uneasiness.

"Nothing." Jake shook his head, leaned closer, and lowered his voice. "I don't think we're alone."

She exhaled and her gaze focused behind him. "Thank God you feel it too."

Yeah, he felt it and his sixth sense never lied. Someone was watching them.

"Come on." He captured her hand, pulling her behind him at a fast clip. While walking, his gaze narrowed. He scrutinized the brush, surreptitiously snapping additional pictures, hoping for the least little clue as to where someone hid. The who and the why might take more time. Right now, he meant to vacate the area. He'd return later without an innocent bystander and do more searching under the cover of darkness.

"I thought your car was parked near the road." Her nod indicated the opposite direction he'd taken.

"It is." He'd led her a good distance from Kiera's car and they were now out of visual and hearing range from their unseen observer.

"Then why are we going this way?"

"I saw something earlier I want to check out," he said in a low voice, not altering his steps. He also wanted a few more pictures. Since someone lurked nearby, he wanted to be subtle about how he did it. "It should only take a minute."

His hand still gripped hers, but this time he held on and continued walking.

Jake eventually slowed. His gaze fell twenty feet to the right. He now knew what bothered him. He ambled closer and dropped her hand, then crouched to study the ground, the entire time clicking away to capture what he saw. Flattened grass, broken twigs, bent branches. Small signs shouting at his senses.

"Looks like some kind of scuffle took place here." Rubbing her arms, Michelle cast a furtive glance around.

"Yeah, it does," he agreed. The location wasn't more than two hundred yards from Kiera's car. The two had to be connected.

Jake touched his pocket. The slight bulge from the bag of drugs he'd concealed from the sheriff now weighed heavier. What the hell had Kiera gotten involved in?

"Let's go." Straightening, he grabbed her hand again, using the grip as a lifeline. He needed something to stabilize his plummeting emotions. Too many questions filled his jaded brain. "I saw what I came to see."

~

At the car, Jake reached for the door handle. When his elbow grazed her breast, Shelly lurched, almost stumbling in her haste to move away. Steadying hands gripped her shoulders.

"Ooh." She winced. "That hurts.

"Sorry." He let go, then tenderly peeled the sleeve away, unveiling a nasty bruise. "You should get this looked at."

He had the gentlest touch. His gaze sought hers and for one long moment, they just stared at each other. In his brown, bedroom eyes, Shelly spied a remnant of what had briefly sprung between them all those years ago. Then the glimpse evaporated. She blinked and stepped back, unsure if it had been real or simply wishful thinking.

"It's just a bruise." Clearing her throat, she tucked stray hair behind her ear. "I'm fine." She slid inside the car.

"I waited too long to come back," she said, to fill in the silence after he'd seated himself beside her. Though she voiced the sentiment, she lied through her teeth. He didn't need to know the thought of returning had never been at the top of her to-do list. She buckled her seat belt.

"What do you mean?" He inserted the key into the ignition and started the car.

"I should've forgiven Kiera sooner, then maybe I could've helped somehow."

"Maybe." While releasing a huge sigh, he shifted gears and hit the gas pedal, pulling onto the highway. "But I'd rather talk about something other than Kiera and could'ves or should'ves, if you don't mind."

She nodded. How sad to realize he'd said almost those exact words that summer. Memories of her stupidity leaped to the forefront of her mind. Flinging herself at Jake hadn't been her smartest move. What was worse than being his rebound? The whole town knew he'd turned down the poor kid for the rich one, thanks to Kiera. And Kiera had made sure she'd suffered…for daring to rise above her status…for daring to respond to the attraction…for daring to dream of happily-ever-after with a man like Jake.

Was she a glutton for punishment? Why had she come back?

"Tell me about your life." The rich cadence of his voice drew her out of her depressing thoughts.

"What would you like to know?" She harbored the idea that he'd used the topic as a diversion to keep their attention off what had just passed between them. Obviously, nothing had changed in how they'd dealt with their underlying attraction. Pretend it didn't exist.

"Elaine mentioned you're living in Atlanta now."

"Yeah. I am." She flashed what she hoped passed for a confident smile and stole a glance in his direction. His focus was glued to the road. He appeared much too relaxed.

Shelly rolled her eyes. Well, if he could act as if that time hadn't happened, so could she.

She should have kept to his methods of pretense back then. Or maybe not. She had Mikey as a result, something she'd never regretted, but she'd learned a hard lesson in return. Standing at the wrong end of a romantic triangle and loving someone who was in love with someone else had been like an acid eating away at who she wanted to be.

Running away had been the only way to stop the self-destruction.

"Big change from Campton. Was it hard making the transition from small-town girl to city girl?"

"Maybe. I can't remember." Actually, she was only too happy to land in a city where busybodies didn't know everyone's business, especially when they seldom got their facts straight. What a relief to have neighbors who knew nothing of her life. Mikey blended in with other kids who lived with one parent. "Atlanta's home now. I like the idea of walking into a department store or restaurant where the salesperson or waitress has no clue about my past."

"I never thought of Campton in those terms. But I can see your point." When she only grunted without responding, he hesitated an awkward moment, then asked, "So, what do you do in Atlanta?"

"My sister and I own an antiques store. My mom helps out. She's our best employee."

Shelly kept a smile pasted on her face. "Monica always jokes about cloning her." Since chumminess wasn't in her best interest, she didn't add more.

Jake returned her smile, but his wasn't as stiff.

Shelly blew out a lengthy breath, stuck her chin in her hand, and focused on the passing scenery.

In silence, they sped in the direction of Elaine's house. Thank God he didn't have a need to fill in the quiet, just seemed to accept she wasn't about to expand on her autobiography. Eventually, he turned right onto a dirt road…the same road leading to the trailer where she'd spent most of her childhood. Curiosity had her glancing down the narrow, tree-laden lane.

"It's still there," Jake said, stating the obvious.

"Yeah." The bleak eyesore appeared exactly as the image stored in her mind. More memories flooded back, of earlier times when she'd shared the minuscule two-bedroom house on wheels with her mom and sister. Years of tenants' abuses hadn't helped the ugly space. It worsened if you added in a landlord who didn't comprehend the word maintenance. Shelly had known, because she'd looked it up.

She sighed. Now as an adult, she realized her fate could have been a lot worse. After all, she had a strong mother who loved her daughters.

Still, in her mind, having both love and money would have been nice.

"Money doesn't mean much in the scheme of things. I'd trade any amount to have your father back." She could still hear Maggie's response when either she or her sister would complain about their lack of funds. Shelly's father had died of cancer, leaving behind huge medical debts and no life insurance. Only five at the time, Shelly had vague memories of her father and never really missed him. Not like her mom had. According to Maggie, money couldn't buy love.

Except maybe Jake's love. Okay, that was a bitchy thought, but she was entitled. Heck, she'd always had a sneaking suspicion that Jake stuck with Kiera because of her place in the town. An easy illusion to entertain, she realized just then. Had she deluded herself out of some sick need to compensate for what she'd lacked?

"Looks out of place, doesn't it?" she offered, stating another obvious. "I've always wondered what Ed and Elaine really thought of having such an eyesore so close to their property." The palatial Delaney house looked as though it belonged along the ocean in Palm Beach, Florida, rather than the rustic setting.

He shrugged, his expression saying he accepted the rural lifestyle. Trailers didn't fit in with any of the houses nearby, but everyone tolerated them. Neither low-rent apartments nor neighborhood associations existed in these parts, and money, or lack of it, defined those who lived here.

Kiera's family, along with Jake's, dated back to the town's beginning.

Shelly's family had always been trailer park trash, if you listened to the gossips.

Her mom had never paid attention to gossips. Actions counted to Maggie, not money. How a person behaved spoke loudest. "Being poor isn't a crime," Maggie used to say. "It just means you have less of what others have." Great words to live by.

Her mom never deviated from living her words, also never lived above her means after vowing to pay back every penny owed for her husband's care. Deep down, Shelly was proud of her mother's noble words and actions. Yet, she'd had to go to school and face all those kids, even poor kids, who'd loved to point out how little her family had.

Thankfully, Jake pulled into Elaine's driveway. The moment he shut off the ignition, Shelly jumped out of the car, relieved to finally put some space between them so she could breathe. This was going to be a long, long night.

~

He reached down and felt for a pulse. There was none. He looked at the asshole who had just fucked up their operation. "She's dead. Why the hell did you kill her?"

"She was trying to get away. I had to stop her."

"Not with an overdose, you idiot." Shit. How could the moron not learn, with two similar incidents ending the same way? The timing couldn't be worse, with that bitch's OD taken care of only hours ago. "You should've called me or Ivy if she was giving you trouble."

"I thought I could handle it."

"Yeah?" Straightening, he kept his hands at his side, waiting until the urge to pound the shit out of him subsided. "You handled it all right. Now we got a real mess on our hands. We've barely squeaked by with the other deaths. Hell, we've been lucky to avoid every goddamned drug enforcement agency swarming the area, and what's worse, state troopers are peeking into every crevice right along with them. Use your fucking brains."

He glanced back at the lifeless woman at his feet. A real beauty, spunkier than most. What a total waste of flesh. "Since she's dead, we're out money. Big money, and I'm not about to lose more. You got that?" He'd known she was a fighter from her caution in slipping into his trap. He'd gone too fast, rushed the process because he was short a girl, and now he had to start from square one, find another to replace her. But again, the timing was for shit.

"I just thought—"

"That's the trouble. You don't think. Goddamn fuckups. That's what I'm saddled with," he spat out, reaching for more patience. Once he calmed down, his mind spun. "We can't just dump her in the woods this time. Wrap her up and wait until things die down outside. Then take her to Cumberland and put some weights on her."

"Cumberland? Shit, man, that lake's too far away. It'll take too long."

"You should've thought of that before you shot her up and killed her."

"Why can't I use Barren?"

"Too close to the others, if her body's ever discovered. We can't afford more scrutiny. Get Billy to help."

"Billy? You know he ain't all there. What if he talks?"

"He won't. Not if you handle him right. He's our insurance." He gripped his gaze with a firm stare. "But for God's sake, don't kill him too. If you do, I'll hunt you down and kill you myself." He took a set of keys from his pocket and threw them in his direction. "Tell him you're going fishing before you drug him. He loves to fish. My pontoon's in my backyard on a trailer. Make sure you use the deepest part of the lake. I got other problems to take care of."

He turned, yet heard the other man grumble under his breath. He halted and pivoted, making eye contact. "You fuck this up and you won't get another chance," he warned, the sharp edge of his voice ripping through the night. "You got that?"

~

A servant Shelly didn't recognize set about pouring wine in the Delaney library. Emily, Jake's daughter, was in bed. The entire evening, especially dinner, had been a few long and emotional hours of watching Elaine's attempt at normalcy. Grief hung about her so thick, Shelly wondered if the distraught woman's life would ever return to normal. She wished she could ease her pain.

To make matters worse, Jake's quiet presence grated more on her peace of mind.

"It would be nice if you could stay for the funeral." Though Elaine smiled, dull sadness still lurked in her eyes. That's the way she dealt. Put on a brave face and strive to grieve in private. "It'll be next Tuesday. The medical examiner assured me he'd be done with her autopsy."

Shelly took a sip, stalling. Tuesday was one day less than a week away. She owed Elaine, and wanted to be here for her in her time of need, but the last thing she wanted was to remain in this house any longer than necessary. Not with him being so near. She looked up, an excuse on the tip of her tongue, but Elaine's hopeful expression stopped her cold. Her gaze traveled to Jake, who'd raised his eyebrows and was watching her intently, just as he'd done all night.

"I can't promise anything, but I'll try." Shelly sighed in resignation. "I hate to impose, though. I'll most likely have a car tomorrow, and I can get a motel room," she offered, undeterred from at least trying.

"Heavens, no. You're family. I wouldn't think of letting you stay in a hotel."

Of course she'd say that.

"I talked to George," Jake said. "Your car's not totaled, but it's pretty mangled. He can repair it, but it'll take some time and he'll need to order parts. Or he'll tow it, if you'd rather someone else do the work."

"I know George's been around forever and will do a good job," Shelly said. "I'll discuss it with my insurance agent, then give him a call." At this point she had no idea what she'd do, but lingering in Campton while waiting on repairs wasn't in her best interest either.

"I'd love to visit you in Atlanta, Shelly, once the funeral and all this business dies down." Tears filled Elaine's eyes. "Oh, heavens. Look at me! You'd think I'd be all dried up by now, with all the tears I've shed." She dabbed at her face with a tissue, wiping the drops away. She blew her nose and tried to present the proper Southern charm in her smile, but the wobbly effort did nothing to cover her grief. "I miss your mother. How is Maggie?"

"She's fine. Monica's fine." Shelly felt obligated to fill them in on the last six years. After all, Elaine had made such a valiant attempt at cheerfulness. "We bought an antiques store together a few years after I moved there."

"Oh? Kiera was never interested in Delaney's. Other than spending money there. I finally sold it after Ed died. Had no heart to keep it going on my own." Elaine shook her head. "You and Monica were the best salespeople I ever had. Outside of your mother, that is."

"Maggie works for us now." Shelly offered her own wobbly smile. Her energy waned. She just didn't have it in her to add any more cheer to the somber mood other than, "She's our model employee."

"You're lucky to have each other. The three of you were like my second family, and now with Emily going to live in Nashville full-time with Jake, I'll be all alone."

"Nashville's only an hour away," Jake interjected, after staying silent for so long. "You're welcome any time. You have been since the divorce. You know that, Elaine."

"Divorce?" Shelly's eyebrows lifted a fraction of an inch.

"Yeah. We lasted eighteen months," was all Jake said, turning back to Elaine. "And Emily can stay here when she's not in school or when I need to work. Kiera's death won't change things."

Shelly swallowed hard. He and Kiera had been apart for years? Why had Elaine never told her in her Christmas cards? Why had Jake never looked her up after his divorce? The answer was too obvious. She'd completely misinterpreted their relationship. Relationship? Who was she kidding? Jake had always belonged to Kiera, and Shelly had been a stupid fool for manipulating him, using Kiera's tactics. Her behavior hadn't been any better than the trailer park trash everyone accused her of being. She brought her wine to her lips and sipped to hide her embarrassment.

Elaine nodded, smiling wistfully. Shelly wasn't sure Elaine had heard Jake's comments as she stared off into space. Thankfully, it signaled their conversation had come to a natural end.

Seconds later, Elaine stood. "If you'll excuse me, I need to lie down."

Shelly left her unfinished drink on the table and escaped to her room.

~

The air conditioner kicked on, chilling the bedroom's air, but Shelly still couldn't breathe.

Sleep had been elusive, next to impossible when her mind wouldn't shut down.

She paced. The room closed in on her. She needed space. Intent on finding some, she moved to the sliding glass door. The moment Shelly stepped onto the huge deck that circled the back of the house, humid warmth hit her. It felt good, not at all stifling like the cold, drier air of her room. She walked to the balcony's railing as she mulled over Kiera's last words.

Remember the money tree. What had she meant? Following Kiera's edict, her thoughts drifted to an earlier time, those happier, more carefree moments in their friendship.

The mental picture brought on a smile. She'd forgotten how gullible a kid she'd been…

"So, we'll be rich?" Shelly remembered asking, as she'd stared with awe at the bit of green she and Kiera had planted. The memory was so clear, she was suddenly reliving that time…those feelings.

Both had tamped down the pile, adding more dirt to fill in the indentions of the hole they'd dug.

How would it be to never have to worry about money? To never be hungry, to walk into a store and buy anything you wanted? Not because it was serviceable and necessary, but because it was frivolous and extravagant? Shelly liked big words and used any opportunity to practice them. They made her feel important and words didn't cost anything but a bit of memorization.

She looked down at her ugly shoes, well-worn and formerly belonging to her older sister, the same as every item she had on. Her gaze slid over to Kiera's darling sandals. A birthday present, she'd said. Kiera had also unwrapped the latest Nintendo system, along with two new games and a computer.

For her eighth birthday, Shelly had gotten cake and a handmade card. A computer wasn't in her immediate future unless the tree yielded something sooner, rather than later.

"When can we start picking the money off the branches?" Shelly couldn't wait until it bloomed. Then she wouldn't be poor any longer. Money would solve her family's problems. She could pay off all of her dad's hospital bills. The Matthews family wouldn't have to pinch pennies. She could buy new clothes to wear to school, so the kids wouldn't make fun of her hideous hand-me-downs.

"No, silly," Kiera said, in an older, ten-year-old voice that always made Shelly feel like a stupid third grader, as if two years gave her infinite wisdom.

Shelly rolled her eyes. Yeah! Infinite. The word she'd learned in school fit in this instance, but not to define Kiera's brains. When related to numbers, they went on into infinity and she'd prayed for more than an infinite amount of money.

"It's not real. I thought you knew that."

"I did." Shelly lifted her chin and swallowed her disappointment, determined not to let her friend see how devastating her revelation was. For days Kiera had talked of nothing but planting the money tree, and how when it bloomed Shelly's problems would be solved. Optimistically—another good word she'd learned and tried to live by—Shelly had taken Kiera's claims to heart. She hated being poor. Being poor made it next to impossible to stay optimistic.

"According to legend, the money tree is something that brings riches in the form of luck."

An owl's call broke into Shelly's musings and brought her back to the present. Back to the fact that Kiera was dead. Back to the reality of Jake sleeping somewhere in the house.

She rubbed her arms and stared into the moonlit night as the insects played their music.

Her gaze roamed over the dark shadows defining the edges of Elaine's property. The money tree's bushy silhouette added to the grays in the enormous yard.

She smiled. Even after all these years, it still thrived. Why had Kiera mentioned the tree? Tightening the robe Elaine had let her borrow, Shelly headed down the stairs. She padded across the damp grass, which cooled her bare feet almost to the point of making them uncomfortably cold, contrasting with the warm, humid air. The thought of going back inside for shoes flitted into her mind, but she discarded it, too intent on checking out the bush.

When she neared it, she searched the ground. The moonlight aided her ability to discern differences in the shadows, but didn't provide enough light to see clearly.

Another owl hooted in the darkness. The tree frogs and crickets stopped their screeches, adding an eerie element to her surroundings. Goosebumps formed on her arms. She rubbed them, stilling the sudden chill running up her spine. The prickly sensation intensified.

Hairs on the back of her neck stood on end. She sensed she wasn't alone. She'd had the same feeling earlier in the day while hiking to Kiera's car in the woods.

Her hearing sharpened. She squinted, trying to focus on the shadows of grays and browns.

She slowly pivoted, now certain someone watched her.

Chapter 4

Jake's muscles tensed. He gripped the railing and resisted the urge to slink back inside after spotting the exact moment Michelle's gaze locked on his.

Escape was impossible now.

She had to guess what he'd been doing. He didn't know how he felt about being caught spying. He hadn't been able to stop himself from stepping into the shadows when her balcony door had slid open. Mesmerized, he'd watched her graceful body float toward the railing. She'd spent a long moment before finally drifting down the stairs and onto the grass like an apparition.

Blowing out regret in his sigh, Jake relaxed his shoulders, wishing he'd handled both women differently all those years ago. But no one got do-overs and experience had taught him one of life's tough lessons. Above all else, a night of unforgettable sex solved nothing, only complicated matters, especially when the downward spiral of his previous relationship hadn't stopped spinning.

The argument that pulled Michelle into his spiral was etched into his brain. Like he could ever forget the moment some of the lightest weeks of his life began? Nor could he forget that some of his darkest years followed those same weeks.

Michelle's presence had churned the memories to the surface again, memories that wouldn't die, especially that last fight with Kiera.

Right now he could see her arguing so clearly, as if it happened yesterday, not six years ago.

~

"I don't see why you're being so fucking stubborn," Kiera had said, after they'd just had hot sex in one of their spots in the woods, not too far from her house.

"You know why." By this point, Jake had become immune to Kiera using her body to get her way. Still, he'd taken what she'd offered without even blinking, which only made their relationship sicker in his mind.

"So what if I got a little carried away last weekend? Shelly should've kept her mouth shut."

"Why? Because she cares about you? You're lucky to have such a good friend. I'm sorry, Ker, but I agree with your parents on this." She needed some kind of intervention.

"Fuck it. I'm fine and I'm not going." She crossed her arms over her naked chest, clearly annoyed.

Sex hadn't dissuaded him, so she switched tactics, using a snit. If her eyes had been loaded guns, he had no doubt he'd be a dead man given the look she threw his way.

"You have no choice." He stood and grabbed his pants, yanking them on and zipping them up in clipped movements. "You're out of control, Kiera." She got that way every summer. While away at college, she wasn't so bad.

"So that's it? You're going to fuck me and leave?"

He sighed and put on his shirt. "You can be such a bitch sometimes, you know?"

"Come on, Jake. You're telling me you can live without this for six weeks?"

Kiera rubbed against him suggestively, laughing and using her tongue to trail the side of his face. She worked her way to his ear and bit his lobe in a calculated, stimulating fashion. "I don't believe you can," she all but purred, cupping his balls and stroking his shaft over the soft denim of his jeans. "Think of all the fun we can have."

He gripped her wrist, stilling her hand. Sent her a look that matched his stern voice. "It won't work. You can be as nasty or as sweet or as sexy as you want, but I won't change my mind. Not this time."

She yanked her arm free and sneered, while stepping back and snatching her shorts. "I was just having a good time and you've turned into another parent." She threw a T-shirt over her head, pulling it down to cover her perfect breasts, not bothering with a bra.

"You have a problem and it needs to be dealt with." Jake buttoned his shirt, ignoring the sexy picture she presented standing not two feet away with her hands on her hips and puffing with pure vexation. It wouldn't do to give in now, no matter how well she knew how to use her tongue to get him off.

"I do not. If you don't help me convince my parents I'm fine, then you can just go and find someone else to screw, because we're through."

"That's all this is to you, isn't it? Fun and games?" he shouted, losing some of his control. "Grow up and take some responsibility. You were stoned out of your mind when you passed out, or have you forgotten that little detail?"

She wasn't high now because she'd been on her best behavior all week, trying to talk her parents out of sending her off to a drug treatment facility for the summer. In his opinion, she needed to go. He was as worried about her increased drug use as the Delaneys were.

"We're through." She walked up to him and poked him in the chest, almost snarling. "Do you hear me?"

"Yeah. Loud and clear." He rolled his eyes, reaching for patience, and added firmly in a low voice, "I'm not changing my mind and I'll be here when you get back."

"Screw that. If you think I'll want you then, you can go to hell," she yelled, stalking away, her back ramrod straight. Kiera did righteous indignation better than anyone. "In fact, I hope you rot in hell, Jake Collier." Her last words were thrown out over her shoulder after she'd slowed, going for maximum effect in another burst of temper.

Suddenly, he saw movement out of the corner of his eye. He glanced over and Michelle stepped into view.

"Look who's here. Sweet little Miss Innocent to take over where I've left off." Kiera pushed past her friend. "Since you've always coveted him, you're welcome to him. That is, if you can handle him." Kiera stormed out of sight, yelling something about the two of them deserving each other.

"Hi, Jake. I heard Kiera's shouts and…" Michelle stopped a few feet in front of him, brushed a strand of hair off her face, and stared at a point beyond his shoulder.

Exactly how much Michelle had heard, Jake wasn't sure, but the red stealing up her face told him she'd caught enough. Kiera could be an absolute bitch at times.

"I'm sorry to interrupt." She paused and cleared her throat. "I didn't mean to cause trouble. I probably shouldn't have ratted her out to her parents."

"No. I'm glad you did. Someone needed to." He exhaled on a long sigh and wiped his face. His shoulders slumped in weariness over the exhausting toll usually required in dealing with a woman who could test the patience of Mother Teresa. And he was no saint. "But can we talk about something else besides Kiera, and could'ves or should'ves?"

~

There were a lot of things he should have done and didn't, Jake realized now, six years later, as Michelle started toward the deck. She'd thought they'd broken up. What would she think if she'd known how sordid and sick his relationship with her friend had really been? He certainly didn't think she would have continued gazing at him in that same hero-worshipful way.

The vision of Kiera passed out in Michelle's arms, which had led to her forced rehab, had given Jake a glimpse of the two friends together. The contrast had kept him awake every night that summer. Over time, he realized Kiera's behavior had driven the love right out of him. But she'd needed him. He couldn't desert her. Not then.

His biggest regret, one he'd have for the rest of his life, was in not speaking up about Kiera's drug use earlier. Then maybe her problem wouldn't have escalated to the point it had.

Michelle tucked an errant golden strand of long hair behind her ear drawing his focus as she neared the deck. Though shadows hid her eyes, he knew her attention zeroed in on him, just as his was on her. She appeared no different now than she had so long ago, except she'd blossomed, like a rose fully opened. Of course, he couldn't deny he'd always noticed her. His gaze moved lower as a twinge of attraction registered. He looked away when he realized he was ogling her round, full breasts. The act was too reminiscent of that last summer.

"Couldn't sleep?" he asked, when she reached the top step.

"No. I was remembering the past. We planted that bush together," she said, obviously talking of Kiera and herself. Michelle turned and pointed in the direction she'd come from.

His gaze followed her hand. He stared into the darkness.

An awkward silenced ensued until she cleared her throat. "I'm really sorry about Kiera's death. About the way she died."

"Yeah. Me too."

She stuck her hands in the silk robe's pockets and rocked back and forth on the heels of her feet. The edges of the collar drifted lower to expose her shoulder.

His smile was quick, the move continuing to remind him of that last summer, the exact moment after Kiera had stalked off. Michelle had stuck her hands in her jeans pockets and rocked back and forth, a vision so clear, he could still hear her ask, "Maybe we could hang out together, sometime after work?" Her beautiful, warm smile had been too potent a draw and her innocent question had spiraled into an affair of the heart he hadn't expected.

Jake had figured no harm could come from a little flirting and hanging out. Not when he'd always treated Michelle as the little sister he'd never had. So instead of sending her packing, which is what common sense and decency had dictated for big brothers, he'd done the opposite.

Worse, he'd caught himself fantasizing too many times.

About his little sister. How sick was that?

And to add to his sins? In their short time together, he'd fallen in love with her

Unlike Kiera, Michelle had been easy to be with, a golden girl, so cheerful and uncomplicated. Well, not quite uncomplicated, considering what happened.

He should have stopped the craziness before it got crazier. Instead, he'd rationalized the situation. If he couldn't have Michelle, he'd at least have the next best thing. Time with her.

"So, you live in Nashville now?"

Michelle's question pulled him out of his disturbing thoughts, and he shook off his gut-wrenching guilt of not keeping her at arm's length until he'd sorted it all out.

Unfortunately, she'd been irresistible to someone like him and his jaded soul. He hadn't deserved her warmth or her vibrancy, but he'd craved both nonetheless. Had basked in them, if only for a night, which was all he'd allow. More would have only contaminated her.

"Yeah. I have been for a while." He smiled and didn't offer more. The last she'd known he was working for Delaney, training to take over the cabinet factory as heir apparent for Ed. Exhaling, Jake added, "I find it unsettling that you and Kiera never reconnected before this, when you used to be such good friends." The two had always been like night and day and the older they got, the more their differences emerged. Still, they'd been as close as sisters, and though they'd fought like pit bulls, they'd usually kiss and make up within an hour.

Two years younger, Michelle had never exhibited Kiera's wild tendencies. Maybe their friendship took on a different dimension around the same time Jake's relationship with his ex began changing. The idea eased some of his guilt over avoiding Michelle after their brief affair. No. He could never call what he'd shared with an angel something so meaningless. The time spent in Michelle's company had made him think he'd died and gone to heaven. Too bad he'd been slated to spend an eternity in hell.

He'd always wondered why Michelle had abruptly left town like she had. Without a word.

No good-byes. No "I still want to be friends." No "Thanks for the memories."

Of course, what else could he expect when his actions hadn't been those of a friend, and the memories he'd given her had only added to his sins? He hadn't been truly free to offer memories in the first place, not when Kiera hadn't been done with making him suffer.

"I know getting back in touch with you was something she'd talked about and wanted." Deep down he'd wanted the same thing, because he'd felt responsible for tearing the two apart. He couldn't help thinking he'd been a little too honest during his last candid conversation with Michelle.

"Still focused on Kiera," she murmured, then added in a louder, almost caustic voice, "What difference does it make, especially now?" She shook her head and met his gaze without flinching. "I realize that was a cold thing to say, but I think I'm entitled."

His sad smile formed. "I'm sorry, Michelle." She'd have been much better off if he'd continued ignoring the attraction. "I should never have acted so irresponsibly and put you in the middle of my problems with Kiera back then." He offered remorseful expression. "I'd always hoped those few weeks hadn't been the main reason you left, but I know I'm being unrealistic to think they wouldn't affect all of us." After all, his actions had kept him from looking her up after his divorce. She didn't need him and his guilt messing up her life.

"It's in the past and no longer relevant." Her stiff words matched her smile.

"I see." He nodded.

"No, I don't think you do." Her gaze sought the bushes, where it remained for endless minutes. "But I do. We were all young and stupid." Shrugging, she refocused on him.

"No argument there, but I don't remember you being quite as stupid as the rest of us." Most of the kids he and Kiera had hung with back then had been totally into partying, with Kiera running at the head of the pack. Jake had tried to control her craziness as best he could, but he had to admit, he gave in to it too often because that was precisely the element he'd loved about her. Yet, he'd never imagined how far she'd take it. Who knew a wild party Kiera had heard about would be a life-altering event.

In the uncomfortable silence, his mind traveled back to the summer he'd recognized as his turning point with Kiera. The months before he'd started his last year of college were the beginning of their end…his first indication of trouble in paradise. Jake had long outgrown getting drunk and had more important things on his mind, like keeping his football scholarship. Yet nineteen-year-old Kiera hadn't listened to reason and they'd fought about her going to a party without him, using Tom Baker's interest to get her way.

Jake hated admitting jealousy had driven him back then. Hated more that he'd still been horny enough to ignore manipulations and react exactly as she'd orchestrated, no better than a slave with a ring through his nose. Manipulation had been Kiera's specialty, one she'd used and exploited to hold him more securely than the thickest chains.

Damn, he'd been such a stupid fool to think that what they'd shared during their teens would remain uncomplicated and not turn sordid. If Jake hadn't played Kiera's game—had at the very least called her on her bullshit and ended their relationship right then and there—he couldn't help thinking everyone's outcome might have been different, especially his and Michelle's. Too late, he'd realized his ex had had a dramatic flair, saying and doing things for effect. Like telling him if he hadn't been so against her going to the party, she'd never have gone. And if she'd have never gone, then she'd never have taken her first hit of speed because Jake hadn't been there to stop her. In the end, he'd fully believed he'd been part of the problem, had owned his part in her addiction. He should have been watching out for her.

Glancing at Michelle, Jake cleared his throat and said as sincerely as he could, "I really am sorry for the way things turned out."

"So am I, Jake." She smiled up at him and his heart lurched.

For a brief moment, he was in the past and almost gave in to the temptation to lean toward her, wanting more than anything to let her light warm him.

"It's late." She abruptly turned to go, as if sensing his thoughts. "I'll see you in the morning."

"Good night." Swallowing more regret, Jake watched Michelle slide and latch the door. He fought the urge to follow, wondering what would have happened if the past could be rewritten.

A twig snapped in the distance.

He straightened, focused on a section of the yard, and listened.

Another twig snapped. And then another.

Could be an animal, but intuition told Jake it was of the two-legged variety.

He silently slinked down the wooden stairs, stayed in the moonlight's shadows, and crept to the edge of the bushes. Then moved faster. By the time he reached the determined hiding spot, whatever—or rather, whoever—was gone.

Jake searched the moonlit ground, noting evidence of crushed grass and bent twigs, and crouched to pick up a telltale cigarette butt, still warm to the touch. A hint of cigarette smoke lingered, tickling his nostrils. His instincts weren't off. Someone had lurked here.

He glanced back at the house right as Michelle's light flickered out.

Who had been watching and why?

He looked at his watch, had just enough moonlight to see the time.

Twelve thirty.

Too keyed up to sleep with her so close, he headed for his SUV. Now would be a good time to check out the area around Mueller's Cave.

While driving, he pulled out his cell phone and punched up his partner's number. When Rich Heslin didn't answer, he left a message, giving him a brief update on the day's events.

Rich would contact him when his cover allowed communication.

He parked in the same spot he and Michelle had earlier, and turned off the ignition. Minutes later, with the aid of a bright flashlight, he hiked back to the spot they'd seen the Camry, but the spot was empty. In its place was crime scene tape. Baker had been busy.

No surprise there. Jake had reported the car's whereabouts to the sheriff.

Slowly, he pivoted, throwing light within the circle the yellow barrier created as he went. The pipe he'd seen earlier was gone. He slipped under the tape and walked toward the area, keeping the light on the ground in front of him and scanning the brush carefully now. Everything appeared untouched, but it was too dark to see much detail, even with the added illumination.

Just then he heard more than the sounds of the night, more than leaves rustling or cicadas humming. He pulled out his nine millimeter Glock and started in the direction of the noise.

"Don't shoot. It's jus' me."

"Billy?" Jake recognized Joe Durbin's brother. "Where's Joe?" he asked, re-holstering his weapon. Joe, the older of the two, had to be around somewhere as he and Billy usually rode together.

"Don't know. I'm guarding."

"Oh? What're you guarding?"

"Umm." Billy appeared to be deep in thought. He scratched his head and then shook it, completely befuddled. "I dunno. I'm supposed to keep strangers out."

"Out?" Jake searched Billy's face, looking for… "Damn," he blew out, running a hand through his hair in frustration. He'd never get a straight answer. He should have more patience with the guy given his past, but patience was in short supply tonight.

It was no secret Billy had the mind of a ten-year-old since a bicycle accident with no helmet had caused brain damage when he'd been about twelve—a local tragedy to be sure. It still amazed Jake that parents in town hadn't required helmets after the experience, but he surmised until more kids suffered the same fate and the laws changed, most would think it a freak accident and not something that could happen to their child. He certainly wouldn't have been caught dead in a helmet back then.

Rural living at its best, he thought, sighing and glancing around.

So, where the hell was Joe? The sheriff's deputy never let his younger brother wander too far, which meant he was probably doing the same thing, investigating, and explained why Billy stood guard within feet of the pipe that was no longer there.

He was about to go and search the guy out when Joe stepped out of the shadows.

"Collier." He nodded.

"Durbin." Jake indicated Billy with his head. "Is he on the force now?"

"Ha-ha," he shot back, clearly not enjoying the joke. "Keeps him out of trouble when I have to work. What about you? Kind of late to be out for a stroll, isn't it?"

"We both know why I'm here."

"Oh?"

"Ease up, Durbin. I'm investigating, same as you. In fact, I'm the one who told Baker where to look for the Camry."

Just then, Deputy Doug Larson came into view and stood in the shadows, watching.

Jake nodded. "Larson."

Larson returned the nod, but didn't move from his spot.

"Well, we're done with the scene, so have at it," Durbin said. "Maybe you'll turn up more to help us with the KSP's theory."

"The state police have a theory?" He'd talked to the head trooper earlier and Nelson hadn't mentioned anything about a theory.

"Yeah." Durbin hocked a mouthful of tobacco spit into the bushes. "Who'd have thought it of your ex? With all her money? And when she had everyone believing she'd recovered?" He turned to Larson and winked, adding another piece of chaw into his mouth.

Larson grunted, his sly grin saying the two lawmen shared a secret.

"What do you mean?" Jake would definitely have to give Nelson a call.

"Come on. Don't tell me you missed it when you spotted her car."

"I still don't follow."

He looked first at Larson, then Durbin for clarification, but all he got was more confused when the deputy added, "Baker has a lot of questions. If you ask me, the answers are obvious. Anyone with so much shit found in her car wasn't as lily white as she pretended." Durbin snorted. "It's always the ones who act so pious who have something to hide. Walkin' around town like she was Ms. High and Mighty. Hell, she was high, all right. But on drugs, not on staying clean."

"That makes no sense."

"Need me to draw a picture? I saw enough powder to pull more than a slap on the wrist in front of a judge, that's for damn sure. She was dealing."

"What?" Jake hadn't held back his shock in the one word. He was more than a little confused now. Earlier when he'd looked through the windows, the seats had been empty.

"She was in over her head. Hell, my money says she had something to do with those other ODs," Durbin ranted, not paying any attention to Jake's confusion. "Christ, what a bold move to leave shit on the seat, sittin' out in plain sight. But she was always more than bold. You ought to know."

"No, I don't know." Jake gritted his teeth, fighting his rising annoyance. Someone went to a lot of trouble to make it appear as if his ex was into more than she was.

Why? He turned to look at the spot where he'd seen the pipe.

"So, what else did you guys find?"

Both deputies' amusement died.

Durbin's gaze narrowed into a scrutinizing glare.

Jake met his stare unflinchingly, unwilling to offer more than, "I'm just wondering. Since you have this all figured out."

These lawmen seemed to ascribe to Baker's thinking, acting as if their very positions warranted more than they deserved.

Jake shrugged, simply not in the mood for sharing. Not with jerks who thought their shit didn't stink because they wore a shield. A rural deputy's job paid slightly above minimum wage. Larson was okay. But Durbin had never been the brightest bulb in the chandelier, which made Jake wonder all the more if being stupid ran in the family. Sometimes Billy acted as if he had ten times the brain, even with his injury.

He spared one more glance toward the center of the tape. "Well, you've got my number if you figure anything else out." He would call it a night and compare notes with the sheriff later.

"See ya, Billy. Enjoy guarding." He felt his phone and remembered the pictures he'd taken on his cell.

Billy's face split in a toothy grin. "I like guardin'."

Jake nodded to Joe and started back in the direction of his car. "Tell Baker I'll catch up with him in the morning." He intended to return to Elaine's and load the snapshots into his laptop, something he should have done earlier. He'd been too preoccupied with his daughter's questions and Elaine's grief over Kiera's death to remember them. Now, he couldn't forget because before he met with Baker, he wanted to be prepared. Hopefully by then, Rich will have returned his call. He and his partner could work on getting backup into the area to check for his missing white pipe.

Not that he didn't trust the sheriff's office to do a proper job.

No! This was personal. Like Baker, Jake was a thorough man.

Chapter 5

"Order's up," came a shout as Jake pushed the heavy, screeching door open, drowning out the bell's tinkle. Smells of ground coffee, bacon, and maple syrup wafted under his nostrils as his glance swept the room. Seconds later, he spotted the sheriff in a booth nursing a cup of coffee.

Peggy Ann's Place was considered Campton's only fine dining establishment. Fine dining in this case meant you got good, hearty Southern cooking, not ambience. Peg was mighty proud of the plates, silverware, ceramic salt and pepper shakers, and cloth napkins she provided, saying though they weren't fancy, at least they weren't paper. Which was true, Jake thought, as he ambled toward Baker.

Of course everything about the place, from the cracked, fake red leather on the stools at the counter and on the seats at the booths to the faded black-and-white checkered linoleum floor leading to the jukebox in the back, shouted diner. An old one at that. Peggy Ann's hadn't seen a face lift since the fifties, but no one seemed to care as long as the surroundings were clean and the food remained tasty.

"Collier." Baker's nod indicated the seat across from him. He looked like he'd spent the night in a blender. The deep shadows and furrows etched into his face meant he probably hadn't gotten much sleep. "I took the liberty and ordered you some coffee," he said, when Jake stared at the second full cup resting on the table.

"Thanks." Jake sat and tossed Baker the manila envelope containing the pictures he'd printed the night before. Then he picked up the cup of steaming liquid. He needed a jolt of caffeine. Elaine had never mastered the skill of brewing decent coffee; neither had Maria, the Delaneys' housekeeper. Besides not sparing the grease in her cooking, Peg's coffee could give Starbucks competition and was always plenty strong.

"What're these?" Baker asked, his eyebrows rising an inch.

"Pictures I snapped right after I came across Kiera's car. Durbin said you found meth in it." He still hadn't heard from his partner and his mind hadn't shut off as to the picture someone was trying to paint of his ex. Why go to the trouble?

Jake was a doer, someone who plowed forward with a plan, and until he had an idea of what he was looking for, he couldn't formulate a plan. He hated this stage of the process. Made him feel edgy. Ineffective. It was the worst feeling in the world, wanting to do something, yet having to hold off, to sit back and assess. Jake was quickly learning he wasn't particularly adept at patience.

He damn sure wasn't about to let Baker portray Kiera as public enemy number one without at least presenting evidence that proved otherwise. He'd talked to Nelson, the lead investigator for the Kentucky State Police, and the guy didn't think Kiera's OD was related to the others, citing differences in their MOs. Nothing of this case pointed to the ordinary, which made it hard to get a handle on exactly what was going down.

Drug traffickers had certain patterns they followed to avoid detection.

True, those patterns were always evolving, becoming more sophisticated, more difficult to detect. Usually dead bodies from ODs were so far down the distribution chain, they were impossible to trace back to the original source. Rich, his partner, believed a major meth distribution ring operated somewhere within a fifty-mile radius of Nashville—highly organized, much like the cocaine cartels of the eighties, and not just some rednecks burning the shit from a few trailers out in the sticks. Campton and Mueller's Cave were miles outside of the radius, but it could fit, especially if Kiera's death was somehow connected to the other two.

While Baker unclasped the envelope and let the pictures slide free, Jake waited, purposefully not mentioning the photos of the pipe he'd excluded until he spoke to Rich and threw a few ideas past him. He wasn't ready to make any assumptions, not after he'd spent much of the night mentally searching for any clue in Kiera's behavior. Yet, his obsessing had only highlighted her dedication in helping him. No. Kiera was no dealer. She'd stumbled onto something that had killed her. That something was related to the case he and his partner were working on. He'd stake his badge on it.

"The camera doesn't lie," he murmured, as Baker scanned each picture thoroughly. Jake was now doubly glad he'd held back the bag of meth he'd found on Kiera earlier. "I don't see any drugs sitting on the seat, do you?"

Baker shook his head, still engrossed in the photos. Once done, he placed the pile back in the envelope and sighed. "Can I keep these?"

"Yeah. I've got copies."

"Why the hell would someone go to so much trouble to set Kiera up?"

"I don't know. You tell me. You were closer to her in the last six months than I was."

"Well, she wasn't dealing." Baker swiped his face with a hand and blew out a frustrated exhale. "I didn't need these pictures to know that, and they only corroborate my belief. Her death wasn't an accidental OD. The ME sent blood samples out to be tested to see if the chemical makeup of the drug was the same as in the others. Tox screens'll take some time, but worth the wait. I'll bet there'll be similarities matching the shit planted in the car. Then we'll be able to prove a connection."

"Oh?" Jake hadn't expected the sheriff's position to mirror his thoughts. "You still think there is one, even though Nelson has ruled it out?"

Maybe the guy was better than he gave him credit for. After all, a sheriff was only as good as his staff, which in this case consisted of idiots wearing badges, in his opinion, with Durbin the being the lead idiot. They were all on the same side, working much like a unified team for the same goals, but the Kentucky State Police tended to trump sheriffs in the rural game of law enforcement. Higher up the chain of command, with additional funding and extended resources, the state agency had more clout, not to mention more money to hire better investigators.

All organizations had their fair share of screw-ups, but cops like Durbin faced more competition if they wanted to join the state police force, which usually meant staying at the bottom rung of the law enforcement ladder and settling for becoming a deputy at less pay and prestige.

"Don't you?" Baker asked, drawing his attention back to connections.

"Yeah, I do. What'd you make of the area surrounding Kiera's car?" Despite not offering anything of his suspicions until he had a better handle on what they were, Jake was now more than interested in the sheriff's thoughts. The guy knew every nook and cranny, every holler and most likely every cave, including Mueller's. He'd closed too many rural labs not to.

"I had the cave's opening un-boarded and gave it a thorough check." Baker's lips curled into a scowl. "Saw no indication of anyone being in the cave since old man Jenkins boarded it up. But there's evidence around the entrance and in the nearby woods of activity. Just haven't figured out what. Foot-matted grass, cigarette butts, and even a few empty liquor bottles. Told Durbin to keep an eye on the area at night for the next few days to see if anyone shows up. My guess is, it's probably just kids hanging out."

"Hmm. Then I wonder why her car was there," Jake said, thinking out loud.

"Question of the year. When we find our answer, we may have our key to this whole frickin' puzzle."

Jake decided to hike in later under camouflage, in case someone was still watching, to do more digging on his own now that Mueller's had been un-boarded. He had to agree with Baker. This case was a puzzle, where none of the pieces fit, and one Jake and his partner wouldn't normally be involved with.

The DEA was federal. An agency geared toward big drug traffickers who peddled shit from out of the country or across state lines. In these parts, meth was a growing problem with sales and distribution staying within a smaller radius, rarely crossing county lines, much less state lines. Until recent years, neither Tennessee nor Kentucky attracted the kind of illegal business border states like Florida, California, or Texas dealt with. Unfortunately, the evidence proved they were catching up fast.

ODs weren't usually under the jurisdiction of federal agents either, but given the first OD vic had been the daughter of a US senator who'd pulled enough strings to warrant an investigation by a federal agency, he and Rich were saddled with the case. Rich decided to go in undercover. He was a master at disguise and could blend in anywhere, and no one in town had ever met him. Jake decided to stay visible. Since he knew this area, knew the local people and had ties here with the Delaneys and his daughter, it didn't make sense to do otherwise.

The senator had stated that his daughter had run away to become a singer. He and his wife were shocked to learn she'd been found dead in southern Kentucky. When last they'd heard from her, she'd been singing in a Nashville bar.

Other similarities emerged in the case, the biggest being both women who'd died had had enough drugs on hand to make them look guilty as sin, and like Kiera, the vics had had too much to live for to do drugs. Or so their parents claimed, a detail Jake hadn't taken as total truth at first, considering his jaded viewpoint based on experience. A parent's view of a grown daughter tended to be biased and based on favorable memories. When those sweet little girls grew up, they sometimes changed as they matured, like Kiera had, and each had the potential of becoming nothing like the angels their parents remembered. Until Kiera showed up in a very similar position. She hadn't been using. He'd risked his career on her sobriety and he'd still risk it to this day. Too much coincidence for him to think otherwise, and Baker had that same instinct.

What if the other victims' families' convictions were on target? He'd read their files and the affidavits so many times, he'd memorized them. He'd also read the autopsies as they pertained to the drugs found in their systems and the manner in which the women died.

"I got bigger problems if this is all tied to those women's deaths." The dread in Baker's tone drew Jake's attention. "This whole frickin' case is morphing into a nightmare."

"Sounds like something else happened."

Nodding, Baker took a long drink of coffee. He set the cup down. "Got a notice this morning from Nashville PD on a missing woman. Parents haven't heard from her in almost two months when she called all excited because she had a line on a job singing in some bar."

"Any idea which one?"

"Yeah. Della's."

"Della's?" The same bar Rich had targeted and where he had become an evening fixture, going in undercover. Another interesting coincidence.

"Umm hmm." Baker pulled out his notebook. "NPD reports one Kimberly McDowell talked to her mom for twelve minutes on April twentieth, saying that's where she was headed. The McDowells haven't heard from her since. According to cell phone records, that was the last call made from that number." He laughed, but little humor came out in the sound. "Of course, they're not from around here, so they don't know shit."

Jake smiled. The bar was a landmark. There were a lot of dry counties in this part of Kentucky, but Della's wasn't situated in one of them. For as long as anyone could remember, too many guys from both dry and wet counties had tried to sneak into the bar, hoping a fake ID would get them a drink before their time, but Della wasn't stupid. No one ever got past her radar.

She was old as Moses and twice as religious, despite running a bar. After all, her religion wasn't Baptist, but Catholic as she'd proclaimed to anyone who'd listen.

As far as Jake knew, Catholics like Della loved whiskey and wine. Unlike a few bar owners in these parts, she'd never bought illegal bootleg, nor did she condone selling it. Those who did were stealing from the government, but that was never her concern. In her opinion, moonshine wasn't on the same plane as drugs.

He'd given Rich a hard time about his belief that the bar was somehow tied to the deaths.

Hell, the whole county knew Della's position on drugs. "Drugs are illegal," she'd always said. "If a person wants to get high, they can come and drink good Kentucky bourbon in my bar along with every other goddamned redneck." If she caught wind of anything that smelled of drugs, she reported it, hating what they did to kids in such a short time. Jake doubted her bar would be used in such a manner. Not unless she'd done a complete one-eighty. He'd finally given up trying to explain to his partner when he'd realized his protests hadn't registered.

Rich had heard the name once too often while undercover on another case for it to be a coincidence. What better place to hide an illegal operation than in the backwoods of Kentucky? The bar was on the edge of the county, a few miles from Campton and closer to where the bodies had turned up.

Jake had considered the theory a stretch at first, but now? Hell, nothing made sense to him. Della's was a starting place, and Jake had to admit, Rich's hunches tended to be right on more times than they weren't.

"So, do you think she got the job?" he asked Baker, getting back to the missing girl. No one but Jake knew of Rich's involvement, his safety being the most obvious reason.

"I don't know." The sheriff sighed heavily and picked up a fork to start on the plate of hash browns and scrambled eggs Peg had just placed in front of him. He pointed the utensil at Jake, as if using it to emphasize his next words. "If not Della's, it's gotta be another bar, and we both know how many bars between here and Nashville provide live music on the weekends."

Too many, Jake thought. Most weren't owned and operated by someone with Della's scruples. Jake had frequented quite a few of those bars as a teen and he had no doubt Baker had his share of experiences. Sleazy places that supplied a lot more than hard liquor. Hard drugs and harder women were too readily available for anyone with the money.

Almost every guy between the ages of sixteen and twenty-one utilized fake IDs and spent much time and money drinking and screwing in those places. Hell, he knew offhand of at least a dozen or so that could be used as a front for the prostitution—sex slave—drug distribution ring they were looking for. The names had changed over the years, as had the owners, but the kids always knew which bars bent the rules.

After chewing a few bites, Baker swallowed, then took a drink of coffee. "I'd planned on interrogating Della after I eat. You wanna tag along?"

"No. I've got to check on my daughter and make a couple of phone calls. I'll catch up with you later to compare notes." Jake scooted out of the booth. Rich would definitely be interested in the latest connection, courtesy of NPD, about a missing singer and Della's.

"Before you go," Baker said. "I was wondering if you have any information on the name I gave you last week?"

"Oh, yeah." He pulled a notebook much like the one Baker used out of his pocket. "Roger Peters, right?"

"Uh-huh, that's him. My quick background check didn't yield much more than a Bowling Green address. A few charge cards and some paid utility bills, which is why I asked for your help. It's like he didn't exist before that."

"He exists, all right. According to my source at the FBI, you have some good instincts to home in on him." He flipped to a page and added, "Peters is a bit on the slimy side. Passed the bar, licensed to practice law in three states—Georgia, Tennessee, and Kentucky. He's made a name for himself defending small-time scumbags. Knows how to use cash without drawing a lot of attention, which is probably why you couldn't find much on him. The guy's been under the scrutiny of the FBI and the DEA for a couple of years."

"Hmm. Not exactly a model citizen, is he?"

"Trust me, he knows his way around any side of the law that benefits him. Smooth as silk. Slippery. Nothing sticks to him, but we both know he wouldn't be on their radar unless they suspected him of something. You want me to dig deeper? I can talk to someone who's involved, who knows more than what's on paper or in the files."

"Nah, you've given me enough to form an opinion."

"You think he could be part of this?"

"Maybe." Baker shrugged. "He's only been hanging around for a few weeks or so, well after the second body was found. I'm not willing to totally discount him as a suspect. Makes me sick to think how easily a guy like him skates so freely."

"Happens all the time. We can only play by the rules, Baker. Sooner or later he'll make a mistake and the second he does, whoever's in charge of watching him will swoop in and nail him. When the FBI or DEA goes for a bust, we have to have an airtight case with all the i's dotted and every t crossed or we don't even mess with it." Jake snorted and shook his head. "Too many vultures out there just waiting to say we've abused a scumbag's rights or some other shit to get him off."

"Well, thanks for the info. I'll make sure to keep a real close watch." Baker went back to his breakfast.

Jake left Peggy Ann's, checked his text messages on the way to his SUV, and noted one he'd waited over sixteen hours to receive.

He steered the Durango onto the road heading out of Campton and drove toward I-65. A few miles down the interstate, he pulled into a rest area and immediately hit the restroom.

At the urinal he heard, "You always did have the worst aim."

He chuckled and finished his business before walking to the sink. The guy who belonged to the voice did the same.

"So, I see you got my message," he said, as Jake dried his hands on a paper towel.

"Yeah." Jake threw the towel in the wastebasket on the way to the stall, peeking through the crack. He nodded to his visitor who moseyed over to the door and flipped the lock, ensuring privacy.

"You look like shit," Jake said.

Rich flashed his thousand-watt smile. "All part of the act."

"Better you than me."

"What's up? What's so important you had to meet?"

Jake filled him in on Baker's news about the missing girl and Kiera's death, and handed over the bag of meth along with another set of pictures, complete with a couple showing the pipe. His partner had been the only person he'd told about his ex's involvement, so he didn't need to spend a lot of time on explanations as to why he'd withheld evidence. Once Rich heard about the second planted bag in her car, he completely agreed to keep it quiet, saying he'd take care of it.

Rich had contacts everywhere, including those who could have the shit analyzed and broken down in a matter of hours, much faster than the usual method of waiting days, sometimes weeks, or even months in the backlog of evidence in the system that needed analyzing.

Rich didn't know what to make of the pipe. "Baker checked out the cave?"

"That's what he said. Durbin was there last night, along with Larson. I'm going back later for my own look, just to make sure.

My intuition doesn't lie. Someone's watching it, so I plan on being evasive. Baker didn't spend his formative years in the cave like I did, doesn't know about all of the hidden passages. If someone's using it to make the shit, I'll find some clue."

"Man, how screwed up is that?" Rich grunted. "Right in the sheriff's backyard. Cements my hunch that something big is going on in these backwoods. I still think Della's Bar is involved," he said, not backing down from his original suspicion, formed after accidentally stumbling over an interesting website. A webcam, always showing the same interior but transmitting from different well-hidden spots around the US, graphically captured erotic displays of two going at it. More disturbing than the porn show was the hint of what they were selling. The music in the background added to the scenes as much as the unidentifiable couple getting it on.

"Sex, drugs, and rock and roll," Rich added, his thoughts obviously roaming along similar paths. "I've seen and heard of just about every sordid depravity during my stint as a DEA agent, but this is pretty bizarre."

Jake nodded, agreeing. How could he not when the digital files he'd viewed were so explicit.

Pleasure—most likely meth or some derivative of the drug—was being peddled as an aphrodisiac along with the ultimate male fantasy. The most gorgeous women, touted as sex slaves, supposedly knew exactly what men wanted, and given the show, these weren't false claims.

"Wealth has its privileges," Jake murmured, considering the buy-in cost for a night of pure ecstasy, including an ample supply of the drug to aid in the process, along with instructions on using it for maximum effect. "It's clearly a high-end business."

Rich dried his hands, aimed for the trash can, and tossed a direct hit. "There's nothing high-end about prostitution or drug abuse."

"No," Jake replied. "And the desire to get wasted isn't exclusive to those without money." Drug addiction tended to lower standards, annihilating inhibitions holding back the animal inside of every human being. A person under the influence seldom controlled the beast, going so far as to participate in horrendous acts he or she would never imagine doing if sober.

Hell, Jake had experienced the beast without the benefit of any drug, including alcohol, so he could only imagine the worst.

Unfortunately, for their investigation anyway, the means of joining this exclusive sex club were as highly guarded a secret as the location. It took more than the one hundred thousand dollar entry fee Rich had discovered when his attempts to infiltrate the inner sanctum and gain membership had failed.

"Definitely an ironic twist," Rich said, sporting a wry grin.

Despite this entire case derailing with too many dead bodies and the idea of a sex slave business mixing with dealers cooking meth and other drugs so close, Rich's attitude never changed. It was all a game to be played. No one played it better than Rich Heslin.

"Oh yeah, before I forget. Baker asked me to dig into Roger Peters. I gave him all the information I had."

"Does he suspect him?"

Jake nodded. "You gotta admit, he fits the profile."

Rich laughed. "Guys like that always do. They're almost a cliché. And you know what really fascinates me?"

He didn't expand until finally Jake grinned and prodded, "No, but I can see you're dying to enlighten me."

Rich's laughter rumbled deeper and humor flashed from his eyes. "The way a guy like that attracts more women than a porch light attracts moths on a summer night."

"Some have no discriminating taste."

"Maybe it's his charm."

"I doubt it." Jake shook his head as his grin stretched. "It has more to do with what I call the Harley factor."

"The what?"

"Harley factor." Jake chuckled. "Have you ever seen an ugly woman on the back of a hog? He can be as repulsive as shit, looking like he stepped out of the gutter, with tattoos covering his body, oily, stringy hair, and a beer gut the size of a full-term pregnant woman's belly, but the babe riding behind is always hot."

"Hmmm, you make a strong point about discriminating taste, but I doubt Roger'll start driving a hog just to pick up hot babes. Why would he, when he doesn't need the prop? He only needs to smile pretty and rely on his charm." Rich's humor faded and suddenly he was all business. "Is that it?"

"Yeah. What about you? Learn anything new?"

"I'm keeping tabs on a couple of interesting people, and considering this new information, I'm leaning toward someone local being responsible." Rich broke off and remained silent a long moment, lost in thought. "Do you know a Bobby Winters?"

Jake straightened and made eye contact in the mirror. "You don't think he's connected to all this?"

"I have no idea." Rich shrugged. "But I do know he's one slick dude and he's latched on to our Roger. A match made in heaven, in my opinion. I thought I'd get your take on him before homing in on him."

Jake grunted. "He's a year younger, so I never hung out with him much, except the usual...you know, parties...friends of friends. And now? I only know him by reputation." In that respect, little had changed in ten years. "He's a respected businessman, but he's always struck me as being on the sleazy side and not someone I'd want my daughter to date."

"Hmmm. Funny how slick guys all seemed to recognize each other." Rich stroked his chin, stared into space, and then sighed. "Bobby's also tight with the Durbin brothers and they seem like law-abiding citizens with big brother Joe being a deputy and all, but I'm not ruling out anyone just yet. I'm still in the discovery phase and the process can't be rushed. A lot of sleazy people come and go at Della's. More than enough new faces to draw suspects from."

"Well, when you get past the discovery phase, give me a holler." When Rich nodded, Jake added, "I'll get back to you via e-mail or text on what I find out at the cave."

"Appreciate it." Rich started for the locked door. "Things should start getting interesting with Peters now that the locals have spotted him. Makes me wonder what will happen next."

Jake threw out a laugh. "I'm sure it's all entertaining."

"Hey, I gotta take my thrills where I can. Nothing beats watching the locals watching suspect number one and two."

"Just don't let them know you're watching."

"Have you so little faith?" Rich said, before he slid out the door.

Seconds later Jake left the restroom. His partner was nowhere in sight.

~

Shelly prolonged her shower until the water was no longer even lukewarm. Then, after dressing and unable to procrastinate any longer, she headed in the direction of the wonderful scent of coffee, hoping for a temporary diversion of the long-ago memories of her throwing herself at Jake that had haunted her dreams and now her thoughts.

At the top of the stairs, she placed her face in her hands as heat streaked along her spine at mental images that just wouldn't die. How she wished Jake hadn't been on that deck last night. Her senses stood on edge. Like a bow pulled too tight, her muscles tensed and no amount of deep breathing would let her relax.

What did he think of her? If he didn't already despise her, he probably would once he discovered she told Mikey he'd abandoned them. At least that was the way she'd taken it back then. She didn't want Jake to hate her. She'd rather hate him. If only she could, then she could forget him.

Shelly rubbed her temples, unable to hide from the truth. She still cared. She'd never been able to forget him. Lord, she could still smell his scent. A spicy, tangy fragrance that mixed with sweat and was totally Jake.

Amazing how a scent had the power to take her back to the time when she'd had him all to herself. Unfortunately, Kiera had returned to snatch him back. No matter how badly Kiera treated Jake, he would always love Kiera, which left Shelly with nothing but a memory and the seed of her stupidity.

As long as Shelly held on to her anger toward her dead friend, she could pretend that Jake had had no choice for abandoning her. She could pretend she'd meant something to him. She could pretend Kiera had coerced him into marriage. Viewing the scene with the eyes of a rational adult, she realized her pretenses had some humongous holes.

She rounded the corner and spotted Elaine sitting with Emily at an oak table in the breakfast room, less formal than the dining room they'd eaten in the night before. "Good morning."

Her voice held more cheer than was in her heart. She'd get through this. She had no choice.

Elaine nodded without verbally acknowledging her greeting.

Emily wasn't as reticent. "Hi, Aunt Michelle," she said, using the title her father had instructed her to call Shelly, continuing with a lengthy monologue about a TV show. The five-year-old didn't seem to grasp the reality that her mother wouldn't be returning and was all smiles this morning, a complete contrast to her grandmother, who appeared mired in grief.

Shelly grabbed the pot and poured coffee into the mug left on the sideboard. She took a sip and returned Emily's smile before making some contributing comment about Dora the Explorer.

Mikey loved Thomas the Train Engine, so Shelly understood the young, imaginative mind.

"Dora likes to travel. Someday I'll be just like her," Emily said in reply.

Shelly nodded and noted a few more comparisons between her son and Kiera's daughter. Emily had Kiera's dark looks, complete with the promise of growing up to be as beautiful, where Mikey was fair. The stamp of Jake's genes in the shape of her eyes and the cut of her chin were features she shared with her half-brother. Definitely not a connection she wanted to think about.

Maria, the Delaneys' housekeeper, came into view just then and pulled her attention from discovering additional resemblances.

"Good morning. Do you still like your eggs over medium?" Maria walked through the archway to the open kitchen and stopped at the refrigerator at the far side of the double rooms.

"You remembered." Shelly smiled as she sat in a chair across from Elaine.

"*Sí, señorita.* You are one of the family and not easy to forget." She grabbed a carton of eggs, then moved to the stove where she turned on the burner and commenced cooking. "It is good to have you here, especially since the *señora* is now gone. So sad."

Placing her napkin on her lap, Shelly gave a distracted nod and listened with half an ear while Emily chattered like a magpie.

Mikey was always more talkative in the mornings, too. Another similarity she wouldn't dwell on.

While she sipped coffee, her previous thoughts snuck back inside her brain, along with last evening's run-in with Jake. Her face flamed. No amount of time could undo her stupidity.

Yet, Shelly hadn't expected his apology. Not last night and not spoken so openly regarding those glorious weeks when she'd had him all to herself without Kiera's intrusion. She groaned silently and closed her eyes. How lame and jealous she must have sounded last night. But what else could she have said when Jake had homed in on precisely why she'd never returned?

"Daddy said he'd take me to the park this afternoon." Emily's words drew Shelly's attention.

Elaine flashed a sad smile and patted Emily's hand. "That's right, sweetie."

She glanced at Shelly and added as if in explanation, "Jake had some business to take care of, but he still hopes to keep things as normal as possible for her."

"I'm glad," Shelly said, thankful for Elaine's mention of his whereabouts this morning. At least he wasn't here, tormenting her further. Not that his absence kept her from thinking.

She sighed and dug into the plate of food Maria stuck in front of her. Yet, the task of eating did nothing to keep the thoughts at bay. Her brain simply wouldn't shut off to the past and to her mistake of trusting Jake.

Shelly also should have known better than to trust Kiera's words damning Jake, because when Shelly had run to her for advice after discovering she might be pregnant, Kiera had cold-heartedly gone back to him, forgetting every word about despising him or telling Shelly she was welcome to him. To cement her hold, Kiera had ended up pregnant as well, then had the gall to goad Shelly with the news.

Jacob Collier had belonged to Kiera, and Shelly had accepted that outcome.

As far as friendship went, Shelly had had enough. She'd put up with Kiera's drug use and empty promises to change. She'd put up with the way Kiera had treated her in the end, like a servant or someone even lower. They'd been worlds apart financially, which hadn't helped, but Kiera had far exceeded the bounds of friendship when she'd tenaciously held on to Jake just to keep him from having a relationship with Shelly. Jake had been no better, falling at Kiera's feet again when she'd treated him like dirt beneath her shoes.

Oh yes, Shelly needed to remember why she'd left and stayed away in the first place.

"I didn't catch that." Shelly looked up, realizing Elaine had spoken.

"I said, it would be nice if your mother and sister could drive up for the funeral." Her expression seemed so hopeful.

"I can't promise anything." She purposefully hadn't mentioned the funeral during her call the evening before. "It's tough for the three of us to be gone at the same time." Geez, that's all she needed. For her mom and sister to come, and of course they'd bring Mikey. Then her secret would be out. She'd always told her son he'd meet his dad some day when the time was right, but this seemed the worst possible time. If she hadn't wanted to be a charity case back then, she certainly didn't now. Not when Kiera's death had taken Kiera out of the picture. Shelly   had no intention of being second place. Ever.

"Will you at least ask? I'd love to see them both."

"Sure."

Shelly's cell phone blared. Glancing at the caller ID, she groaned inwardly. She might not have a choice. "Speak of the devil," she said with more enthusiasm than she possessed. "I think that's Mom now. Excuse me a minute." Pushing the On button, she brought the phone to her ear and turned away from the table. "Mom?"

"It's me. Not Grandma."

The moment she heard her son's voice, she lowered hers. "Hey, honey. What's up?" She stole a furtive glance at Elaine. She was busy with something on Emily's plate and paid no heed to her or her phone call.

Shelly let out a relieved breath and her attention returned to Mikey, who was chatting up a storm about the water fight they were going to have at the slumber party that night.

"Can I?"

When she realized she hadn't heard the entire question, she asked, "Can you what?"

"Buy a new super soaker."

"Don't you already have one?"

"Yeah, but it's lame."

"It squirts water, right?"

"But, Mom, I need a better one that shoots farther. Kevin's got one. Target has them in stock and Grandma says she'll take me if you say it's okay. Please?"

She looked up. Maria held up a pot of coffee, her expression asking if she wanted another cup. Shelly nodded, and presented her back. Her voice dropped to a decibel higher than a whisper. "Tell Grandma it's okay. Look, sweetie, I'll call you later and you can tell me all about it. Okay?"

"Thanks, Mom. Bye. I love you."

"I love you too. Bye." She was about to tell him to put her mother on, but he'd already hung up.

Well, she thought, shrugging off disappointment. So much for missing Mom. She disconnected the call, pivoted, and tucked the phone into her pocket. She picked up the cup of coffee Maria had just poured.

"Emily, will you run and get my needlework, dear?" Elaine said.

The child jumped up as Maria held out the carton. "Cream?"

"Sure." Shelly waited for a dollop, then stirred. She took a sip, but almost spit it out when Elaine said, "I take it from that phone call you never had the abortion?"

"That's a personal question. Why do you ask?" She prayed the heat streaking up wasn't a blush, because then Elaine would read the truth in her face. The older woman had given her the money, had advised her to have one, and added ten thousand dollars to the amount so Shelly could have a clean start in Atlanta where Monica had been living. It hadn't taken much for Shelly and her sister to talk her mother into following. If nothing else, the money had done the trick. She and her sister had lived on next to nothing during her pregnancy, both working at an antiques store. When the owner had decided to sell, they'd approached him with an offer. Since the old man liked them, he'd bent over backward to make it work. She and her sister had saved every cent they could, until they had enough. After all, Maggie had taught them well about thrift.

Shelly smiled. The money tree *had* brought them riches in the form of luck. She had a son she loved more than life itself and she had a secure job she shared with her two best friends. Life couldn't get any better. Well, it could, she thought, as Jake's image flashed. But happily-ever-after with him wasn't in her future. Not then. Not now. Not ever.

"I'm glad," Elaine said, ignoring her earlier question and obviously making her own assumption.

Shelly gasped. How had the older woman guessed her secret so easily?

Elaine only smiled wistfully and reached across the table to pat Shelly's hand. Her eyes glistened from unshed tears beginning to form. "I was a fool back then to listen to Ed. He'd always been so indulgent with Kiera and spoiled her rotten. I knew it would cause trouble in the end. Lord knows I wasn't ignorant of Kiera's problems. I just never imagined they could be so bad." She shook her head and exhaled a heavy sigh. "As I think back on it, I was never sure if I advised the right person to have the abortion, which makes me doubly relieved to learn you didn't. You were always so responsible." A tear broke free, sliding down her face. She brushed it away. "I could never regret Emily. But I knew marriage and a baby would only make things worse. She was too young to be a wife and a mother...too selfish."

What could Shelly say to that? Yet, she knew exactly how Elaine felt because she never once regretted her choice, no matter how scared she was at first. "I...um...I...couldn't go through with it," she finally said, once she was able to speak. Mikey was part of Jake. How could she destroy something created during the best moments of her life? "Your advice was sound, and I appreciated the money. It helped with the down payment on our store."

Elaine stared off into space with a pained expression. Then she nodded. "I worried about my part all those years ago. Imagine, me encouraging an abortion. I should've stayed out of it. Can you forgive me?"

A noise drew their attention.

Shelly's heart almost stopped beating when she glanced up to see Jake step through the door.

Chapter 6

"Why aren't we starting back up? An interruption will cost thousands."

Water trickled from ten feet away, sounding much like a faucet left on low. Despite the temperate fifty-degree air inside the cave, he felt the heat of his annoyance riding along his back. Everyone else had agreed with his reasoning and he shouldn't have to explain it again. He was the backbone of the business, and under his direction they'd prospered. He wasn't any happier with the shutdown, and in his opinion, if the asshole in front of him hadn't fucked up, this wouldn't be happening.

The guy had pocketed close to a million dollars in three years, and now was worried about a lousy few thousand? Instead of blasting him like he wanted, he simply smiled and said, "We'll weather it." Didn't he already have a contingency plan in place? Now wasn't the time to be bold. No! It was a time for caution. He understood the need for caution. His caution had made them all wealthy men.

"For how long?" Unwrapping a piece of gum he'd pulled out of his pocket, he stuck it in his mouth.

"A couple of months."

"A couple of months?"

"Six at most. Once the heat leaves without finding a clue, we're back in business, same as before."

"But we can't afford to shut down for so long. What'll happen to our customers?"

"We concentrate on getting rid of existing stock and we take back-orders. Our customers will wait because they can't buy our exclusive product anywhere else. We can't risk exposure."

"Can't risk exposure? Why? The cave's already been checked out, and as intended, no one found anything. Where are your fucking balls? We're talking about thousands of dollars a week."

"Cost of doing business."

"Cost of doing business? You sound like a frickin' accountant. Figure out something else. Closing down is a lousy option. It's all that bitch's fault. You should've dealt with her earlier."

"Maybe." He watched him pace back and forth in the confined, damp space, making him dizzy and reminding him of a caged tiger. Not the best time to quit smoking, in his opinion. The guy was too jittery and nervous already. "But it changes nothing. You're not seeing the whole picture." He shrugged, his hands going out palms up as if to say his hands were tied.

"Screw the whole picture. I'm only interested in hard, cold cash."

"So am I. None of us counted on trouble coming into town and making contact. Without knowing what she knows and with Collier and the others so close, we can't take any chances until we neutralize the threat."

"We should've stuck to selling drugs. I never liked all the other shit. Trying to cover it up is what brought in Collier and the others in the first place."

"You forget this is a partnership and if you didn't like all the *other shit*, you should've gotten out before you pocketed the profits." He walked over to him, waited until he stopped his pacing, and then made eye contact, letting the warning show in his gaze. "Now that I have your attention, I'll explain once more, so there is no misunderstanding. Unfortunately, we've encountered a few unforeseen setbacks." He kept his voice low, calm, and precise, as if he were talking to a small child. "Unexpected deaths, along with having to terminate an additional problem, have alerted too many people, which is why we're taking evasive action. You'll shut up and do as I say, or you'll lose a hell of a lot more than money. I won't jeopardize any part of a business enterprise I've spent years building. You got that?"

"I still don't like it." He broke their mental connection and resumed pacing.

"The sooner we get Matthews out of the way, the sooner the heat subsides and we're back in business. We don't have the luxury of ignoring the bitch's dying threats to bring us down. Whether she was bluffing or not no longer matters. Her contact with Matthews is what raised the temperature around here to well over boiling in the first place."

"Why not handle the heat like we've always done? They know jack shit about what's going on. Just throw them a few more bones to satisfy them, make 'em feel like heroes."

"I intend to." He nodded, figuring how to arrange a decoy lab's discovery with enough similarities to convince lawmen on the hunt. "If it works, we start back up earlier, but we can't afford any more mistakes. As to the shutdown? I've planned a few contingencies to ensure survival." After all, he had an investment to protect. "In the meantime, I'll keep my eyes open for other opportunities, other ways of gaining merchandise. We may have to amend our approach a bit. Another contingency."

"Yeah, yeah. You and your frickin' contingencies," he mumbled.

"Don't worry. You'll be compensated in the end. Look at this as a small holiday."

He grunted, slightly mollified, then turned to leave. "I'll wait for you at the truck."

He watched his departure, thinking money always talked. Paved the way on his road to success, he'd discovered early on. He never ceased to be amused by how accurately he could spot those who'd take easy money over breaking the law. Of course, first he'd had to convince them they wouldn't get caught, something he was good at. He'd had too much experience at convincing people to do his will not to have sharpened the skill.

They'd capitalized their business with making and selling crystal meth in the beginning, but none of them were stupid enough to produce the garbage long term. No. Now they produced pleasure, dealt in quality not quantity, and sold only to those who could afford it and those who were less likely to abuse it. In his opinion, the shit idiots burned in kitchens and trailers around the country was just that. Shit. Those morons knew nothing of the chemicals they dealt with. Fortunately, an understanding of chemicals, and their makeup, along with some experimenting on end users, provided full knowledge of which drugs worked best to maximize pleasure, while minimizing the side effects. He'd tested his end product, using human guinea pigs to refine his pleasure pill over the last ten years.

He halted at the hidden entrance and glanced back at the small, pristine lab. A perfect setup.

"All part of my contingencies," he whispered, pushing the rock-encrusted door back into place. Stalactites and stalagmites blocked the access. As had already happened, anyone searching would walk right past, thinking it a section of stone, without ever guessing a finger of the cavern held the state-of-the-art equipment used for much more than cooking mere meth.

He'd built a multimillion-dollar operation that utilized the anonymity of the Internet, the best tool to come out of his generation. His customers, high-end users, paid any amount of money for a feeling and provided new customers through word of mouth. He provided the pleasure. On all levels. Amazing how far some men with unlimited amounts of money would go to sustain pleasure. Obviously their money wasn't enough to get them off, a fact he exploited. Even more amazing to him, when they discovered they could get away with it, they'd buy it, do it, and then recommend it to a friend who was just as depraved. His profits centered on this. Discreet word of mouth from satisfied customers was key.

He had no more time to worry over this part of the business. His human merchandise needed his full attention now. With the area being overrun with Feds and state police, he had to make sure they avoided detection until he could unload them.

Chapter 7

Had Jake heard their conversation?

As he stood framed in the doorway, Shelly studied his face, seeking some sign, but he only smiled and looked down.

"What? Do I have something on my shirt?"

"No." She took a sip of coffee, casting her eyes straight ahead, fully relieved he obviously hadn't. "Elaine and I were discussing my life in Atlanta."

"Really? Care to share the information?" He moved to the cupboard and grabbed a cup, proceeding to pour coffee, but Maria shooed him out of the way and took over the task.

"Go sit." Her nod indicated the table. "I'll bring you a late breakfast."

"It's just girl talk," Shelly said, as he pulled out a chair next to her. "Stuff you wouldn't be interested in."

"You'd be surprised what interests me."

Noting an angry edge to his words, Shelly glanced at his face once more, wondering if he'd heard the words about aborting a child they'd conceived. But again, his face was a blank mask. He was either a master at hiding what he was thinking or he hadn't heard.

Emily ran into the room, interrupting the moment. "Here it is, Grandma." She triumphantly handed Elaine a pile of material and colorful threads. "Daddy, you're back!" Her excited squeal followed as she jumped into his arms.

Jake hugged her, before settling her in his lap. "George called."

He waited until Shelly looked at him again, then added, "Said he talked to you earlier, right after you spoke to your insurance agent."

"Yeah. I guess I don't have the right coverage." Shelly shrugged. Her policy didn't include a rental, and she'd have to pay more than a dollar a mile towing charge for anything over a fifty-mile distance, which would tap into her savings, since she was already paying the deductible. Not for the front windshield—that required none, but going off the road was considered collision and if she'd been going slower she could have avoided losing control, according to the agent she spoke with. "They'll only tow as far as Bowling Green, so I might as well utilize George. I know he'll do a good job."

He also offered her a free car to use while hers was in his shop, which meant she'd probably be stuck here. She felt funny about driving a loaner the six-hundred-mile round trip to Atlanta. She'd love to be better off financially to afford options, especially after six years. Not to mention, she hated leaving her son for any length of time.

Everything always revolved around money, or the lack of it. Extra cash was still too hard to come by. She'd discussed it with Maggie and Monica. Both assured her Mikey would be fine. It wasn't as if she never traveled. All three took turns going on buying trips for their store. "He's too busy with his friend's sleepover to give missing you a thought," her mom had said, adding, "Stay put. It's a silly waste of money to drive back and forth." Shelly's conversation with Mikey just moments ago reinforced the idea. He was perfectly happy without her, which erased some of her uneasiness about being gone for a few days.

Plus, Elaine seemed to need her.

"If you want, I'm heading out in a bit." Jake picked up his fork after Maria set a plate in front of him. "I can drop you off at George's garage."

"That'd be great." Shelly smiled. Having just swallowed the last bite, she pushed back from the table with the thought of escaping. At least for a while. "When are you going?"

"Let's see." He glanced at his watch. "Once I'm done eating, I need to make some quick calls. Give me half an hour, okay?"

"Sure. After all, you're the one doing me the favor." She left the three and decided to check the money tree while they finished their breakfast.

Shelly stepped out the family room door, connected to the

deck at the other side of the house from her bedroom. Brisk air hit her, much cooler than the night before, with the sun still hiding behind the deciduous trees. The air smelled clean as it always did after a cold front mixed with the heat. An early morning thunderstorm resulted, along with lower humidity for a few days. She followed the shady path as birds chirped and insects buzzed around her.

In the light of day, nothing of the eeriness from last night remained, easing her fears.

At the tree, she stopped and peered at the round disks she'd thought would eventually turn into real dollars all those years ago. A sad smile formed as she realized how much her dream seemed like a lottery player's. She'd wanted it to bloom money and had thought it would happen simply because it was such a fervent wish. Yet, the odds at the lottery were actually better. At least a player's one in ten million shot was something that could actually happen.

She walked around the leafy fullness.

Remember the money tree.

An answer had come at three in the morning. Not long after they'd planted the bush, they'd hidden secret messages, buried in a spot known only to two silly kids. Even though the habit had long since died, that had to be what Kiera had meant.

Crouching, Shelly reached under the bush as far as she could, patting the ground and pulling at the grass as she went. Eventually, a large piece of sod sprang free in her hands, and she knelt, leaning in to examine the small hollow in the dirt below. From the square hole, she pulled out a ziplock plastic bag containing a book. She pulled it out of the bag and opened what appeared to be a journal of some kind, written in Kiera's scratchy hand.

The first page dated two years ago had her name and the purpose of the book—an aid to help sort out her feelings of her extreme past in an effort to become the mother her daughter needed.

Reading such personal thoughts, Shelly felt like a voyeur, someone who, after driving by an accident scene with mangled cars, had to slow down to gawk. And like that sick person, she couldn't stop herself from invading Kiera's privacy. Why else would she give her the weird message if she hadn't wanted her to read her personal thoughts?

Didn't matter one whit that Shelly was rationalizing her behavior. Something inside her wouldn't let her put the journal down.

She flipped through the pages that followed a chronological order, just like a diary up to the final entry, written only days earlier. She skimmed it, hoping for more clues as to why this had been so important. All she got was ramblings about how excited Kiera had been that Shelly was finally coming home.

Shelly sat back, crossed her legs, and continued reading. After a few seconds, she wiped at her eyes because suddenly they were blurry. She hadn't expected Kiera's words.

> I've been thinking a lot about those extreme days when I was so zoned out and clueless to the pain of those around me. Pain I caused. The hardest part of this process was to look into the mirror of Kiera Delaney's life and see what I'd done...who I'd become. Certainly not the person I set out to be. Does anyone set out to be a drug addict? Addict. Such an ugly term, and one that was difficult to own up to. Part of addiction is using something as a crutch to hide behind. I can't hide my worst any longer. My cruelty toward Shelly is the mirror I regret the most, and looking into it has been more daunting than anything I've done so far. Yet I have to do it. I have to face the person I loved like a sister and tell her how sorry I am for not being the same friend she always was to me.
>
> I remember the day we met and how much pride she had, holding her head high despite taunts from the bullies in the school. She was two years younger, but seemed so much older. I've always admired her for her bravery, knowing I could never have been as strong as her. If I had been, I'd have never hidden behind drugs or outrageous behavior.

Shelly's mind drifted back to the mentioned day. She remembered being scared to death to start school.

Her dad was in heaven, never coming home again. Which was a good thing, seeing as he wouldn't know where they'd gone. They no longer lived in the same house she'd grown up in, having just moved into the trailer. She and Monica were going to a new school.

Monica had warned her to expect a little teasing. Left to her own resources outside the kindergarten classroom, Shelly was too afraid to go in. She had good reason. That was when she got her first taste of how cruel children could be.

Shelly watched the other kids put their lunches in a cubby and went to do the same.

"Barney's for babies."

"He is not," she defended, at the sneer of one of her favorite characters. She loved her lunch box.

"That looks old and beat up," said one little jerk, whose father Shelly later learned worked in a high capacity at the cabinet factory Kiera's family owned. "Where'd ya get it? Someone's trash pile?" He laughed at his joke, punching his friend on the arm.

"Nah. She lives in one," his friend said, laughing back. "Ya know? The trailer next to the Delaneys. My mom says they're just what the county needs. More poor white trash moving into the area."

"You're just a…a…" Shelly sputtered a moment, having no glib retort because embarrassment rose up to stop thoughts from forming. And there it started, until her guardian angel stepped in front of the kid and shoved him.

"Take that back, you poopy-head. For your information, you're the trashy ones, being so mean." She put her hands on her hips. "And ya know what else? I like Barney and I'm not a baby and her lunch box is worth way more'n yours."

"Let's go," the teacher said, interrupting. "Quit teasing the younger kids and get to class." The two boys moved quickly, hurrying inside their classroom on the other side of the hall while the teacher stood at the door. She smiled at Shelly and added before disappearing, "You too, sweetie. Put your lunch away so we can get started."

Shelly nodded, placing the Barney lunch box, one Monica had outgrown, inside a cubby. She turned back to the older girl who'd come to her rescue and brushed a tear away, trying to keep more from coming. It was the first time she realized what being poor really meant.

"Thanks. The lunch box is old and I guess Barney is kind of for babies." Still, it was hard being called trash or being so disloyal to a character she loved.

"Forget those jerks. They dunno beans about anything," the girl stated, with the assurance of someone who had a new lunch pail picturing the latest cartoon rage. "Billy Durbin and Bobby Winters are both poopy-heads. You're the new kid who moved in at the end of the road, aren't you?" When Shelly didn't deny the claim, she went on, sticking out her hand, "I'm Kiera Delaney. Just ignore those two and if you can't, call them poopy-heads. They hate that."

Shelly chuckled at the memory now. A traumatic event for any five-year-old, which is why it was so vivid after twenty-one years. But she just thought of something new. Calling those two Kiera's nickname had drawn more taunting. After all, they'd hated being called what amounted to the equivalent of shitheads almost as much as Shelly had hated being reminded of her low status in the town.

For the first time in her life, she looked at the incident from a different perspective and realized maybe...just maybe...she'd played a role to keep the animosity alive. Not wanting to think about that now, she went back to Kiera's journal.

If Shelly and Jake can forgive me, then it means I've come full circle and I've achieved my goal.

Damn. This wasn't the kind of stuff she wanted to read. Not now. Shelly wanted to hate Kiera. Yet, reading the excerpts unleashed strong memories of earlier years when her childhood friend had been entirely different from the calculating woman who'd lured Jake back into her clutches.

Suddenly, she felt a presence. Still sitting, she glanced over her shoulder, stunned to see Jake behind her, his gaze resting on the book she held in her hand. She'd been so intent on memories, she hadn't heard his approach.

He crouched, nodding to the journal. "That Kiera's?"

"Yes." What else could she say? He had to recognize her handwriting. Plus, he'd been present when Kiera had given her edict about the money tree. "I thought there might be something to explain the craziness of her actions from yesterday."

"And?" He watched her face closely.

She shook her head, closed the book, and sighed. "No such luck. From what I can tell, it's just a diary of thoughts about how she wanted to atone."

"Can I see it?"

Having no choice, she handed him the diary. He flipped through it, much as she'd done. He spent a few moments on different pages, before settling on the page she'd been reading.

Shelly felt heat go up her face, wondering what he thought of Kiera's last words.

"I think she meant for me to know how she felt." She didn't expand other than to add, when it looked as if he was going to keep the book once he'd closed it, "I'd like to finish reading it."

Jake didn't say anything at first, just eyed her while his brain obviously churned. "I'll make sure you get it back. I'd like to have an expert take a look at it first."

"An expert? Why?" Shelly's gaze narrowed in confusion. "Do you think there's more to her overdose? What's going on?"

"I'm not sure." Indicating the book with a nod, he said, "I'm hoping this might give me a better clue."

"Then why not let me keep it for a day or so and give it a once-over? After all, I knew Kiera better than anyone. If I find anything useful, I'll hand it over right away. What can it hurt?"

He thought about her suggestion for a moment, then shrugged. "Okay. A day or two shouldn't matter." He stood.

She took the book he held out. "I'm ready to go whenever you are."

When Jake didn't drop his hand, she gripped it, allowed him to haul her up, and ignored the burst of pleasure shooting straight to her center the contact caused.

Once upright, she immediately let go and brushed debris off her shorts to disguise her reaction, praying her face wasn't a glowing pink. At times like this, she hated being so fair. Her mother was always quick to point out how every emotion showed in her expression. Shelly lowered her eyes, disguising those too, and turned to walk silently beside him back into the house.

Chapter 8

"I'm mostly waiting on parts," George said, thirty minutes later after showing Shelly into his office.

Jake had dropped her off at the garage and mentioned checking in once he finished his business, just to make sure she was okay, he'd said. For some reason, his concern fed some sick, underlying need to have him care. Of course, that was so like him. The ultimate nice guy, making sure she was taken care of. No wonder she still harbored feelings for him. If he'd been a selfish jerk or even a little on the cold side, she could have written him off and forgotten him.

"Air bag and front bumper," George said, yanking her back to the reality of her crashed car. When she met his gaze he added, "Once they come in, it'll take a few days. Paint will take the longest. Has to bake and cure. Can't rush that, otherwise it'll show in a couple of years."

As he went on about repairs, the thought of a motel room flashed again. Or maybe she'd get lucky and Jake would stay out investigating whatever he seemed to be investigating. He'd never said. She wasn't quite sure what he did, but whatever it was, it had something to do with Kiera's OD and Sheriff Baker, as she'd heard him mention both names too many times while he'd been on his cell phone.

Maybe he'd followed his dream. Or maybe he was trying to clear Kiera's name.

She snuffed out the flare of jealousy and rationalized his behavior. Of course he'd defend the mother of his child. In fact, knowing how this town talked, if there was the slightest chance of another scenario for Kiera's demise, he'd latch on to it like a tick to a dog in May, just as Shelly would. She understood the need to protect a child.

George stood. "Is there anything you need from your car?"

"As a matter of fact, there is." She suddenly remembered the book she'd left. If anything, it would keep her occupied in case of another sleepless night.

"It's out back." He started out with her, but the phone rang. He stopped to answer. Seconds later, he put his hand over the receiver. "Last row. It's open. I need to take this, but I shouldn't be too long."

Shelly nodded, pushed her way through the door, and headed for the last row. When she spotted her car in the distance, her pace increased.

Movement out of her peripheral vision had her turning and she glimpsed a utility truck parked beyond the fence. Nonchalantly, she slowed, placed her hand in her purse, and pulled out her cell phone to capture proof. A picture. Not that anyone would believe her, but the truck looked exactly like the one that had forced her off the road. If she could figure out who'd been driving, maybe she could talk to him. Didn't matter that the idea had more holes than a sprinkler and no sane driver would admit to causing her crash. Still, she had to try. At this point it seemed a better alternative than doing nothing.

After snapping away, she pocketed the phone and resumed walking. She'd only taken a few steps when a shout hit her ears.

"Look out."

Someone shoved her, tackling her from behind. Her hands instinctively went out in front of her as she hit the graveled ground, too stunned to think about the engine hoisted on a crane that swung around, broke loose, and crashed with a loud thud mere feet from where she'd stood only seconds ago.

"That was too close for comfort." The voice, one she didn't recognize, broke through her haze of fear. He stood and bent to help her. "Are you okay?"

"I think so." Shelly took his offered hand, let him pull her up, and winced. Pain shot through her bruised shoulder, dulling the throbbing coming from her hands and knees that had taken the brunt of her fall. "Thanks." She glanced at the smashed motor and shivered. "You saved my life."

George rushed up to her, concern etched onto her features.

"I don't know what to say other than I'm sorry. That crane shouldn't have swung like it did. And the cable definitely shouldn't have snapped."

Three heads turned toward the crane. A severed cable dangled in the breeze. The control cab stood empty and there was no one in sight.

Shelly wiped the dirt off her shorts, smearing blood in the process, and tried not to think about how hard she'd hit the gravel beneath her feet. The small rocks had to have scraped every bare spot on her body.

"I'm fine. Nothing broken," she murmured after taking a stiff step. Slowly, she worked out the kinks and the pain subsided to a dull ache. "Just shaken up."

This was the second time in less than twenty-four hours she'd returned from the edge of fright. Though in decent shape, she wasn't used to such jarring, first from a car accident and then from being tackled. Her gaze rested on the empty crane again before roaming to the crumpled pile of metal. Of course, if she hadn't been tackled, she'd be dead, so she wasn't complaining.

"Thank God you were in the vicinity to help, Roger," George said. "Otherwise, it could've been serious."

"My pleasure." After brushing off his dress slacks, the man turned to Shelly and smiled. "I'm Roger Peters. I noticed you earlier. It's amazing what lengths a guy has to go to for an introduction, though."

Shelly flashed an indulgent smile, recognizing the come-on and enjoying the trip his eyes took in obvious approval. Having spent enough time in singles bars with her sister, while Maggie babysat after telling her girls they were only young once, male interest wasn't that uncommon an experience. Still, receiving such a stare always made her feel normal.

Didn't matter that it seldom went anywhere. Usually after a few dates, she lost the desire to take a relationship further. She wasn't a prude, by any means. However, she was picky. As stupid as it sounded, Jake Collier was her benchmark of the perfect male and a hard act for any man to follow.

"I'm Shelly Matthews." She stuck out her hand, but noticed it was scraped and bleeding. She dropped it. "I'd shake, but I don't want to mess up your clothes any more than I already have," she said, also noting smudges and small tears in his expensive wool pants.

"Guess I should've introduced you, seeing as how you saved my customer and also saved my ass from a lawsuit." George's expression turned sheepish. "Send me the bill for a new pair of pants," he grumbled. "Least I can do."

Roger laughed and clapped George on the back. "I will. And considering I might be the one filing your lawsuit, you owe me doubly."

"Roger's new to town," George explained. "Works out of Bowling Green and lives down the road a stretch."

"I see." Shelly nodded. New to town could mean anything from a week to five years, and down the road a stretch could mean anything from a block to twenty miles.

"I'd say saving a life calls for a celebration. How about meeting me for drinks, so you can thank me properly."

Shelly glanced back at Roger and grinned. He was good-looking enough, with a tall, muscular build and dark blond hair. Plus, he had saved her life, which earned her gratitude and a chance. "Sure."

"Was there something you needed?" George asked Roger, interrupting a weird moment when the guy wouldn't release her eyes.

After another long pause, Roger's focus wandered from her to George. "I had a couple of questions."

"Okay. Give me a few minutes." George glanced at Shelly and offered a fatherly smile. "Your hands are bleeding, missy." He motioned with his head in the direction of the office. "Come on in and let's take a look at those knees. Those cuts look more serious."

Her gaze moved lower, resting on her knees as blood oozed from scrapes she no longer felt.

"I have some antibacterial cream to put on them after we wash away the dirt." George placed his hand on the small of her back. Before he started walking, Roger handed Shelly a card. He'd written directions on the back for the bar, as well as the name.

"Six o'clock. Don't be late." He started off in the opposite direction, adding over his shoulder to George, "I've already talked with Kay in the office. She answered my questions."

George guided her toward the building. Halfway there, Shelly suddenly remembered the utility truck. She pointed to where she'd seen it. "George, do you know who owns that truck?"

"What truck?" He squinted and followed her hand with his eyes. "I don't see any truck."

She looked to her left and sure enough, the space on the other side of the fence stood empty. "It was right there. Before the crane broke."

George shrugged and continued walking. "Well, it's gone now."

Shelly lagged behind, filled with questions.

Why would she see the truck right before the cable snapped? Had it really been an accident? Despite feeling a bit paranoid, she wondered why all of a sudden the utility truck was now missing. Maybe the guy saw her taking pictures and hadn't liked it.

Shelly took one more look at the empty space over her shoulder. Then she caught up to George, who'd stopped and waited. As he led her inside, other thoughts about coincidences entered her brain. One death-defying incident could be construed as an accident, but two? Were they connected?

No! Campton wasn't a mecca for intrigue. Her imagination was simply on overload.

~

On the drive back to Elaine's, Jake called Michelle's cell. The cave could wait. He hadn't been able to get her out of his mind most of the morning, and with this latest development, he wanted to satisfy his urge to make sure she was safe.

"Hi, Jake," she said, answering after the fourth ring and sounding more perky than he expected. "What's up?"

"I just spoke to George. Are you okay?"

"I'm fine. It was a freak accident and my guardian angel was looking out for me again."

"Where are you?"

"I just turned onto the road leading to Elaine's."

"Good." He was about five minutes behind. "Stay there. I'm

on my way. I'd like to talk to you about what happened."

"There's nothing to talk about. I was in the wrong place at the wrong time. I have every intention of holing up in my room and spending the afternoon reading Kiera's journal."

"I have my reasons, so humor me, okay?" When she stayed silent, he added, "It shouldn't take long. I only have a few questions."

Jake hung up and pressed the accelerator harder, not liking the anxiety riding his spine. The sensation alerted instincts that never lied. Somehow Michelle fit into this whole puzzle, but he didn't see any connection—other than being at the wrong place at the wrong time.

He parked, then raced up the porch stairs two at a time, determined her reluctance to answer questions wouldn't stop him from easing his fears.

"Why are you so concerned about a freak accident anyway?" Michelle asked later, as Jake paced in Elaine's living room after listening to her full accounting of the hoist breaking. "Like I said, it broke loose after swinging around. I was in a dangerous area and should have been looking out."

He sighed, not going anywhere but absolutely crazy and becoming more frustrated by the second. She didn't seem to grasp his unease and he didn't want to tell her the whole truth of what he'd learned once he'd finished his reports and had called George. The crane's snapping wasn't the freak accident she'd readily assumed. In an effort to clue her in without panicking her, he said, "George is fanatical about safety. He thinks the hoist may have had some help in falling."

"But that would mean it wasn't an accident."

"My point exactly." There was no gentle way to inform her other than to just blurt it out. "Especially when you tell me you saw a utility truck similar to the one that ran you off the road."

"He didn't run me off the road. He cut me off and his tools most likely weren't secured."

"What if that wasn't an accident? What if it was meant to happen? You said it yourself, you came this close to dying." He held up a hand with his forefinger and thumb an inch apart. "It's too much coincidence this truck is in the vicinity before a partially cut hoist spun and broke. And when the dust settled, it was gone. Why?"

"You're scaring me."

"Good. That was my intention. You need to be scared so you won't blow this off as just happenstance. This whole mess is terrifying, and I don't like the thought of you being attacked. Not once, but twice."

Her eyes grew as wide as quarters as his warning sank in. "You think someone is targeting me? To hurt me on purpose?"

Jake shrugged. "I'm not sure, but why take chances?"

"I got a picture of the truck."

"You did?"

Nodding, Michelle lifted her cell phone out of her purse and clicked a few buttons. He could kiss her for having the foresight to snap a picture, but he restrained the urge. Getting too close wasn't a good idea. Not when she looked so adorable, offering him the phone with such a sweet smile.

"See? I think I even got the license plate."

Pushing out his distracting thoughts, he looked at the screen. Sure enough, there it was in living color. He handed it back. "Can you e-mail me, so I can blow it up?" With a plate number he could get a name, and with a name, maybe a lead.

"Sure. Just give me your address." After a few seconds of fiddling with her phone, she peered up at him expectantly and he rattled off the e-mail address. "Done."

"At least you're here now, safe and sound." Jake lifted and rolled his shoulders, as a bit of tension left his body.

"For the afternoon, during which I plan to read." Michelle waited until he glanced her way again before she smiled and added, "But later I'll be busy. I have a date."

"You have a date?" He couldn't keep the surprise out of his voice. His jaw locked and the tension he thought had dissipated suddenly flared up again, tightening in a knot at the top of his spine. He reached around and massaged the spot. She'd most likely dated a lot of men in the last six years. Why should he care whether she had a date now?

"Yes. With the guy who tackled me and saved me from being crushed. Did I forget to mention him? He asked me out for drinks, only I haven't quite decided if I'll meet him or not."

The way she threw the news out now made him realize it

wasn't an oversight. She'd held the information back on purpose. George hadn't mentioned anything about this phantom guy, having cut their conversation short because several customers had interrupted.

Jake was more than curious. "Who is this guy?" And what the hell had he been doing at George's?

"Just my guardian angel." Shrugging, Michelle smiled. "George says he's new to town."

"Does this paragon have a name?"

"Roger Peters."

"What?" He blinked and stared, too stunned to hear the name he and Rich had been discussing earlier. The knot of tension progressed higher to pound along his temples, settling into what felt like a brain-splitting headache. "You're going out with him?"

His fingers moved to his forehead. In an effort to ease the throbbing, he rubbed. Damn! Just what he needed. To save her from that charming miscreant.

"Yes. He seemed nice enough."

"Nice enough?" Jake laughed, but the harsh sound held no humor. The two words didn't exactly describe the guy he knew him to be and the information he'd relayed to Baker wasn't something he could share. "What do you know about him?" he asked instead, appealing to Michelle's common sense. She'd never been one to take undue chances. Surely she hadn't changed that much in six years.

"I know George likes him and I know he saved my life. Which, in my book, is enough to say yes to a drink."

What could he say in response? He forced himself to take a deep breath.

"Just be careful." He groaned inwardly. How overly protective those words sounded floating past his ears. Hell, why not advertise his thoughts? He was acting no better than a jealous fool or worse. It was only a drink, and she was a grown woman after all.

"You act as if I'm an idiot."

"Yeah? Well, after two accidents that don't seem so accidental, I wouldn't be going out with strangers."

"What are you implying?"

Michelle couldn't be so obtuse, could she? "A guy like that could talk you into bed in no time," he yelled, finally losing all objectivity.

"Excuse me?" She stared at him open-jawed, her mouth forming a perfect *O* as the incredulity filling her eyes changed to a dawning awareness. "You're worried about my virtue?" She laughed and put her hand over her heart. "Oh, Jake, I'm touched."

"Shit," he blew out, wiping his face. Now he sounded like a raving lunatic. Rich's theory of a sex slave ring was starting to affect his thinking. He couldn't tell her the truth about what he was investigating, so he did the next best thing. Tried to warn her away. "Just be careful, will you? You know nothing about this guy."

"Hey, what's to know? He saved my life and asked me out for a drink. I think showing up is the least I can do."

She stood, and from the determined glint in her eyes, he knew their talk was over and nothing he said would change her mind.

"I have a journal to read. And once Elaine retires for the night, I'm going out. For drinks with a good-looking guy."

Jake squeezed his fingers into a fist, resisting dual impulses as her emphasized parting shot filtered past his ears. The urge to hit something overwhelmed him, as did the urge to run after her and shake some sense into her.

Why should he care? He didn't. Period. He didn't even know her any longer. Six years had provided the distance to get Michelle out of his system, and all he had to do was wait until Kiera's funeral, after which she'd go back to Atlanta and he'd go back to Nashville once he solved this case. Just because they'd grown up together and he felt a strange sort of protective instinct toward her, didn't give him any special privileges to control her life.

Instead of trailing after her and making a bigger fool of himself, he headed for his room and his computer. Of course she'd find Peters attractive. Hell, he had no doubt what had attracted a guy like him. No man with any life left at all would pass up an opportunity to buy Michelle a drink.

"Forget her. Just forget her. You have a job to do," he

muttered, pressing the On button to his laptop and waiting the full minute for it to boot up. He checked his e-mail to retrieve the picture, then quickly enlarged it. Jake scribbled out the now legible numbers, grabbed his cell phone, and punched in a preset number, pushing out thoughts of Michelle being devoured by the male vulture she was meeting later for drinks.

"Hey, gorgeous," he said to Linda Phillips, a woman he had an ongoing relationship with when their schedules meshed.

"Hey, sexy." He could tell she was smiling at the other end. "Long time, no hear."

"Sorry I haven't called. I've been busy." Jake didn't have to explain further. That particular element was why they'd been friendly lovers for so long. Both liked their space. Neither wanted strings. Linda, he could handle, because she wasn't looking for long term any more than he was. He'd already warned her communication would be nil before he'd left Nashville, so he didn't spend too much time on needless niceties now, other than reciprocating with the few basic questions of how each was faring. "I've got a license number I need you to check on."

"Wait," she said, suddenly becoming all business, which was why he liked her so much. He might even go so far as to say he loved her in a placid sort of way that he could control. She never expected more than he could give, and he extended the same courtesy, never asking for anything, always enjoying what she put in. "Let me grab a pen."

Like him, Linda worked crazy hours in law enforcement. They'd met at a symposium in Nashville and had realized they lived minutes apart. The two had other commonalities, single parenthood being the biggest draw. Emily got along with Linda's older daughter, and they had no problem blending households when time allowed. Jake didn't delude himself in thinking their relationship would ever evolve into a deeper one. On either side. But it sure beat those lonely nights when thoughts of how he'd screwed up his chances for happily-ever-after got the better of him. Time spent with Linda made life bearable, and he figured if he ever decided to have more kids, she would be his best candidate. They had a running joke between them. When and if she ever decided on the same thing, she might consider candidacy.

"Okay, shoot." Her voice pulled his focus back to his reason for calling.

He rattled off the number.

"As soon as I have an answer, I'll e-mail you, just in case you're out of cell range."

"Thanks. I owe you." Another drawback of rural living, he thought. Technology was long in coming in some parts. Too many areas around here had dead spots where cell phone service was next to impossible.

After a few more words back and forth, he said his good-byes and hung up. Then he set to work on trying to stay busy as thoughts of Michelle snuck back into his mind. A guy like Roger Peters was the last thing she needed. But since he wasn't much better, he tried to dismiss the idea of jealousy. He wasn't jealous. Long ago he'd lost the right to care enough to endure jealousy.

Chapter 9

On the monitor, he watched Kimberly's angel of mercy enter the room.

"Tonight's your lucky night, sweet thing." Her tone was soothing, much like a mother speaking to a baby. "Your visit here may be coming to an end, and you'll go to someone who loves to make you feel exquisite."

Kimberly tilted her head as if to listen to her soft voice.

He chuckled at how quickly she'd succumbed to their methods, much faster than the others. After studying various figures in recent history, guys like Branch Davidians leader David Koresh or Paul Jessup, who'd led his group of lecherous old men to marry underage girls, he'd been fascinated by the social structures they'd created that allowed such deviancy—ways in which mass murderers like Jim Jones in Jonestown manipulated people into going so far as to kill their own children.

He'd developed his own form of mind control. Of course, it always helped to have God on their side. Except that he couldn't afford to take the time to cultivate the idea of finding heaven. He put his victims through hell instead, using basic human drives like hunger, thirst, and even sex as tools, so that when they got a taste of what they thought of as heaven, they'd do anything to keep it, even if it meant selling their souls, or in this case their bodies, both of which he owned.

For now.

If the SLA could get Patti Hearst to rob a bank, he could get his stable of gorgeous girls to be whores. All eventually met the same fate as Kimberly, going to whoever paid the most, all feeling dependent on those who bought them. After all, he also knew how to use their mix of drugs and psychological mind games for maximum effect.

"Would you like that, Kimberly?"

"Yes," she replied to the angel, closing her eyes.

Under the influence of his drug, she had to be aware of everything in the room. Sounds would seem louder, more intense, colors brighter, and when something touched her, he knew she burned in that spot.

Kimberly's angel followed protocol, rubbing musky, scented oil over her body. The smell was meant to invade her nostrils and seep deep inside of her and add to her sensations. Right now she probably burned all over. And just when the angel determined the burning might become too much, her touch softened, soothing the burn, but not extinguishing it.

Only one thing would extinguish the excruciating, mind-numbing yearning.

"No!" She squirmed, trying to sit up. "This isn't right."

"You mustn't fight it," the angel cooed. Her hands became rougher, more insistent, taking away Kimberly's will to struggle stroke by stroke. "You know resisting does no good."

He smiled, watching. Women like Kimberly were always torn…always struggled. In the beginning. He relished viewing the progression. The struggle of hating what was happening slowly diminished, as the dawning awareness of what was to come set in. An absolutely fascinating process. Few could resist the pull. They'd come to love the pleasure. Yearn for it. Do anything for it.

"Just enjoy. He will enjoy you. How can he not, when you're so beautiful. You know exactly what to do. This is your chance to shine. It will mean you're ready to move on. And when you do, you will always know the pleasure you've come to love." The angel hesitated a moment before asking, "You want that, don't you?"

"Yes."

Of course she did. Her brain wasn't working right. Her memory was distorted. Her every waking moment spent waiting for the angel's return. By this point, they controlled her thoughts, wouldn't allow her to think clearly, only allowed her to want what they wanted her to want. To be taken care of. To please. To enjoy. All her desire to fight, to remember, gone, stolen by a combination of drugs and mind control.

Kimberly was no different from those who'd gone before her. Waiting became her waking nightmare. Waiting in anticipation, knowing what would happen next, her body craving the intense pleasure.

Yes. By design, waiting was terrifying, the thought of doing without unthinkable.

Poor Kimberly. Deep down, she might consider what she did as somehow wrong, yet unable to determine quite why. She wasn't tied down and could easily escape. She wouldn't. Not like the others had. He now could spot the symptoms of those who could fight his drug. Kimberly was hooked. If the haze diminished, she'd think too much about what she'd be missing.

Certainly, the thought was enough to chain her to the room until the haze resettled and she wouldn't have to think about her actions. He had no doubt that she had no will to do anything but what he and the angel asked of her.

Nothing mattered, except attaining the pure bliss of the act. An act they controlled.

~

Shelly drove the eight miles to the bar, looking forward to some time away from the craziness of the last two days. Elaine had been reclusive most of the day, spending the rest of her time with Emily. Shelly had felt like an intruder. She'd tiptoed around or remained in her room reading half of Kiera's journal, which had given her some insight into her friend's state of mind as a recovering addict, but had offered nothing to explain the current circumstances.

Elaine had begged off dinner, claiming to be too drained to be good company.

Shelly had needed to get away from Jake, whose presence had never ceased to rattle her.

While parking in one of the few spots available, their conversation played over and over in her mind. Why had he warned her off drinks with Roger?

Was he jealous?

She snorted. Fat chance.

No. He'd been more concerned about the accident not

being an accident. Maybe he wasn't so far off, as she'd been a little weirded out by it too, especially after learning the hoist had had some help in snapping. That little detail didn't add to her sense of calm.

Roger couldn't be responsible. He'd risked his life to shove her out of the way, and she wasn't about to let Jake's overactive imagination scare her into not enjoying a charming man's company.

Shelly stepped out of the car. Music blasted from the wooden building, which along with the crowded parking lot, told her this was the most happening place in Campton, or anywhere within twenty miles.

She glanced briefly at her watch. A quick grin formed. Seven minutes after six.

Perfect timing. Less than ten minutes late was enough to be fashionable, without appearing desperate or being too rude.

Roger suddenly materialized beside her once Shelly entered the packed, smoky room. It was happy hour according to the sign above the bar, one that also advertised live music Thursday through Saturday.

"You're late." He yelled to be heard over the band playing onstage. Couples filled the small dance floor just to the left of it, adding to the lively atmosphere.

Shelly smiled. "Am I?"

He was lucky she'd come at all, but he didn't need to know she'd debated the decision much of the afternoon.

His prompt presence meant he must have been watching for her. Roger was better looking than she remembered. His chiseled handsomeness, firm jaw, and deep-set, arresting blue eyes were enough to draw the envious stares of other women around her. Her smile stretched. Maybe, just maybe, Jake was jealous. After all, he hadn't gone into his overly protective mode until after she'd mentioned Roger's name.

He must know the guy, she mused.

Geez, wouldn't that be something? The tables turning and Jake eating his heart out instead of her?

"Until I saw you walk through the door, I wondered if you were going to be a no-show." Roger leaned in, just inches from her ear, so close the warmth from his breath brushed her skin.

He placed his hand on the small of her back, guiding her through the noisy bar to a table far away from the band where they wouldn't have to shout as much to be heard.

"I would never be so thoughtless as to not show up without a call. I finally decided nothing short of a drink would thank you properly. After all, a girl doesn't get saved by Prince Charming every day." Shelly sat in the chair he'd pulled out. "I just wish you hadn't ruined such a nice pair of slacks to do it."

"Well worth the price. A guy doesn't get the chance to save a beautiful damsel in distress every day."

"Flattery will get you far, you know."

"How far?"

She laughed, enjoying the way Roger's eyes assessed her. "Not that far." Shelly liked him. He looked good in his faded, butt-hugging jeans. Damn good. The navy T-shirt stretching over a broad chest and a couple of bulging biceps told her he'd spent his fair share of time in the gym. She hadn't made a mistake in taking the chance on meeting him.

"You don't even know how far I was thinking."

More of her laughter rose up and he joined in, adding, "What can I get you, beautiful?"

"I'm driving, so I'll nurse a glass of red wine."

"Cabernet okay?" His eyebrows quirked up a bit.

She failed to keep the surprise from showing in her eyes. "They have it here?" Geez, listen to her. If the locals ever caught wind of her attitude, they'd laugh her out of town. She could just hear them now. White trash putting on airs. She'd come a long way in six years.

Roger grunted. "We're in Campton, Kentucky, not the Outback."

"Sorry." Shelly offered an apologetic shrug. "I guess I am being a bit pretentious."

"Yeah, well the place does have a few rough edges, which in this case can be deceiving, so I forgive you. Very few know or care that Della has a decent selection of wines."

"I'll have to be more careful in forming opinions, then." She took a furtive glance around while he ordered, wondering about perceptions. She'd been too young to visit bars before she'd left town, and despite being crowded and lively, this one did look a little rough.

Similar rough-looking bars in Atlanta featured any kind of beer or hard liquor, but very few high-end wines. Not that she'd visited many, mainly venturing into the safer, more professional hangouts, where suits and styled haircuts were the norm for men rather than chains and tattoos.

Of course, Roger had no visible tattoos and his hair was styled, but he seemed to fit in too well with this crowd. Maybe that was why Jake had warned her off?

Her grin was quick. Having a drink with him was a little like taking a trip on the wild side, and Shelly determined right then and there, it might be more fun to experience the unpredictable.

The cocktail waitress placed little paper napkins on the table. "I'll be right back with your drinks," she said, before turning and rushing away.

"So, Roger, what do you do, besides rescuing damsels?" Shelly met his bold gaze, holding on to her smile. Who knew where this adventure would lead?

"I'm a criminal defense lawyer."

"Ah!" Damn. A lawyer? That explained the exchange he and George had had about lawsuits. Her heart sank. Just her luck her joyride jolted to a harsh stop. Shelly hated lawyers based on the few she'd dated in Atlanta. She hadn't met one who didn't think he was God's gift. Even more disappointing? She'd hoped Roger would be someone with a darker profession, someone to take her mind off Jake.

"Ah?" Roger studied her face. "What does that mean and why are your eyes glazing over? You're forming another opinion, aren't you?"

Shelly had the grace to blush, feeling heat rise on her cheeks. "Sorry." She, of all people, shouldn't judge. She cleared her throat and picked up the glass of wine the waitress had just plunked down in front of her, hiding her embarrassment in taking a long drink.

He tsk-tsked, shaking his head and waiting until she chanced another glance at his face. When she met his amused gaze, he grinned. "And after promising not to form opinions." He picked up her hand and studied it. "So, tell me. Why do you dislike lawyers?"

"I don't," she lied, lifting her chin a notch, challenging him with the declaration.

"Ah, ah, ah." Roger brought her hand to his lips, kissed it, and then massaged her fingers, sending little tingles up her arm. "Don't deny it. I'm the guy who saved you. Remember?" He smiled, his dimples forming. "And as such, I deserve the truth."

He had a strong grip. Secure and confident, reminding her of Jake.

No. Shelly wasn't going to let Jake intrude on this opportunity. After all, Roger had a bit of danger about him. That element in itself was thrilling, also making her a tad wary, especially since Roger held on to her hand, stroking her fingers in a move she'd quite determined was intended to stimulate. He seemed just a little too smooth.

Another interesting tidbit to ponder.

She unobtrusively studied him, trying to discern what it was about him that drew her while repelling her at the same time. The thought brought her up short, but once formulated, Shelly became even more guarded. Still, she was well aware she might have jumped to conclusions too quickly about him and his profession. She had to admit she was overly jumpy due to her earlier experiences and Jake's warning. The guy deserved a chance. She'd just have to remain cautious while enjoying his company.

"So, tell me," Roger urged, finally releasing her hand. "What do you have against lawyers?"

"Nothing, now." She laughed. "Because I never met any like you before."

"Good answer." He took a swig of beer and stood. "Come on, let's dance."

Much later, Shelly glanced at her watch. "Oh, damn." It was after nine and she'd been having such a good time with Roger, she'd forgotten Mikey. She never let him go to bed without a call to say good night if she happened to be out of town.

"What?"

"I forgot to call my son," she blurted out without thinking. She grabbed her purse, searching inside for her cell phone, wishing she'd kept silent, judging by the speculation forming in his eyes. Yet, despite not wanting the world to know, all she felt was relief. Roger was new to the area and didn't seem like the type to gossip.

In fact, she realized just then, she'd used her admission to put up a roadblock. In past experiences, most guys ran in the opposite direction at the moment of truth. Nothing halted the single male on the make faster than mentioning motherhood. Shelly liked Roger in some bizarre, dysfunctional way, but she wasn't going to bed with him. He made her too nervous. She'd caught his calculated stare once too often, giving her a good indication he was weighing his options and his chances. In that respect, he was a typical guy and a bit of a disappointment. Not that she was a prude. She'd just never been into casual sex and had no intention of sleeping with anyone without forming a strong relationship first.

"Son?" His gaze narrowed. "You're not married, are you?"

"No." Shelly stiffened and stared at him, dumbfounded. "Why would you ask that?"

"I don't know." Roger sat back and shrugged. "After spending the last few hours with you, I just can't believe any guy would let you go. I certainly wouldn't, especially if you were the mother of my child."

"You're being too nice." Shelly laughed to cover the weird feeling the comment produced. She glanced around, avoiding his gaze. "Um…listen…I…um…I hope you won't mention it around town about my son." She planted a forced smile on her face, going for normal. "Campton isn't Atlanta. Most here don't know I have a five-year-old. I'd prefer to keep it that way."

"Ah! I get it. A secret." Roger's big hand splayed across hers, highlighting their differences in size. Shelly was much smaller than him. "Your secret is safe with me. I won't tell a soul."

"Thank you." She tried to pull her hand away, but his grip tightened.

Just then, the cocktail waitress strode up to the table. "Can I get you anything else?"

Shelly stood, finally able to yank her hand free, and all too glad for the interruption. "I'm fine." No doubt about it, he made her nervous. "I'll be right back. I have to make my phone call." She prayed along the way to the restroom that Roger meant what he'd said about not telling anyone about Mikey.

Inside the small room, Shelly leaned against the door and exhaled a sigh of relief. She never should have come tonight. Hiding the fact that she had a son was harder than she'd ever imagined. How could she think to keep the news from Jake, when she'd all but given the news away to a complete stranger after one drink and a few hours of conversation?

One glance in the mirror, which highlighted her colorless complexion, prompted her to quickly wash her face and pinch her cheeks. She added a bit of blush and lipstick, then reached for her cell phone. When one bar appeared on the screen, she headed for the door to make her call outside. Only it wouldn't open. She pounded on the door, pulling harder as a streak of panic spread in the form of goose bumps over her skin.

Why would someone try to trap her in here?

Jake's warning entered her mind, as did the idea that this wasn't accidental either.

"Help!" Shelly yelled, using her fists to make as much noise as possible. Even with the pounding, her efforts did little to be heard over the loud music. Suddenly a sweet smell assaulted her nostrils and she looked up at the air vent. A wave of dizziness rolled over her along with nausea. What was happening to her? Acting on a fear-filled instinct, she grabbed a handful of paper towels, wet some, placing them over her nose and mouth so that they stuck if she held her head high. Then taking the others and without breathing, she stepped onto the toilet. She had just enough strength to pull the vent out, quickly covered it with the rest of the towels, and shoved it back into place.

Shelly then got down on her hands and knees close to the door, using her wet mask as a shield in order to breathe in air coming from the two-inch gap at the bottom. Her thoughts were jumbled, but somehow she understood it was important to keep inhaling the fresh air. For a brief instant, she had no idea where she was or what had happened.

Eventually, her mind cleared and a majority of the dizziness faded.

A while later Shelly heard pounding. Her name floated on the air, sounding like it was coming from a long tunnel.

"Shelly? Are you in there?"

More pounding reverberated, as Roger's voice registered.

"Yes." She stood, feeling stronger, and looked down, noting she'd been on the grungy bathroom floor. Why? She couldn't remember. Shuddering, she wiped at her knees before dropping the wet paper towels in the trash, then moved to the sink to wash her hands and face, catching a glimpse of herself in the mirror.

The pounding continued. The urgency had her ignoring the pale image staring back. She rushed to the door to open it, which surprisingly was no longer locked.

Had she imagined the last few minutes? She wasn't sure of anything.

"That was a long phone call. I didn't scare you away, did I?" Roger laughed. Then he glanced at her face and all humor drained from his expression. "Are you okay?"

The question, so like Jake's, rolled over her, making her wish he were here instead of Roger.

"Yeah. I'm fine." Shelly smiled and checked her watch. How long had she been gone from the table? She couldn't remember. It had to have been more than fifteen minutes, but in reality it seemed like only seconds had passed. How weird was that?

She certainly wasn't about to bring on more concern and ask. "It's a little stuffy in here." She stepped past him, trying to walk without stumbling. "I just need some air."

Out of the corner of her eye, she saw George and several other faces she recognized from her last summer, along with a couple she couldn't identify, all staring intently in her direction. Had one of them wanted to hurt her? It didn't make any sense. She glanced at Roger, who by now was walking solicitously by her side gripping her elbow, as more questions entered her mind. Shelly kept them in, not wanting to let him know how freaked out she was.

All she wanted to do was go home, but suddenly she was too afraid to drive by herself.

When she was about to head back to their table, Roger steered her in the opposite direction and out the rear of the bar. The door slammed behind them, cutting off most of the noise and emphasizing one fact. Shelly was now all alone with him.

What did she know about this guy?

Nothing.

Her heart raced as a sudden streak of terror hit. Shelly wiped her sweaty palms on her shorts, wishing she hadn't been so stupid.

Here she was at Roger's mercy, allowing him to lead her toward a vacant picnic table with a spotlight shining above that did little to chase away the shadows. At least she wasn't going to die in total darkness.

"Sit."

Warily, she sat, prepared to bolt the moment the threat became more real as adrenaline pumped through her system. She damn sure wouldn't make it easy for him to kill her.

Yet all he did was pace, much like Jake had earlier.

"I like you, Shelly Matthews. And because I like you, I'm going to give you a strong piece of advice."

"Okay." Her chin inched higher and her gaze narrowed. Advice was better than being drugged and killed. She groaned inwardly. She'd been watching too many CSI shows.

"Stay away from Della's. Go back to the Delaneys' and try to keep out of trouble until you go home to Atlanta."

"Excuse me?" Her total shock registered in the two words.

"What happened in the bathroom?"

"Nothing," she lied. "Look, I'm fine. Nothing happened. You don't have to warn me away from Della's like I'm some kind of stupid kid too young to know better." Jake used to do that all the time, all those years ago, and she didn't appreciate being treated like she had no brains or couldn't take care of herself now any better than she had back then.

Besides, she'd gotten out of the bathroom alive, although she couldn't quite remember how or what had transpired to make her feel like she'd somehow narrowly escaped. How could she tell him that? He'd really think she was an imbecile who needed babysitting.

"Nothing happened? Even though you were gone for twenty minutes?"

Shelly glanced at the ground, knowing the truth shone in her eyes. "So?" She shrugged. "I just wanted to call my son and I couldn't get reception. Then I had to go to the bathroom. There was a bit of a wait," she said, adding to her lies. "Once I finished, I noticed my face needed a little makeup. That's when you pounded on the door." When in doubt, mix the truth with the lies, she thought, remembering that much. She yanked out her cell phone, trying to act put upon. "Do you think I might make my call now?" She punched up her home number, and while waiting for the call to go through, added, "Then we can go back in and finish our drinks." Shelly really needed another glass of wine for the courage to carry off the rest of her pretense.

Roger eyed her for a long moment. Finally, he sighed. "No problem. I'll wait over by the door."

~

When the woman he knew to be Shelly Matthews left the bar, Rich wondered if he should follow her. He hung back instead, deciding to see what the others he watched did. At the same time, he checked his pocket for the small transmitter he'd retrieved, intending to e-mail a copy of her conversation with Peters to Jake. He might find it interesting. Rich certainly had.

Something went down earlier when she'd visited the ladies' room. He was sure of it. Her body's signals hadn't lied, had shouted her apprehension loud and clear.

He fully intended to check it out.

When no one moved from their spot for the next fifteen minutes, Rich headed for the restrooms. No one left to follow Shelly either, so more than likely she was okay to drive home alone. He waited until a drunk woman stumbled out before slipping inside the small room and locking the door. Rich felt around the mirror, noting nothing of interest. He glanced at the heating vent. It appeared to have been set hastily back in, one end not flush with the ceiling. A check of the wastebasket wielded unused paper towels. He picked one up and sniffed.

Hmm. Interesting. Smelled sweet…like chloroform, maybe. Rich took out a plastic bag from those he always carried for just such circumstances, stuck a couple of the towels inside, sealed the top, and placed it with the others in his pocket.

Next, he unlocked the door and opened it an inch. Good. A clear hallway.

Seconds later, he settled into a chair at a corner table and nursed another beer, keeping an eye on Bobby Winters and his friends. Rich was still considered an outsider, but he'd become chummy enough with the locals to play a game of pool and shoot the breeze, so the label had already begun changing. The longer he remained a fixture, the more invisible he became. Most in the smoke-filled bar left him alone to drink and watch.

He'd probably get little sleep tonight. The bar closed in less than an hour, after which he'd e-mail Jake and then make another drive to Nashville.

~

At the Delaneys' circular driveway, Shelly gunned the engine until the car reached the house. She turned off the ignition and heaved a sigh of relief, only too thankful the headlights in her rearview mirror hadn't followed.

Several times during the twenty-minute drive they'd gotten closer, easing back when an oncoming car's lights would pop up in front of her. This happened several times. She increased her speed after each one as the car behind narrowed its gap. Finally, she'd spotted a car ahead, going in the same direction. After that, the car following kept a steady distance.

Shelly sat frozen for a long moment, just staring into the night. Her eyes adjusted to the darkness, as thoughts about her evening flitted through her mind, along with both of her "accidents."

She rubbed her temples and wished for the millionth time she could remember those few minutes in the restroom, but the memory was gone…like it never existed. Seeing George at the bar had her wondering about him. Funny how his call this morning had come at such an opportune time and he'd hurried onto the scene after the hoist broke. Maybe he hadn't counted on Roger riding to the rescue on his white horse and shoving her out of the way. Both times. After all, he'd rushed to check on her in the restroom too. Or had those been Roger's ruses to put her at ease and off her guard? Oh, damn. Listen to her. She was turning into a nut job.

Why would anyone want to do her bodily harm?

No. Shelly couldn't believe it. There had to be another explanation. She bent to grab the door handle and spotted Jake sitting in a rocker on the front porch.

She exhaled a long breath and jumped out of the car, forcing herself to keep breathing as she walked. Jake looked too damn sexy, rocking back and forth, silhouetted in the shadows.

"You're up late," she said, her foot hitting the last step. It was after one o'clock. Shelly knew this because she'd waited to leave the bar until well past twelve to avoid this exact scenario.

Jake nodded. "I wanted to make sure you made it home safely."

Shelly gave a soft snort, shaking her head. Still playing the hero. How she wished he'd stop the charade so she could move on. At times like this, she found it hard to remember that he wasn't her hero. Not really. He'd been Kiera's. "I'm a big girl, Jake."

"I can see that."

She ignored the sexual implication as well as the heated sizzle his eyes telegraphed with the statement. Up close, she could see his day's growth of beard. Shelly stilled an urge to push the strand of dark hair off his forehead, wondering if it was still as soft as she remembered.

Don't let him affect you.

Her gaze moved lower. His jeans were old and faded, soft denim sheathing his legs and butt like a second skin. He'd rolled up his shirtsleeves, revealing strong forearms now clutching the arms of the rocker. The top buttons of his shirt lay open, displaying shadows she knew to be a dusting of soft, downy hair.

Don't let him affect you. She repeated the mantra in her mind a few times, inhaling a steady breath. Shelly smiled, working to keep her voice from revealing her thoughts, and added, hoping she sounded more relaxed than she felt, "I've been taking care of myself for a long time, but I appreciate the concern."

She started past him, but Jake stopped her with, "Want to share a nightcap before you head up to your room?"

"Why?" The discernible uncertainty of the one word hung in the air.

Damn, she thought, as his spicy scent wafted under her nose, immediately taking her back to that last night. Funny how a smell could produce such a vivid memory, and funny how he hadn't changed colognes after all this time.

Shelly wished Jake didn't affect her. Why couldn't someone

like Roger interest her enough to replace him? She took another deep breath, catching even more of his male essence. Butterflies suddenly flapped inside her tummy, spurring the blood in her veins to race faster at the thought of spending time with him.

Remember, Shelly. It's not in your best interest.

"I'm tired." She couldn't deal with Jake tonight. Not after spending the last three hours satisfying Roger's concern over her safety. She hadn't been able to figure him out, but one thing she knew. She'd made a humongous mistake in not leaving when he'd given her the opportunity, after warning her away. Once they'd returned to their table, he'd asked question after question about her life in Atlanta and earlier. The guy was definitely nosy. She'd survived, skirting his nosiness, but at an emotional cost. Right now, she had little patience left and no endurance for the man who'd always made her heart skip beats.

The rest of her excuse rode on the tip of her tongue, but before she could verbalize it, he said, "I wanted to ask you a few more questions about what happened at George's garage this morning. That is, if you're not too tired."

Jake's voice held an edge of jealousy, something Shelly would love to believe, but didn't.

His request brought back to mind the hazy incident in the restroom, along with what had happened on her way home. Suddenly a drink seemed like a perfect idea.

Shelly pasted a fake smile on her face and turned, meeting Jake's gaze. "Sure. I'd love a nightcap." Too keyed up to sleep, she rubbed her arms, then opened the front door and went inside with one thought. She wanted his opinion. Earlier, after returning with Roger to their table, she'd had the weirdest feeling of someone watching her. For the rest of the night, she'd been unable to dismiss the idea. Yet, every time she'd checked, she'd found no evidence, which only added to her paranoia.

"It would be good to talk to someone about tonight." She followed Jake into the Delaney library, hung back, and watched as he continued toward the bar at the other end of the room.

His take on her thoughts might help her sort out fact from fiction.

Jake looked over his shoulder. "Oh? Trouble with Roger?"

"No. Not really." This time she couldn't miss the sneer

when he mentioned Roger's name. He was jealous. The thought was staggering.

At the bar, he glanced at her with raised eyebrows. "What's your pleasure?"

You, she almost blurted out, but stopped in the nick of time. "Wine is fine. I prefer red."

He nodded and picked up a bottle, filling a wineglass. "So, what happened?" He grabbed another bottle, uncapped it and poured amber liquid, most likely Kentucky bourbon, into a tumbler.

Shelly eyed the bourbon longingly, dying to immerse her worries in the oblivion of a couple of shots, but the last thing she needed was straight alcohol to weaken her already lowered sense of self-preservation. Hadn't the past taught her anything? She could barely tolerate one drink without feeling the effects. Since she'd had two glasses of red wine earlier, and despite having them over the course of several hours, hard liquor would only complicate matters.

Maybe talking to him hadn't been her brightest idea. Handling Roger had been child's play compared to how ill-prepared she suddenly felt to deal with the sexy hunk striding too confidently toward her, holding out a too-full glass of red wine.

She sighed, relieving him of the wine, and admitted, "I think someone's been following me. Even on the way home."

"Oh?" His eyebrow shot up. "What makes you think someone's following you?"

Shelly sipped while he sat across from her, eyeing her until she had no choice but to explain her feelings, ending her tale with the lights in her rearview mirror, and adding, "If you throw in what happened in the restroom along with the earlier incidents, I'd say I'm entitled to being more than a little edgy."

"Restroom?"

Jake's gaze never wavered from her face, making her feel a tad stupid for not heeding his earlier warnings.

"Forget it. It was nothing." Shelly shouldn't be here, so close to him. She definitely shouldn't be having more wine. While her mind screamed to stop, she continued bringing the glass to her lips, left with no will other than to drink, no matter that these extra ounces might put her over the top. Now that the danger had passed, she didn't need further berating for not minding him like some naughty child. After all, she wasn't even certain of what took place. "Nothing that I couldn't handle."

Jake considered this. "I advised you not to go tonight."

Bingo. "I'm well aware of your advice." She smiled and gulped a mouthful, despite the consequences of feeling more than the slight buzz, telling her she should slow down. "From now on, I'll pay more attention to it." Mikey was the biggest proof of how far she'd go once the buzz started. Her grin expanded. Geez, he was tempting. So was the wine. "And here I am, safe and sound, so I'd rather talk about something else besides advice, if you don't mind."

Shelly took a few more sips, the liquid sliding down her throat, warming her, and filling her with more confidence.

Jake was still eyeing her as if she were some kind of puzzle. "Okay. Let's talk about you, then. You never did tell me much about your life in Atlanta."

She returned his careful scrutiny, still sipping, wondering what he'd do if she told him the truth. That she was a single mother, taking care of his child.

Shelly mentally rolled her eyes. Sweet Jesus, the wine was going to her head quicker than she'd imagined. She inhaled deeply, holding on to her smile. "What would you like to know?" So what if her voice sounded flirtatious. She could handle her attraction. Hadn't she just handled Roger for hours without succumbing to his sexy dimples and glib tongue?

He chuckled, then shrugged. "Give me an average day in the life of Michelle Matthews."

Her gaze turned speculative as she continued studying Jake more intently. "Hmmm. An average day? My days aren't very exciting." What about him? What was his life like now? He seemed guarded and dangerous. Both elements added to his appeal. "I'm sure my life is boring compared to yours."

"I doubt that." The lopsided grin he still sported did strange things to her insides. "In all the years I've known you, you've never been boring, Michelle."

The silky smoothness of his compliment rolled over her, the huskiness of his voice worming its way through to her core and adding to the warmth the wine had already produced. "Maybe, but I've always wanted to be dark and mysterious." The way Kiera had been.

"Oh?" His eyebrows rose and she nodded at the implied question. Slowly, he shook his head. "Uh-uh. That's not you. I'll never believe you've changed so much."

The statement brought her up short. Her focus flew to her hand and she studied it, fingering the wineglass. Finally, she sighed. Taking another sip, allowing a bit of liquid bravery to wash over her, she grinned. "Maybe you're right. I haven't changed. But something has been bothering me for six years." Her gaze sought his.

When she didn't say anything for the longest time, he quirked a brow. "Well?" he prodded, keeping his eyebrow up, giving the silent command to continue.

She swallowed and, aided with the courage of another mouthful of wine, ventured forward. "I'm curious. What happened, Jake?"

Shelly couldn't stop the question from leaving her mouth. Just like tonight, confusion over what had been pretense and what had been real filled her as other memories returned. Maybe this was the wrong time to ask with so much shit going on, but damn it all, she wanted to know.

No! She had to know.

Why hadn't she asked that very question six years ago? Before she slunk off to lick her wounds and let Kiera win?

Why?

When Jake had spent too much time before that summer trying to act uninterested. The night they'd made love she'd felt something and she could have sworn he had too. And now, with him sitting close, sharing a late night drink and with their attraction still sizzling, Shelly demanded, "Why did you go back to her? Your lame excuses never really satisfied my naive soul."

Jake studied her face, clearly thinking, then exhaled, pulling a hand through his hair. He looked down at his glass, twirling the contents. She wasn't sure he'd say anything until his eyes met hers once more.

"You really want to know?" he asked, not bothering to pretend he didn't understand her question, thank God.

Her chin inched up and she held his steady gaze, wishing she didn't find him so attractive. "Yes. I deserve an answer." He was every bit the hunk she remembered. His presence still made her heart beat faster. Probably always would. "And I'd prefer the truth, if you don't mind."

Shelly should have insisted on the truth all those years ago, if only to assuage her deep-seated feelings of inadequacy. She'd been the aggressor, aided with an alcohol-induced stupor fueling a need to tell him how she felt. Unable to voice her feelings, she'd shown him instead.

Unfortunately, it had been one-sided and she'd learned one thing about guys that night. If you got enough beer into them, they were just as amenable to sex as any drunk virgin, maybe more so as the level of a man's inhibitions started from a lower point than a woman's. In the end, their month-long fling had been a huge disappointment.

Fling?

Disappointment?

Lord almighty, who was she kidding? It had been much more than a fling and she'd been devastated when Jake could barely look at her afterward, knowing he'd slept with and had had a semblance of a relationship with someone other than his precious Kiera. She'd only been a convenient rebound after their breakup. Someone to fill in while Kiera had been in rehab.

"Kiera needed me. You didn't."

Her jaw dropped. Shelly gaped at him with an open mouth. It took her a moment before she could speak. "That's your best answer?" Wine-induced or not, she wasn't quite sure she'd heard him correctly. "Kiera needed you?" She snorted. "Yeah, right." His answer wasn't at all what she'd expected.

"It's the truth. Or part of it." He wiped his face with a hand, leaning forward, looking a little uncomfortable. "What do you want me to say? I was a stupid jerk who messed up. I trusted the wrong woman. But once I did, my path was set. I couldn't reverse and change direction."

"What do you mean, you trusted the wrong woman?" That sounded as if he'd made a choice. He'd never let her think there'd been any choice at all, so she didn't believe him. Not when Kiera had status, which had to have been an added allure.

Jake's dad had worked for Ed Delaney, as had Jake after he'd gotten his master's degree. Shelly had nothing to compete with that, so she'd withdrawn. "I thought you cared."

"I did." He shrugged. "Which is why I bailed. I couldn't saddle you with my problems. You had your entire future ahead of you and didn't need me and my screwed-up life adding to your burden."

"And marrying Kiera had nothing to do with money? Nothing to do with your position in Ed Delaney's company or with the clout Ed held in the county?"

"I'd be lying to deny it, and we both know it." He sighed. "I've already admitted to being stupid. What more do you want?"

"Nothing." She realized it was the truth. "You screwed up, Jake."

Shelly stood, set her empty glass on the table, and shook her head. Sadness filled her.

Even though the air still crackled with that same sizzling attraction that had always surrounded her and Jake, she realized another fact just then. Attraction wasn't enough. She wanted it all. She deserved it all. For the first time in her life, she turned to walk away, knowing she'd done the right thing in leaving all those years ago. Jake didn't deserve her love. He never had. She walked toward the library door, repeating over her shoulder, completely forgetting the earlier threats, real or imagined, "You really screwed up."

Chapter 10

Jake watched Michelle's retreating back. He grabbed the bourbon along with his drink, headed outside, and fell into a chair on the dark deck, wishing the desire to open her door and try to explain wasn't his most pressing thought. The past would not intrude. Not when he had a job to do, which included keeping her safe.

He sensed her involvement in this, but that made no sense.

Hell. Nothing made sense. His stomach clutched, dread gripping him tightly, as Michelle's parting shot filled his brain.

You screwed up, Jake.

Yeah. He'd screwed up, all right. Big-time.

He could never undo his past mistakes. Never. Damn it all if her presence hadn't lanced the shield covering his twisted heart, poking a hole big enough to leave him vulnerable and needy again. For too long, he'd thought he'd buried the feelings Michelle stirred. Yet Jake had only been deluding himself. Self-lies and pretenses had accomplished nothing and no longer held the memories at bay. They slammed into him, an acid of reality eating away at his gut.

Thoughts of those few weeks, where he'd shed the chaos of Kiera and their demented relationship to stand under Michelle's radiance, filled him with sadness and more yearning.

Some of the most carefree and happy weeks of his life had ended the same way they'd begun, ugly and painful. He could never outrun the past.

Jake swallowed another long sip, wondering why he was torturing himself.

The image of Michelle's determined expression and straight back, as she'd left the room voicing her declaration, reinforced the sentiment. He'd never get another chance to screw up. Not in this lifetime and not with Michelle Matthews.

Jake's cell phone vibrated through his jeans. He poured another liberal amount of bourbon into his glass and slammed it down his throat, praying that the memory of taking her innocence and then pushing her away would subside. He'd been totally screwed up back then. Too late, he'd come to his senses.

Sighing, he shoved regret to the side and pulled his buzzing phone out of his pocket. His partner wasn't exactly the person he wanted to talk to just then, preferring to drown his misery with bourbon without any interruptions. Duty, however, wouldn't let him ignore the call when it could be important. He poured himself another drink and put the phone to his ear. "What's up?"

"I'm on my way to Nashville and wanted to give you a heads-up."

"Oh?" Rich's solemn voice didn't sound promising. "Why? What's happened?"

"Tell me about Shelly Matthews. How does she fit in?"

He bit back what he really wanted to say and asked, "What do you mean?" Why would Rich be homing in on Michelle, anyway? "She shouldn't fit in at all." Not in his mind. "She's an innocent bystander who got sucked in because she met Kiera right before she died."

"Someone's after her and it's tied to this."

"Tell me something I don't know." When Jake caught himself snarling, he inhaled deeply. Once he felt calm enough, he spent a moment updating Rich about how she'd been there when Kiera had collapsed, also filling him in on her car accident. "That's why she was at George's this morning."

"Are you aware she spent the evening with Peters?"

"Yes." His spine straightened. Every cell in his body became as taut as a board. He gripped the phone and forced himself to breathe. To relax. "I couldn't stop her from going without alerting her to what I know." He sucked in another steadying breath. "Your point?"

"I'm worried about her. She visited the restroom and was gone for over twenty minutes. None of my targets did anything to make me suspect them, but something went down. My gut tells me so. When she finally left the bar, I searched the room.

Other than a few paper towels with a sweet scent that might or might not be some kind of drug, there was little else to glean. Not from my vantage point. I'll know more once I have a lab corroborate my suspicions."

"Hmmm." Jake's mind spun. "Michelle mentioned something earlier about the restroom and she arrived here claiming someone followed her home."

"She's in danger," Rich said, voicing Jake's exact thoughts. "I e-mailed you a file a few minutes ago. I tried to clean up the background bar noise as best I could. Listen to it, then call me back. I'll be on the road another hour or so. We can talk while I drive."

Jake hung up and stared into the dark night. A snaking sensation of foreboding cooled his blood. He should stay away from Michelle, just as he should have six years ago. Far, far away because the yearning grew. Every time he saw her, her radiance enticed him, like the leaves on a plant reaching toward the sun.

He sipped his bourbon, seeking solace in its warming effect, and reaching for the courage to face the information Rich had mentioned, unable to completely discard the idea that the file would change his life forever.

What a ridiculous notion, he mused. Alcohol must be affecting his reasoning. He downed the remaining liquor in two big swallows before setting the empty glass on the table and standing. The burning heat sliding the length of its journey actually felt good.

With a resolute sigh, Jake stalked inside to check his e-mail.

~

For the second straight night, Shelly paced, too tense to sleep, unable to relax. She shook her hands, then wiped them on her shorts, squelching the desire to sneak downstairs to retrieve a glass of bourbon. Submerging her emotions in alcohol wasn't the answer. Still, she was tempted.

Out of the corner of her eye, she caught a bit of brown. Kiera's journal sat discarded on the bureau. Maybe reading more of her friend's past would help her deal with the present.

Shelly reached for the book, intending to settle in for the night. She'd eject Jacob Collier once and for all from her thoughts, keep to herself these next few days, and get through them as best she could. As her fingers touched the leather, a streak of light flashed across the walls of her room. The book all but forgotten, she went to the window and peered out. Seconds later, another beam shot out from the woods beyond, illuminating the backyard for a brief instant.

Someone was out there. Then she saw Jake slink down the deck stairs, heading in the direction of the lights, clearly with a purpose.

Why? What was he doing?

She stared out at the yard for several minutes. When nothing happened, Shelly grabbed a flashlight and without thinking, rushed through the door to follow Jake's footsteps further into the woods. Going outside was a much better diversion than obsessing in this enclosed room.

At least tonight, unlike last night, she was fully dressed, including sandals, which made running along the damp grass easier.

Shelly slipped past the money tree, staying hidden in the tree-filled brush. Splashes of brightness from Jake's flashlight peeked out of the darkness every now and then, keeping her on track. She'd gone a good distance when the lights abruptly flickered out as she caught sight of Jake's form before the night swallowed him.

She slowed and trod more tentatively, no longer certain the decision to investigate had been one of her brightest. She took several more steps and halted, shining her light into the shadows. Gradually spinning, she glanced back at the house, suddenly cognizant of how far from its safety she'd strayed.

A sense of isolation loomed.

She clicked off the flashlight and waited, still listening and watching, trying to discern where Jake had disappeared.

Nothing.

No Jake.

No light.

No sound.

Even the insects had gone silent. It was eerie how the sounds had dissipated from her consciousness without her awareness.

Had they been there moments ago? She wasn't sure.

She retraced her steps, working to make her way back to the house, remaining in the shadows.

A twig snapped, stopping her in her tracks.

Shelly pivoted and peered into the dark woods in the distance. Her heartbeat quickened. Like the night before and earlier this evening, she sensed someone watching. She doubted that someone was Jake.

After several deep breaths, she listened, her mind on full alert. Panic set in. Her imagination of what dangers lurked just feet away fed her fears.

She turned and ran, now more afraid than ever. Shelly darted for the cover of the bushes, not sure of why, only sensing that if she didn't, something dreadful was about to happen.

The second she changed direction, a noise whizzed past her head. A piece of bark flew off a tree to her right. She flinched.

As she put up a deflecting arm, someone grabbed her waist and shoved her forward.

Her legs buckled from the extra weight.

Oh, God! She was going to die.

With no way to stop her forward momentum, the ground came up to meet her fast. Pain shot through Shelly's arms as she blocked the fall with hands that had already taken an earlier beating.

Every muscle in her body hurt. It took a moment before she could think again. The vicious throbbing raced from her knees to her butt, followed a path up her back to her elbows and out her fingers, and then ebbed slightly.

Being tackled was getting old. At least this ground held grass rather than gravel.

When she tried to rise, an immovable block of what had to be a man hampered her effort as another whiz sounded. Dirt and grass sprayed from the ground just a few feet away.

"Stay down," a voice she identified as Jake's hissed. "Don't you know enough to duck when someone's shooting at you?"

"What?" She started to say more, but his hand clamped over her mouth at the same time his comment registered.

"Shush," he whispered, his mouth inches from her ear.

Oh, God! Someone was shooting at her? Why? Shelly

squeezed her eyes shut tight and forced herself to relax. This couldn't be happening.

Jake was breathing hard, as if he'd been sprinting. "I'll take my hand away if you promise not to say anything."

Nodding, she sucked in a gulp of air, not daring to make any noise when he loosened his hold.

Fear clutched at her heart, sending her heartbeat galloping faster than horses out of the gate at the Kentucky Derby.

"We have to get to cover." As he whispered, he rolled, keeping her with him. A few more rolls and they were on the other side of a tree.

"Oh," she cried out, as pain flared in every joint. Though to give him credit, Jake had tried to buffer her fall to the hard ground with his body.

"Are you okay?" he whispered seconds later.

"Yeah." Her voice was just as soft. "I think so."

In the moonlit darkness, Shelly could see the concern in his eyes. Thank God he'd tackled her. She didn't want to think of the second bullet most likely hitting her if he hadn't been behind her.

Shelly sat against the tree as Jake kneeled next to her, running his hands along first her arms and then her legs. She glanced at his face and spied no emotion, yet felt every stroke, recognizing his gentle touch from that night so many years ago. She quickly squelched the thought. If he could ignore the attraction, so could she. She wouldn't think about how she'd love to stroke him back.

Jake leaned back on his heels and spoke softly. "Nothing appears to be broken."

"No." She shook her head, flashed a small smile, and prayed her beating heart that no longer had anything to do with being frightened wasn't loud enough for him to hear. "I'm only bruised."

He grunted. "Sorry if I hurt you. But it couldn't be helped. You were right in the line of fire."

Shelly brushed her hair behind her ear. "I guess I owe you."

He looked around, studying the dark terrain carefully. He turned back to her, concern still etched into his features. "Do you think you can run, staying low and under cover?"

When she nodded, Jake pulled out a gun.

Her eyes widened. That was a big gun. She hated guns. Guns killed people.

He stood and helped her up. "Go now." His nod indicated the direction of the house.

Now? He wanted her to go back to the house? Without him? "You're not coming with me?" Her fervent whisper held none of her rising panic.

"I'll only be a minute. Whoever was shooting is probably long gone, but I want to make sure and have a look around."

"Why can't I wait here?"

"I'll feel better if you're inside." Jake took her flashlight and nudged her forward. "Hurry. You should be safe enough. I'll be right behind."

Shelly rubbed her arms, suddenly cold now that Jake's warmth no longer covered her body. "Be careful."

Then, following his orders about staying low, she bent over and ran as fast as she could toward the house.

Chapter 11

Jake made sure Michelle was almost to the house before he turned to stalk through the woods. His temper flared, hotter than a just-lit barbeque doused with lighter fluid. Stilling the urge to hit something, he strove to find the asshole shooting so he could pound the shit out of him.

Adrenaline pumped through his veins as he ran, adding to his earlier fury after listening to Rich's digital file. Livid was a mild description of how he'd felt. Hell, he was still furious. Earlier, while standing in the shadows, about to call his partner, he'd seen the same lights that must have alerted Michelle, only he'd been ahead of her. Thank God. If he hadn't been stealing in the dark and seen the figure shooting, she might now be dead, a victim of a rifle wound.

That thought infuriated him because then another child would be motherless.

He'd purposely sent Michelle back to the house, not trusting himself to be around her. He could have easily wrung her neck over his discovery, and her stupidity for placing herself in danger hadn't helped his anger any.

How could she?

Her voice telling Peters she had to call her son still echoed in his mind.

Michelle had a five-year-old son? If that were true—and he had no reason not to believe what he'd heard—who was the father? Had he fathered a son six years ago? Had their heated encounter all those years ago culminated in a pregnancy? The conversation he'd interrupted this morning between Elaine and Michelle suddenly made sense. He thought Elaine had been talking about Kiera, but it had to be Michelle. Michelle had gotten pregnant. That had to be the answer, almost a foregone conclusion, despite using protection. She'd been a virgin that night, and she wasn't the type to go from bed to bed.

Shit. He had a son. Why had she never told him?

Jake tried to block the pain the thoughts evoked and focused on the guy using her for target practice rather than on something he had no control over.

He slowed, then finally stopped and flicked on Michelle's flashlight. Light flooded the bushes beyond. He scouted the area until something shiny caught his attention. Crouching, he focused the light from a closer distance. A couple of spent shell casings lay in the grass, inches apart. From a rifle. He used a twig to avoid smudging prints, pocketed them, and rose.

Listening, he circled with the flashlight.

Night sounds and shadows were all he noted until the light revealed a dark object that looked to be a baseball cap, similar to the one Billy Durbin had worn the night before. With no bag or gloves to use, he carefully lifted, rolled, and tucked it into his pocket.

The shooter had obviously fled, so Jake gave up his search. Had Billy been stalking Michelle? Or was he just an innocent bystander? Maybe Linda could lift legible prints off the casings. She understood how slow the system could be at times and he could count on her in a lurch. Not that he'd ever had to before now.

With the danger all but gone and nothing else to divert his attention, Jake's thoughts instantly returned to Michelle and her conversation with Peters. Jake turned and strode at a fast clip toward the house, slowing halfway to yank his cell phone out of his pocket and place a call to Rich.

The minute Rich came on the line, he said, "I heard the contents of your file. You should know another attempt to kill Michelle Matthews was just made. Only minutes ago." He continued talking as he walked.

"Hmm." Rich was quiet, clearly thinking. "What do you make of it?"

"Shit. My take? It's obvious. Whoever's after her thinks she knows something. But that makes no sense. They hadn't seen each other in years. Their only connection was when Kiera passed out in her arms."

"Maybe Kiera gave her something?"

Jake pointed Michelle's flashlight at the ground to avoid tripping over roots and rocks. "Nothing that I could see. Besides, if she had something incriminating to hand over, she'd have given it to me. I'll ask to be on the safe side." As he stared ahead, the journal came to mind. Did that have something to do with the attempts on Michelle's life?

"What about the kid?"

Rich's question pulled Jake's attention back to the digital file. "The kid?"

A disbelieving snort shot through his ear. "The five-year-old son, remember?" His partner did patronizing really well when he wanted to. "It was part of the conversation I sent you. Shelly Matthews made it plain as day she didn't want anyone to know about him. Maybe there's a connection there."

"There's no connection. I'd know because we grew up together. You're spending too much time at Della's and your imagination's getting the better of you."

Dead silence. "You grew up with her?" Rich didn't bother to soften the accusation.

"Yeah," was all Jake offered. He wasn't about to enlighten Rich. Until he knew more. "Kiera's last words to Michelle were to remember the money tree. When she checked under it, she found a journal."

"A journal?" Rich waited a beat, then added excitedly, "That's it."

At first, Jake wasn't completely sure. But now? "The idea fits, especially if she wrote something incriminating. Shit." His fury flared again. He halted at the bottom step of the deck and gripped the flashlight, stilling another urge to hit the wooden post in front of him. He began pacing, too agitated to go inside. "Why didn't Kiera just tell me her suspicions, instead of taking this on alone?"

"Fear?" Rich said softly, deflating some of his anger. "You gotta admit, your ex had a credibility issue. Maybe she uncovered something big and didn't think anyone would believe her. I mean, look at the hard time I had selling you on Della's."

Jake rolled the thought around. "Maybe." It made sense.

"Anyway, Michelle knew Kiera better than anyone and she's going through it to see if it leads to anything." His thoughts then shifted to what he'd found on the ground only minutes ago. "After scouting around, I picked up Billy Durbin's hat, along with a few shell casings."

"You don't really believe he's involved?"

"No. For the obvious reasons." Billy didn't have a mean bone in his body and everyone knew it, including Rich. "But if Billy was there, you can bet your last dollar Joe wasn't too far away. Whatever this is, it's enough to kill over. Kiera's death is real. The bullets flying were real."

"Hmm. A mental trail is forming as we speak," Rich said. "Maybe Joe's investigating the locals and is on to something."

"Maybe." Jake grunted. Durbin was a shit-for-brains kind of guy who acted like he was Supercop, yet too stupid to realize he wasn't. Jake still had a hard time believing anyone local was involved in what they were investigating.

"Like you said, where Billy goes, Joe follows." Rich's voice crackled in Jake's ear. "I'm still working on the Winters angle. Little bro hangs with Bobby Winters on occasion. Could be a connection. Not a strong one. Hell, everyone seems to take care of Billy, including Bobby."

"I see you've been doing your homework," Jake interjected. Bobby and Billy had been good friends since grade school, despite Billy's mishap.

"Yeah, what I call Campton 101. Riveting shit. And this is where my thought process gets interesting. The more I think of Bobby, the more I wonder about him. He's sweet on Ivy Jackson. From what I've gathered, Ivy started as a cocktail waitress a few years back and now books Della's talent as well as waiting tables one or two nights a week—during the busy hours only. Add in missing women, singers looking for work. Getting drugged in a bathroom and led out the back would be easy to pull off." He hesitated. "A perfect setup. I love it when a plan comes together. I feel like George Peppard."

"Who?" Jake climbed the four steps two at a time. "You know, the A-Team leader with Mr. T and the crazy guy. It's on cable."

"I don't waste my time with TV." Jake grinned. Leave it to

Rich to comment on some ancient show with all the shit flying around.

"You should. It's a great show. No one ever dies."

Jake's gaze narrowed and skepticism came out in his voice. "No one ever dies?" He leaned against the rail and glanced out into the dark yard, seeing only shadows. The insects chirped—a background noise that belonged to the night.

"Yeah. The team blows the shit outta everything, but they never kill anyone."

Jake smiled and rolled his shoulders, working out some of his pent-up frustration. "Humph, sounds as unrealistic as your plan that's coming together. What you're suggesting about Bobby and Ivy is a stretch. A rubbery one."

Rich laughed. "I hate to remind you, but those were your exact words about Della's involvement."

"Yeah, but if you're right, it's rather ugly."

"Nature of our business. Manufacturing and distributing illegal drugs involves much ugliness. So does selling sex. And unlike the television show, real people are dying."

"I just can't imagine kids I went to school with as cold-blooded killers. Plus, Bobby's a big muckety-muck at the factory. He doesn't fit the dealer mold." Sure, Bobby had done his fair share of partying back then, but that didn't mean much. Hell, at one time, he'd partied hearty, too. Just like every kid in the county. Bobby was a sleazoid and not someone he'd choose as a best friend, but that didn't make him a drug-dealing pimp, any more than Kiera's past made her a dealer now. "He has too much to lose and doesn't need the money." Most drug dealers he'd come across were sycophants who'd rather make money off the misery of others than work at an honest living.

"You've been gone awhile, Jake. People change or they may have been totally different from the way you remember them."

Wasn't that the truth, Jake thought, remembering how Michelle had kept his son from him all this time. He certainly never would have expected that from her. Kiera, yes. But Michelle? He'd always considered her perfect.

"Bobby's job could be a cover. What better one to have," Rich said, pulling him back to their conversation. "The guys you have to watch are those with the cunning to hide in plain sight, using respectability as a cover."

"That's a scary thought."

"What if Kiera knew something we didn't? After all, at one time, she bought her shit from someone local, yet with her credibility issues, she couldn't very well accuse anyone without proof."

"Another scary thought." Jake didn't want to think about how he probably would have scoffed if Kiera had come to him accusing anyone in town they'd hung out with as kids of anything, let alone Bobby Winters.

"Scary or not, it's worth checking out. I'm already working on Ivy's background."

"I wonder where the guy in the utility truck fits in."

"My money's says there's a connection to Della's and Ivy. Once we find it, the puzzle may make sense."

Jake nodded. In fact, now that he had a few names for Linda, she might find a connection faster.

"So, what are you going to do about Shelly Matthews?"

Rich's voice registered. Good question. "I intend to make sure she stays safe." He quickly formulated a plan to have her disappear for the next few days. He offered Rich a verbal sketch of his plans.

Elaine would understand, if it involved finding out what really happened to her daughter. The woman had been a godsend over the years in taking care of Emily when he'd had to go undercover. Doing the same now would offer more than lip service that nothing had changed. He still needed her help, and it would give her something to focus on besides Kiera's death. "While I'm working, I'll make sure Michelle stays busy and out of trouble reading the journal. I'll keep you posted as to what she finds."

Jake disconnected the call, then opened his cell and punched in Linda's number. "Hey, gorgeous," he said when she answered right away. "You're working late." He was expecting to get her voice mail.

"Hey, yourself. Kerry's with her dad. I couldn't sleep and had nothing better to do than work. I know I'm anal, so don't rub it in." She hesitated. "I was just about to e-mail you with some info on the truck tag."

"Great."

"Hah. Not so great. It's registered to a Lynwood Products out of London, Kentucky, for what good it does."

"Oh?" Jake exhaled on a sigh and rubbed at the tension building in his neck.

"The company's bogus. Doesn't exist, neither does the principal owner. Gerald Meyers. At least there's no DMV record on him."

"Both exist." Someone drove the truck that sent Michelle off the road.

"Yeah, which is why I'm still digging, but it'll take some time. I've uncovered the vehicle identification number, but so far the VIN hasn't helped much. This guy is a pro. The number's buried, hidden in layers of bureaucratic red tape." There was another brief pause. "But then, he doesn't know that someone who knows how to use a shovel is looking for him."

Jake gave a halfhearted attempt at a smile. "I have faith in your abilities. Would a name or two help? They may connect to the tag. Make the search easier."

"You're my hero. Shoot."

"I had a feeling." Jake's grin was quick. Her tone of voice left no doubt she was smiling as she wrote when he rattled off the names. Linda loved puzzles. "That's why I called you." She was also a computer genius who headed a task force in Nashville averting the crime wave of the future. Identity theft and hackers. Crooks were going so high-tech that those catching them had to go higher. "Let me know when you get a lead." He waited a moment and cleared his throat.

Linda's amused voice shot through the phone. "What?" When he didn't offer anything, she prodded, "Come on, out with it."

"Since Terry's with Mark, how about a favor?"

"Depends on what it is."

"I've had a busy night. Someone used me for target practice." He didn't expand on why. Just added, "Once the dust settled, I found a couple of shell casings. It'd be great if you could check them out for me. Problem is, I'm moving fast and so is Rich. Can you meet me halfway? It'll mean driving. Two hours at most, and I'll understand if you decline. I can work something else out." He didn't add that he was hesitant to turn them over to the sheriff because doing so would raise too many questions he didn't want to answer just then. "It pertains to the missing singer NPD is searching for. Rich thinks the two are connected." The jury was still out for him. Right now, Jake didn't know what to think.

"Are you shitting me?" Linda snorted. "Of course I'll meet you. You know I'd run through fire for you, Jake. How many times have you saved my butt with your observations?"

He smiled. "I didn't do much more than point stuff out from a different perspective. You'd have figured it out eventually."

"You saved me mucho times, so a two-hour drive is nothing in comparison."

"Thanks. I owe you."

"I like the sound of that."

"I'm sure you do." He chuckled, then gave her instructions for where they could meet. "I'll see you in about an hour," he added, still grinning.

~

Ten miles after Rich Heslin disconnected his call with Jake, he pulled off the interstate, drove across the Victory Memorial Bridge spanning the Cumberland River, and headed into downtown Nashville. He drove another half mile, parked in a metered spot, but at well past three a.m. he didn't feed the meter.

A musky, fishy odor assaulted his nostrils as he walked. The smell of the river at night. For some reason, the dark intensified the sensation.

Minutes later, he slid a key card into a slot, unlocking the door to one of the three-story buildings lining the street several blocks off the water. He walked the distance of the dark halls to the elevator and took the short ride to the basement.

The steel doors opened to a large room full of activity, not as busy as midday, but the lit background and few bodies scurrying about indicated the lab worked around the clock, unlike the business part of the company situated on the floors above.

No one paid him any attention, used to seeing him off and on over the years. He kept his pace steady until he reached a big office at the end of the hall.

"Hey, Betsy." He threw the plastic bag with the paper towel he'd picked out of the trash across her lab table where she sat on a stool peering into a microscope. "I knew I'd find you here."

"Why wouldn't you?" She exhaled a quick snort. "I work here." Lifting the bag, she asked expectantly, "What's this?"

"That's for you to find out. I need to know what's on those paper towels. Think you can give me a quick idea?"

Betsy separated the zip lock, sniffed, then slanted a narrow-eyed gaze at him. "I'm going to lose my job if you keep this up," she scolded, taking a good-sized piece of towel out of the bag with tweezers. She separated the pieces into two, sticking one in another plastic bag and the other in a vial with a few drops of some substance.

Shaking it, she capped and set it in a tray, resealed Rich's bag, and handed it back.

He stuck it in his pocket. He'd turn it in as evidence when he got the chance. By the time he did, Betsy will have come up with an answer to most of his questions, saving him precious days.

"Once is a favor. Twice I'm being crazy, but come on, Rich. This is getting to be habit. You're taking advantage. Again."

He grinned, stepped closer, then leaned both fists on the counter on either side of her, nuzzling her neck, kissing his way to her ear. "Please?" he whispered, biting on the lobe. "I'll owe you big-time and I promise an Italian feast at Valentino's."

Laughing, she pulled away. "Down, boy! As I recall, you already owe me two nice dinners. This'll make three. Maybe I don't want Italian." She pushed at his chest, which did nothing to get him to move. "Come to think of it, I'm not even sure I want two."

He took a small step back, but kept her prisoner in between his arms. "Pretty please?"

She laughed harder. "You're wasting your efforts. Go work on someone who can appreciate your smooth tongue. It doesn't faze me anymore. I don't want or need the grief for what comes after."

"Aw, come on, babe. Don't be a bitch. I need your expertise. I have a bad feeling about this." He waited a minute, then went in for the close. "I need to know what's going down. Now. I don't have the time to wait for the system to work."

"Or the patience," she grumbled. "You and your instinct." Shaking her head, she offered a resigned sigh. "I shouldn't let it or that killer smile affect me when I could get fired in a heartbeat for aiding and abetting. And so could you."

"We won't." He lifted his arms and let her go. Her quick smile told him she'd come through for him. Betsy Heslin always did. He was the one who could never come through. As a husband. She never held it against him, though. That was what he liked best about his ex. They might not have dealt well as a married couple, but as friends, he could have no better. Betsy knew her way around a lab. She analyzed chemicals like a critic tore apart a movie or book, section by section, layer by layer.

"You know you're not following SOP. There's a process in place. Not to mention the little detail called chain of command. I should make you wait, just like all your buddies."

The DEA sometimes utilized this lab when theirs got backed up, which happened more times than not if trials were pending or if the assistant attorney general needed the information to determine if they'd go to trial in the first place. The American justice system had a few cogs, but despite those drawbacks, it worked better than anything else out there, in his opinion.

Samples of the shit he'd given her earlier were already in the system, but who knew how long they would take to be processed. He hadn't lied. Time was of the essence. The sooner he knew what he was dealing with, the sooner he and Jake could stop it.

"You won't, because I've hooked you on this. You're as stumped as I am." Betsy lived here. Never stopped analyzing if something caught her attention, like the shit Jake had given him earlier that day, along with small samples found on the two dead bodies he'd also managed to get to her a few weeks ago. "Besides, you'd be pissed as hell if I left you out of this, when my instinct tells me this shit is key to my investigation."

His motto? Knowledge was power. But timing was

everything. Gaining knowledge early in the game gave him his edge. Knowledge that came too late could be useless or disastrous.

Connections like Betsy provided a more timely knowledge. Rich broke the rules of bureaucracy all the time, but only when he knew it wouldn't hurt his case. "I've researched other women's ODs in the region and unearthed ten prostitutes' deaths in five years."

He'd use any edge in chasing the bad guys, especially when those bad guys didn't have his limitations. "And even more interesting? They all have similar MOs with the case I'm working on now, identical if you take away the fact that they were hookers. So, you see why I need you?" Too bad he had no samples from those deaths his ex could analyze. If he did, he was sure she'd prove a link.

"God, I hate it that you know me so well." Betsy heaved an exasperated sigh. She was the late night supervisor for CBU Labs, working third shift in the wee hours of late night and early morning. A calming environment, as she put it. Rich had a different take on her lifestyle and teased her about being a vampire in an earlier life. His ex didn't even function until after ten or eleven in the morning, and only then with massive doses of Starbucks.

"So, your message said all the samples matched." Which meant his—and Jake's—hunch had panned out. Thank God the powers that be with the lab loved Betsy and basically let her run the entire nighttime setup, much to his good fortune. A fact he exploited, making his job easier.

"Yeah, they do. Identically. Down to the percentage of phosphorus, pseudoephedrine, better known as ephedrine, and iodine. Very interesting and not feasible unless all the samples were created from the same batch. At least, that's my humble opinion." She sat on her stool and scooted toward her inbox. "I took a closer look at the blood samples you provided and came up with something even more interesting."

Jake had provided small samples of the first two victims' blood, knowing Rich's source would come through much faster than the weeks, sometimes months, it would take to get results in the system.

Betsy reached for a folder. "See what you think."

Rich caught the file she tossed, leaned a hip against the counter, and opened it. "What am I looking at?" He threw a questioning glance her way. "Looks like Greek to me."

"Sorry." She grinned. "I'll try to explain it in terms a Neanderthal like you can understand."

"Flattery doesn't work on me."

She grunted. "There are other trace elements in the two blood samples of chemicals not usually present in street meth."

"Another drug?"

"That's my guess. The makeup of both samples isn't identical enough to come from the same drug lot, but close enough to tell me they were made with the same recipe."

"Hmm. Interesting."

"Isn't it?"

"Do you have any idea which drug?"

"MDMA, better known as Ecstasy, is the closest match. The sample contains minute traces of safrole, the key ingredient in MDMA, but in my opinion it's not Ecstasy. There are a few other compounds I don't recognize that change the makeup of the drug. To figure it out, I'll need to do some research. Someone with a pharmaceutical background is playing with some pretty sophisticated and controlled chemicals that aren't readily available."

"Okay." He rolled this information around in his brain a moment. "So, if I dug up a few samples of blood that may contain the same drug, do you think you'd be able to recognize these compounds, even if it's been a few years?" If he were lucky, autopsies were performed on the hookers who died. He wasn't holding his breath. Prostitutes' ODs seldom raised the kind of alarm or questions as deaths of other women under the same circumstances, so why bother with an autopsy.

"I think so." She nodded. "If they had them in their system when they died. Won't know till I try." She grinned and quirked a brow. "You really think you can get me samples?"

"If they exist." He winked, flashing a grin. "I won't know for sure till I try, now will I?"

Oh yeah. Betsy was hooked on this mystery. The idea solidified when her nod indicated the plastic bag she'd put the piece of paper towel in. "If I were to give an educated guess on your napkin, I'd say it's full of lorazepam or Ativan. It's a benzodiazepine that acts fast."

His eyes glazed over as she rattled on as words like anziolytic, sedative/hypnotic, anticonvulsant, and muscle relaxant filtered past his brain.

"Probably was mixed with atropine," she added, again getting technical, talking about Atropa belladonna and other such sources.

"Okay, cut the big fancy words and just give me a quick rundown."

Betsy shook her head and mumbled something about Neanderthals and science not mixing. "Both are fast acting and dissipate just as quickly, similar to what is used in colonoscopies. I'll even go out on a limb here and say it was administered in aerosol form or a gas, given the way it was absorbed on the paper. It's too evenly spread. That's pretty sophisticated, too. In my humble opinion, you're not looking for a redneck burning shit in his kitchen. Whoever's messing around with this stuff knows his way around a Bunsen burner."

"Add in that women are dying, it's more than a scary thought," Rich said, remembering Jake's response.

~

"Jake! You scared me." Michelle looked up, hand over her heart, her face as white as a sheet when he'd noiselessly entered her room via the deck. "Did you find anything?"

"No. Get packed," Jake said, not caring that he'd scared ten years off her life. She clearly wasn't expecting him to come from any direction. "We're leaving."

"What?"

As Jake's anger seethed, he worked to keep his voice modulated. "It's not safe for you to remain here." Hell, he fought the urge to take her by the shoulders and shake the truth out of her. "For some reason you're a target, and I won't place my daughter or Elaine in danger. So, get packed."

He saw her overnight bag sitting on the floor, picked it up, and tossed it in on the bed. "Come on. Move. I don't have a lot of time."

Her eyes grew as big as saucers and her back went ramrod. "You can't just barge into my room and start ordering me around."

"Don't test me tonight," he ground out. "I'm not in the mood." Something in his mannerisms and tone must have alerted her to the fact that he wouldn't back down, because in a heartbeat all of Michelle's bravado fled. She meekly nodded, moved to the dresser, opened drawers, and began packing.

Thank God he wouldn't have to carry her kicking and screaming from the house. He stormed to the window and opened the slats in the blind with his left hand. He peered between them at the shadows in the yard, clenching his right hand into a fist until the desire to strangle her died.

"Where are we going?" she asked.

Jake turned back to see her stuffing her bag with the clothes she'd brought. "Away."

Expecting another outburst, he was surprised when she only nodded and silently continued packing, before heading for the adjoining bathroom.

While she did that, he hurried to his room and grabbed his bag. The only thing he had to add was his shaving kit, which he quickly filled.

He hadn't been gone from Michelle's room for more than a few minutes. When he returned, she was peering out the same window facing the deck he'd been looking out, clutching her bag.

"Okay, I'm ready," he said. "Let's go."

She reached for Kiera's journal and tucked it into her side pouch.

As she walked past him, Jake snatched her bag and trailed a few feet behind. In the living room, he stopped.

"I need to leave a note for Elaine and Emily." He quickly scribbled one out. Once done, he picked up both bags, then nodded for her to go ahead. He followed her out the front door, all the way to his SUV.

"Are we just going to drive around, or do you have a destination in mind?" Michelle asked him after they'd been driving for ten minutes.

"You'll know when we get there."

"Fine."

Jake glanced over to note she'd crossed her arms and was now staring out the window.

He punched the accelerator hard. The entire time he sped along the country road, heading for the interstate, the same question burned a hole in his gut, filling him with his earlier rage. Why the hell hadn't she told him they'd created a baby together?

As much as he tried, he just didn't see how Michelle could be so cold-blooded as to keep his child from him. He'd expected such selfish actions from Kiera and had known how to protect himself from them, but he'd had no defenses against Michelle, who'd obviously used the same tactics.

Michelle wasn't who he thought she was. She'd done the unforgivable, and damn it all, it really hurt to have to face the fact.

~

"Thanks, Linda," Jake said forty-five minutes later, after giving her the spent shells.

She nodded. "Once I get them to the lab, I should have prints in a few hours. That is, if there are any, and if the guy is in IAFIS," she said, mentioning the fingerprint database the FBI managed.

"We could get lucky." He hugged her, then opened Linda's car door. "You don't know how much I appreciate this."

"I hope things work out." Her nod indicated Jake's Durango, parked at the rest stop. An overhead streetlight illuminated Michelle's sulking form in the front seat. "Is she the one?"

"Yeah. Michelle Matthews. Someone wants to kill her and I'm trying to keep her safe."

"No." Linda shook her head, offering a small smile. "I mean, is she the one who changed your life. Made you cautious?"

Not expecting her question, he searched her face for a clue as to what she knew. "Where would you get an idea like that?"

"It's okay, Jake. You mentioned her staying with Elaine and I put two and two together from other details you've told me. She's your ex's friend, isn't she?" Her smile stretched. She trailed the back of her hand down his face, patting it in almost a motherly fashion. "I fully understand. I have my own baggage." Her gaze returned to the SUV, her smile becoming wistful. "Maybe you should come to terms with your past. She seems nice. Might be worth the effort."

"You're way off base." He snorted. Michelle was nice, all right. Nice enough to keep his son from him. He eyed Linda, wondering about her suggestions. She probably hid a few not-so-nice secrets herself. Of course, if he were honest, he'd have to admit…his weren't any nicer.

Shit.

The whole goddamned world had gone to hell. No one was nice anymore.

No one.

Common decency had flown out the window. Wasn't this case enough proof? Indulgent rich people were buying drugs and sex slaves over the Internet, and someone was trying to kill Michelle because she… Hell. Jake scrubbed a hand over his face in frustration. He had no clue as to why. He only knew he had to protect her. Because…it had to do with karma.

"Well, whatever…just be careful." Linda sounded unconvinced. She hugged him and added a quick peck on the cheek before hopping into her car. "I'll let you know what I find out."

Jake stood staring as she backed out of the space and drove off, wondering at her perception. Eventually, he sighed and glanced at his watch. At four in the morning, he needed to get Michelle to safety, then get some shut-eye so he could work in a few hours. He had too much to do to let emotions get in the way.

~

"What the hell is wrong with you?" Michelle asked, almost shouting, as Jake hurried her out of his SUV after parking.

She was tired of feeling his cold rage. And to add insult to injury, she'd had to watch him meet his girlfriend.

He slammed the car door. "Nothing's wrong." Seconds later, he was leading—forcing would be a better term—her up a gravel path.

"It's not nothing and you know it." She tried to yank her elbow out of his grip, but his hold tightened, and he only urged her faster. She glanced around, noting a house in the woods, given all the shadows of trees surrounding them. With what appeared to be an awesome view of a lake, illuminated in moonlight. Any other time, she'd deem the scene romantic, a reminder of their time together. But not tonight. Tonight, Jake's actions were anything but.

"I'm trying to keep you alive." He practically growled, which along with the fierce glower he fired her way, made her think he'd rather kill her than follow his edict.

The same moonlight highlighted his white teeth, reminding her of a wild beast acting on instinct, leaving little trace of the caring man she'd always thought him to be.

"I am alive." She glared back, giving one more tug on her elbow. "I don't appreciate the rough handling. I've got bruises all over."

"You don't seem to realize what's happening here. Women are disappearing and dying. Is that what you want?" Jake's grip immediately softened, but not his voice. The sharp sound cut through her mind with a razor's edge, slicing its way to her very soul. "Despite not understanding why, I'm trying to save your sweet little butt, so quit fighting me."

She blinked in an effort to stop the tears she felt lurking. His every enunciated syllable expressed his disgust and disapproval, as did his every facial feature, from the snarl on his lips to the disdain that hardened his gaze. Her chin inched higher. "Why are you being so mean?"

"No reason." Given the way he spat the two words, Shelly couldn't believe he didn't have one. "Just keep moving till we get inside."

"Fine."

The instant they'd made their way across the front porch of someone's vacation home, he reached into his pocket for a key. After unlocking the door, he pushed it open and grabbed her elbow, almost shoving her inside.

Shelly jerked her arm free in an effort to avoid his touch, then crossed her arms and snapped, "I don't need your help." She slipped further into the huge foyer and stood in the dark, while Jake dropped her bag in the middle of the floor and turned on a light.

"I'll be back in a few. Don't go anywhere."

Every cell in her body tightened, and she fought the urge to kick him as he strode past her. She took a look around, noticing an upscale, richly decorated room. Wood floors, a cozy stone fireplace, plush furniture, and earth-tone colors. A wall of windows overlooked the lake. Shelly rubbed her bare arms. She wasn't cold. Just bruised and agitated. From her position, she could see into the state-of-the-art kitchen. Top-of-the-line appliances and granite countertops. The place reeked of money, including a museum-like feel. No one could possibly live here. It was too sterile for human habitation.

"At least tell me where we are," she called, hearing him rummaging in the other room.

"Isn't it obvious?" he shot back, his tone patronizing. "We're at a lake house."

She stamped her foot and held her gaze on the outside, sucking in air to keep from exploding further. Despite having badly scraped hands, if he were standing in front of her, she'd had no doubts about taking her best swing at him, her mood was that foul.

Shelly stared into the dark night as darker thoughts filled her mind.

Jake knew about Mikey. He had to know. That was the only explanation for the abrupt change in his behavior. Nothing short of that would cause his earlier hot stare to freeze into a glare colder than dry ice.

But how? She stiffly paced, feeling every bruise, and realized in a sudden flash of insight the how didn't matter. What did matter?

Shelly eyed the hallway where he'd disappeared, thinking.

She had to get away from him. The sooner the better.

Her focus returned to the wall of windows.

Get away? Yeah, right! The moonlit lake and surrounding forest could be one of a dozen in the area. They all looked the same in the dark. With no means of transportation, she was stuck.

Why in the hell didn't I pay attention while he drove, her

mental voice shouted.

One thing was for certain. She planned to stay out of his path.

Shelly waited until he came back into the room.

"Water's on now and I turned down the air. It may take an hour or so to cool off, though." He advanced to the open kitchen, peered first into the cupboards and then into the fridge. "No one's been here in a while. I'll need to get some things in the morning."

"You seem familiar with this house. Is it yours?"

Jake grunted an assent, riffling through drawers.

"And how long are we going to be here?"

"Don't know." He slammed one drawer and opened another.

"So are you some kind of agent? Is that why you have a gun?"

His answer was another grunt. When he didn't offer more, just kept to his searching, Shelly sighed. What was it about the male of the species? Getting any useful information out of him seemed no easier than dragging details out of her son when he'd offer similar one- or two-word answers to her questions about his day.

"I assume you have a place for me to stay?" She met his gaze with raised eyebrows. "I'd like to go to bed." Ignoring sore muscles that rebelled with pain at any exertion, she bent to pick up her bag. She probably wouldn't sleep, but she could read Kiera's journal. Hadn't finishing it been one of Jake's demands on the drive?

"Upstairs." Jake nodded to the staircase. "Take your pick of bedrooms."

"Thank you." Shelly retreated in the direction of the stairs. At the top, she spied several bedrooms. After a cursory inspection of each room, she picked the best for her purposes, complete with a lock.

"Good night," she yelled as she turned, then jumped when she realized he'd followed her and stood too near.

Jake eyed her thoughtfully before stepping past her and saying over his shoulder, "Good night. I'll see you in the morning."

She hurriedly stepped inside, shut the door, and flipped the lock with a loud click. Not that she needed to, when he seemed to want to be well away from her as much as she did him.

Chapter 12

He stopped the truck at the edge of the gravel driveway. By the time he'd turned off the ignition and climbed out, Ivy stood in front of him. She'd obviously been waiting for him, given her smile.

"You're late," she said.

"I had a few things to take care of this morning. It's been busy. I only have an hour or so, then I've got to get back."

"Poor baby." She slid an arm around his neck, drawing him near to plant a kiss on his lips. When she meant to break away, he gripped her head, holding on, increasing his mouth's pressure, and forcing her to provide a real kiss.

"That's better," he murmured, biting her lip, then sucking. He released her and looked around.

Very few knew he leased these two hundred wooded acres, miles from the nearest paved road, and he meant to keep it that way, never changing the agreement when his great-aunt died five years earlier. A records search would only yield an obscure name. No one questioned it, especially the owner who'd moved to Florida, as long as the yearly rents were paid.

"How are they?" he asked, referring to their human merchandise. Together they headed for the house, situated in a small clearing. The structure was outdated, built in the 1950s. But it had what they needed. A full cellar he'd subdivided into ten windowless, richly decorated chambers, with only one way in and a bolted lock on the door.

"Behaving as they've been instructed. Very cooperative. I hated to see Kimberly go."

"So her sale went smoothly?"

When she nodded, he sighed, almost sad, mentally assessing

Kimberly's rapid progress. She'd been a challenge at first, and one he'd savored. But once his domination was complete, he'd lost interest. She was just like all the others at this point—a trained whore to be sold to the highest bidder.

"We had a busy night, full of regulars," Ivy said, heading up the porch stairs. "And very lucrative."

He bounded up the steps after her and into the house, listening as Ivy updated him on the johns who'd arrived the night before by plane. They landed on a hidden strip less than a mile away, eager to engage in a fantasy. It was a lot like visiting the Best Little Whorehouse in Texas from the Dolly Parton movie, except they were in southern Kentucky and his women were more like mindless sexual dynamos who'd do anything to please.

"No problems with taping?" he asked, glancing at the monitors when they entered their viewing room. As usual, the evening's activities would have included a live transmission. All part of the agreement and a necessary precaution he'd set up, as one camera always captured a john's face, so there was no doubt as to the aggressor. This wasn't part of the broadcast, however. Men with enough money to buy an evening with a sex slave wanted anonymity and seldom posed a threat, but why tempt fate? Business was business. Each got what he wanted. His buyer got his rocks off and he got free advertisement as well as an insurance policy. He sold to only satisfied customers. In four years, millions of dollars had changed hands without any complaints.

"Smooth as a baby's butt." Ivy flipped the switch that brought seven of the ten screens alive with color.

"Senorita?"

"See for yourself while I deal with Juanita," she said, turning to of one of the four illegal aliens hired to help Ivy. The Mexican women fixed meals, kept the house clean, and made sure the customers followed the rules and stayed below at night.

Money had its uses, he thought, watching her talk to the woman in fluent Spanish. Made things easier, as did the circumstances. He knew human behavior enough to know none of his hired help would breathe a word about what they saw or heard, too dependent on the thousands of dollars Juanita and her husband, along with the others, earned each month. Most of their money was sent home to a small village in Mexico. It certainly didn't hurt that they spoke no English, nor did the threat of being deported instantly if they ever did figure out a means of communicating.

He moved to another monitor and pushed the Play button to view different sections of the DVD recorded the night before. A satisfied smile settled upon his face. His singers had learned to sing with their bodies and had learned to love it.

Ivy finished with Juanita and came to stand behind him, her eyes fastened on the recording.

"They outdid themselves last night," she said.

He nodded. Such naturals. All youthful beauties and nothing like the seasoned hookers he'd worked with to test his methods. These enticing, alluring sex kittens presented an almost innocent appeal, blending what he termed "the Madonna and the whore" that his customers craved. Certainly none had the hardened exteriors so prevalent in his earlier subjects, who'd been too low class for his targeted customers. They'd also had a low tolerance to the drugs his team had created.

He'd developed his first singer quite by accident and it had worked so successfully, he continued. Of course, he'd become highly selective, picking out only women with backgrounds and personalities conducive to his needs. Meaning, no one cared if they disappeared. No one seemed to miss either the hookers or the singers. Until recently. "We're in this together." Their operation worked so well because they were a team and he was their leader. "We can't afford any more trouble."

"They never give me any trouble."

He smiled. "Of course they don't." Not when she knew exactly how to handle them. He looked at the other screens. "Everything appears normal."

Yet, he had a foreboding feeling and he always listened to his instinct.

His cell phone rang. The lit caller ID indicated the code name, Montoya, who was pressing him for an answer. He let the device ring and turned back to Ivy. "Montoya says he'll pay double for as many women as he can buy if I can deliver them tonight."

Hot American women were worth their weight in gold on the black market, especially those he'd broken in. By the time his slaves were ready to make it to their final destination—an out-of-the-way bordello in Mexico in this instance—they were so far gone they'd never make their way back into the country.

"Four are ready for sale now and one is close. The last two need more time."

"We don't have time. Montoya's request is a perfect solution to our problem. I'm closing up and getting rid of everyone tonight." He usually limited sales to two or three at a time due to controlling live inventory.

"Tonight?" Ivy scrunched up her nose and frowned. "But I need at least another week for the full transition."

Ivy was right and precisely the reason he'd always resisted Montoya's pressure to sell more. Their method of developing sex slaves took time and effort. The more time they had for tweaking the mind, the better the end product, and the less chance of some memory remaining of their time in transition. "We'll have to make it work. He wants to schedule his plane to arrive around three a.m. That way we can still pull in another decent night with the usual customers." Those customers would be gone by then. He hesitated. Montoya wouldn't be happy when he heard the news about closing, but he was a reasonable man, and as a businessman, he'd understand his position. He had bigger worries, like surviving.

"It's risky."

"Not as risky as being found here. Mexico's a long way off and there's little possibility of tracing them back to us, once they're sold."

"You really think we should worry over being found out?"

"Yes." He didn't like her questioning his motives, but he tolerated her insolence because he needed her.

Ivy Jackson had gained Della's trust. She hired and fired the bar's talent, homing in on suitable candidates he'd sent there. The bar was key to obtaining merchandise as well as johns. So was the joint effort of those involved. In order to remain anonymous and avoid detection, they stuck together. Between them, they multitasked, took turns at the cave, at the house and doing the dirty work, like causing necessary accidents or scoping out talent. Without each of them performing their specific tasks, their setup wouldn't work. All aspects of the business ran smoothly...or it had before he'd miscalculated and three of their slaves had died. Unlike the prostitutes' deaths, these dead women were like waving red flags at the law enforcement bulls, generating nothing but interference and increasing their risk.

Their need to divest and lay low grew by the hour, especially since he wasn't sure what Matthews knew. "The longer Matthews remains a loose end, the more worried I get."

Kiera Delaney's threat hung about his neck, heavier than a fucking anvil. He still wondered how the bitch had found his love nest. And where in the hell had she stashed her evidence? Too bad they'd had to kill her before he found out. Definitely a tragedy, when she'd have made an exquisite slave.

"You're worrying needlessly. Matthews doesn't know anything," Ivy said, obviously picking up his train of thought. "How could she? Kiera only had seconds before passing out. I was there, remember, watching and listening. But now, because of last night, Matthews is wary." She shook her head, her hands going palms up, to add weight to her words. "I don't know how she knew to stop the airflow and avoid breathing in the drug in the bathroom to come out of it before Bobby had a chance to get to her, but I do know the drug worked. I saw the few minutes of live feed from the DVD. She clearly had no memory of what took place. So we wait. There's always a next time."

"Maybe." He didn't want to upset her with the news of another failed attempt. Ivy had been against doing anything as drastic as shooting in the dark from the beginning, saying all they had to do was wait for the right opportunity and Matthews could simply disappear, the same way the singers did. Sold to the highest bidder. Easier said than done after so many botched tries and no time left for brainwashing.

"The threat has to be neutralized. Our future depends on it." Only death would be final enough for him, but he didn't verbalize the sentiment. Dealing with Matthews had become a meaty bone of contention between them. She'd had misgivings about outright killing to protect their investment. He had no such misgivings.

No one wanted exposure, least of all him. He'd guided their

growth from the shadows, an aspect that had led to their overwhelming success, and he had no intention of allowing anyone to destroy a profitable venture that had taken years to develop. Especially a friend of Kiera Delaney's. Not one who knew so much of her past, and not when he'd been part of that past at one time. He couldn't be certain of what Kiera had talked of back then. What she'd revealed to a best friend. He wasn't willing to take the chance of Matthews making any kind of connection.

"As I was saying, we sell the girls to Montoya, and wait until things cool off before starting anything more in that area," he said, drawing her away from delving further into his plans for Matthews. "I have a line on a new customer and a way to make more money in the meantime. Says he's intrigued by the concept of what we're selling."

"Was he recommended?"

"Not in the usual way. He found us. I haven't met him, but you may have. He's been hanging out at Della's."

"I don't like it. How does he know about you?"

"He doesn't. He made mention in passing to our go-between."

When her face wrinkled in displeasure, he held up a hand. "Hear me out first. I understand your concerns." He smiled. She was as cautious as he, which is why he depended on her. In five years she'd become a fixture at Della's, waiting tables on the weekends, the busiest nights, scoping out their potential clients, who'd always been instructed to hang out at the bar during that time. Until she was satisfied.

"It helps to have the sheriff's office in our back pocket. My research indicates he's no ordinary customer and the interested party he represents is a client who loves our videos and wants to help us expand our business." He chuckled. "Seems we've developed a bit of a reputation over the Internet. Word of mouth has always been our strength. I plan on sucking him in, but I doubt the usual blackmail will work with this guy. He's a lawyer. Shrewd. Aware of both sides of the law. While Collier and the state police are spreading out in these woods, we can take our time in deciding. Yet, in the end, we may have no choice but to trust him. I'd like to start that aspect up again as soon as we can to avoid more losses."

"Trusting anyone is a big risk."

He shrugged. "Not if we handle it right." Hadn't they done so when they'd branched into new territory, using the Internet to remain hidden, going for men with big money and some kind of dysfunction? They'd figured a way to handle that risk and now they were all wealthy. "Money and dysfunction still add up to profits. That element will never change."

The beauty in their entire setup was that no one who bought knew who was selling, but the sellers knew the buyers. Except for Montoya, who he knew by name only, and even then, Montoya knew nothing of their identities. Everything was handled electronically. They'd planned well, hiding their identities and using the rural area to their advantage.

"Besides, who would believe that Della's, just a bar in the backwoods run by a crazy woman, is a front for our lucrative business? Even if evidence points in that direction, it's easily explained and dismissed."

Ivy snorted. "I guess the risk depends on the money involved and how soon he can react once we're good to go."

"My sentiments exactly. Timing is the real issue," he said. "I'm positive we can do business with Peters and stay cautious at the same time. I view it as an opportunity for expansion after this mess is over."

"Then give him a try. Communicate by e-mail. Have Bobby give him the address."

"Okay. And you agree to selling all seven to Montoya?"

When she nodded, he turned to the video monitors, seven small screens showing the remaining women, and smiled. "You've outdone yourself." Each appeared ready to meet her fate. A night of ecstasy or an eternity spent pleasing Montoya. "We'll simply have to make sure they enjoy themselves enough, until they're long gone from here, without leaving any trace of their months with us."

"Too bad we're losing them." Ivy looked at the monitors and sighed. "I rather liked seeing how far they'll go to please me."

He chuckled. "You've become a sadistic bitch over the years."

"Not sadistic. Curious. The process is an interesting study in human behavior. Would've made a great project in behavioral psychology," she said, speaking of the class both took in college where they met. They'd been together ever since.

"Maybe," he said. "But we'd have been marked down for not anticipating potential problems." This was reality, not some hypothetical situation dreamed up by students looking for ways to make money. "We've far surpassed classroom projects, turning ideas into millions."

Unfortunately, the reality of three dead women meant millions in lost revenue, as well as creating a huge logistical problem with avoiding detection. All because some could fight the drug's effects better than others. He hadn't planned for that contingency, only because he hadn't known about it. "In time, six months tops, once those singers' deaths become a distant memory with their case files packed away due to lack of any real trail to follow, we'll be back in business. And we'll have benefited from our costly mistakes."

Suddenly, movement from one of the screens drew his attention. "What's with Sally? She looks restless."

"Not restless. Needy." Ivy laughed and grabbed a bottle of pills. She held them up, heading for the basement. "It's time for their *medicine*."

He watched her go. Once she was out of the room, he punched Call Return.

"Get the job done and take her out." The person on the other end didn't bother pretending he didn't recognize his voice or misunderstand his order. "Just do it while Ivy's busy. Am I clear?" The instant he got his positive response, he disconnected, then hit the button to bring up Montoya's number.

"We're on for tonight. Have your pilot follow the same instructions as last time. He'll be met at the landing field. I'll expect half payment to be in the account before midnight and the rest after liftoff."

Chapter 13

It was after nine by the time Shelly opened the bedroom door and followed the strong scent of coffee. That and the smell of cooking bacon permeated every square inch of open air. Her stomach growled as she walked.

She rarely ate bacon, but couldn't resist taking a slice from the pile Jake had cooling on the counter.

Grinning, Shelly chomped on the tasty morsel and grabbed the coffeepot to fill the mug he'd left out. Nothing tasted better than artery-clogging bacon when starving.

"You cook?" She nodded at the bowl of whipped eggs and chopped vegetables sitting next to the pan. He'd obviously made an early morning grocery run.

He grunted in what sounded like a positive reply, before turning back to the stove.

She tamped down her rising annoyance. Why should she care that he was still ignoring her? Hadn't she dealt with his indifference before?

"I could get used to such service," she said sweetly. Two could play his game. She'd just pretend she didn't care.

"Yeah, well, don't get too used to it, because we're trading off. You're in charge of lunch."

"Oh?" A smile tugged at the corner of her mouth. "I don't do cooking."

"If you're hungry enough, you'll cook."

She shrugged, wondering how long Jake would endure her efforts before taking over all the cooking once he tasted hers. Her grin stretched. She really *was* a lousy cook. The worst. In fact, there was a running joke in her house. According to her mom and Monica, Shelly hadn't mastered the skill of boiling water, let alone cooking.

Thank goodness for fortified cereals, and frozen foods in plastic bags and microwaves, otherwise she and Mikey would have starved long ago. She glanced around. Not a microwave in sight. He probably didn't eat Honey Nut Cheerios, either.

"Since I cooked, you can set the table."

"Sure." He'd find out soon enough. She headed for the drawer he'd opened.

In no time, he'd dished out the food, then carried both plates to the table, but that was the extent of his politeness. Jake sat and picked up his fork, focusing totally on his meal and what went into his mouth.

Shelly sighed and dug in. Right now, she was too hungry to care that he was being a jerk.

Ten minutes later, he stood. "I need to take care of some things," he said, indicating a breakfast spent in complete silence was over. "I shouldn't be gone more than a few hours." He couldn't get to the door fast enough. "Don't leave the house. If you need something to do while I'm gone, wash the dishes and then finish reading Kiera's journal."

"Asshole," she said under her breath, then stuck out her tongue at him as the door closed. Childish or not, it took away some of the ache. At least for a few seconds. She retreated to the window and watched him climb into his Durango without sparing another look back at the house, or another thought of her, it seemed.

The peacefulness of her surroundings wasn't lost on her, but the moment he drove off, an ear-splitting quiet pervaded her senses, pointing out the emptiness in the large space. Shelly stepped out onto the deck, walked to the railing, and inhaled deeply. Her gaze took in the serene setting. So peaceful, yet so full of life. Along with the hawks circling high above, she spied a couple of tiny bluebirds playing, chasing each other, and landing on branches not ten feet away. The cicadas' loud buzzing overrode the usual morning insect noises. Her eyes focused on the dense green forest, searching, before sweeping the calm mirror-blue of the lake. Despite being in the middle of so much activity, loneliness swallowed her whole. Everywhere around her, life went on. Sunshine beat against her face, rays warming the earth, but she'd never felt colder.

Had she really known Jake all those years ago? Or had she fallen in love with an ideal? With a picture of perfection of what he should be in her mind?

Tears burned behind her eyes. She brushed them back, refusing to let Jake's actions bother her any more than they already had. She'd never figure him out. Nothing had changed in six years, except he was now some kind of agent. He'd told her he hated working at the factory and wanted to work in law enforcement, so at least he'd followed his dream.

She looked at her watch. Still too early to call. Mikey had spent the night at a friend's house and wouldn't be home yet.

Sighing, she glanced once more at the green and blues surrounding her. Following his earlier comment, but not because he commanded it, she rushed inside to retrieve Kiera's journal. The idea of reading on the deck appealed to her, dispelling some of her gloominess.

Shelly sank into a comfortable lounge chair and opened the book, remembering how far she'd read, up to Kiera's fancy wedding and fabulous honeymoon after she'd come back from detox.

> The first year of my marriage to Jake went okay, basically because I stayed clean and played house until Emily arrived. During that time, Jake had moved up at the factory, taking over more responsibility from my dad. But by then, I sensed I'd lost him. Lost his love. His whole focus, as it should have been, was Emily. I love Emily, but I had mixed feelings about my daughter right after she was born. She'd taken the last little bit of Jake's attention and I couldn't deal with it. Eventually I went back to anesthetizing my pain, rather than facing my mistakes and owning up to them. I blamed everyone, had an excuse for everything.
>
> I had pretty much ruined my chance at being a wife Jake could love with my continued drug use, but I still had my daddy. I was still his baby girl and no matter what I did, he still loved me...still believed my excuses. Then suddenly, he was gone, too. I guess I had decided

my life was over at that point because I stayed high for months, wanting to die. Who knows? Maybe I thought if I died I could meet him in heaven, until I realized I'd probably go to hell for all the sins at my feet.

Shelly blinked. Her eyes blurred with unshed tears. Ed Delaney's death had definitely affected Kiera to the point of her making significant strides in the struggles to return from what Kiera termed the hell of addiction. That and Elaine Delaney, who now controlled the purse strings and no longer aided and abetted her habit. Elaine demanded Kiera get help, or she could kiss everything good-bye. Jake had been the first to call Kiera on her bullshit, as she'd put it. He simply wouldn't let her addiction disrupt their daughter's life.

With the help of a savvy counselor, Kiera began to understand her motives. Lying and existing on empty promises shattered what used to be loving relationships. Kiera had destroyed so many, without realizing she'd squandered the chance to get them back until it was too late. She'd also used her addiction as a means of controlling those around her.

Shelly grasped the unhappiness described. Manipulating others was obviously dissatisfying. Shelly read on, completely absorbed with Kiera's process of climbing out of the bottomless pit of her drug problem, also Kiera's exact wording. In detailing the ugliness of what it was like to live on the dark side of looking for a high, Kiera wasn't easy on herself or her actions.

I've read most alcoholics and addicts never fully recover, but can exist without their crutch if they place themselves in higher hands. I prayed. I prayed so hard that I knew God had to hear me. I was so afraid of dying alone and going to hell. It's true. What I read. Believing in Him keeps me strong enough to fight a daily struggle. One I had for almost two years without a hit of anything before Jake would let me see my baby. And the worst part? When I finally held Emily in my arms, I was so ashamed of myself. That was when my faith in God was really tested. Because no worthy mother can just toss her child aside for a fix like I did.

Being so unworthy made me crave my crutch. How I survived, I really don't know, except for the grace of God and praying harder. Funny, I never put much faith in believing in a higher being before. Now I know. Those who've felt this power know. Like I do. I hold on to it when times get tough.

I'm proud to say I've made much progress. Jake is even willing to share custody. He set the bar high long ago and that has never changed. During my fight back, I have to admit, he was a strong anchor to hold on to. He's a little God-like in that respect. He let me try, while also expecting me to rise above what I'd become. He expected me to be worthy, so I was. Little by little, I became someone worthy of a beautiful girl. I promised myself (and God) on Emily's fourth birthday, I'd never do anything to destroy what I'd worked so hard to achieve. In fact, looking back, I believe Jake's firm denial of refusing to allow my behavior to taint our daughter was my catalyst for change after my dad died, even though it took me a year or so of counseling to figure it out.

The next section shifted to her struggle to repair the relationship Kiera had all but destroyed with Elaine. Shelly continued reading, while wiping at the tears now freely falling. She had always viewed Kiera's drug problem from a skewed perspective, only reacting to how it affected her personally, without understanding the full magnitude of a person's suffering once addicted. How horrible Kiera's life must have been at one point, having given up so much in the search of the perfect high.

Shelly's heart ached for her ex-best friend, feeling the same pain Kiera's admissions produced, feeling her disappointment in herself and in others. Almost a parallel to Shelly's own life, she suddenly realized. Except Shelly hadn't cut her ties to those who loved her, but she'd run from the things that had hurt her, just as Kiera had done.

The realization caused her to reflect. Self-reflection meant facing the truth. And as Kiera had written, looking in the mirror of your past mistakes was daunting. In the end, when Kiera needed her most, Shelly had bailed, too worried over her own pain, never looking beyond.

Shame filled her at how she'd judged her friend. Just as others had judged Shelly. Kiera had always been there for her, until she got mixed up with drugs. Deep down, Shelly knew her own motives hadn't been pure. She'd used Kiera's problems as an excuse and had done everything in her power to seduce Jake. And what was worse? She'd do it again in a heartbeat. So, what did that say about the kind of friend she'd become?

More tears filled her eyes, making it impossible to read any further.

Chapter 14

Jake steered his SUV onto the main road, having just left Elaine's house. He reached for his phone. He'd spent a few precious hours with his daughter and Emily was now playing with a friend. Jake wasn't sure how Emily felt about all this. On the outside, she appeared as chipper and happy as ever, talking nonstop the entire time, asking question after question about her mother.

Though she seemed to understand that Kiera wouldn't be returning, Jake knew her young mind hadn't fully grasped the finality of death. Her pain would most likely come on slowly, at which point his role would then be to help her deal with it as best he could. Talking and being open with feelings was hard for him, but he'd do his damnedest, so that Emily wouldn't lose her spark like Kiera had done for a few years.

"Is Durbin working today?" Jake asked when Tom Baker answered on the other end of the cell phone, interrupting his musings.

"He had the morning off," Baker said. "Should be in at four when his shift starts." His voice faded. Jake heard him answering someone else, most likely the dispatcher. The two spent a moment talking back and forth, before the cell phone crackled to life again. "Sorry. I just got in." Tom waited a heartbeat, then asked, "Why're you asking about Durbin, anyway?"

"Was he working last night?"

"Yeah. He's still keeping an eye on the cave along with Larson. Both twelve-hour shifts ended around four a.m. Now, answer my question. Why're you interested in his whereabouts?"

"I have a few questions to ask about some lights I saw. Just wondering if he saw them too," Jake lied.

"What kind of lights?"

"I don't know. They streaked across the sky. Maybe floodlights."

"Were you close to the cave?"

"No. I was at Elaine's. Caught them from the window. When I went out to investigate, someone took a couple of shots at me." He didn't include Michelle's presence because he didn't want her exposed. Driving into town to make a statement would make her too big a target.

"Shit," Tom blew out. "Just what I need. A bunch of goddamned poachers who can't even wait a few months before legally killing Bambies in the woods. You'd think they'd at least have the brains not to shoot at innocent bystanders to keep from being caught."

Jake sighed. Dealing with poachers wasn't under the sheriff's jurisdiction, but he'd probably investigate. Year-round hunters who ignored laws weren't uncommon in these parts. State and federal game wardens in the area were just as stretched as other officials. Department of Natural Resources enforcers were overworked and underpaid. Most local public servants were dedicated men and women who knew each other and tended to keep their eyes open to help out if they could, drawing on any resource at hand to enforce laws that kept peace in the county.

"Well, let's hope the deer are smarter than the idiots with the lights," Jake said, despite being pretty sure that whoever fired the shots wasn't using lights to lure deer, but he didn't see the need to enlighten Tom. Until he had more corroboration to back up his suspicions. He damn sure wasn't about to accuse a respected businessman like Bobby Winters of anything without it. Campton was a small town and those locals in charge tended to close ranks and protect one another from outsiders. Which is what he'd become, he suddenly realized, noting the distrust in Tom's demeanor during most of their phone conversation. Rich had been right about that. And hell, he knew they'd all protect Billy. "So, what's going on with the case? Anything I need to know?"

"I spoke to Ivy Jackson. She's in charge of hiring and firing. Has been for a few years," Baker said, updating him on his progress at Della's. "She remembered Kimberly McDowell. Said she auditioned, got the gig, but never showed up the first Saturday she was supposed to start. She just figured with her voice, she'd gotten a better offer." Baker sighed into the phone. "Happens all the time in this business. Or so Ivy tells me."

Baker rambled on, talking about the others he'd interviewed, employees and bar patrons alike. Jake listened and made the appropriate noises, especially since Tom had mentioned Ivy's name, without letting on what he'd already discussed with Rich. To do so would create a barrage of questions Jake couldn't answer, even going so far as possibly compromising his partner's investigation. No one suspected Rich was undercover DEA.

"We're working this case together, so keep me in the loop," Baker said. "You got that?"

"Yeah, I got that." Jake glanced over at the baseball cap resting on the seat. Billy Durbin's cap, he was sure. The sheriff might be pissed in the end to have been left out of that loop. Yet, given the level of violence had risen, Jake wasn't about to blow Rich's cover. After all, these guys had gone to school together and were still tight buddies. One careless comment from loose lips was all it would take. Women's lives depended on Jake's secrecy now, so Baker would just have to accept his reasons. And if not? Well, Jake didn't give a shit. Good investigator or not, he still couldn't stand the guy.

He ended the call and punched the gas pedal. His navy Durango sped along the narrow road leading to Joe Durbin's house. In minutes, he pulled into a gravel driveway and parked in front of a neat little box, complete with a gable in front providing a tiny covered porch. Not much different from the trailers dotting the landscape, except this house didn't roll.

"It's a little early for a social call," Durbin said, stepping outside. Barefoot and shirtless, he wore jeans that rode low on his hips and hadn't bothered to pull a comb through his bed head.

"This isn't social. I have a couple of questions." Jake ignored the twinge of guilt for interrupting Durbin's sleep with his door pounding and reached behind, tugging the baseball cap out of his back pocket. "I found Billy's cap. I wanted to return it." When he held it out, something flickered in Durbin's eyes, before disappearing behind a smirk.

SANDY LOYD

Durbin spared a quick glance at the hat, shook his head, then looked away. Seconds later, he hocked a mouthful of chewing tobacco into the bushes. "Not Billy's." He stuffed a new piece into his mouth.

Jake narrowed his eyes. "You're sure?"

"Yes."

"Maybe you should take a closer look."

"Don't need to." Joe's annoyed gaze landed on his again, daring him to refute the denial. "It's not Billy's."

Jake stuffed the hat into his back pocket. "Where was your brother between the hours of two and three last night?"

"Here—in bed."

"Here?" Since Jake had already talked with the sheriff, he knew Durbin couldn't know that for sure, which meant he was lying through his teeth. Eyeing him closely, he noted the guy wasn't as cool and collected as he pretended all of a sudden. A sheen of sweat trickled down the side of his face, despite a cool breeze, and Durbin's focus kept darting from one point to another. He wouldn't meet his gaze again. That, along with the rapid clenching and unclenching of his fist, was a dead giveaway of agitation…or nerves. Was he guilty of something more than lying, or had big brother slid into his protective mode covering for Billy? Giving it one last shot, Jake asked, "Are you sure? Did you actually see him?"

"Isn't that what I said?" He finally met his gaze and glared, his back straightening. "You got a hearing problem, Collier? Or is your problem with understanding simple words?"

Jake smiled. Now the guy utilized anger to hide his lies. "Simple words are easy. What I'm having trouble with is figuring out how you can be in two places at once." When it dawned on Joe just what he was getting at, he added, "Did you think I wouldn't talk to Tom?"

"So I took an unauthorized break and checked on Billy. What of it?"

"I'm just trying to be thorough. Someone took a couple of shots at Michelle Matthews last night, and not ten yards away I find this hat, a hat that looked an awful lot like the one Billy had on the last time I saw him."

"That's why you're on my doorstep, harassing me so

goddamned early? 'Cause some fucking redneck had lousy aim? Too bad he didn't hit her. If you ask me, he'd be doing society a favor, taking out white trash instead of killing a deer."

Jake ignored the guy's slam at Michelle and concentrated instead on how Durbin just used the same excuse Baker had. "Yeah, well, listen up," Jake warned. "Kiera died under suspicious circumstances, and I'm not about to let the same thing happen to Michelle. Are we clear?"

Durbin grunted. "You're living under a delusion about your precious ex. Kiera got herself killed because she was into shit she shouldn't have been."

Something in his tone alerted Jake. His gaze narrowed. "What shit?" He studied Durbin's facial features, looking for something…anything…that would give him a clue. Oh yeah. It was there in his eyes. Durbin knew much more than he let on. His gut never lied.

"Drugs." Durbin spit out another repulsive mouthful of what Jake also considered to be shit. A hundred times worse than smoking and just as deadly, given all the mouth cancers in the area. When the deputy smiled, tobacco-stained teeth, darkened from years of chewing, marred an otherwise good-looking face. Yet he seemed oblivious to this imperfection, and Jake's disgust climbed to new heights as Durbin said, almost sneering, "Illegal ones if you get my drift, and she should've steered clear of those selling the shit. She got sucked back into using just like any junkie would. Being a Delaney didn't do squat for her in the end." He met Jake's gaze, his full of rancor. "And if you ask me, your white trash girlfriend should get outta town. Doesn't take a genius to figure if someone's shooting at her, staying ain't safe."

Jake couldn't determine whether it was a threat or not as Joe stood grinning like the Joker in Batman. Shaking his head, he turned and headed for his Durango.

Durbin was mixed up with this; Jake would stake his badge on it. Now belted inside and about to turn the key, the vibration of his cell phone coming from his pocket stopped him. He dug it out and snapped the device open. "Yeah, Rich, whatcha got?"

"I just wanted to fill you in on what I found out after we talked last night."

~

Rich ended his conversation with Jake after explaining Betsy's findings and her thoughts on the combination of drugs found on the towels he'd taken from the bathroom at Della's. In return, he found the information Jake relayed about the bogus truck plates interesting.

Rich drove on a back road toward Bowling Green and the office he was using for this op. The couple of hours of much-needed sleep he'd grabbed in his rental house had refreshed him. A mile out, he caught a glimpse of a utility truck parked at a gas station/food mart.

The truck's description matched the one Jake had just mentioned. Driving one-handed, he slowed and reached for his notebook. He flipped to the right page and compared license numbers. They matched. He swung a U-turn and pulled up to an empty pump. On his way to prepay, he had his cell phone out as if he were placing a call, and snapped pictures of the three occupants inside the store. He put the phone to his ear, speaking to no one, and walked up and down the aisles in search of nothing, the entire time keeping his attention surreptitiously on the trio. Patiently, he waited until all three had made their purchases. The guy he'd targeted, the one he thought might belong to the utility truck, paid for a drink, guzzling it down as he walked to the pumps. While the truck filled, the man finished his drink and tossed it in the trash.

Rich looked at the pimply-faced kid behind the counter who couldn't be a day over eighteen. His nod indicated the truck driving away. "That guy paid with a credit card, didn't he?"

"Yeah." Pimply-face's gaze narrowed suspiciously. "Why?"

"Can I see the transaction?" When Rich flashed his badge, drawing the usual awe, pimply-face nodded and reached into the cash register.

"It's electronic, so there's not much on it."

Rich smiled and noted the name sewn into his pocket, not wanting to call him the name he'd given him for obvious reasons. "Thanks, Raymond." He wrote what little information the slip provided into his notebook. He stuck the phone to his ear, turned away from the kid still paying homage to his badge, and punched in Malone's cell number. Eric Malone was one of two geek types assigned to the case. Mitchell Jarvis was his partner. "I'm 'bout a mile out. Got a transaction I need you to trace." He gave the specifics and asked, "Think you can get me more info on this guy?"

"Give me five and I'll call you back."

"Thanks, but I'll be there in less, so tell me in person." Rich snapped the phone closed and handed Raymond a five for the chips and soft drink he'd grabbed. "Keep the change."

The bell tinkled as the door hit his back. On the way to his car, he veered near the trash can and retrieved the empty can his suspect had thrown away, just in case he might need the prints. But Rich knew Jarvis and Malone would likely trace the transaction before he arrived at the office.

He climbed inside his car, stuck the key into the ignition, and paused long enough to e-mail a picture to Jake. Next, he called Jake's cell, getting his voice mail. While easing away from the pump, he left a quick message.

Minutes later, he turned into the strip mall parking lot.

"Hey, Malone, Jarvis," Rich said, entering and nodding at the two tech guys from the Nashville field office monitoring equipment in a hidden back room.

Both looked up and returned his greeting.

Rich arched a brow. "Come up with anything?"

"On the credit transaction?" Jarvis asked. When Rich nodded, he added, "Yeah, but I got something you might like more."

"Oh?"

"Thanks to your heads-up late last night, we hit pay dirt. Bobby's whereabouts are boring. He's at work. But your friend Ivy's been busy since we placed a tracer on her car early this morning." Jarvis typed, his fingers flying over the keys. In seconds, a picture flashed on the screen. Using the mouse, Jarvis sharpened the scene, revealing a fairly large house surrounded with a forest of trees. It looked like the only structure for miles. "This is what we get when we type in the GPS coordinates where she stopped after driving for fifteen minutes." He then scrolled the page to reveal a map of the area. "See for yourself. X marks the exact spot. The property backs up to the cave

Collier's interested in. Road in is miles away, though."

"Hmmm." He studied the screen, noting the distance between Della's and the *X*, along with the close proximity to the cave. "You think that's where they're having their drug-crazed orgies?"

"I'll give up my firstborn if it's not." Jarvis maneuvered the cursor to the corner, focusing on what appeared to be a landing strip. "And here's how johns come in and out."

"By airplane?"

"Works for me, if money's no object."

"Wouldn't that attract attention?"

"Not out there." He did a sweeping motion with the mouse and the arrow circled the green on the screen, showing a path a plane might take. "A small plane flying above a few thousand feet wouldn't make much noticeable noise. And by the time he'd be lined up for landing, he's over trees."

"Good job, guys." Rich rubbed his hands together, thinking of the clean bust when the bastards were caught by surprise. "So, how long before we'll be ready to go in?"

"Depends," Malone said. "Right now, there's not enough evidence for a search warrant. All we'd do is alert them. But that'll soon change. We know where they are and we know how they transmit their activities." He cleared his throat, as a hint of pink touched his cheeks.

Rich hid a smile. None of them were choirboys, but they'd all seen the live feed from the webcam and some of the shit caught on tape would make even the devil blush.

"Anyway," Malone continued, "I'll go in after dark tonight. I figure if I can get within listening range to intercept and record their signal, then bingo. We got our probable cause. I'm sure I can get enough to make a good case, especially if I link it with the live feed. Last time I checked, selling either illicit drugs or hot hookers is against the law in Kentucky. And if we get lucky and find drugs when we bust in, it'll be a slam dunk for the AAG."

Rich's face split into a wide grin. They'd all win major points with the AAG. Assistant attorneys general tried federal cases in federal court, and those Rich had come into contact with over the years salivated over cases like this. Easy wins. Video evidence was damning. No one, a grand jury included, watching the live feed from the webcam would believe sex wasn't being sold across state lines, and according to the message, drugs played a big part in the experience.

"You'll be careful?" Rich asked, knowing it was a stupid question the moment it left his lips. "Three dead bodies mean these people won't play nice if confronted. And we can't ignore the attempts on Michelle Matthews." He didn't have to add his suspicions about the prostitutes' deaths, having already mentioned them in detail, even going so far as to plot out the locations where the bodies were found with the two, noting definite patterns within the five-year period. Gut instinct told him they were connected and made him voice his concerns.

"You worry too much, Heslin," Jarvis chimed in. "We know how to fire a weapon."

Rich nodded. That much was true. As trained undercover operatives, Malone and Jarvis could handle themselves, but they spent most of their time on backup surveillance. They were the best in the business, usually working in nondescript vans or vacant buildings gathering evidence, well away from the unknown dangers drug dealers posed when standing next to them.

"So, what about the credit transaction?" Rich asked, trying not to think about the fact that this was an accident waiting to happen if anything went wrong.

"Coming right up," Jarvis said. "The name helped make the search easier."

"Can you believe his name is Jerry Mathers?" Rich snorted. "Weird coincidence if you ask me, having the same name as the Beav."

"Huh?" Jarvis asked, his expression as clueless as Malone's.

"You know? *Leave It To Beaver*, the show from the sixties on cable?" Both shook their heads. "Oh, that's right. You guys waste your wide screen on playing those video games." He sighed. "How sad." He shook his head and tsk-tsked. "You don't know what you're missing."

Jarvis grunted, giving Malone a look that said, "We could say the same, Heslin," before clicking the mouse, his expression hardening into all business once again. "Haven't had time to do a thorough background on…" he hesitated a moment, then grinned, "…the Beav, but I did find a connection to our own Ivy and Bobby when I googled each name. Amazing what shit you can find about people when you google." He glanced at Malone and winked. "Though to be honest, if the *Leave It To Beaver* guy was there, I didn't note it. Was too busy looking for a younger man living in this region."

Rich ignored the comment and glanced at the screen. "You have been busy," he murmured, noting the information now popping up. "So, they all went to college together?"

"Yep. Mathers graduated eight years ago. Summa cum laude in chemistry. Got a job with Waddell Pharmaceuticals right out of college. According to this, he's been there ever since."

"I haven't seen him in Della's. My guess says he's a silent partner." Definitely worked, considering Betsy's information. "Dig up what you can on the company. Find out what his role is. And while you're at it, find out who owns the property."

"There's a lot of information to sift through." Jarvis scooted his chair closer to his computer and began typing. "Could take some time."

"Do your best." Rich pulled out his cell. He punched in Betsy's number and listened to her voice telling him she was out. At the beep, he said, "Hey, Bets. Give me a call when you wake up. I want to see if you got any more information and I have a few questions." Finally, the puzzle was beginning to make sense. But where did Billy Durbin fit in? Or Joe Durbin? He turned back to both men. "Add these two names in your search and see what comes up."

"What're we looking for?"

Rich shrugged. "Any connection either might have to Mathers or Waddell Pharmaceuticals." He remained silent, his brain churning. "You know, now that I'm thinking about it, add a couple more names. Might as well be thorough."

Chapter 15

With no more excuses to stop him from driving back to the lake house and Michelle, Jake pointed the SUV north, hoping she'd stayed out of trouble.

He parked in the shade and switched off the ignition, but didn't move. He stared at the house, framed in the late-morning light. His house. His prize for marrying Kiera, and Ed's guarantee that Jake would stick to his agreement. A house he'd been angry enough to take, which didn't make his deed any easier to bear.

His fist gripped the wheel. Oh, how he hated this house.

And now Michelle was in there. Why had he brought her here when he'd sworn never to return once he'd left almost five years ago? Why hadn't he sold it?

In a flash of insight, he finally understood why Michelle had disappeared and had never told him about her pregnancy. Why would she do anything else? How could she have competed with the hold Kiera and the Delaneys had on him? Looking at his house, he knew she couldn't.

For too long, he'd pretended he'd been noble in marrying Kiera due to her pregnancy. Yet deep down, he'd known the ugly truth. All he'd done was cave, giving in to guilt, using the ease of going along with the Delaneys' plan as a crutch, because he hadn't had the guts to say what he'd really thought and to tell Kiera how he'd really felt. Not until after Emily was born.

He climbed out of the car, his shoulders slumping as he slammed the door and walked toward the house.

"Michelle?" Jake glanced around. The kitchen shined. Smiling, he went from room to room, searching. When she wasn't in the bedroom she'd picked out, a streak of unease rolled up his spine. He strode to the window and peered out, then breathed in a sigh of relief after spotting her on the deck below.

She didn't look up when he stepped outside. Scanning the length of her, Jake let his eyes drink in her golden beauty. Long, willowy legs graced a lithe body. When he caught himself staring at her perfect round breasts, his hand fisted, squelching the desire to touch her to see if she was as soft as he remembered.

Movement drew his attention higher. He focused on her face as Michelle turned and greeted him with a warm smile. Their eyes met. For a brief instant, he caught something in her expression he used to see all the time back when she'd idolized him.

Michelle closed the journal. "Did you have a nice morning?" Her tone had too sarcastic an edge for someone who appeared so angelic just seconds ago, and it amazed him how quickly her expression hardened.

"Nice enough." Jake cleared his throat. "Thanks for cleaning up." His nod indicated the journal. "I see you've been reading."

He rolled his eyes. God, could he sound any more asinine? He sighed, fell into the chair next to her, and worked at pretending he didn't find her attractive.

"Isn't that what you wanted me to do?"

The smile he offered was quick, even if halfhearted. "Yeah. Did you learn anything?"

"A lot of information I'd rather not know, but nothing as to what you were hoping for." Her features softened into a wan smile. "I still have about twenty pages left, though."

"Good," he murmured, nodding. He examined his fingernails, struggling with the urge to continue ogling her breasts. From his seated angle, he had a picture-perfect view of one soft mound peeking out of her bunched-up shirt.

"Shit," he blew out, wiping his face and standing, purposefully eyeing the breathtaking scenery as he walked to the railing and leaned against it.

Jake shoved his hands in his pockets and studied the lake.

"Can I go for a walk, or is that against the rules."

He shrugged, glancing over his shoulder. "I could use a walk."

"That wasn't an invitation." Michelle stood glaring, chin held high, sparks almost shooting from her eyes.

He grinned. For some reason, he found her disdain amusing. "Haven't you had enough alone time?"

"No. I prefer my own company, if you don't mind."

"You'll go with me, or you don't go." Hip against the rail, he pulled his hands out of his pockets, crossing his arms. It made no difference to him. "I'm not letting you out of my sight."

She started down the stairs at a good clip. "Fine."

Jake trailed after her, remaining ten to twenty feet behind and noting a straight carriage that had always given him the impression she had a bit of royalty flowing through her veins.

Class, his mother would say. In her opinion, class wasn't bought. If nothing else, no matter how much money Kiera had had, Michelle had always outclassed her, despite a poverty-stricken beginning. He had a sneaking suspicion that element probably played into why the two no longer stayed friends once Michelle left. Kiera didn't like anyone to top her.

A classy woman wouldn't keep his child from him, he suddenly remembered. The pain the thought brought on pierced his calm and his anger flared up all over again. The impulse to shake her and ask why was more than a passing urge. Jake didn't, just silently followed her instead.

They'd walked almost a half mile on a dirt and gravel road darkened by the noon hour shade from leafy, mature trees hiding the sun.

Jake looked around. "We should start back now. Nothing appears out of the ordinary, but why push it?" This part of the lake was still deserted and would be until later that night when all the weekenders wanting a piece of nature burst into town.

"Sure," Michelle murmured, abruptly turning. A speck of white caught his attention at the same time she pointed and shouted, "Look. A doggie."

At the side of the road, Michelle stopped and leaned over to slap her knees. "Come here, sweetie."

"You can't just go around picking up strays," Jake warned, examining the mutt critically. Stray dogs were always a problem on the lake. People just dropped them off, under a misconception that if the animals were in the wild they could fend for themselves. Nothing could be further from the truth. "He could have rabies or something."

SANDY LOYD

"He doesn't," Michelle stated with conviction.

The dog whimpered, eyes never drifting from Michelle's face, clearly afraid, yet most likely too hungry to care. His ribs stuck out, pointing to the obvious. He definitely hadn't seen a meal in a while.

"He's just a big ol' baby." She patted her knees again. "Come on." With head bowed, a sure sign of subservience, the mongrel slowly scooted in front of her. "That's a good boy."

Michelle bent and stroked the mutt. "He's so sweet." His tail began thumping like he was beating a drum with it.

Of course the dog responded, Jake thought grimly. How could he not with Michelle's persuasive skills? The sweet coaxing sound shot straight to his groin, which along with the compassionate expression taking over her face, reminded Jake of how she'd once offered both to him. He rolled his eyes, mentally ordering himself to quit thinking along those lines.

The dog eventually curled his tail under his belly as he rolled over, giving her more access, his big brown eyes begging to be cared for.

Jake wasn't keeping any damned dog in his house, especially one who stank—not a dead animal smell, but close to it. "Geez, big guy," Jake said, rubbing behind his ears, earning a grateful lick on the hand in the process. "You look like you've had a few rough days." Okay. So he was a sucker for lost causes.

"He's precious."

"Yeah. Precious," he grunted, eyeing Michelle thoughtfully, noting the warmth emanating from her eyes. What would it take for her to view him in such a way again?

He shook his head, clearing it. Why should he care? He didn't want her stroking him like she stroked the dog, dirty and mangy as it was.

Liar!

Shit! Jake turned toward the house. He didn't. Case closed. She obviously didn't want him, and he certainly didn't want her.

Bigger liar!

Damn. He was in trouble.

No, no, no, no, no. He could handle her. He could handle the attraction.

Liar, liar, pants on fire!

178

"What should we name him?"

"What?" Her words drew him out of his sick thoughts, but he wasn't sure he liked what he heard.

"He needs a name."

Jake held up a hand. "No, he doesn't. You can't keep him. He doesn't belong to us."

Her expressive face all but shouted her concern. "He needs us." Michelle had always had a soft spot for anything in need.

His gaze moved higher to lock on to her eyes, their ocean-blue depths dragging him under.

Instantly, blood raced south and more thoughts from that night rushed back in a flash of white-hot sizzle. Damn, it was hard not to think of sinking into her warmth when she gazed at him like that. With familiar adoration, the same expression that made him think he could solve world hunger if he'd just put his mind to it.

Raking a hand through his hair, he straightened and looked away to break eye contact.

"Please, Jake." She placed her hand on his arm. Heat warmed the spot as their gazes locked once more, the dog all but forgotten, the idea of kissing her now his biggest thought forming.

Get your mind out of the gutter, Collier. You're here to protect her and nothing else. You will not defile her again.

Had he always been such a horny bastard? Of course he had! Well, that was about to change. Let her keep the damn dog, if doing so would make her happy. Then, once this was over she could go back to her life, and he to his.

But can you live without seeing your son?

The question slipped into his brain. She obviously hadn't wanted to include him in their lives before now. If he was nice enough, maybe he could forge a friendship out of this experience and she'd want him around.

"Okay, you win. We'll take him back to the house, clean him up, and feed him."

Niceness seemed to have its place. The smile she bestowed on him made him feel like he'd fed half of China, when in reality all he'd done was agree to feed one damn dog.

"Listen." Jake cleared his throat, going for nicer. "I'm sorry

I've been such an ass," he said, his expression softening. "This whole thing has got me acting crazy, you know?"

She flashed another warm grin that tugged on his insides now, just as it had only seconds earlier. "I guess getting shot at can do that to a person."

The effect was no different than all those years ago. Six years hadn't dulled the craving.

They returned to the house at a much faster pace, where Jake mixed a few raw eggs from the carton he'd purchased earlier that morning. He added half the package of ham he'd picked up for lunch. He fed the starving mutt before drenching him—it was a he, vying for Michelle's attention, as any male who got to within a foot of her would do—with the hose and adding herbal shampoo to get rid of the dead-animal smell.

"Here, let me." Jake took the loaf of bread out of Michelle's hands, having watched her flail about in the kitchen a good ten minutes after drying the dog. She hadn't lied earlier about not cooking. He didn't see how anyone could not know how to slap some ham and cheese between two slices of bread, brush them with butter to heat on the stove, but no woman looked more out of place in his kitchen.

"You're a smart man, Jacob Collier." Michelle laughed and hoisted herself onto the counter as the mutt curled contentedly at her feet.

He grunted and set to work, making grilled ham and cheese sandwiches, while dog and woman observed his every move.

Smart dog, he mused. Fido never strayed more than a few inches from her, except when he'd consumed the food.

"I can't believe you don't cook. It's..." Jake broke off and eyed her. "It's unnatural. Everyone should know how to cook."

"I microwave." Her chin inched higher, her grin spreading from ear to ear. "Doesn't that count?"

He looked to the heavens, chuckling and shaking his head. "You poor thing."

"Hey." She actually looked affronted. "I get by."

"I like a decent meal when I eat, and I don't do..." his lips curled in distaste, "microwave." Jake winked. "But who knows. If you hang around me for too long, it might rub off." Using the spatula, he turned one of the sandwiches over, still shaking his head. "One can only hope."

Her laughter hit his ears. The soft sound traveled all the way to his gut, where it nestled in his groin.

"Don't count on it." When he quirked an inquiring brow, ignoring the heat her actions generated, she laughed harder. "Maggie calls me a lost cause. Monica says I was dropped on the doorstep." She sighed. "Seems my mom and sister got all the cooking genes in the family."

"And what genes did you get?" Hell, he knew he shouldn't flirt, but it was hard not to when she looked so damned cute, spouting off about how proud she was of her lack of cooking talent. He couldn't care less about cooking because he knew exactly where Michelle's talents lay.

Don't even go there, Collier.

He exhaled on a long sigh and returned to grilling the ham and cheese sandwiches.

"Since you're cooking, I'll set the table." Her straight back as she opened the silverware drawer, along with her business-like tone, meant she'd picked up and was going along with his change of direction.

Thank God. Wouldn't do to repeat the past. Even if they could ever recapture what they'd once shared, he had to remember one fact. A child complicated things. Between them, they had two. He needed to be friends more than he needed sex.

For the second time that day, they sat at the table to eat. As the dog repositioned himself next to Michelle's chair, Jake wondered about his son. What did he look like? Blond and fair, favoring Michelle, or was there any resemblance to him? What was his name? Did he like sports? How would he feel about meeting a half-sister? A father?

Michelle's voice suddenly cut into Jake's thoughts. "I feel like I've been prying into her life." When his gaze narrowed in confusion, she held up Kiera's journal, and it dawned on him what she was talking about.

He grunted a reply. "I doubt Kiera would have told you where to find the journal, if she hadn't wanted you to pry."

"Yeah, I guess." Another sad smile formed. "Maybe she knew I'd understand."

"Do you?" He'd often tried to understand Kiera's motives.

Fell short, then stopped trying altogether.

"Yes. I think so. After reading her thoughts, I've decided money, along with its privileges, can be just as big a detriment as being poor."

Jake couldn't argue that point. "She was a complex woman who didn't deserve to die so early."

"I'm curious." Michelle lowered the journal. "About your relationship with Kiera. In the end, I mean."

Her statement caught him off guard and all he could do was stare at her, too dumbfounded to say anything coherent. He finished chewing the bite of sandwich and swallowed. What *had* Kiera written? Had she understood his motives? She'd known how he felt about Emily and his need to protect her. But had his ex guessed at the other?

"That is, if you don't mind my nosiness." Michelle tucked a strand of hair behind her ear, her face reddening slightly.

Jake smiled as she suddenly focused too intently on her sandwich. The blonde beauty never could hide her emotions. It had been something he'd found so attractive about her. "Hell, at this point, be as nosy as you want. I have nothing to hide any longer," he said, realizing the minute the words were out, he meant them. Why hide? Hiding hadn't done a damn bit of good. If he brought the past out in the open where he could see it, he might figure out where he went wrong, so he could move beyond and not repeat the same mistakes. "Ask away. I'll try to be honest."

Michelle eyed him intently. "Kiera mentioned that after Emily was born, she lost you. I'm trying to understand. What happened? You'd told me you loved her."

He thought about the question for a long moment. The answer wasn't any less complex than those involved, the woman asking about the woman he'd married, or their respective relationships. "Yeah, as sick as it was, I did." He couldn't lie. "I'd always loved her, you know? Loved her wildness, loved her brashness. Loved sex with her. But by the end, I didn't love her enough." Not like he'd loved Michelle. But Jake didn't voice his feelings, saying instead, "I shouldn't have married Kiera." Michelle didn't need to know the total truth of how he'd felt or the depths to which he'd sunk.

Michelle's eyebrows drew together. His revelation clearly stumped her.

"It's a long, sordid story I may let slip over drinks some night, when I'm too wasted to care what you think of me," Jake interjected, when she was about to ask a question he had a hunch he didn't want to answer. Honesty had its limits. He'd taken the easy way out, taking the flash and the dollar signs, something to regret forever. Jake thought he'd had it all. Money, sex, recognition, and the exalted life that came with the Delaney name. What a joke, especially after he and Kiera had created Emily and his nightmare had really started.

Jake's cell phone rang. The timely diversion saved him from having to get any more personal. He yanked the phone out of his pocket, noting Linda's ID. "Excuse me. I need to take this." He pushed away from the table, stood, and walked to the wall of windows. Studying the water, he answered, "Yeah, Linda? Whatcha got?"

For a minute there, he'd been so close to saying something stupid.

"I just got word," she said. "The lab lifted a thumbprint from one of the spent shells. I have a name."

"So soon?"

"We got lucky. The guy's in the system, has been since he was a kid."

Jake pulled his notebook out of his pocket, along with a pen. "Okay, shoot."

She rattled off the name and address. "According to the information I have, he's twenty-seven. This last known address was fifteen years ago."

"I know the address." He closed the notebook and put it away. "Are you sure?"

Her annoyed huff shot straight through his ear. "I can't believe you just asked me that."

He sighed and looked out at the water. "I'm sorry. I just wasn't expecting that name."

"You know him?"

William Hamilton Durbin. "Yeah." Jake knew the name. He raked a hand through his hair, resting it on the back of his neck, rubbing. "Thanks for the work. I owe you."

She laughed. "Call us even."

He disconnected and noticed Michelle's interest. He ignored her questioning look, clicked to voice mail, and listened to Rich's heads-up about the picture he'd e-mailed. He sat back down to finish the half-eaten sandwich, thinking about Linda's revelation. Why would Billy be shooting at Michelle in the middle of the night? This case was turning more bizarre by the minute, and the lady across from him was right smack in the line of fire. Why?

The second Jake swallowed his last bite, he rose. "I'll be in my office and then I'll be heading out for a couple more hours." He would log on and retrieve the picture before calling Rich. "Will you be okay?"

Michelle patted the mutt's head. "Don't worry, the dog and I will be fine."

Of course, the dog would be fine. He would have her for company. Jake pushed the thought away. "Lucky dog," he murmured, picking up his plate. He wouldn't stoop to the level of being jealous of a damn dog. But as more of her soft voice filtered past his brain, he realized he was green with envy, especially when his gaze landed on her hand, stroking the length of the dog's now white fur.

"We'll have a fine time, won't we, Precious?" she cooed.

Jake spared the mutt a quick glance. Maybe he wasn't so lucky. No male dog with any dignity wanted to be called Precious. "Remember. Don't leave the house. I'll grab some dog food for *Precious* on my way back, as well as food for dinner," he said a little louder over his shoulder, chuckling on his way to the kitchen, glad to have something to laugh at when nothing seemed funny.

Michelle stood. "While you're busy, I'll clean up, then finish with the journal."

"Great." He put his plate in the sink, then halted in the kitchen doorway. "If you need anything, I'll be in my office. At least for a bit." He focused on exiting the room quickly, otherwise, he'd lose his resolve.

"Geez, Collier. Get a grip," he muttered, flipping on the light before plopping into the leather chair and reaching for his laptop. Wireless wasn't an option on this part of the lake yet, so he had to work the old-fashioned, slow way. With a phone line.

He plugged the jack into the side of the machine. He could just imagine the comments he'd get if anyone in his division saw him now. His co-workers already teased him about residing in the dark ages, going so far as to call both Rich and him dinosaurs who wouldn't embrace technology. In his mind, the term dark ages was relative to the end user. Since he'd rather write stuff in a notebook than in some little gadget that needed batteries to work, he ignored all teasing.

He fidgeted, tapping a beat to the tune in his head with his fingers, anything to keep his mind off the woman in the other room as the machine booted up.

The second he could, Jake clicked his e-mail. This home office was definitely high-speed challenged, he thought, wishing it would hurry.

Sighing, he waited longer.

He embraced technology. He used high speed, something that hadn't been available anywhere ten years ago. A cell phone and high speed were about as much technology as he was willing to learn about. But not for the reasons his co-workers cited. He texted. But rarely. Not when drug dealers tended to note any overt use of technology, trust being a huge issue. It was a matter of survival when in the heat of the job. Too much information was stored in those gadgets and deleting what was stored could be a total pain. If it wasn't on hand, it couldn't be compromised and used against you.

It took another two minutes for the picture to load. When it did, he was floored to recognize the individual Rich captured on his cell.

The doctor in the ER.

He googled the medical center, bringing up its list of doctors. Since this website was used to generate business, it had photos as well as accreditations next to the doctors' names. Dr. Thomas wasn't even a close match, appearing thirty years older, with little hair—and gray—not a full head of black like the man in the picture Rich had e-mailed.

So, what was this Jerry Mathers doing at the hospital?

He grabbed his cell, then hit Rich's preset number.

"What do you make of it?" Jake asked his partner, after relaying the information and listening to Rich fill him in on what

Jarvis and Malone had discovered about Mathers. "He was in the ER right before Kiera died. Too much of a coincidence, if you ask me."

"You think he might have killed her?" Though Rich asked it as a question, it sounded more like a statement of fact.

Jake grunted. "Given the circumstances, it fits. One minute she's hanging on, the next she's dead."

"Yeah."

Jake sighed, not wanting to add the rest. "Billy's prints were on the shell casings I found last night."

"Hmm. More interesting." Rich hesitated. "Seems little bro isn't as lily white as big bro says he is."

"Billy's elevator doesn't go to the top floor. He definitely doesn't have the brains to do this on his own. He's being led."

"And you think big bro is the leader?"

Jake leaned back in his chair. "Definitely a high probability. If not, he knows who is. I'd stake my badge on it." Suddenly Jake remembered the older lady in the waiting room and he sat up straighter. "This guy Mathers spoke to a woman in the ER that day Kiera died." He thought for a moment. "Gardiner. That was it. Her son's name was Wayne Gardiner. Can you get me a phone number or an address? I'd like to talk to her."

"You think she might have seen something?"

"Possible."

"Hold on a minute and I'll give it to Jarvis." Rich broke off and Jake heard him talking in the background before coming back on the line. "He's looking right now. I've got to tell you, my gut's agreeing with yours on this."

Jake didn't want to believe it, but usually their instincts were spot on, and precisely what made them such a good team. "Bobby, Ivy, and Mathers. When you add in Joe's threats, we have the Durbin brothers, and it gets crazier." He remained silent, thinking. "Kiera must've stumbled onto their operation. That's why they killed her. To shut her up."

"That fits. The property on the map Ivy drove to backs up to the property the cave sits on. Road in is several miles away, but as the crow flies it's not far. On foot, it's less than half a mile."

"I plan on taking a look inside the cave. I meant to do it

yesterday, but got sidetracked with Michelle's accident."

"Good idea. And I've got another one. Since Joe Durbin's so protective of little bro, maybe we should shake his tree and have NPD take little bro in for questioning, see what shakes out." Silence followed a brief moment before he added, "In fact, the more I think about it, the more I like it." Jake could only imagine Rich's smile. "A drive to Nashville with a police escort ought to do the trick."

Jake sobered. "How long do you think it will take?"

"Few hours. Depends on how busy they are or how important they think Billy is to their investigation. Wait a minute. Jarvis has something." Rich stopped talking. "Ah, shit. Looks like your witness, Mrs. Muriel Gardiner, is dead. Victim of a rollover accident not ten hours after Kiera's death. Seems these people are awfully efficient at disposing of witnesses in what could be termed accidents."

The blood in Jake's veins ran cold. "Not good."

"No," Rich stated firmly. "If they've earmarked Michelle Matthews, you'd better watch her."

"She's safe for now." No one knew she was staying with him at his lake house, which bought him a little time to investigate the cave. Jake said his good-byes, closed down his laptop, and started for the kitchen. He rounded the hallway and spotted Michelle washing dishes.

She glanced up when he halted in the doorway.

He offered a smile that didn't reach his eyes. "Like I said earlier, I've got to go out." His smile faded to a frown. "Stay inside."

Michelle scrunched up her nose and shook her head. "It's so nice, I was planning on reading on the deck."

He resisted the urge to argue. "Okay, but stay on the deck. No wandering away."

He heaved a relieved sigh when she nodded and said, "Sure," seeming to sense from the severity in his tone she needed to follow the request. He turned toward the front door and had to mentally urge himself forward.

"I shouldn't be gone long." He didn't want to leave her alone. "I'll pick up some dog food for *Precious*."

Jake dragged himself into his Durango, started the engine,

and pushed the gas pedal hard, the entire time resisting the temptation to go back inside.

Chapter 16

Now alone, Shelly glanced at Precious and smiled, remembering Jake's definite sneer at her chosen name. It didn't matter that he might have a point. She rubbed behind the dog's soft white ears. Though he was precious to her in the form of instant companionship, the name wasn't exactly manly.

"You males have to stick together, don't you, boy?" She eyed him thoughtfully. His ears perked up. "Well then, I guess I'll have to think of another name." What would Jake name him? She wondered. He'd called him Fido. But she shook her head, scrunching her nose. His tail thumped, drawing another smile. "You're no Fido," she murmured. The tail thumped louder.

"Since you're my buddy, how about I call you that," she cooed, stroking his back, which was silky smooth now that he'd had a bath.

Buddy peered up at her, his brown eyes worshipful, telling her she could call him ugly and he'd still wag his tail like crazy.

She laughed. "Then Buddy, it is."

Shelly glanced at the journal and sighed. It was time to finish, no matter that she now dreaded the chore. "Come on, Buddy. Keep me company while I read."

The second she shifted out of the chair, the dog trotted right beside her, his tail moving faster, if that were possible. He happily followed her as she headed for the deck's double doors.

Buddy plopped by her side when she slipped into the comfortable lounge chair. The afternoon heat felt good against her skin after being in the air-conditioned house for so long.

Shelly opened the journal to the spot she'd left off, wondering about Kiera and Jake's relationship.

"What about us?" Shelly didn't want to think about the

SANDY LOYD

questions she'd asked Jake all those years ago.

"There *is* no us. What happened was a mistake." His voice, always at the forefront of her thoughts, wouldn't be silenced. Nor could she forget how he'd looked her in the eye while speaking, breaking her heart in the process.

The most wonderful night of her life had been a total mistake in his view. He'd never veered from his intention of marrying Kiera. So, what went wrong when Kiera had had exactly what Shelly had coveted?

"Don't think about it," she said under her breath, turning to the book as a tear slid down the side of her face. She brushed away the moisture and clenched a fist. Even after six years, she still did not understand.

Worse, she hated herself for wishing for a different outcome, that Jake had picked her instead of Kiera. She'd never understand how he could go back to Kiera after all they'd shared that night. How could something so damn good have been a mistake?

"Just face facts and move on," she whispered, stroking Buddy. The dog seemed to sense her misery. He put his head in her lap, nudging her hand with his nose, and whimpered as only a dog could to get his point across.

She didn't want second place in his heart any more now than then. In fact, now would be worse. Not just because she'd be competing with a dead woman, but also because that dead woman had been her friend at one time and had deserved better treatment.

"Don't worry, Buddy. I have Mikey. He'll like you." The thought elicited a wide smile. Her conversation with her son earlier had been short. But enough. Mikey had made her feel wanted, saying too many times in their five minutes how much he missed her.

She exhaled heavily and started reading.

The next two pages detailed nothing new, until the journal's focus shifted to Kiera's dealings with Shelly, and the words suddenly became personal.

Shelly had it all; only she was too wrapped up in being poor and what she materially lacked to realize it.

The sentence brought her up short. Was that how Kiera had viewed her?

Shelly didn't want to think about how accurately the statement described her. Why subject herself to this torture? She should just leave. Take a bus ride to Atlanta and let Maggie and Monica come back for her car.

But then you're taking the coward's way out. Again! The thought stopped her.

Kiera was being totally honest, having homed in on one of Shelly's weaknesses and in a heartbeat, clarity struck. She needed to be just as honest. With this in mind, she went back to the words, praying no one else who knew her had picked up on Kiera's intuition.

> I ruthlessly played on her insecurities. It was the only way I could think of to stop the worst from happening. But the worst happened anyway. I lost the two people I loved the most, my best friend and the love of my life, both from the same act of futility, ironically enough.
>
> I regret so much from those days. My counselor says I'm not being real. That in order to heal, I have to be strong enough to face all that I did, bring every bit of the ugliness of my actions out in the open and face it, so I can stay strong enough to resist the lure of drugs in the future. But she doesn't understand how much I hurt. How cruel I was when I lashed out. Or how desperate. As I write this, I'm filled with sorrow and remorse. I was such a spoiled bitch. I wish I could attribute my actions to my addiction. But I can't. And no matter how much I hate the memories, they are mine. If I don't own up to them...face them, I might as well go back to using, because any addiction is a vicious cycle that never stops until overcoming the why's. Unless death intervenes.
>
> In my case, I wonder if death wouldn't be easier.

Start with one regret and go from there. That's what my counselor says. Easier said than done, I shouted to her on our last visit.

I then laughed because once I started thinking, I realized there is too much shit to narrow it down to one regret with Shelly.

One act I'll regret to my dying day, and not just because it backfired. I thought if I got pregnant, I could keep Jake to myself. Yet, by the time I learned I was pregnant, he was already gone.

True karma, as my counselor would say, but doesn't, because she's trying to help.

I squandered both love and friendship for all those years, only to find when I needed them most, they were gone.

Jake thought I didn't want to go into rehab because I wouldn't grow up. I'm sure there is truth in there, somewhere, but I didn't want to leave him alone with Shelly. I saw the way he'd look at her. In all the time I'd known him, he never looked at me like he did her.

I used to accuse Shelly of coveting Jake, but what I left out and didn't dare tell her? By that summer, Jake coveted Shelly. I knew it was only a matter of time before he dumped me to pursue her. I also knew if I got pregnant, I might have a fighting chance, something to hold on to him with. So, before I left for rehab, I exchanged his condoms with defective ones I'd gotten over the Internet, praying I'd get pregnant and that a child would hold him. I felt I had no choice.

Of course, I certainly never expected Jake to sleep with my best friend while I was away. Who knew Shelly had the guts? And more importantly, what had happened to the Jake I'd come to depend on? More karmic justice? That's my take, because in the end, the laugh was on me. I got what I deserved, but it still hurt. More than I ever thought possible. I made sure Jake and Shelly suffered. I blamed her. I had to blame someone. And I hated her for stealing Jake. Except, looking back, I know it wasn't theft. I handed him over on the silver platter of my stupidity. My arrogant belief I could do whatever I wanted and have whatever I wanted just because I wanted it. My selfishness. My arrogance. My drug habit. All of those things combined helped push Jake away.

Yet, that wasn't the real reason I lost him. It took me years to understand I never had him. Not really. Not like Shelly.

I deliberately ruined whatever might have been between them because I couldn't handle that truth. I cried to my parents and they rushed to help as they always did, cleaning up my messes.

I look in the mirror now and know I told the person I loved like a sister to leave and not look back. Told her he didn't love her. Told her she wasn't good enough. Even told her to abort her child, giving her the advice, so Jake wouldn't know and if he ever did learn of it, he'd hate her. Hell, I'd have done anything to get rid of her and secure my chances.

In hindsight, I realize how low I'd stooped. My lowest hour. And in the end, we all lost.

How does one atone for such horrendous cruelty?

I called Shelly, begging her to come home, knowing she's a bigger person than I ever was. I have one chance to bring Shelly and Jake together. If I do this one unselfish act, I will be able to forgive myself. Though I am fully prepared for the worst, I pray that once Jake and Shelly discover the extent of my selfishness, they will still have it in their hearts to forgive me. I'm writing it here in order to practice seeing the truth, grasping it completely in my mind, so there will be no misunderstanding. Shelly and Jake belong together.

I dread with all my heart the day I will have to speak out to them both and admit my sins, knowing that will be the day I'll risk losing them both forever.

Thank God, those were Kiera's last words. Shelly didn't think she'd be able to take any more of Kiera's honesty.

She wiped away tears.

Jake loved her? All those years ago, Kiera had been threatened by her? Shelly had a hard time believing it, but obviously, Kiera had believed it.

She also understood Kiera's reasoning because she understood Kiera, but one truth hurt more than the others.

Shelly had it all; only she was too wrapped up in being poor and what she materially lacked to realize it.

It appeared Kiera had understood Shelly just as thoroughly.

Chapter 17

"Are you fuckin' crazy?"

"Will you calm down," he soothed in a low voice, though inside he seethed. Their venture was going from bad to worse.

"Don't tell me to calm down," Bobby yelled into the phone. "You're sitting in Bowling Green, far away from everything and I'm the one they'll be pointing a finger at."

The man's shrill, penetrating tone did not help his rising annoyance any.

"He threatened me."

He grunted. "Empty threats and you know it. He won't do anything because it could harm his brother. It's our insurance policy. You know that."

"What if you're wrong and he talks? This has gotten out of control."

"You're not being rational." He inhaled deeply, reaching for patience. "He won't say a word."

"I don't like it."

His grip on the phone tightened. "You don't have to like it," he ground out. "You'll shut up and do as instructed. Understand?"

"What about Collier?" Bobby shot back. "He isn't Joe. There's no controlling him. He knows something."

He sighed, knowing he had a point, but unwilling to risk upsetting him further. "He doesn't know shit."

"Then why was he by the plant earlier, asking me questions?" His voice held accusation.

"He's fishing. Just like we knew he would, and you should've easily answered any and all questions."

"What if you're wrong? What if he's pieced a few other

details together?"

"Panicking isn't the answer." More blood rushed to his head as his concern spiked. "If you had taken care of Matthews like you were supposed to, we wouldn't be in this mess." He clenched his jaw, feeling their entire organization unraveling at the seams. "I thought you knew how to fire a goddamned rifle. A girl could do better."

"After Collier came out of nowhere and pushed her out of the way, I couldn't get a clean shot. Did you want me to kill him too?"

Might not have been a bad idea, except for one thing. Killing Jake Collier would stir up the law enforcement hive already too active in the area. If one of their own died, they wouldn't stop looking no matter how long it took. "How did he find out about Billy in the first place? How did he know to goad Joe with that little detail?"

"I didn't have time to grab the shell casings, and Billy lost his hat when we were running."

"That's sloppy and shit like that will kill us," he sneered. "We can't be sloppy. Paying attention to details has always been our strength." It was Bobby's mistake that brought in more scrutiny in the first place for the four of them and here he was complaining. "You only have yourself to blame. If you'd have done your job like you were supposed to…" Not just last night but with the women, but he didn't say the thought out loud. "Collier would've been too busy taking care of her to pursue you through the woods. We would've had the shells to use as blackmail for Billy. Then we wouldn't be in this mess."

There was dead silence on the line until Bobby finally said, "I'm disappearing."

He snorted in disbelief. "I wouldn't advise it. Running like a scared rabbit will only draw more attention to yourself."

"You think I should stick around and get nailed?" His short laugh shot through the line, but it held no humor. "I'm not stupid."

"You have a job to finish. You need to complete that job."

"Easy for you to say when they don't know about you."

"After tonight it won't matter. Then you can go to hell for all I care." He pressed the cell phone's End button, then punched up Ivy's number.

They would have to deal with Bobby Winters. Sooner rather than later.

~

Jake hit the main highway, driving toward town and the cave. He eventually parked, having pulled far enough into the woods so his Durango couldn't be seen from the road. This was the first chance he had to check out the cave and figure out where the white pipe came from.

He exited the vehicle and began the hike to the entrance, staying cautious as he walked.

Wouldn't do to let Baker's deputies spot him. For one thing, Doug Larson was friends with Joe.

He spied Larson first and slipped farther into the brush without alerting him to his presence. Seconds later, he entered the dark cavern, a place he hadn't stepped into since that last summer when he and Michelle had run for the cover of the cave because of a sudden downpour.

He switched on his flashlight.

Memories slammed into him, hitting him harder the deeper he walked.

Damn! Why did the mental pictures plague him at every corner?

Didn't matter that the memory filling Jake was created before he'd gotten in over his head with Michelle, but their time in the cave did nothing to stop the quicksand of her allure from sucking him in more.

He'd never forgotten their conversation, spoken right on the rock he just passed, especially since what he'd shared made him realize how much he hated his life at that time, hated working for Ed Delaney, hated who he'd become.

The vivid moment in time an impetus for finally breaking away once he'd discovered his grave error in marrying Kiera. To this day, his revelations to Michelle still echoed in his mind.

"Sometimes I feel as if I'm wasting my life," he'd said.

"Why?" she'd asked.

Good question, he'd thought, as he'd lit a lantern they'd kept hidden when they visited. Nothing had seemed right any longer.

As if it was yesterday, he still remembered his answer…could still see her smiling face…

~

"I never thought I'd be some pencil pusher working at a cabinet factory." Jake exhaled a short snort. "I know that sounds stupid. I mean, it's a good job and all. But…"

Michelle sat on the rock in the cave next to him, her attention riveted to him, the depths of her ocean-blue eyes gleaming in the shadows. "But what?"

"Nothing." Ed Delaney had always kidded him about being the son he never had. Ed had definitely picked him for his successor. Jake just didn't know if that's what he wanted, but until he figured it out, it was a job. "I shouldn't be knocking a good job."

She touched his arm as she spoke. "It doesn't sound like nothing."

He shrugged, remaining silent, letting the heat of her fingers warm his insides.

"If you could do anything, what would your dream job be?"

Her question, spoken with such sincerity, required an honest answer. "You promise you won't laugh?"

Michelle laughed, then sobered. "That was…" She put her palms up, as if to say she didn't know what it was.

Jake fastened his gaze on her engaging smile. Couldn't look away as she added, "Just know it wasn't directed at your dreams. I never laugh at dreams. Not when I have a few of my own."

He nodded, considering his next words. "Last year at school I went to a federal job fair. You know, CIA, FBI, DEA, all those initials." The laugh rolling out of his chest was only halfhearted. "One thing about the government, they use every letter in the alphabet."

He'd never told anyone of his interest in law enforcement. Not Kiera, not his mom and dad, and certainly not Ed Delaney. They'd never understand his reasons, but somehow he knew Michelle would, so he admitted, "I've even given a lot of thought to becoming a drug agent. You know. Because of Kiera—and some of the other guys who got messed up with the shit."

Hell, he'd never felt the urge to indulge, but he'd sat by and watched friends get fucked up, being too young and stupid to stop them. By the time he'd grown enough balls to speak up, the damage had been done. Just like with Kiera. "I pray detox works for her."

"So do I." Her hand gripped his arm. "But no one can do it for her. Kiera has to really want it too."

"Yeah. I know." That didn't ease his guilt any.

When Jake had learned of Kiera's experimenting, he'd gone to his dad and asked outright about amphetamines. His dad had told him what he'd known, thinking it the same speed or similar to what his truck-driving employees from the factory had used back in the 70s and early 80s. But this drug, though similar, was more deadly and more addictive, Jake had learned too late. His further research revealed how very little it took to hook a kid, especially a wild kid like Kiera. Since he hadn't been there to watch over her, he'd felt totally responsible and had no choice but to help her.

More than anything, he wanted to help other kids too, which might ease more of his guilt.

He took a deep breath, meeting Michelle's earnest gaze. "Kids are the target market. I figure it's by design, when the shit is so readily available." He shrugged. "Get 'em young, you have a customer for life. Like the tobacco companies."

~

A bat flew out of the shadows, pulling him out of the memory. Jake flashed the light around, wondering why he had the feeling something was going on in this cave when everything appeared unchanged. He continued walking past stalactites and stalagmites, flashing his light along the rock-encrusted ceiling and walls, unsure of what he was searching for, but knowing he'd know it if and when he saw it.

His mind wandered back to his reasons for becoming a DEA agent. Doing his job well had given him some solace for his guilty soul. Unfortunately, he'd never be able to undo what happened to Kiera.

In his opinion, addiction was a slow and exceedingly heartbreaking method of suicide. For all involved, especially loved ones like him and the Delaneys who had to watch, helpless to do anything to stop the self-destructive process.

No one should have to face the temptation at such a young age. Drugs just seemed to infiltrate the schools earlier these days, when kids are too stupid and immature to know the dangers. The war was never ending, but Jake still had to fight the battle or die trying.

After thirty minutes of slowly investigating the passages, working to keep the memories from overwhelming him, he finally found something different. Footprints in the damp earth led him deeper into an offshoot of the cavern that few knew about. Eventually the footprints ended. At this point the ground was made of rocky slabs of limestone that seemed worn with use. A closer check revealed what looked to be the remains of a dismantled lab. Jake flashed the light near the rear of the cavern and saw the white pipe lying on the ground, most likely used for ventilation. He made a mental note to tell Baker his boys had missed something in their earlier inspection.

Jake worked his way back the way he'd come and then entered another vein of the cave. It wasn't long before he spied wooden steps leading up. Cautiously, he followed them and came to some kind of makeshift entrance. He pushed at the trap door. It gave easily and the bright light that hit him was blinding. Squinting, he poked his head out.

A house stood in the distance, not fifty yards ahead through a clearing.

Everything looked quiet.

The place had to be where the women were held, but he couldn't get closer to check it out with so little cover.

According to Rich, Jarvis and Malone had planned to stake it out later tonight.

His cell phone buzzed as he lowered himself into the cave. He pushed back out for more light and better reception. Tom Baker's ID flashed on the screen.

Jake punched the On button. "Yeah?"

"What the hell did you do?"

He stiffened, unprepared for the anger in Baker's voice. "What do you mean?"

"NPD picked up Billy for questioning. Joe's gone on a

rampage over at the Delaney factory, swearing to kill Bobby Winters, and is now holding him at gunpoint. So, I need to know what you said to rile him and why NPD is involved."

Jake swore under his breath that Rich's plan had shaken out such an extreme reaction. "I just showed him a baseball cap. Thought it might be Billy's."

"That doesn't explain why Nashville is questioning him."

Jake swallowed hard, not wanting to admit he'd gone behind the sheriff's back. He sighed. "I took a couple of shell casings I found to NPD for prints and told them how I happened to come by them."

"And you didn't think to enlighten me?"

"No. Not when you were so sure it was deer hunters doing the shooting, and it seemed as if Michelle Matthews was the target." Jake didn't bring up what he'd found in the cave. Someone in Tom's office wasn't doing his job. Doug Larson got Jake's vote, since he and Bobby were friends in high school, but now was not the time to address it.

"Matthews? She's part of this? Another fact you failed to let me in on. What the fuck are you doing? Have you forgotten we're working together? This is my town, Collier, and I have the goddamned right to know what you're goddamn doing."

"I'm well aware of how this town is about Billy Durbin. Would you have done anything if I'd have told you Billy was out in the woods shooting at innocent bystanders?"

"Shit," the sheriff exclaimed in a disgusted grunt. "Well, it's a moot point now because by not telling me, Joe's gone ape-shit and I've got a hostage situation." Another snort shot through the phone. "You know how Joe is about Billy. He's not listening to reason and your actions lit his short fuse. I gotta go. You'd better pray I can snuff it out. Otherwise, I plan on making your life miserable."

"I'll be there as soon as I can."

The loud click in his ear told Jake he'd hung up.

Jake hefted himself out of the cave, taking the risk of being seen this far from the house, as it'd be much faster to travel aboveground.

He hurried in the direction he determined from the angle of the sun to be where his car was parked.

After finding his SUV, he gunned the motor and shot off down the highway. Holding the speedometer at seventy on the narrow country road designed for no higher than fifty-five was no easy feat. Jake didn't let off the gas, sensing if he didn't get there soon, he might be too late.

He and Rich needed Joe Durbin alive.

Minutes later, he skidded into the factory parking lot. It hadn't taken five more to learn Baker had pegged the situation correctly. Durbin held Bobby at gunpoint, threatening him with his life, because, as he put it, he'd had no business bringing his brother into his mess.

"Joe," Jake yelled. "Killing Winters won't do Billy any good."

"You don't understand."

"Yeah, I do. Let's talk about it."

"No. It's too late for talking. They've screwed with him and with me for the last time. I'm tired of the bullshit. It stops here and now. Billy's innocent. He'd never hurt a fly and these bastards are setting him up." Joe turned to Winters, who looked like he was ready to wet his pants, and snarled, "I could kill you for that alone. And die a happy man, knowing I took out vermin with me."

He aimed his gun but Tom Baker, who Jake saw out of the corner of his eye, shouted, "Collier's right, Joe. I don't know what the hell you think to accomplish."

"What I should've done years ago," Joe shot back.

"Come on," Baker urged. "Going off half-cocked won't solve anything." He hesitated. "Talking is easier than killing or dying." When his words didn't stop Durbin, the sheriff nodded to a sharpshooter on the roof of the building across the street. The sharpshooter returned the nod. "Put the gun down, Joe," Baker yelled. "I don't want anyone killed. Especially you."

"You'll have to do better than that, Tom. This ends here. Right now." He fired, hitting Winters at the same time the sharpshooter got off a shot.

Unfortunately for Jake, both bullet wounds looked fatal.

Chapter 18

Jake climbed inside his car after doing a lot of fast-talking about why he'd withheld vital information. He wasn't sure if Tom bought his excuses or not, but the sheriff let him go because Jake finally admitted to needing to safeguard Michelle Matthews and why.

Of course, he'd had to listen to a barrage of accusations about not keeping the sheriff informed.

Tom's warning shot about never doing it again rolled off him. Jake didn't work for the asshole. Besides, Tom should have known of, or at the very least suspected, Bobby and the Durbins's roles in this. He should have been able to foresee the tragedy and head it off. After all, this *was* Tom's town.

Jake sighed, shaking his head. He'd have to warn Rich about Larson and have the state police deal with his involvement.

Still, he had to give Tom credit. The sheriff trusted his deputies. If Joe Durbin knew what was going on, and Doug Larson was in on it, along with Bobby and Ivy, the three most likely used Billy to keep Joe in line.

Jake understood the blind spot. No one wanted to point the finger at another officer without proof, nor did anyone want to admit to a cop being dirty. Cops barely made enough to get by and money was a potent lure. Thankfully, the majority of those on the force didn't sign up for the job to get rich.

Jake steered the Durango toward the lake house, driving the narrow, tree-shaded road too fast. About a half mile away, he parked off the road, feeling compelled to remain cautious. He jerked the door open, jumped out of the SUV, and started running.

At the house, he rushed up the steps two at a time, not stopping until he was through the front door. He checked first the living room and then her bedroom before spotting Michelle on the deck, in the same lounge chair he'd seen her earlier. Fast asleep.

Half a moment later, he stood over her, silently observing.

In sleep, she appeared so peaceful, almost angelic. A true golden girl, haloed with dark-blonde hair and blessed with a beautiful pale complexion, marred only by a few freckles. They dotted her nose and were only noticeable from up close. His gaze traveled the length of her long, willowy body. Focusing on Michelle's chest, now rising and lowering with slumberous breathing, he clenched a fist and looked away.

He took a deep breath and relaxed into the chair's cushion, unable to quell his rising sense of dread over the dead bodies that kept piling up. Jake wished he could gaze out at the scenery forever and forget that he hadn't stopped Durbin from overreacting. His and Rich's plan had exploded in their faces, netting them no new information other than they'd been on the right path.

Jake stared out at the blue lake, surrounded with a sea of green trees. The yellow ball of the sun shone bright in a cloudless sky, adding to the crisp beauty. The air seemed cooler today, a little on the dry side for this time of year.

Though he despised his house, he loved the lake and the area. The peaceful and serene environment never failed to produce a sense of relaxation. Something he lacked in his life, he suddenly realized. Any time that wasn't connected to work was spent with Emily, and kept him from taking the time to enjoy nature.

Jake remembered long, lazy summers spent swimming, boating, and just plain enjoying what this part of Kentucky offered. Maybe that's why he couldn't bring himself to sell it. The lake was a perfect place to bring a kid. Or kids, if Michelle ever shared their son. "One could only hope," he muttered, glancing back at her. Then he saw the open journal on the table between them.

His curiosity stirred.

He picked up the book and his eyes were drawn to a sentence that caught his interest.

Jake rested his legs on a footstool and leaned back into the cushions, too engrossed to do anything else but read.

He finished and set the journal back on the table, trying to grasp the magnitude of what Kiera's last words meant.

His mind spun, working to keep the acid of knowledge busily eating a hole in his gut from swallowing his optimism whole.

How could she?

He didn't want to believe Kiera could do such a thing, but the proof was in the results. Two pregnancies when he'd always been more than careful about protection, which now made some kind of mad sense.

Such a goddamned waste of time and heartache. He gazed out at the water, seeing nothing, and wondered if his life would ever be the same again.

He felt a cold sensation and glanced down. The dog had repositioned himself next to his chair. The mutt stuck his head on Jake's lap, nudging his hand.

"Hey, Precious." He spoke softly and stroked. "How're you?"

Minutes later, Jake was still absently stroking the dog when Michelle's hand moved to her chest, pulling his gaze.

His attention roamed higher to rest on her face.

Her eyes opened. Slowly, she threw off all dreamy thoughts. Her expression changed, as the reality of him sitting next to her and staring at her, hit.

"You're back." She stretched. Her half-lidded eyes emanated warmth and her smile beckoned.

The same yearning that sucked him in six years ago pulled at him now, squeezing his insides tightly. Damn, he felt like he'd gone back in time, as a rush of longing swamped him and he smiled.

Giving in to temptation, he leaned toward her and grazed those sleep-swollen lips that begged him to kiss her.

When mouths fully connected, a sense of coming home filled him.

For two days he'd been dying to taste her, wondering if

kissing her would be as good as he remembered. Reality was better. For someone who'd spent too long in hell, he felt as if the gates of paradise had opened, along with her mouth, drawing him in further.

A wet nose worked to separate them, shattering the spell and yanking him back to reality. He broke their connection and leaned back, sighing. "Seems Precious doesn't like to be usurped in your affections."

"Not Precious," she said, laughing. "Buddy."

The soft sound of her laughter entered his brain and zinged through his system at the speed of light.

He inhaled deeply, stilling the urge to sink into her warmth. This was not the time, nor the place. He cleared his throat as Buddy started jumping, prancing, and barking. "Well, *Buddy* may have to go do his business."

"I'll take him."

They rose together.

"I'll go with you." He wasn't about to let her out of his sight. Not now. Maybe not ever.

Michelle bent to grab her cell phone and put it in her pocket, then picked up the journal and closed it. Hugging the book, she breezed down the steps, heading for the lake. Jake got the impression she assumed he hadn't read Kiera's revelations, in fact didn't want him to read them.

He wasn't about to enlighten her and lagged behind, thinking. Jake might never be ready to discuss Kiera's deeds, and at the same time, he understood Michelle's motives. By remaining silent, she was obviously protecting him from more heartache.

Yards ahead and still clutching the journal, she picked up a stick and threw it.

Buddy bounded after it every time with the same enthusiasm as the first throw.

Her laughter floated back, wrapped around his ears, and held him spellbound. He'd never tire of the sound. Lord only knew he had no business wishing to hear more.

Jake sighed, wishing he hadn't kissed her, because now he couldn't get the thought of having her out of his mind. Sucking in deep breaths, he concentrated on the surrounding scenery and ignored the lure of her soft, encouraging voice praising the dog's prowess.

The air was fairly calm, the cicadas' eerie buzz droning in the background.

When they neared the lake, Buddy dove for a stick Michelle tossed a ways out into the water.

She laughed. "I thought he might be a water dog."

The game continued for countless minutes as Buddy swam toward them, stick clamped between his jaws. The dog eventually grew tired and trotted with his stick into the weeds for a rest.

When Jake noticed Michelle plopping down on a big flat boulder, much like the one they'd sat upon at one time, thoughts of their lovemaking flashed. Warmth flooded his veins, seeping south. Jake eased next to her, keeping a safe distance in between, and wondered if she remembered.

He stole a glance at her face. The pink sneaking up her cheeks answered his question. Jake opened and closed his hand, stilling the urge to touch her.

He cleared his throat, drawing her focus.

Their gazes locked.

Though her face darkened, so did the blue depths of her eyes, expressing one thing loud and clear. Michelle wanted him as much as he wanted her. He was in deep shit, because he couldn't control the impulse to lean toward her, unable to stop until his mouth was an inch from hers. She smelled so good. Lemony. The sweet, tangy scent invaded Jake's nostrils, inflamed him further, and warmed his insides.

She didn't hesitate to wrap her arms around his neck, inviting him the rest of the way.

The moment their lips touched, energy sparked through him. He deepened the kiss. No longer capable of resisting the temptation of touching her, his hands roamed of their own volition. Stroking. Feeling. Caressing. Begging.

In the meantime, Michelle was doing some touching of her own, driving his need for her beyond his endurance. He'd surely explode from the craving.

Stop! his brain yelled.

He broke the kiss, breathing heavily, his heart racing.

Closing his eyes, he rested his chin on her head, holding on to sanity by a thread. He had to keep his need in check. He was here to protect her, not seduce her. She was the mother of his son. That thought had him smiling, because it gave him something to hang on to.

Buddy lay some ten feet away, sound asleep. His soft snoring filled the air, blending in with the buzzing insects and chirping birds. A fish jumped out of the lake, the plop resonating along with the water's distortion when it dived back under.

Jake released the angel in his arms and sighed. Nothing was resolved and they needed to talk. Yet he hesitated. If anything, this newfound contentment seemed tenuous. He wasn't about to risk destroying the moment with so much conflict. There was plenty of time for talking. Later.

He closed his eyes and let his mind rest.

A second later, the roar of a car's engine broke through the afternoon's noises…no, not a car…a truck. The motor and sound was too loud to be just a car. Jake sat up and looked around.

Buddy's ears perked up and he growled.

Weekenders wouldn't begin arriving for at least another hour. Remembering Durbin's threat, he stiffened.

Michelle sat up, her body tense. "What's wrong?"

"I don't like the sound of that engine." He stood and nodded toward the house. "I want to see who it is." It could easily be the meter reader, but Jake was taking no chances. "Wait here, okay?"

Michelle nodded. "Sure."

He reached for his gun and hiked up the hill.

At the top, he noted a parked utility truck. Seconds later, Mathers came running from the direction of Jake's house.

Using the trees for cover, Jake hurried back the way he'd come.

~

"Let's go, Michelle," Jake said, sprinting toward her. "We don't have a lot of time."

"What—?" Not expecting his terse tone after such an idyllic

hour, Shelly froze, noting how every muscle in Jake's body seemed on edge.

One glance at his face reaffirmed her earlier thoughts when he'd headed for the house. Something wasn't right.

Air stuck in her throat, preventing her from exhaling. "What is it?" she asked as he halted in front of her.

He listened for a moment, then spoke in the same firm tone. "Throw the stick for Buddy that way to get him moving." Jake pointed to the east.

Shelly glanced behind her. Bushes and trees blocked her view of the house. "Why?" What had he seen?

She hesitated until he practically growled and gripped her elbow, pulling her off her perch. "Do it now. We've got to get out of here."

She grabbed both a stick and Kiera's journal. Shelly threw the stick as far as she could. Thinking it a game, Buddy bounded after it and she followed, almost running with Jake by her side.

Thank God the dog was cooperating.

Jake seemed to grasp she'd never leave him. Buddy had become her friend and Shelly was sure Mikey would love him. She clutched the journal tighter, going deeper into the brush, working to keep up with Jake. He followed along the shoreline of the lake, which was actually a meandering river that had been dammed forty or fifty years ago.

Shelly chanced another glance at him after they'd traveled a handful of minutes, and noticed his drawn gun. She closed her eyes, trying not to think about how big it was or why he might need it.

Seconds later, his grip was back on her elbow and he pulled her to a stop. "Wait. Get down."

She crouched next to him, the urgency in his voice forcing her to quickly obey. Her sides were near to bursting and hurt from running so fast. She sucked in huge gulps of air and worked to catch her breath.

Like an alert cat in the jungle, Jake stood as still as stone and listened.

Scared senseless, Shelly watched his face intently.

Were they going to die?

Her heartbeat pounded in her ears. Even as it slowed, the

steady thump was so loud she was sure it could be heard in the next county.

Suddenly, she had no more time to think. Jake grabbed her hand and tugged her into a standing position.

"Run," he coaxed, his fervent whisper needing no interpretation.

Shelly ran, almost letting him drag her because he was so much faster. The two dodged bushes, using the dense greens and browns for cover. The entire time, she fought to keep up.

Buddy never veered more than a few feet from their side, staying hidden with them, seeming to sense the danger. They'd barely gone the distance of a city block when suddenly the earth erupted in a violent explosion with enough force to send them flying a few feet.

Clarity replaced Shelly's confusion. In the heat of it, Jake had somehow covered her with his body. He lifted off in a sudden move and sprang into an upright position.

Smoke and fire filled the air behind them. It took her a minute to grasp what had gone up in flames. The house where she'd spent the day with Buddy. If Jake hadn't come back when he did, she might now be dead.

"Why is someone trying to kill me?" She realized she'd voiced the question out loud when Jake clenched his jaw and said, "I don't know. But I'm damn sure going to find out."

He stood, offered a hand, and yanked her to her feet. Then he took off running again.

"Stay with me." It wasn't a request. More like the determined command Jake was so good at giving. "We have to get out of the area."

Shelly had no choice but to stay with him, as his grip was lock-tight. At the top of a small hill they'd climbed, she took a hurried peek behind her. From this vantage point, she saw what she couldn't see earlier. The smoldering flames flared bright orange and yellow through the trees.

Again she wondered why someone had gone to the trouble of blowing up Jake's house. It made no sense.

It had to be the journal. No! She discarded the thought immediately. She'd read it thoroughly and there was no mention of anything to warrant the kind of violence now taking place.

People didn't kill over an addict's desire for atonement.

Shelly spared a brief glance at Jake's face. His determined expression, so like her son's, told her he no doubt knew much more than he let on. She was weary of being a target.

The minute they were safe, she vowed as they continued to run, he would tell her what he knew.

Eventually they came to a paved road, but Jake kept to his same rigorous pace.

"Wait." The horrible stitch in Shelly's side wasn't subsiding. "Please slow down."

"No."

She flinched at his brusque tone. Please don't let him regret kissing me, she prayed. She couldn't bear it if he regretted what they'd just shared.

He caught her gaze and sighed. Wiping his face in what could only be a frustrated gesture, he added a bit more softly, "We can't slow down just yet. I want to be clear of this road by at least a mile. Whoever blew up the house probably doesn't realize yet you weren't in there, but if so, then they may be searching for you."

Shelly couldn't stop the tears from seeping out of her eyes. The exertion of holding them in over the last few days was suddenly too difficult. "Why is someone trying to kill me?"

"Shit," Jake murmured under his breath.

His expletive was clearly aimed at her tears, which only drew more. "I'm sorry." He gripped her shoulders and pulled her closer. "We don't have time for discussion." He bent to kiss her, his lips adding to his contrite tone.

He broke their connection. Disappointment was her only thought until he gently nipped her nose, her cheek, her chin, before straightening. Then nodding in the direction they'd been traveling, he swatted her butt. "We have to move. Your life depends on it."

Okay, he didn't hate her. Not after that kiss, and not after glancing into his eyes and seeing total concern. Jake was only trying to save her life and here she was a blubbering mess, hampering his best efforts.

Shelly wiped the rest of the wetness from her face and followed him through the brush. The entire time, she couldn't stop the idea that he was used to this kind of thing, an idea reinforced with the gun he now wore in the hidden shoulder holster.

Jake had obviously become the agent he'd hoped to be.

Chapter 19

Jake finally slowed and glanced at Michelle. Exertion highlighted her face better than a neon sign. "We can stop here. I think we're far enough away." They'd traveled more than a mile along the perimeter of the lake.

He'd pushed her hard and she had no clue as to why. Plus, he could tell she didn't understand his anger. It wasn't directed toward her. It was directed at this whole goddamned mess, but he wasn't about to enlighten her as to what he'd discovered.

Not now.

Now, he needed to get a grip and figure out how to keep them alive.

He let go of her hand to pull his cell phone out of his pocket, and punched up a number before he brought it to his ear.

"We got problems," he said when Rich answered. He turned away from Michelle and lowered his voice. "Mathers found Michelle. I need a place to hide her. Fast." He spent the next minutes detailing the explosion and how they'd barely escaped alive. "I doubt he realizes she's escaped, which bought us some time."

"How do you think he tracked her?"

"I touched base with Baker earlier, he asked me to give Ginnie a heads-up on my location. Larson probably got the information out of her." Virginia Stephens was the county dispatcher. Had been for twenty years, so he wondered how it was possible. Not much got past that old crone. "Hell, the leak could've come from Durbin too, since that was before NPD took Billy in."

"Hmm. What about cell phone triangulation?"

Jake snorted. "You're talking about a sophisticated tracking method for a backwoods operation."

"The operation may be headquartered in the backwoods, but Mathers and company are mighty sophisticated, so we can't discount anything."

"What do you propose I do with Michelle to protect her? Durbin's dead, so he's no longer a suspect." Right after Durbin had died, Jake had called Rich, recounting everything.

"Where are you?" Rich asked.

"I'm on Nolin, about two miles from the dam. Thirty miles north of Campton." He gave a brief description of his location and how to get there, since Rich wasn't familiar with the area.

"Let me make some calls. I've got a line on what I think is going down tonight, but I don't want to keep you on your phone. Turn it off, just in case. Then turn it on one hour from now, so I can reach you. Hopefully, I'll have everything arranged by then."

"Thanks." Jake cut the connection as well as the power, with full confidence in Rich's ability. His partner always came through.

An hour later, after turning on his cell phone, Jake paced. Michelle and Buddy were safely hidden from view. He'd told her to stay put until he returned with his truck.

A ring tone interrupted his pacing. He answered.

"I'm a couple of miles from where you told me you'd be."

"Great. I'll be watching the road." He continued walking a ways from the road. A car occasionally flew past, most from Louisville or Bowling Green, coming to the lake for the weekend. At least they appeared to be.

Less than five minutes later, he spotted Rich's car. He leapt out of the bushes. "Thanks for the lift," he said after climbing inside.

"Where's Matthews?"

Jake cinched his seat belt. "Hidden. I'll pick her up after I get my Durango. I was hoping for a quick peek at the destruction and didn't want to risk taking her back that way." He looked out the window after giving Rich directions to where his SUV was parked. "Bastard blew up my house."

"He's dangerous." Rich hesitated. "Think we should pick

him up?"

"No. We'd alert him. With a good lawyer, he'd simply walk as we have nothing on him that's not circumstantial. I only saw him head for his truck. Intuition told me to get out. I don't have any proof he actually caused the blast. Most likely he tied into the propane tank at the side of the house." That's how he'd do it, if he were trying to blow the place to smithereens. "Besides, after tonight, we should have plenty of reason to hold him and keep his sorry ass in jail. He's running out of fear. I can feel it. Why else would he kill Michelle?"

Rich sighed. "He obviously thinks she knows something."

"I've been with her for two days and she knows nothing."

"What about this journal you told me about?"

Jake shook his head. "Nada. It's just my ex's way of trying to make amends for her horrendous behavior all those years ago."

Rich nodded, his attention going back to driving.

"So, are you the father?"

The question caught Jake off guard. He damn sure wasn't expecting it. "Nosy bastard, aren't you?"

Rich kept his attention on the road. "Just connecting the dots. You were friends with both, right?" He spared Jake a quick glance.

Jake shrugged, neither agreeing nor disagreeing.

Rich laughed. "I get it. She's a looker. Your ex was a looker."

"Don't start. It's complicated." Heaven only knew how complicated.

Rich's laughter increased. "Nothing about sex should be complicated. You're either attracted or you're not." When Jake remained silent, Rich tsk-tsked. "Not fooling me. I know you, remember? But I suppose you're right about complications. Love triangles are always complicated."

"You don't know jack shit."

"Yes, I do. Interesting family." Rich grinned. "Met his brother, Aw Schitt."

Jake frowned and grunted. "You're a laugh a minute."

"I try."

Jake only shook his head and resumed staring out the window.

By this point, Rich had turned onto the gravel road leading to where his house used to be. Rich kept driving past the nosy weekenders who'd stopped and turned into gawkers. Smoke filled the air, along with the crackle of flames and the hiss of water as the volunteer fire department worked at putting out the remaining flames. The explosion pretty much wiped out the house. Thankfully, the surrounding grounds were still sodden from rain several days ago, so the fire hadn't spread and was easily contained, and looked to be now burning itself out rapidly.

Rich pulled up to the spot he'd hidden his Durango.

Nothing looked out of place and the SUV seemed untouched.

As Rich put the car in park, Jake remembered the dog food and the groceries he'd picked up were still in the backseat. At least they'd have something to eat, the dog included.

"Okay, here's the deal." Rich caught his gaze, his own shining in excitement. "E-mails from the organization and Peters are going back and forth. Seems they're closing up shop for the time being, but are interested in doing business at a later date.

"This is going down tonight. Jarvis and Malone will set up close to the house near the cave as soon as they have the cover of darkness. Our orders are to prepare for anything. Once we get substantiation, we go in. I spoke with Cummings after the latest turn of events and he agreed. We'll have plenty of backup so nothing else can get fucked up."

Jake nodded. Cummings was their boss and someone they needed to placate at times, especially when deputies and suspects started dying.

"Jarvis and Malone are electronically searching for the millions Mathers and Ivy have probably set aside. They're scared. They're desperate. They've got nothing to lose and they can easily disappear if spooked."

Jake's brows rose. "What do I need to do to be ready?"

Rich pulled out a set of keys. "Take care of Matthews." Then he grabbed a cell phone from the console, along with a sheet of paper with handwritten instructions. "Safe communication and directions to Malone's fishing cabin. It's not the Ritz, but it's safe. Stay with her until you hear from me. *Capische?*"

Jake took the items from him. "I want to be there when you take these bastards down."

His partner nodded. "Fair enough. I'm not sure of the exact time. It all depends on what happens after dark. I'll call when I have something positive. The cabin's not that far away, which is why we thought it would be perfect for this."

Jake reached for the door handle, then stopped and turned back to Rich. "What about Baker?"

"What about him?"

"He's not going to like it that you came into town and took away his thunder." He'd already gotten a taste of his anger earlier. Since Baker had never forgotten how Jake had taken away his football scholarship, he could only imagine his response once major arrests were made and the sheriff wasn't in on them.

Rich's jaw tightened. "You're shitting me, right?" He met his gaze. "The guy has been clueless to what's going on right in his own backyard. I don't give a damn if his feelings are hurt because we did his job for him."

Jake smiled. "You gotta admit, this isn't your usual redneck crime. And we'd be clueless too, if not for Lady Luck."

Sometimes luck was all a lawman needed. That and a bit of determination. Rich definitely had determination. Tom had determination too, but Jake didn't bring it up. He remained silent, holding Rich's gaze and praying their luck would stay with them.

Rich finally sighed and wiped his face. "I'm still not excusing the guy. He'll just have to understand. We don't know how deep this goes or who all is involved. Since Durbin died and your house blew up, I have a hard problem completely trusting anyone in his office. Too many ties to keep things a secret." He clenched a fist and pounded the steering wheel with resolve. "Before the night is over, I intend to know what kind of shit Mathers is pushing and who those women are. I'm not about to risk another body or risk the suspects fleeing because someone tipped them off."

"I agree." Just the fact that his lake house was hit was proof enough for Jake. "I'll wait for your call." Jake jerked the door handle and emerged from Rich's car.

He quickly slid behind the wheel of the Durango and started

the engine as Rich pulled away. Jake drove in the opposite direction until he got closer to the crime scene.

Jake shifted into neutral and watched the fireman he determined to be in charge spit out a wad of chew.

As disorganized as the volunteer squad seemed to be, they still managed to extinguish the fire. Jake was grateful no other properties were affected. He had insurance. He could rebuild.

The men appeared to be wrapping up. At this point they were placing a makeshift fence, as well as "Do Not Cross" crime scene tape, around the perimeter to keep out looters and kids. Their time was free, but anything they used had a price tag.

He put the SUV in drive and pressed the gas pedal. He'd stop by their office later to pick up the bill and thank them.

Right now, Michelle was waiting for him and he needed to ensure her safety before he did anything else.

~

Jake parked near the spot he'd left Michelle and climbed out.

"Michelle? Buddy?" he called, walking toward the lake.

He spotted her a moment later.

She stood and brushed debris off her backside. "It's about time. I was beginning to think you weren't coming back."

"I wouldn't leave you." He turned to the dog. "Come on, Buddy, in you go." He opened the back door. The dog needed no further invitation.

Michelle advanced to the other side and Jake followed. He reached for the door handle, stopped, then bent to kiss her.

"Just so you know," he murmured at her surprised look. "I missed you."

She nodded, flashing one of her killer smiles. Without another word, she climbed inside.

Neither spoke as he shifted gears.

"Where're we going?" she asked, after they'd driven for a while in silence.

He handed her the directions. "Here, you tell me."

Michelle navigated as he drove south toward Bowling Green. With her help, he found the road leading to the cabin, and he used the term loosely. The structure now in view appeared tiny.

He shrugged. "No one knows about this place." It had a roof and four walls, so he wasn't going to complain. "Home sweet home." Jake put the gearshift into park, shut off the ignition, and glanced at her to gauge her reaction. "I know it's not much. But it's safe."

Michelle nodded. "You forget I used to live in a house with two other people that wasn't much bigger…and it had wheels."

"Good. I'd hate to cramp your style."

He climbed out as her quick retort filled his ears, shooting a rush of heat straight to his center. Damn, if he didn't enjoy being with her, he thought, running around to open first her door, then Buddy's. He bowed, extending a hand toward their humble dwelling. "After you, my lady."

Michelle brushed the wrinkles out of her shorts. "So glad to know chivalry isn't dead."

He slammed both doors. "I'll get my payment somehow."

The hint of red stealing up her face over his innuendo was adorable.

Jake couldn't help but lean in for a kiss after gripping her shoulders to hold her in place. She tasted exactly as she had earlier. More heat shot through his veins. "I'm positive I'm getting the better end of this deal." He drew back and captured her gaze, letting her see the message his eyes conveyed. He meant to continue later.

She offered a semblance of a smile. "Payment goes both ways."

Buddy chose that moment to burst in between them.

Sighing, Jake dug into his pocket for the keys, then handed them to her. "Go on in. I'll get the groceries I bought earlier."

"My hero. I could get used to such service."

Jake grabbed the bags and followed. He would have been more amused, except this wasn't a laughing matter.

The cabin was much bigger than it looked from the outside. The only room with a door was a tiny bathroom, tiny meaning he'd have to suck in air to shut the door, but there was running water and electricity. "At least we have hot water." Jake indicated the small water heater next to the corner shower.

Nodding, Michelle shoved her hands into her pockets, rocked back on her heels, and glanced around. "I should call home."

"You can't. It's still too risky to turn on your phone." Jake set the groceries on the counter and opened a drawer, rooting for a can opener. One wall lined with cabinets denoted a kitchen area, complete with sink, small stove, and refrigerator.

He found what he searched for and checked the cupboards for anything to add to their makeshift meal. Canned food lined the shelves.

Good old Malone. The guy was always prepared. His gaze landed on the TV and latest Nintendo game console underneath.

Jake gave a mental snort. He had better things to do with his time than play video games. He planned to enjoy Michelle's company. At least for a few hours while he waited for Rich's phone call.

Dinner by candlelight, a walk through the woods in the dark. Both sounded romantic and would be if they weren't running for their lives.

"First things first," he murmured, grabbing the dog food and opening it. Jake spooned out half the can, stuck the rest in the fridge, and set the plate down for Buddy.

He glanced at Michelle. "What would you rather have with your chili?" She'd positioned herself next to a chair and now stood staring at him. His eyebrows shot up teasingly. "Green beans or canned corn?"

She shrugged. "Surprise me."

Buddy wolfed down his meal, then curled into a ball beneath the table next to Michelle. With one long, contented sigh, the dog placed his head on his paws and closed his eyes.

Michelle rubbed her arms and exhaled a deep sigh. "Why is someone trying to kill me?"

In two steps, Jake was beside her and she glanced up at him with tears brimming in her eyes.

He wrapped his arms around her. "I don't know the full details yet, but we'll know soon."

"I'm so scared."

He had a million questions he wanted to ask, but Michelle was in no condition to answer them. "It's okay," he said, trying to soothe her fears. "I won't let anything happen to you. I promise." He kissed the top of her forehead and she leaned further into his body.

"Kiss me, Jake. Like you did at the lake."

Her whispered words were like water to a thirsty man. He nuzzled her neck. "It's not a good idea."

"I don't care. I just want to feel alive. Please, Jake." Michelle turned her head and worked her way to his lips in full invitation. He couldn't resist deepening their contact the second she opened her mouth. Instantly, he was hard.

He broke the kiss, grazing her lips. "Are you sure?" he whispered, nipping his way up her face to her closed eyes, along her cheek to her ear, where he spent a moment, using his tongue.

Michelle slid her arms all the way around his neck. "I…umm…yes. I'm sure."

Jake needed no other invitation. He picked her up, strode to the bed, and tossed her on it. The bed bounced when he followed, collapsing on top of her.

Her laughter rang in the air and was music to his ears. He would never tire of the sound.

Michelle Matthews was like a drug he couldn't get enough of. Every time he got close to her, he wanted to be inside her. He shed his jeans at the same time she rid herself of her shorts. He slipped her top from over her shoulders and discarded it behind him, along with his own shirt. Jake bent his head toward breasts that called to him. He wondered if he'd always feel like this as he sank into her heat. And like that other time he'd been inside her, he couldn't stop the wave of lust from picking him up and hurling him toward completion.

He loved her. For too many years, he'd loved her. He never should have let her go in the first place.

Chapter 20

He paced. Fear slid over his body, blanketing his calm with dread.

Bobby was dead. Joe had killed him and gotten himself killed for his trouble.

Okay. Those turns of events weren't disastrous. He'd make the best of the situation and look at the silver lining. Two mouths had been silenced. Now that things were getting crazy, mouths tended to talk and had the potential of disclosing hidden facts.

He had bigger problems. Michelle Matthews still lived. He felt it in his gut. He grabbed his cell phone and punched in Ivy's number.

"You'll have to handle the business tonight. Can you get off work?"

"Why?"

"Bobby's dead. Everything's falling apart."

"What?" She never watched TV, so she had no way of knowing and the shock of his announcement carried in her tone. "How? When?"

He spent the next few minutes updating her, as well as trying to soothe her overreaction to the news. When she finally calmed down, he said, "I need to deal with Matthews, even if it takes me all night." He knew she didn't want to hear that, so he added, "We can't afford to let her live, Ivy. She's the only link to me and in turn, a link to you."

A loose end he needed to silence once and for all. Kiera had been too positive he'd go down and he couldn't discount her bold claim that still echoed in his mind, growing louder by the hour.

"You'll be caught," she'd said. "You can't hide forever,

cloaking yourself as a do-gooder for mankind in your exalted position."

Yes, he could, he thought. Hadn't the four of them been doing that for years? Because of human nature, something they all understood. Most people were stupid and didn't see what was right in front of them. Didn't see what was happening right in their backyards. But Collier wasn't stupid. He'd figure it out sooner or later. Before that happened, the man had to die.

Ivy would just have to understand. "If we're caught, we could go to prison for a long time." He had no intention of going to prison. "So, you need to make sure everything runs smoothly tonight while I take care of the links."

"Okay. I'll call in sick and be at the house."

"Good." With Matthews and Collier dead, the only other threat of exposure would dissipate once the women were gone. "Oh, and by the way," he added, "I got an e-mail from Peters. Says he'll be happy to accommodate us with anything we want."

"God. That's rich. Bobby's dead and you're talking about business."

"What would you have me do? Curl up and die with him? I couldn't stop the outcome, so I'm preparing for tomorrow."

There was dead silence on the phone until she asked, "Why did he have to die?"

He swore under his breath and his jaw clenched. He relaxed it. "Your questions sound like an accusation." He rolled his shoulders and relaxed further. "I didn't kill him. Joe did, remember?"

"You might as well have."

"I'll ignore that comment because I know you and Bobby were friends. But don't fuck with me. We're in this together. You got that?"

"Yeah. I do. Look, I can't talk now. I'll catch you later."

The loud click in his ear told him she'd hung up. He shoved the phone into his pocket, wondering if he'd have to deal with her too. No. He owned Ivy, just as he'd owned Joe Durbin. If he went down, so did she.

He started the truck. The receiver for the tracking device he'd stuck on Collier's Durango beeped and he smiled.

The Matthews bitch was with him. Had to be.

After putting the vehicle in gear, he drove south with one thought.

Both Collier and the woman were as good as dead.

~

"What else did he tell you?" Rich asked Andrews, the Nashville PD detective who'd questioned Billy. Rich had wanted to be present, but he couldn't break cover, so he had to be content with secondhand information over a cell phone with the lead investigator on the case of the missing singer, Kimberly McDowell. Rich had filled him in earlier as to Billy's actions, and Andrews had agreed to his plan to pick him up for questioning. But it quickly became a wasted effort with dire consequences. No one had expected Joe Durbin's knee-jerk reaction.

"He said he went fishing the other night," Andrews said.

"Fishing?"

"That's a direct quote. We figure it was Lake Cumberland, because apparently they drove a long way and the lake was big."

Fishing? Lake Cumberland? Rich shook his head, more confused than ever. "What about last night? Did he say what he was doing then?"

"They went deer hunting."

"They? Did he say who he was with?"

"No. But he told me he lost his hat."

"Shit." Something he already knew. "That's it? Did he say he pulled the trigger?"

"Hell, no. I couldn't get a straight answer out of him. The guy talks in riddles. I'm not sure he even knows what day this is. I finally decided he was a dead end and had one of the patrolmen give him a ride home. You're welcome to come in and listen to the tape if you want."

"I might do that." But not now, Rich thought, sighing. "Thanks for the info."

The moment he hung up, Jarvis' shout from the van registered. "Hey, Rich. You should hear this."

They'd parked among trees and brush, close enough to the house to set up surveillance, yet far enough away to avoid notice.

When Rich walked through the van door, Jarvis nodded at the machine in front of him. "I recorded it. It just came over the radio scanner." He punched the Play button.

"Code three. Get an ambulance out to the Durbin place fast." Tom Baker's voice shot through the device. "I need help. Oh Jesus, he got a hold of Larson's gun and shot him with it. He's gone fucking crazy, yelling about how Larson killed his brother."

"Who, Sheriff?"

"Billy Durbin. Goddamned bastard tried to take me out too." There was a brief pause before his shout was heard in the background. "Wait, Billy. Don't run. You'll make it worse on yourself." If Rich didn't know better, he'd swear the sheriff was crying. "Hell, he's headed toward the high school. He shouldn't get far. I shot him."

"Oh my God," came the dispatcher's horrified response.

Without knowing what to make of it, Rich glanced at Jarvis, who shrugged. "Why would Billy kill Larson, then try to shoot the sheriff unless he was part of this?" And if Billy was a half-wit, then how could he be part of this? Maybe Billy wasn't the half-wit they all took him for.

Rich clapped Jarvis on the shoulder. "Nice work. Now find out all you can about Billy Durbin." If Billy had a connection to Ivy or to Mathers, Jarvis would discover it. Rich reached for his cell phone. "We're missing something in this whole thing. And we can't afford to miss anything when people are dying."

~

"Michelle?" Jake's voice infiltrated the quiet.

After making love, they'd eaten by candlelight, then taken a walk, which ended in a second round of lovemaking. Feeling totally satisfied, Shelly was too comfortable to answer.

"Are you awake?"

"Umm hmmm."

"Open your eyes, sweetheart. We have to talk."

"Famous last words." She sighed and opened one eye, squinting. Dusk had settled into dark, but there was just enough light spilling from the candle on the table to see his concerned expression. "Later."

She closed her eyes and turned, nestling her butt into his groin. She felt his erection poking her and smiled.

Jake kissed her neck and his warm hand stroked her arm. "I'm serious," he whispered near her ear. "We have to talk."

She didn't want to talk. Not now. Now, she simply wanted to relax.

~

"Do you think you can take him away?"

The shrill voice seeped into Shelly's consciousness, suspending her contented afterglow.

"Kiera?" It wasn't possible. Kiera was dead. Shelly sat up and looked around. She was still in the cabin she and Jake had made love in, but he was gone. Kiera stood a foot away, bathed in candlelight. "What are you doing here? Where's Jake?"

She laughed and sat on the edge of the bed. "You don't really believe Jake could love you? You're nothing but poor…" She picked a piece of lint off her pants, then flicked it away. "…trailer park trash."

"That's not true." Those were Kiera's exact words of so long ago. They'd been hard enough to hear back then when she'd been sensitive to the way people viewed her. "Being poor isn't a crime. We've had some bad luck is all," Shelly said, also repeating her own words line for line. She had to believe them.

"Bad luck or not, you'll never take my place. I am somebody. My family means something here in Campton and Jake is mine. Do you hear me? I won't let you steal him out from under me."

"No!" Shelly covered her ears, unwilling to listen to the same words Kiera had hurled at her before. "You don't really love him," she shouted. "You're just holding on because I'm interested."

"You know that's not true. You stole him from me. How could you, Shel? I trusted you."

Kiera's eyes became pools of sorrow, dragging Shelly under with guilt.

"Forgive me," she cried, her tears erupting.

"How can I? You hurt me, Shel. He's always been mine. You knew that."

"But I love him too." Slowly she shook her head, repeating earnestly, "I love him too."

Laughter pealed in the air, mocking her. "You're so naive to think he'd fall for you. If he had to choose between a pregnant you and a pregnant me, who do you think he'd pick?"

Doubts filled her. Who was she trying to kid? Kiera was right. How could there be anything between them when she was a nobody. What's more, Jake had always belonged to Kiera. Hadn't he admitted to loving her earlier?

"Oh, Shel. You'll never hold him with thoughts like those. Take the money my mother gave you and have the abortion like she urged, then use the rest to make a new start. You'll get over Jake. And your leaving will ease his conscience."

"But I don't want the money. I don't want an abortion. I want Jake. I want his baby." By this point, she was sobbing. "Please...Jake! Please love me."

~

"Shush. Michelle, wake up." Jake's voice penetrated her consciousness, as did his slight shake. "You're dreaming."

A dream? It had been a dream? Oh, thank God. Relief filled her.

She opened her eyes, now flooded with tears, and through the blur saw Jake leaning over her, an anxious expression plastered over his features.

"It's okay," he soothed. "I'm here and I do love you. I've always loved you. Christ, I should've told you earlier."

"It seemed so real." She took several deep breaths. Her head plopped against the pillows as she threw an arm over her eyes, praying she hadn't yelled everything out loud. Her heart still raced from the leftover twinges of a dream that had been too vivid.

"So, they paid you off too?" Jake's question came after an extended silence, his voice permeating the space around them.

"Yeah," she sighed. Why deny it. "I'm sorry, Jake. I should've told you. I have a son. Your son. His name is Michael...Mikey. I got pregnant after that night, but I couldn't go through with an abortion." Memories of her heated conversation with Kiera filled her brain. The dream had brought the incident back in living color.

"I know. I read Kiera's journal."

And what could she say to that? Nothing, because at the moment the right words eluded her.

Her thoughts switched to the journal. Kiera was forever accusing Shelly of coveting Jake.

The truth hit.

Shelly had been completely *envious* of what Jake had given Kiera. Worse. Her motives hadn't been any more pure than Kiera's, her behavior just as twisted, and just as wrong. The idea staggered her. Remembering the dream and Kiera's hurt, her guilt increased a thousand times.

And what about Jake? He'd read the journal. In it, Kiera had claimed Jake had coveted her. If that had been true, Shelly couldn't understand why he'd stuck with Kiera.

As Jake silently stroked her arm, she turned to him, risked asking the question that wouldn't stop running through her head, even though she had a good idea of the answer.

"What did you mean when you asked if they paid me off too? Was that why you let me go after what we shared?" She couldn't keep the pain from either her voice or her expression.

He lifted her hand, studying her fingers as he stroked each one. "It's more complicated than that."

"We have nothing but time and I'm listening." When he still hadn't responded after a long silence, she sighed. "In order to move forward, which I'm hoping you want to do, we both have to own our actions." Shelly placed a brave smile on her face, meeting Jake's gaze. "That's what Kiera did, according to her journal. I seduced you, Jake, knowing full well Kiera still needed you, and knowing you and she had unfinished business." Tears broke free when she realized how horrible her actions sounded coming from her lips. Oh God! How could she have done such a thing?

Jake hugged her, kissing the tears. "Shush. Don't cry."

"Why? I see that night from a different point of view now and it makes what we did seem sordid and ugly, when I'd always believed what we'd shared was so beautiful." She sniffed. More tears spilled from her eyes as Jake's lips moved over her face in an effort to ease her pain. But all it did was make her cry more. "So, what's the real truth?" Could she overcome her guilt and feel free to love him without her sins weighing her down? She didn't think she'd ever forget the dream.

"You're no more guilty than I am and I'm no more guilty than Kiera. We're all to blame. We all got caught up in…" He broke off and laid his head back. "No. That's not true." He rubbed his eye with thumb and forefinger and sighed. "I own the majority of the responsibility. I've always known that. And if you want more of the bare truth, you should know I ran from it, hiding behind Delaney's money, hoping a child would be enough to ease my guilt for not being strong enough. I couldn't stop Kiera from self-destructing. I couldn't stop wanting you while Kiera needed me. I couldn't stop from making love with you. You didn't seduce me, not when I wanted you so much. I allowed it to happen and I knew better."

Shelly squeezed her eyes tight. "Do you think we have a chance?" she whispered. Suddenly she didn't see how they'd get past this.

"Yes. And we'll make it." The bed shifted as Jake sat up. "I promise."

"But how?" Feeling his rapt attention, she risked opening her eyes and meeting his intent gaze, unable to keep the heartache out of hers. "It's too much to take in. Too much to overcome. People are trying to kill me, then I find out that Kiera's actions changed my life more than I ever expected. And worse…I realize it wasn't really her actions, but mine, that did the most destruction."

"It's okay." Jake wrapped his arms around her. "We have a son together. That's a miracle."

As much as she wanted his comfort, Shelly knew she didn't deserve it. "But I kept him from you. I told him you abandoned us." How could she have been so cruel? "I punished you for choosing her when you shouldn't have had to choose. And all these years I selfishly kept my son from his father." More tears flooded her eyes. She shook her head, leaning away, but his grip tightened. "I can't think anymore."

"Don't think. Just feel," he said, kissing her lips, her chin, working his way to her ear. His tongue pushed inside, stroking. "This is what I'd love to be doing to your insides. I ache to have you again."

Shelly felt him respond, his firm erection confirming his

SANDY LOYD

words.

"I love you and you love me. We have each other. We have a son. My daughter has a brother. What more do we need?"

"No." This time when she pulled out of his hold, he let her go. "I can't do this." Easing off the bed, she reached for her clothes. "It doesn't feel right any longer."

~

Jake reached for patience as Michelle dressed. Kiera's death had opened his eyes to the uncertainty of life. Since he'd lost Michelle once, he wasn't about to let her get away again, but at this moment, he was stumped as to what to do next.

"Don't go too far," he warned, when she started for the door.

One fact he was certain of, though. He had no intention of screwing up his one chance to make things right.

She stopped and turned around, flashing a wan smile. "I won't. I just need a little air."

Jake got up and stepped into his jeans, not bothering with shirt, socks, or shoes. In two strides, he was in the kitchen. He dug dog food out of the fridge and put it down for Buddy.

The dog inhaled the food in seconds.

Then, deciding not to let Michelle stew too long, he headed for the door. He'd give her space to let her come to the same conclusion he'd reached, but only after he let her know what he'd learned about guilt. Too much only made things worse.

Funny, now that the truth had come out, his guilt seemed lighter. He felt freer. Less encumbered. More able to love and accept what was real and what was illusion.

Kiera was right. He and Michelle belonged together. He just had to get her to believe it too.

He stepped outside. At first, he didn't see her in the shadows.

When he did, he stood, silently observing, and hadn't realized she was even aware of him until she spoke.

"It's an eerie sound. Don't you think? Like some kind of whizzing motor." He listened. Instantly, the whirring filled his ears, became more noticeable. "Yeah, it is eerie. It's amazing that insects can make such a noise, isn't it." Like wind howling

230

through tall buildings or a turbine rotor spinning.

She nodded. "Do you remember the last time you heard it?"

He smiled. "Yeah." Every seventeen years the cicadas came back in full force to make this crazy noise. "How about you?" Their flying around as they buzzed, as well as the dead carcasses everywhere, added to their annoyance. But it was short-lived. Another week, two at the most, they'd be gone, not to come again with this much presence for another seventeen years.

"Umm hmmm." He felt her smile in the dark. "You were so cool. I think I loved you even back then."

Yep, she remembered, he thought. She and Kiera had had a slumber party out in the Delaneys' back yard, one he and the Durbin brothers, Larson, and a few others had crashed with water balloons and fire extinguishers.

He'd gotten grounded for a week, but it had been worth any punishment to hear their screams. Especially hot little Kiera's. That's really why Jake had led them all there.

"Of course, you only had eyes for Kiera. All those years I wanted what she had."

He stayed silent, seeming to sense she was working out some kind of shit in her mind, just like he'd done at one time, only to discover life never went the way he'd thought it should.

"Loving you was just a small part of it." Her extensive sigh came out in an audible exhale. "I yearned for what I thought was missing from my life. Turns out, I had more than Kiera." Michelle leaned against the rail and caught his gaze. "I guess that's why I feel so guilty. I survived relatively unscathed and she's dead. Reading about the last few years of her life, viewing her suffering through her eyes, was hard. I was too wrapped up in what I didn't have to realize how much she needed what I did have to offer. My friendship."

"Aren't we all like that in our youth? A little too wrapped up in ourselves, sometimes too selfish and cruel to worry about the next person?"

"Maybe." She shrugged.

"Life's cyclical. Things happen for a reason. Cicadas only come out once every seventeen years to avoid predators and survive. Survival. Babies are born even when we try to prevent pregnancies. We were all surviving, the only way we know how."

Jake stared at her thoughtfully, determining his next words. "Kiera and I were over long before that night, Michelle. Your staying or leaving didn't change that. Our having sex didn't change things either. For too long, I felt guilty over Kiera's drug battle. Yet I finally figured out I had no control over her, any more than she had control over my feelings for you. I let you go because I let guilt rule my heart. I love you. I've never stopped loving you. I think you feel the same way, given your earlier response. We've got a second shot at this."

He held her gaze, letting her see his sincerity. "Don't let guilt destroy it again. Don't run from love, out of fear, the way I did. You'll only regret it." Smiling, he touched her tear-stained face, barely visible in the shadows. "Sometimes those who need love the most don't think they deserve it."

When he finished speaking, he started back for the door.

His ringing cell phone halted him with his hand on the knob. He paused to answer it, then pushed inside. "Yeah, Rich? Whatcha got?"

"Wanted to give you a heads-up," he said. "Billy Durbin just went on a rampage." Rich filled him in on Billy's killing Deputy Larson and shooting Baker, ending with, "The guy's on the run, might be heading for the cave."

"Damn. What else can happen?" Jake sighed and raked his fingers through his hair.

"You might want to touch base with Baker," Rich added. "He may need you."

"Thanks. I'll give him a call."

"Bad news?" Michelle asked, coming up behind him.

Startled from his thoughts, Jake glanced back at her. He cleared his throat, then hesitated, feeling torn. "I have to leave for a bit." He hated the thought of leaving her, now that they had become lovers. He sensed she needed him. Add into it that someone was trying to kill her, and he was doubly torn. He also needed to check in with the sheriff, to at least act interested in their investigation and offer his services, given what had happened.

Shit. He rubbed his neck. Who'd have thought Billy had it in him? Billy was like an affable giant. Jake had never seen him lift one finger in anger after his accident.

"You have a job to do," he murmured, talking himself into calling Baker. Finally, he reached for his cell phone and punched in Baker's number. After agreeing to meet him ASAP at the cave, he turned to Michelle.

"Come on. You're going with me."

"What?" The look on her face said it all. He'd lost his remaining marbles. Didn't matter. He wasn't about to leave her. Not now. Not ever.

"You're to stay in the car and out of danger. Okay?" he said, once they were both buckled into his Durango.

She nodded and he headed for the cave, making the trip in twenty minutes.

Jake parked off the road a ways from the cave and glanced around. Baker hadn't arrived yet.

He turned to Michelle and said before shoving the door open, "Stay here with Buddy."

He jumped out and hurried toward the entrance. Nearing the cavern, he shined his flashlight on the ground and saw a puddle of black. Could be blood, and possibly Billy's if he'd come this way, but it was too hard to differentiate in the shadows.

It was still hard for Jake to wrap his head around the fact that Billy had killed one man already. There had to be a damned good reason. Billy had never been violent before, so Larson had to have done something to set him off. Which meant his suspicions about the deputy being in on the operation all along were right on. Maybe Billy heard about Joe's death and blamed the deputy. He mentally rolled his eyes. Rich was right. Baker had no clue as to the shit taking place in his backyard.

"Billy?" Jake yelled. He entered the cave cautiously, swinging the beam of the flashlight back and forth as he pulled his weapon from its holster.

"Jake?"

The call came from the left. "Yeah." Jake flashed the light in that direction but didn't see anything. "Where are you? Come on out. I won't hurt you."

"Sheriff Baker's mad at me."

Jake sighed. That answer sounded like the Billy he knew. "That's because you shot someone. I'm wondering why."

"I didn't mean to. I don't remember. I'm confused." Billy came out of hiding to stand under the flashlight's beam, still holding Larson's gun, his shirt saturated with blood.

Jake nodded at the weapon. "Why don't you give me that?"

He shook his head. "I can't."

"Why not?"

"I have to get out of the dark." Billy began pacing, appearing agitated, waving the weapon in the air one second and aiming at him the next. "I don't like it."

"Okay." Moving slowly, so as not to add to his agitation, Jake walked backward, facing Billy. He kept his arms up, a flashlight in one hand and his weapon at the ready in the other. "Let's go outside, then. Follow the light." It was dark outside, too, but not pitch black like in the cave.

If Jake could do this without killing Billy, he would. Too many people had died already. He just wanted Billy out of the cave, then he would worry about relieving him of Larson's weapon.

With the entrance in sight, Jake continued gradually taking steps back, giving him plenty of room.

Jake turned and caught sight of a white utility truck out of his peripheral vision.

Then he froze.

A shape lurking near a tree had his weapon trained on Michelle, still sitting in the Durango.

Mathers.

"No!" Billy's shout pulled the guy's attention. His arm moved at the same time.

Jake had no time to take aim and dived for cover.

Shots burst into the air. Jake rolled and looked up to see Mathers drop to the ground. He then turned to Billy, who just stood there appearing confused after shooting and hitting the guy with amazing accuracy considering the distance and darkness.

With gun drawn, Jake crawled over to Billy just as he collapsed. "Billy?" Jake kneeled next to him, stroking his head, working to comfort him. "Hang on. I'll call for help."

Hearing the slam of a car door, he looked up to see Michelle jump out of the Durango and run toward them.

"Get back in the car," Jake yelled, as he pulled out his cell phone and punched in 911.

Michelle stopped short, relief and confusion on her face, before turning to do as he'd asked. Jake huffed a sigh of relief as the dispatcher came on the line, and he quickly reported the situation and location. He disconnected the call with a flick of his wrist and dropped the phone, pressing his palm against the blood that pumped from Billy's abdomen.

"I hid in the cave, like she told me to when I got scared." Billy's breathing was labored. "She said the cave is special. Protects people like me."

The flashlight illuminated Billy's tear-stained face as he held out the gun. Jake took it from his limp fingers as he added, "I couldn't let him hurt her. Kiera wouldn't like it."

"Kiera?"

He nodded. "She told me to watch out after Lizzie."

Lizzie? Billy must be talking about Elizabeth Jones, the first OD victim.

"I didn't do a good job. They gave me something to drink. I didn't like how it made me feel, so I poured it out like Kiera said to do. He had me carry a big rug into the boat. I thought we were going fishing."

"Where?"

"Lake."

"What lake?"

"I dunno. It was big. We went a long way. I didn't mean to hurt the deputy."

Jake nodded. "Thank you for not letting them hurt Michelle."

"Kiera told me if I protected others, it would make me feel better about Lizzie. I told Bobby not to hurt her. But he lied to me, so I told Joe. Joe's dead. Why did he shoot me?" He drew his eyebrows together in confusion. "Why?" he asked softly before falling limp.

"Billy?" He felt for a pulse. "Aw shit, Billy."

Jake's breath came out in one sad sigh. He wiped at the moisture forming behind his eyes. Billy was dead.

He looked up and noticed someone running toward him with his weapon drawn.

~

Shelly made it halfway back to the car, relieved Jake was still alive. When she'd first heard the shots, her imagination had conjured up all kinds of things and Jake's death topped the list. Right then and there, she realized if she'd lost him, she'd lose her heart.

Jake had been right. She was running from love out of fear of being hurt. The only thing worse than what they'd all done to each other would be to learn nothing from their stupidity.

She only had to remember one thing. He loved her. Running from his love wouldn't solve a damn thing. She deserved love. Jake deserved love. So had Kiera. But Kiera was now dead and her last wish was for the two of them to reconnect.

Out of the corner of her eye, she saw movement. She turned and spied Roger Peters heading straight for Jake, his gun pointed right at him.

Her breath stuck in her throat.

Oh God.

Too late, she realized his intent. "Jake, look out," she shouted.

Roger stopped and spun in her direction. He raised his gun.

She saw intent reflected off his eyes in the shadows.

She froze, staring at death with one thought. He was going to kill her, yet she still had no clue as to why.

She closed her eyes. Please, Lord, she prayed. Let Jake take care of Mikey.

When the gunshot blasted and she was still standing, she turned toward both men, just as Roger hurried past her and Jake was almost in front of her.

He waited while Roger ran to the body lying not ten yards away, reaching for a pulse. Then he shook his head. "Mathers is gone."

Confused, Shelly looked at the two men, who now stood side by side.

"I owe you one," Jake said.

Roger grinned. "Don't worry about it. I never keep count."

"That's because you're always ahead." Jake's nod indicated Roger. "Michelle, meet Rich Heslin, my partner."

"You're Jake's partner?" She eyed him, working to keep her face from showing any emotion. "You told him, didn't you?" It was such a stupid thing to say, but right then her mind wasn't working too clearly. Not when she realized exactly what had just taken place. The guy who'd killed Billy, who also happened to be the same person who'd run her off the road, had tried one last time to kill her, but Roger/Rich stopped him with the bullet she'd thought was meant for her.

Rich only shrugged.

Her attention went from Rich's face to Jake's.

"Why didn't you say something earlier?" She'd been running for her life for two days, only to have an emotional meltdown an hour ago, and now this?

"Why didn't you?" Jake said, throwing her comment back and not flinching under the accusing glare she sent him. In fact, if she didn't know better, she'd think he was fighting to control his temper. But why? She had done nothing but try to warn him.

Jake had known all along about her son, as the memory of the last twenty-four hours infiltrated her brain. How could he not tell her?

Men! Shelly turned and headed for the safety of the car just as Sheriff Baker drove up and parked a few feet away.

Ignoring him, she climbed inside the Durango and sat fuming, waiting for Jake while he and his partner argued with the sheriff. Seems the sheriff hadn't liked finding out about Rich in the same way either, according to the gist of their heated conversation.

When Jake broke off from Baker and Rich Heslin, he stormed toward her, his anger resonating off his body like hot air off a blacktop in the desert sun, sending signals she couldn't misinterpret even in the dark.

He jerked open the driver's side door. Once buckled in, he slanted a heated glance at her. The air crackled with his annoyance.

"Next time I tell you to stay in the car, I goddamn mean it. You understand?"

"You don't own me, Jacob Collier," she shot back, going on the defensive, feeling even more stupid, if that were possible. "I've been on my own for too long to have someone like you tell me what to do."

"Oh? Well, from here on out, you're not alone. You're the mother of my child and as such, you have me to contend with. I'm not going to just disappear. You can run to the ends of the earth, and if you do, so help me God I'll chase you down and drag you back."

Suddenly, Shelly realized this was as much about what went on earlier at the cabin as it was about her not following his orders, and somehow his ranting burst her inflated bubble of irritation.

She was alive and so was he.

"I'm sorry. I was worried about you." Her hand landed on his arm. She squeezed. "I had to make sure you were okay after those shots were fired."

"I can take care of myself. I'd die a million deaths if you'd been hurt." Jake's intent gaze caught hers, giving her a glimpse of the terror he'd felt. "How do you think I would've felt if Rich hadn't broken cover on a hunch that I needed him? If he hadn't been there, and if Mathers had had a clean shot, we wouldn't be arguing now. I was terrified to lose you again."

He reached over with both hands and gripped her face, his expression turning tender. "I love you, Michelle Matthews, and I need you. Don't ever do anything so stupid again."

She swallowed hard, her heart swelling with joy. "I love you too," she murmured, right before his lips found hers in a none-too-gentle kiss. He let every emotion she read in his eyes come out in the kiss…anger, need, desire, fear…and Shelly couldn't help responding to it.

Eventually he broke away, definitely satisfied with her declaration and her reaction, given the grin he flashed her when he released her to start the car.

"So, why was he trying to kill me?" she finally asked, breaking the silence as they headed through town.

Jake sighed. "We believe it's because they think Kiera somehow gave you information."

"As to what?"

"About their drug and sex slave operation." He filled her in on his case, ending with, "From Billy's last words and from what we've put together, Kiera discovered it. Most likely, was why she died. Mathers' death hasn't helped our investigation. It may be over, now that only one of the principals is left alive." He drove on in silence for a mile, then added, "I'm dropping you off at Elaine's. Baker let me go to take you home. You should be safe now, since Rich said Ivy's under surveillance and can't make a move without them knowing about it. I've got to get back to help pick up the remaining pieces."

Shelly nodded. Neither spoke until he stopped in the middle of the curved driveway. "I don't know how long I'll be. Emily should be asleep. We can tell her in the morning she has a brother."

She left the car, relieved, but wondering how to tell Mikey he had a sister. All this time, he thought his father had abandoned them, when in reality, she'd abandoned Jake.

Chapter 21

Jake waited until Michelle was safely inside before heading for Highway 259. At a gravel road, he veered off the main highway following the GPS Rich had given him to locate the van Jarvis and Malone were using for this op.

Jake parked and climbed out of the car. The house wasn't too far away from this spot, neither was the second exit from the cave. Other men, state police and DEA agents among them, hid in the woods. Waiting.

"What's going on," Jake said after entering the van.

Both Jarvis and Malone waved, as Rich answered with, "What a cluster fuck! I can't believe they're all dead but Ivy." Rich's heavy sigh filled the small space. "I wonder if anything will happen tonight."

"It'll happen," Malone said. "It's Friday night. The busiest night of the week according to the website."

"Yeah," Jarvis agreed. "It's business as usual."

"Small consolation," Rich said. "I'd just feel better if I hadn't shot the shit out of Mathers. It would've been nice to have him alive."

"Ivy'll have to do," Malone interjected. "She's in there. We caught her voice off and on for the last hour. But it's still fairly quiet. No sudden movement from the house. Nothing to indicate an alarm."

"Let's hope so." Jake shrugged. "She can't know about Mathers' death." He looked around. "Where's Baker?"

"He and a couple of deputies are out in the woods with the others. I had to placate him somehow. As you saw, he was pissed as shit. After you left, he read me the riot act. Is going above my head, says this is his county…we didn't follow protocol…didn't enlighten him to my undercover work…yada…yada…yada. You know the drill." Rich snorted, waving it off. "The guy's just puffed up. Once we make the bust and he's part of it, his threats will dissipate into thin air, just like the hot smoke he was blowing."

Jake shook his head. "I don't know, Rich. Sometimes you gotta trust others just a bit more." He remembered Billy dying in front of him and wondered. If Baker had been informed from the beginning, would Billy still be alive? And what about Joe, Bobby and Doug? He'd grown up with these guys. Prison was far less final than death.

Then he wondered about what those friends had done.

Selling drugs, he could see. Quick money. The end user is too far away to see the final result, usually a horrendous addiction, which caused suffering to all connected.

But why the other? What was their motivation for enslaving women?

Wearing earphones, Malone put up a hand. "Listen." The sound of a plane filled the small space. "Yep. Just as I predicted."

"Sounds like a twin engine," Jarvis said, also wearing a headset. He grinned. "I bet it's full of johns. Man, these people are too much. How would it be to just fly in, take in a fantasy fuck, and fly out."

"Money has its privileges."

~

"You bastards," Ivy Jackson said, on the front porch of the house three hours later. She marched down the steps, pointing a weapon at Rich who'd just come into view with Baker following close behind.

Officers had stormed the house, catching the johns in the act and unaware, along with Ivy, only she'd been quick enough to arm herself.

Jake eased from view, watching and waiting.

"Stay back. I won't hesitate to shoot."

Both men stopped when she cocked the gun.

"Is Jerry dead too?" she asked, looking directly at Rich, obviously recognizing him as tears rushed down her face. Then she glanced at Tom. "Is that why I couldn't contact him? Because he's dead. Everyone's dead but me." A half laugh burst from her mouth, but her face held no amusement. "Damn! What a stupid fool I am. I trusted the wrong person. Fell for it hook, line, and sinker. We all did." She shook her head. Her shoulders slumped. "Joe was right. I haven't got a prayer. He tried to warn me. Told me to get out before it was too late, but I wouldn't listen. And now it *is* too late," she said, still staring at the two. "I'm already dead, aren't I?"

"NO!" Jake shouted, when he realized what she meant to do.

They needed Ivy Jackson alive. He leapt for her, but he was seconds too late. She'd already pulled the trigger after shoving the revolver into her mouth.

Rich had acted at the same time, getting there an instant before him and feeling for a pulse, but it seemed useless when half her head was blown off, with brains and blood splattered everywhere, noticeable in the spotlights Jarvis and Malone pointed their way.

Even in the shadows, it was a gruesome sight.

Chapter 22

Surrounded by loved ones, Shelly stood in the cemetery, mourning Kiera Delaney's death. Elaine and Jake with Emily and Mikey flanked one side, and Maggie and Monica stood on the other. The day would prove to be another hot one, with the humidity and temperature already over eighty at ten in the morning.

Thoughts of the last week flitted through her mind. The actions of a few who'd died had turned the entire town upside down and shaken its foundation. Joe and Billy Durbin. Bobby Winters. Doug Larson. People she'd known most of her life. She'd never met Ivy Jackson or Jerry Mathers, but their deaths were no less disturbing.

Shelly simply didn't have it in her to mourn them, except for poor Billy. Not when they'd all tried so hard to kill her.

How horrific to learn they were also responsible for such heinous crimes.

"Drugs, sex, and rock and roll," as Jake had explained. "The three together usually mean I stay busy because tragedy usually follows the combination." In Jake's opinion, the vicious cycle never ended.

And behind it all?

Greed. Also a never-ending element in the human condition, according to Jake. Those reaping monetary compensation off the misery of others. Misery *they* caused and exacerbated because one of those involved, Doug Larson, was a lawman, sworn to serve and protect.

That kind of crime was hard to forgive, so Shelly was glad

they were all dead. Their deaths meant justice was served, as well as saving the taxpayers big money in bringing them to immediate justice.

A tear trickled as the minister said a prayer over Kiera's casket.

Dust to dust. Ashes to ashes. The cycle of life. And death.

More tears followed as the metal box was lowered into the ground.

She grieved now for what would never happen. The chance to hug Kiera and tell her how sorry she was had died with her friend.

At least Tom Baker had returned the journal after readily deciding it held no clues. The sheriff was heartbroken and torn up that he'd been so wrong about one of his deputies. Tom felt guilty that Kiera hadn't come to him about Larson, even admitting that he would not have believed it if she had. He and Jake determined Kiera had discovered what they were doing and tried to stop it on her own. A sad realization all the way around.

Shelly had to be content with her friend's last thoughts in her journal, which had in turn given Shelly much food for self-reflection.

She watched Elaine take a shovel and add the first dirt to Kiera's grave, noting the finality of the act. Closure. A basic human need. Everyone needed closure.

Funny how we humans are so predictable, she thought. We react to certain stimuli, especially pain. We all run from pain.

Few faced it head-on, she realized, wiping more tears away. But pain always had a way of resurfacing if one didn't face it and lance it so it could heal. Shelly should have faced hers years ago. She'd always regret not doing so. The hardest part had been facing Mikey and telling him she'd been mistaken about his father.

Shelly glanced at Elaine, who turned to Maggie as the gravesite service finally ended. "It's such a beautiful day. I want to enjoy it and not wallow in something I can't change." Elaine put on a brave smile that didn't quite reach her eyes. "Let's take the kids to the park."

"That's a great idea," Maggie said, wrapping her arms around her. "We can celebrate life. Kiera will always live on in

Emily."

Tears filled Elaine's eyes as she nodded.

"I'm stopping at Peggy Sue's for a sandwich, then I'm hitting the road." Monica glanced at her watch. She'd closed the store and had driven in this morning. She'd never planned to stay longer. "It was good to see you, Elaine. I'm just so sorry it took Kiera's death to bring us back."

Elaine hugged her. "Thanks for coming."

"Drive carefully." Maggie had agreed to stay with Elaine for a few days. Shelly's mom always seemed to know what people needed. An anchor in a storm of emotions. Elaine needed a friend and in Maggie she could do no better.

Maggie turned to her. "Would you like to join us?"

Shelly shook her head, smiling warmly. "You two go ahead." She was thankful for her mother's support in this time of transition, but she wanted some time alone to grieve and more time to deal with her guilt over keeping her son and his father separated. Shelly may never come to terms with that, but she had to try. For Mikey's sake and for Jake, who had completely forgiven her.

Mikey had much to deal with as did Emily. It would be nice for the two kids to share an outing alone with the grandmothers, especially now that both women had something in common—Jake's children.

The kids got an extra grandmother, as well as a sibling. And best of all, Mikey got a new set of grandparents. The Colliers had been on a safari in Africa and out of range of communications when all this happened. According to Jake, they couldn't wait to get back.

"I'll take you home," Jake said, gripping her elbow and leading her to the SUV.

They drove to the Delaney house where Maggie and Mikey were also staying. After parking, he turned to her. "You'll be okay? I can postpone my meeting until tomorrow."

She smiled and shook her head. He'd already postponed it for too long. She placed her hand over his and squeezed. "I'm okay."

He heaved a long sigh and raked a hand through his hair. He looked tormented. Too many had died. They'd barely been in time to save seven women, and Kimberly McDowell wasn't among them. Neither was the senator's daughter, whose disappearance originally pulled in the DEA. A man named Montoya had rented the plane, complete with a pilot who made the regular trip from Nashville once a month. The pilot was in deep shit with the FAA, the Nashville police, and the DEA, if they could find anything to use. Shelly was sure they'd come up with something, once they started investigating. They needed someone to pin it on. Montoya was hidden in Mexico, but they'd find him. So far, the agencies who'd come together to investigate had no luck in tracking the elusive man. Very frustrating for Rich as Jake had said. Rich needed to find Montoya, and he'd determinedly set off to do just that. Jake wasn't so determined, feeling his family needed him more.

"Go. I'll be here when you get back." Shelly kissed him and jumped out of the Durango. She waved as he drove on, then headed up the walkway, thinking of Kiera's journal.

Once inside, she grabbed a ham and cheese sandwich Jake had fixed earlier, trying to push Kiera's last words from her brain. As she ate, another thought occurred to her.

Maybe there was more to Kiera's message before she'd passed out in her arms. True, her friend had wanted to atone, but was forgiveness all she'd wanted? Why hide the journal?

A sudden thought struck. The code. Of course! That was it! She finally figured out what was bugging her about the journal. Subconsciously, she must have recognized the code.

Maybe Kiera put something in code, like they used to do back in school when they'd passed notes. Shelly grinned at the memory. Note passing was something every sixth grader did. And Shelly loved that she'd finally made it to middle school, the same school as Kiera.

Oral communication was nil though, since they didn't share any classes. To get around it, they made up a code, only readable by them in case the teacher or another classmate like Bobby or Joe Durbin confiscated the note. Memories of those days swamped her. Made her miss Kiera so much more, now that their past was put into some perspective. Such a tragedy. Why had they had to change as they got older? Why couldn't things have remained easy and uncomplicated?

After finishing her sandwich, Shelly raced up the steps to her room.

Buddy was at the door, tail wagging as usual. He'd gotten a clean bill of health from the vet and was well-trained. They'd had no luck trying to find an owner. Most likely some stupid idiot couldn't keep him and decided rather than take him to an animal shelter, he could live on his own in the wild. An event that happened much too frequently in the lake country. But instead of dying of the elements, as so many strays did, he got lucky and now he was part of the family.

"Hey, guy," she cooed, stroking his soft fur. "Want to keep me company while I investigate?" The thumping increased. She laughed and retrieved the journal. While she sat at the desk, Buddy curled up under her feet.

More memories from those years filled her. She remembered how everything fell apart when Kiera went to high school, leaving Shelly behind in middle school. Unwilling to be left behind, Shelly started making a pest of herself, following Jake and Kiera around.

Their differing maturing bodies had definitely exacerbated her loss. Overnight, Kiera had become a sex kitten, developing breasts and a knockout figure, while Shelly's five-foot-nine-inch frame held no curves. With no breasts to speak of and her waist and hips only inches apart in size, she'd been in essence a gawky, rectangular stick, not a petite hourglass like hot little Kiera.

Shelly pushed the thoughts away and opened the journal.

Excitement raced through her veins as she scanned the pages and noticed some irregularities. Kiera had definitely left a secret message behind. To the casual eye, it just looked like an affectation of Kiera's printing.

She grabbed a pen and pencil and wrote down the slightly highlighted letters. The real work would come when she had to make sense out of them, figuring out words, sentences, and paragraphs. But Shelly had an edge. She knew Kiera's patterns. Even after all this time, they came back to her, mostly because it was similar to what she used for texting.

Two hours later, her elation soared. She reached for her cell and called Jake, getting only his voice mail.

"Jake. Call me when you get this. You'll never in a million

years believe what I just learned about your case. Meet me at Elaine's. Kiera hid something that I think might help you find Montoya, and at the same time shed more light on why she was killed."

She glanced down at the information she'd unearthed, words hidden in the journal.

> If you're reading this, you know of my sins. It also means Jake was too late and I'm dead. I knew going in that outcome was a high possibility and why I'm writing this here in code.
>
> I found his house. Saw the monitors. Went through his records, then copied them onto a thumb drive. I hid the drive, taped behind the picture Mom has of the two of us.
>
> For years he's been kidnapping women and drugging them to use in his harem. If that wasn't bad enough, he's selling them. He's linked into our cave, running some kind of lab from there, making a drug that's ten times worse than meth and hooking these women so they'll perform.
>
> Shel, that could be you or me. You've got to stop him. Tell Jake where to look.

Shelly paced. Where was Jake and why hadn't he answered her third message. She couldn't wait for him, too full of curiosity to see what Kiera had discovered.

She ran downstairs, grabbed the picture off the wall, and sure enough...there it was, along with another letter. Taped to the back. She ran to the Delaney home office and booted up the computer.

Chapter 23

Jake fidgeted, trying to pay attention to the information Malone had on the screen as his voice droned on and on, adding to his findings. This final report would put their case to bed as far as the Nashville division of the DEA was concerned as it related to suspects Jerry Mathers, Doug Larson, Ivy Jackson, Bobby Winters, and Joe Durbin. Billy Durbin's connection was tragic—considered that of a victim—and therefore treated as such with the documentation.

Della had been horrified to realize what had taken place behind her back, so much so that she shut down her bar and went into seclusion. When Jake last saw her, she looked as if she'd aged fifty years.

They'd all been thankful the women rescued were alive. All seven were now in a detox treatment facility, one that took what the women had been through into consideration.

Still, in Jake's mind, no one, least of all the women, came out of this unchanged. And because a senator's daughter's death had been part of this from the beginning, the FBI and DEA were working together along with the CIA to nail the entire ring. Yep, Jake thought. America's alphabet had joined forces and Rich was leading them. Montoya didn't stand a chance.

Divers had trolled a part of Lake Cumberland that held the closest boat ramp to Campton. Within hours, they'd found another body, a teen missing from Texas. They still hadn't found any sign of Kimberly McDowell, and it was determined that she'd only recently been sold to Montoya.

Mathers' position, as department head in control over destroying not only leftover chemicals but any pills that failed quality control checkpoints in the production process, gave him perfect access. Of course, Waddell Pharmaceuticals had closed ranks, hiding behind a force of lawyers, denying any wrongdoing. They said that anyone who could navigate the web could get the chemicals Mathers used, and his scientific background gave him the knowledge. Hopefully, the company also closed the loopholes that allowed Mathers to virtually create his own drugs from waste that was obviously never destroyed.

According to Betsy Heslin, Rich's ex, he only needed certain ones based on the pills they'd found. She'd isolated the ingredients. Given the drugs the company manufactured, she surmised he probably did a bait and switch. No one would be the wiser, given his position. The proverbial fox being in charge of the henhouse, she'd said. Lord only knew how many drugs Waddell had sold in the past five years actually had the correct amount of dosage. But that was another legal battle and one that would be hard to prove, so Jake figured it would die in the thousands of cases to be investigated. But now the DEA would scrutinize the company, as would the FDA.

Kiera's autopsy revealed that she'd died of an overdose of the same drug as the other singers. Her death was classified as a homicide, the drugs found in her car determined to have been planted by Doug Larson. As a result, she was cleared of any wrong-doing.

Jake sighed. The why's and the how's no longer concerned him. He was ready to move on to the next phase. Men like Montoya would always be there and they'd closed a ring supplying the guy. With so much at Rich's disposal, he'd no doubt catch him, and have a thrilling ride while doing so. Rich thrived on the chase and on the game.

Jake didn't. He preferred to focus his efforts on keeping kids in rural areas, like Campton, safe. He was certain none of this would have happened in his hometown if the drugs hadn't been available at those parties all those years ago. He mentally snorted. Probably still were.

One thing always led to another. How would college kids even think of getting into the drug trade, if they hadn't seen firsthand the demand with their peers?

If he could save one kid from suffering like Kiera had, then he'd feel as if he'd accomplished something.

Save one soul at a time, one day at a time, he thought. That's all I can do in this never-ending battle.

Finally, the meeting ended. While they were filing out, Malone grabbed Jake's arm.

"Hey," he said, handing him a large manila envelope. "Give this to Rich when you see him, will ya?"

"What's this?"

"Inquiries from Western Kentucky University. He asked for the information before the case busted open. Since this one's closed, I'm off to the next."

"Sure. So, what kind of information?"

Malone shrugged. "Copies of class rosters that Ivy and Mathers shared. Rich was just crossing all his *t*'s and dotting all his *i*'s. I couldn't get them online, due to privacy issues, so I had to go in and make an official request. Got the usual bullshit. You know. It'll take time…no manpower…waste of taxpayer's money. Thank God we didn't need the information."

Jake nodded, watching Malone's exit. Yep. The guy hit the bureaucratic nails on the head. Time, manpower, and money. The three were always in short supply when they had too many cases to solve.

He entered his office, plopped into his black leather chair, and threw the envelope on the desk. He took a look around the nondescript, sterile room. One picture of Emily was the only personal item. Maybe there was a reason for that.

It felt right to be here, but he still needed to figure out his future with Michelle. She had a life in Atlanta and he had a life here in Nashville. Although, to be honest, his life would never be far from hers. Nothing had been decided.

His glance hit the envelope. Curiosity got the better of him. Rich always had a talent for sniffing out details. And usually those details led to… He laughed. The case was over.

Still, he couldn't help undoing the clasp and letting the pages slip out.

His telephone rang. "Collier here," Jake said, cradling the phone between his neck and shoulder, eyeing the sheets.

"I'm trying to reach Agent Heslin."

"He's not here. I'm his partner. Can I take a message?"

"Yes. This is Mel Jenkins. I was out of town last week when

SANDY LOYD

the agent called and asked about the property I own back in Campton. I rent it out now."

"Oh, yeah. How are you doing, Mr. Jenkins? This is Jake Collier. We used to hang out in your cave." As they spent a moment on pleasantries, Jake kept scanning. One line in particular caught his attention. So did a name. Leafing through the other pages, he noted the same name in several other classes.

"Agent Heslin wanted to know who I leased the property to. Eva Sanders. But since she died, I believe her grand-nephew has been paying the rent these past five years. I'm sure you know him. Nice young man."

He said the name and Jake's mouth dropped open. "You sure?"

"Yep. My memory's as sharp as it ever was. Met him when he was a boy."

Jake thanked him and hung up. He thought back to that night when Rich had called him with the news that Billy had shot Larson. Remembering the turn of events, a cold sensation of dread washed over him.

What if more in the town were involved?

He pulled his cell out of his pocket and switched it on. He'd shut it down before he went to his meeting.

That was when he got Michelle's messages. All three of them.

"Shit," he murmured, grabbing his jacket and heading for the parking lot and his Durango.

Please, Lord, don't let me be too late, he thought as he tried her cell and got her voice mail.

~

While Buddy slept peacefully curled under the desk, Shelly sat back, totally amazed at what she'd read.

The thumb drive contained records. Accounts in the Bahamas and detailed information on customers and the women, along with what they did to them. Sick was the only word that came to mind when she'd opened some of the files.

No, not sick. Evil. So, this is what Jake had been investigating? How did he do it, she wondered, day after day?

There were some depraved bastards in the world and it

seemed Sheriff Tom Baker was one of the most depraved.

Kiera's letter explaining her actions lay open on the desk...

Jake was so jealous of him but he had nothing to be jealous over. I never liked him and now I hate him. He's an evil man who hides behind an exalted position.

I've always suspected Tom Baker was behind my addiction somehow. He always seemed to be in the background, waiting and watching. Like some kind of predator. I saw him with Bobby too many times not to make the connection. Bobby dealt in college and was my source.

I kept my mouth shut and pretended stupidity, but I thought it odd that Tom cleaned up the area, leaving Bobby alone. I started wondering, then wondering turned into questioning, and questioning turned into keeping my eyes and ears open.

After a while, I decided they were partners. Had to be and it made perfect sense.

So, you might be asking yourself—why should I care? And maybe I shouldn't. But I can't help caring. Knowing he's involved and knowing he's getting away with it, all the while people like me suffer and try to recover from their greed, I have to stop him. But when I mentioned something in passing to Jake and he scoffed at my offhanded comment, I realized no one would take an addict seriously, might in fact think I was trying to cause trouble for someone who'd done so much to stop the meth traffic in the area.

Putting Tom Baker away for good became my goal. A passion that wouldn't die, probably because it's one way I can ease my guilt. Something good springing from something so bad.

Yet, I needed a plan.

Since Tom never hid his interest in me, I feigned interest in him to get closer to him. So far it's worked. But Tom is cagey. I still get the feeling he's watching me. Toying with me like a cat with a mouse, right before he pounces. I've tried to be careful. If you're reading this, it means I wasn't careful enough.

Hopefully you and Jake have reunited. I know he'll believe you much more than he would ever believe me.

Get him, Shel. Please, get him. But at the same time, be careful.

From reading the rest, Shelly pieced together what had happened.

Baker must have figured out what Kiera was doing and killed her. Suddenly, it dawned on her why she'd become a target. He was looking for what Kiera had left behind.

She heard the front door open. Seconds later, she spotted Jake in the doorway, his face pinched with worry. He rushed to her side, placing his hands on her shoulders.

"Are you okay?" he asked, in between deep breaths. He'd clearly been running.

"I'm fine."

Grinning, Michelle held up the journal and a piece of paper. "I've figured it out. Kiera left a message."

"I'll take that, if you don't mind."

Both gazes moved simultaneously toward the sound.

The sheriff stood at the door, his gun pointed straight at them. "It pays to have contingencies and be prepared. I bugged the phone lines."

~

Baker walked further into the room and positioned his back against the wall close to the desk, still aiming.

"You bugged the phone lines?" Jake asked, studying the sheriff's face.

"Yes." Baker nodded at the thumb drive attached to the computer. "I can't believe the bitch made copies. I didn't underestimate her interference like they all thought." He offered a sick grin and said with a conspiratorial wink, "That's why they're dead and I'm still here." He reached into his pocket and took out two strips of plastic with locking ends. "Once I destroy the evidence and deal with the two of you, I can finally relax."

Portable handcuffs, Jake realized, keeping all emotion off his face. "I've got to hand it to you. You had me fooled," he said, in an effort to get him talking. "You had us all fooled."

"Except for Kiera." His grin expanded. "She fought hard. Both times." When Jake's eyebrows rose in question, he snorted. "I thought I had her years ago, but she fought my influence. I figured I just hadn't hooked her enough, but her desire to stay clean overrode the pleasure. I should have taken more notice then. A costly mistake that led to others and some bad luck. Fortunately, my luck has changed."

"Has it?"

"Of course. I've got the gun and you're both here without witnesses." Holding his aim steady, he put one of the strips on the edge of the desk, then waved. "You," he motioned to Michelle. "Pick it up." He turned to him. "And you? Put your hands behind your back." When Jake complied, he nodded. "Now, bind his hands."

"So, what do you plan to do with us?" Jake tried to keep a little room to maneuver, but Baker tugged on it, taking out the slack before relieving him of his Glock. "Nice try." He turned to Michelle, replacing his pistol with Jake's, shoving the other into his waistband. "Now, you. Over here and hands behind your back."

When Michelle moved to where he'd indicated, Baker said, "On your knees, both of you." When neither of them moved, he shouted and pointed Jake's service revolver at Michelle. "Now or I shoot."

Michelle glanced at Jake for direction and he nodded. He had no intention of either of them dying, but placating Baker seemed their only option at the moment.

Both knelt.

"I planned on getting even with you. You've been a thorn in my side for too long. I guess I should thank you first, though, for steering me into the drug business, because when I lost my shot at a scholarship, I had to make up the money somehow and selling drugs has definitely been lucrative." One-handed, Baker bound Michelle's wrists, and the entire time he talked, almost boastfully. "I thought messing Kiera up would even things, but I now realize only your death will give me the satisfaction I crave."

"So, were they all in on it?" Jake asked, ignoring his

reference indicating a role in Kiera's addiction. She was dead and they were alive. He had to stay focused on remaining so. "Durbin, Larson, Ivy, and Mathers?"

"I was the ringleader." Baker's chest puffed out as he boasted, "None of them would have even thought of doing something so bold without me. I made us all millionaires. But Joe was weak and wanted no part of it. I kept him in line because I knew his secret. He caused Billy's accident all those years ago. And implicating Billy only added more insurance. Larson was a straight arrow and wasn't involved until Joe confided in him. Can you believe that idiot Larson had the audacity to confront me? His death came in quite handy. Making it look like Billy shot him took a little finessing, I don't mind admitting. And Ivy?" Baker shrugged. "Well, she had her own sins she was covering. She was shrewd and a perfect partner until her guilt got the better of her. I barely had the time to clean up any signs of my presence from the house. She knew what I'd done and why. I saw it in her eyes and I anticipated her reaction. Her death was also beautifully orchestrated."

"I'm impressed," Jake said. "And Mathers was your roommate in college."

"Enough talking." Baker waved the pistol in his hand. "Here's how it's going to go down. Matthews is going to shoot you with your own gun because you scorned her again. Of course, she'll have no memory and be susceptible to my suggestions, and after I get through with her, she'll totally believe it." He tsk-tsked, shaking his head. "Such a tragedy." The smile he offered didn't reach his cold eyes as he indicated with the gun to keep going. "Face down."

"Killing us won't do you any good," Michelle said, her chin inching higher. "I've already e-mailed the files to Jake's office."

Jake glanced at her and saw the truth of her claim in her eyes. At least the bastard wouldn't get away with it.

Baker eyed her thoughtfully, then shrugged. "I'd hoped to stay in business for a few more years, stay sheriff till my term ends, but I'd planned on leaving sooner or later. Now, I guess it will be sooner. I'll simply amend my plans and kill you both in the cave. That should give me a head start. First, I'll need to make sure you won't give me any trouble."

Unable to do much with his hands tied behind his back, Jake's heart sank the moment Baker pulled a syringe out of his shirt pocket. He couldn't lie placidly and not do something. If he could somehow create a diversion, it might be enough to give Michelle time to run.

The second Baker was in an awkward position, holding the weapon on him, ready to inject him, Jake snapped into action, flipping onto his backside and using his legs to kick both the sheriff and the needle. "Run," he yelled.

The syringe went flying and Baker lost his footing, but he still aimed his weapon and fired, hitting Jake in the shoulder. It burned like a son of a bitch. He ignored the pain and the blood flowing, continuing to kick with all his might as Michelle rolled out of the way, and was on her feet, running, thank God.

Then she stopped.

"You shot him," Michelle yelled, kicking Baker and putting herself within his range.

"You bitch," Baker shouted, slapping her with enough force to send her reeling. She lost her footing and fell.

A split second later, a haze of white blurred his vision and a growl so feral the sound would have sent a streak of fear through Jake, except he recognized the animal. It was Buddy and he'd obviously noted the attack on Michelle.

The dog leapt at the sheriff, latching on to Baker's neck and shaking his head with force. While the sheriff was busy with Buddy, Jake turned to Michelle and whispered, "Grab those scissors and cut the restraints."

"You're bleeding," she said, as tears streamed down her face. But sensing his urgency, she didn't hesitate, fumbling blindly. Jake held still, praying she wouldn't cut him in the process.

Once he shed the plastic, he reached for his weapon that had clattered on the hardwood floor.

"Down, boy," he yelled at the same time Michelle added, "It's okay, Buddy. I'm okay. Here, boy."

Immediately the dog stopped his attack.

Ignoring the pain in his shoulder, Jake took the scissors out of Michelle's hands and cut her binding. One look at Baker and his opinion of the pooch increased a thousand-fold. Baker was an immobile, bloody mess. Jake reached down to feel for a pulse.

"He's bleeding too heavily. I don't think he's going to make it." He placed his hand over the wound, trying to stop the spurting. The dog had hit his jugular. "Hang on," he whispered.

Baker opened his eyes and shook his head. "Can't...you always did have better luck." Then he closed his eyes, going limp. The faint pulse died as life left him.

"Are you okay?" he asked, glancing at Michelle and seeing every emotion he was feeling moving across her face. Fear, the rush of adrenaline from escaping death, as well as sadness for all that Baker's evil had wrought. He also saw his future in her soft smile. "It's over. It's finally over."

She nodded and collapsed, sobbing, in his arm. The other still burned from his wound, but they were alive. And he was done with running. He hugged her to him. When he felt a cold nose pushing on his hand, he chuckled. "You were right about the damned dog. He belongs to us. He's part of the family."

Altogether they made a terrific family.

Baker had been right. He was the luckiest man on earth.

Jake glanced toward the heavens, thanking God. Then, remembering Kiera, he smiled.

Michelle and I will take care of Emily, he thought, sending Kiera a message as well as his prayer of thanks for bringing Michelle and him together again, knowing without a doubt he'd forgiven her as she'd forgiven him. He also knew without a doubt that she was smiling as she looked down from above.

~~The End~~

Thank you for reading *Running From Love*. If you enjoyed this story, please help others find it by posting a review where you purchased it—share a link, tweet about it, Facebook it... Everything helps in this new internet world.

About The Author

Sandy Loyd is a Western girl through and through. Born and raised in Salt Lake City, she's worked and lived in some fabulous places in the US, including South Florida. She now resides in Kentucky and writes full time. As much as she loves her current hometown, she misses the mountains and has to go back to her roots to get her mountain fix at least once a year.

She spent her single years in San Francisco and considers that city one of America's treasures, comparable to no other city in the world. Her California Series, starting out with Winter Interlude, are all set in the Bay Area.

Running From Love is set in a fictional South Central Kentucky town, an area of lakes and caves that she loves and visits regularly.

All of her series, including her romantic suspenses consist of fun, heartwarming stories about crazy friends who, like single people everywhere, are seeking that someone special to share their lives with among thousands of eligible candidates.

Email her at sandyloyd@twc.com or
visit her website at www.sandyloyd.com.
Follow her on twitter – https://twitter.com/SLoydwrites
Like her on FB – https://www.facebook.com/sloydwrites

www.ingramcontent.com/pod-product-compliance
Lightning Source LLC
Chambersburg PA
CBHW050023180626
46810CB00002B/551